TAKE A THIEF

A NOVEL OF VALDEMAR

MERCEDES LACKEY

DAW BOOKS, INC.

DONALD A. WOLLHEIM, FOUNDER

375 Hudson Street, New York, NY 10014

ELIZABETH R. WOLLHEIM
SHEILA E. GILBERT
PUBLISHERS

http://www.dawbooks.com

First Printing, October 2001
1   2   3   4   5   6   7   8   9

DAW TRADEMARK REGISTERED
U.S. PAT. OFF. AND FOREIGN COUNTRIES
—MARCA REGISTRADA
HECHO EN U.S.A.

PRINTED IN THE U.S.A.

To the memory of Gordon R. Dickson
Gentleman and scholar

OFFICIAL TIMELINE FOR THE

by Mercedes Lackey

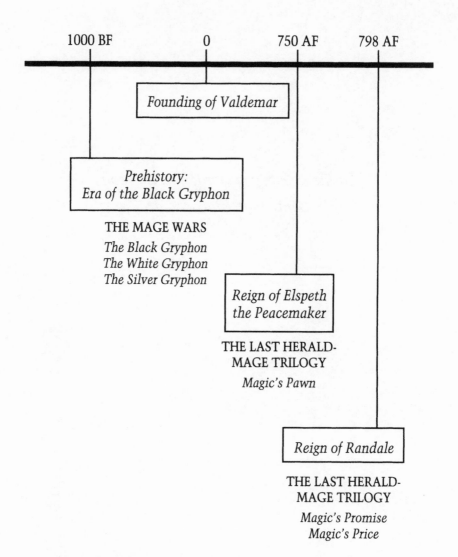

1000 BF   0   750 AF   798 AF

Founding of Valdemar

Prehistory:
Era of the Black Gryphon

THE MAGE WARS

The Black Gryphon
The White Gryphon
The Silver Gryphon

Reign of Elspeth
the Peacemaker

**THE LAST HERALD-
MAGE TRILOGY**

Magic's Pawn

Reign of Randale

**THE LAST HERALD-
MAGE TRILOGY**

Magic's Promise
Magic's Price

BF *Before the Founding*
AF *After the Founding*

HERALDS OF VALDEMAR SERIES

Sequence of events by Valdemar reckoning

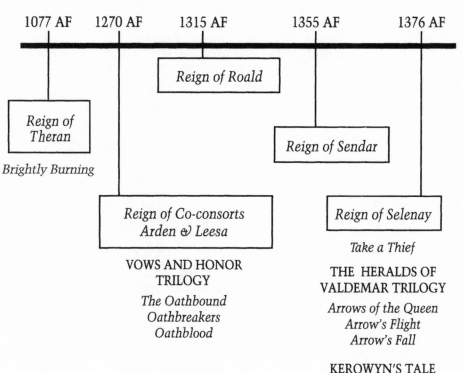

1077 AF   1270 AF   1315 AF   1355 AF   1376 AF

Reign of Roald

Reign of
Theran

Brightly Burning

Reign of Sendar

Reign of Co-consorts
Arden & Leesa

Reign of Selenay

Take a Thief

VOWS AND HONOR
TRILOGY

*The Oathbound
Oathbreakers
Oathblood*

THE HERALDS OF
VALDEMAR TRILOGY

*Arrows of the Queen
Arrow's Flight
Arrow's Fall*

KEROWYN'S TALE

By the Sword

THE MAGE WINDS
TRILOGY

*Winds of Fate
Winds of Change
Winds of Fury*

THE MAGE STORMS
TRILOGY

*Storm Warning
Storm Rising
Storm Breaking*

*Owlflight
Owlsight
Owlknight*

TAKE A THIEF

"GERRUP."

Skif's dreams shattered, leaving him with vague fragments of being somewhere warm, cozy, and sweet-scented. A toe scientifically applied to Skif's rib cage with enough force to bounce him off the back wall of the under-stair cubby he called his own reinforced the otherwise incomprehensible order that he wake up. He woke, as ever, stiff, cold, and with a growling stomach.

It was the beginning of another beautiful day at the Hollybush Tavern.

An' good mornin' to you, too, bastard.

He scrambled to his feet, keeping hunched over to avoid hitting his head on the staircase, his ratty scrap of a blanket clutched in both hands. His uncle's eldest son looked him up and down, and grunted—probably disappointed that Skif was awake enough that a "pick-me-up" cuff to the side of the head wasn't going to be necessary this time.

Skif squinted; Kalchan was a monolithic silhouette against

the smoky light from the open kitchen door, narrower at the top and swiftly widening where shoulders would be on an ordinary human, his only distinguishing characteristics from neck to knee being a pair of pillowlike arms and the fat bulging in rolls over his waistband. Skif couldn't see his face, which was fine as far as he was concerned. Kalchan's face was nothing he cared to examine closely under any circumstances.

"Breffuss," Kalchan grunted, jerking his head over his shoulder so that his greasy locks swung in front of his face. Skif ducked his head and quickly folded his blanket, dropping it on the pad of rags over straw that served him as a pallet. He didn't need to dress; in the winter he slept in every stitch of clothing he owned. Satisfied that Skif was on duty, Kalchan went on to awaken the rest of the tavern staff.

Yah, an' do not a hand's worth of work, neither.

"Breakfast," was what Kalchan had said, but he hadn't meant that it was time for Skif to partake of that meal.

As soon as he was out of the way, Skif scuttled out into the kitchen and began the tedious business of lighting the fires, hindered by the fact that his uncle's penny-pinching ways were reflected in every aspect of his purchases. For firewood, he relied on the rag-and-bone men who swept out fireplaces and ovens in more prosperous households, sifting out the ashes for sale to the tanners and soap makers, and selling the clinkers and partially-burned ends of logs to people like Londer Galko, keeper of the Hollybush Tavern. Nor would Uncle Londer actually buy a decent firestarter, much less keep a candle or banked coals going overnight; Skif had to make do with a piece of flint and one of some other rock. The fact that at least half of this "firewood" had been doused with water—which was, in fact, the law—before the ragmen picked it up didn't make it any easier to light.

Before he could do anything about a fire, Skif went to the pile of sweepings from the floor of the common room that he'd collected last night after the last drunken lout had been rolled out the door. Every bit of dust and fluff that looked as if it might possibly catch fire became his tinder. At worst case, he'd have to sacrifice a precious bit of the straw stuffed into his boots for warmth.

Heh. Sommun' been trackin' in straw. Hayseed from country, prolly. Oh, ayah—here be nice dust bunny, too.

Swearing under his breath, Skif hacked his two bits of rock together, trying to generate sparks, hoping one of them would land in the tiny patch of lint and fluff. When one finally did, and finally cooperated with his efforts, he coaxed it into a tiny flame, then got the flame to take hold of the driest of the wood. He nursed it tenderly, sheltering it from the drafts along the floor, begging it to take. Finally, he set it on the sooty hearth, surrounded it with what was left of the dry wood from last night, and slowly fed it until it was large enough to actually cook over.

Only when the kitchen fire was properly started did the slattern used by Uncle Londer as a cook, dishwasher, and general dogsbody finally shuffle down the stairs from the loft where she slept into the room, scratching head and buttocks at the same time without ever dislodging any of the vermin who called her "home." Skif often wondered why so few people who ate here died. Perhaps it was only because their stomachs were already full of the acidic potions his uncle sold as wine and beer, and once a stomach was full of that rotgut, nothing that came in from the food lived long enough to cause sickness.

The kitchen door stood open to the cold courtyard; Kalchan came in that way every morning, bringing the day's supplies. Uncle Londer never bought more of anything for the inn than he absolutely had to. Now Skif braced himself to head outside into the cold.

Where 'ud it hurt if 'e bought for a week? Wouldn' 'e get it cheaper that way?

Skif ran out into the courtyard to unload the wagon—hired

for the purpose by the candlemark, together with a boy to drive it. The quicker Skif unloaded the thing, the less Uncle Londer would be charged—and if he didn't save Uncle Londer every possible pennybit, he'd learn about it when Kalchan's fist connected with his head.

The boy stared at the ears of his donkey, studiously ignoring Skif, who was so much lower in the social scale than he was. This boy had a coat, new boots, both clean.

Ah, stuck up! Skif thought, and stuck out his tongue at the unresponsive back.

First off, a half-sack of flour, followed by a tub of tallow grease thriftily saved from cookshops where they skimmed off the grease from roasting and frying, and resold to those who could not afford butter and candles. Maisie would be put to taking peeled rushes and dipping them in the melted grease to make the tallow dips that served the tavern as lights, and the cook would use the same grease in baking and on the bread.

Skif moved it carefully and set it down beside the flour; sometimes the stuff was still liquid underneath, and he didn't dare spill it.

Then came a bucket of meat scraps, which would serve for the soup and meat pies.

I don' wanna know what that meat came from. Reckon it might meow. . . .

Next, a peck of withered, spotty turnips, another of dried beans and peas that were past their best and smelled of mold. Last of all, two barrels of beer and one of wine. Both represented the collected dregs from barrels all over the city, collected last night from one of the large merchants who supplied goods to other inns and taverns. Needless to say, this was the cheapest conceivable form of beverage; it even cost less than the sweet spring water collected from outside Haven. It was so awful that Guild cooks wouldn't even use the stuff in sauces; stale and loaded with sediment, it smelled sour even through the wood of the barrel. Skif got the barrels off the wagon quickly, and the boy turned the wagon just as quickly and sent his donkey trotting out into the street. Skif lugged the food into the kitchen where old Moll, the cook, took charge of it all. Only she or Kalchan were allowed to touch the food and drink once it came off the wagon.

Skif had no intention of touching any of it. He never ate here—not that Uncle Londer encouraged him to.

He wasn't done yet; he had to bring in enough water from the courtyard pump to fill the half-barrel in the kitchen—one bucket at a time. He stumbled on the rutted, frozen dirt of the courtyard; his boots, stuffed with straw for extra warmth, were far too big for him. He didn't care; better too big than too small.

Leastwise they don' pinch.

Now Skif went out into the common room to ready it for the first customers, lighting the fire there with a brand from the kitchen fire, arranging bits of wood on either side of the hearth to dry, taking the benches down off the tables, and the shutters off the windows. The oiled paper in the windows didn't do a great deal to keep out the cold, but with snow in the street outside, there was some light getting in this morning, so it was just as well that oiled paper hindered more than it helped in that direction. Skif would never want to see what the common room looked like in the full light of the sun.

As horrible as the food and drink here in the Hollybush were, there were two customers waiting for Skif to open the door. He knew them both by sight; two men who would down a minimum of six mugs of foul beer and choke down a slice of stale, burned bread with a scraping of nameless fat before shambling off somewhere, not to be seen until the next morning. Presumably, they had jobs somewhere and this was *their* breakfast.

They slumped down on the benches nearest the door, and Skif yelled for Maisie, the fourth member of Uncle Londer's tavern staff. As usual, she emerged from her own cubby of a

blocked-up stair that once led to the second floor (which, unlike Skif's, had a flap of patched canvas for a door) followed
by Kalchan. As usual, she said nothing, only scuttled into the
kitchen for the customer's beer and bread, her face set in a
perpetual mask of fear. Kalchan hitched at his trews and
grinned, showing yellowed teeth, and followed her into the
kitchen.

Skif shuddered. As awful as his position was here, Maisie's
was worse.

This was a tavern, not an inn, and the kitchen and common
room were all there was of the place. The tenement rooms upstairs, although they belonged to Uncle Londer, were not available for overnight guests, but were rented by the month. There
was a separate entrance to the rooms, via a rickety staircase
in the courtyard. This limited the tenants' access to the inn
and the fuel and food kept there. Uncle fully expected his tenants to pilfer anything they could lay their hands on, and they
responded to his trust by doing so at every possible opportunity. Not that there were many opportunities; Kalchan saw to
that.

Now Skif was free to leave at last for the lessons that every
child was required by Valdemar law to have until he was able
to read, write, and cipher. Not even Uncle Londer had been
able to find a way to keep Skif from those lessons, much as he
would have liked to.

Skif didn't wait around for permission from Kalchan to
leave, or his cousin would find something else for him to do
and make him late. If he was late, he'd miss breakfast, which
would certainly please Kalchan's sadistic notion of what was
amusing.

See ya—but not till dark, greaseball!

He shot out the door without a backward look, into the
narrow street. This was not an area that throve in the morning; those who had jobs were usually at them by dawn, and
those who didn't were generally out looking for something to

put some money in their pockets at least that early, or were sleeping off the results of drinking the vile brews served in the Hollybush or other end-of-the-alley taverns. The Hollybush was, in fact, located at the end of the alley, giving Uncle Londer the benefit of giving custom no chance to stumble past his door.

There were other children running off up the alley to lessons as well, though not all to the same place as Skif. He had to go farther than they, constrained by his uncle's orders. If Skif was going to have to have lessons, his uncle was determined, at least, that he would take them where Uncle Londer chose and nowhere else.

Every child in this neighborhood was running eagerly to their various teachers for the same reason that Skif did; free and edible breakfast. This was an innovation of Queen Selenay's, who had decided, based on her own observation, that a hungry child doesn't learn as well as one with food in his belly. So every child in Haven taking lessons who arrived on time was supplied with a bacon roll and a mug of tea in winter, or a buttered roll and a piece of fruit in summer. Both came from royal distribution wagons that delivered the supplies every morning, so there was no use in trying to cheat the children by scrimping. But if a child was late, he was quite likely to discover that his attendance had been given up for the day and someone else had eaten his breakfast, so there was ample incentive to show up on time, if not early, for those lessons, however difficult or boring a child might find them.

Skif had no intention of missing out on his share. His stomach growled as he ran, and he licked his lips in anticipation.

Unless luck went his way, this might be the only really edible food he'd get for the rest of the day—and there was no doubt in his mind that the rest of the children in his group were in the same straits.

The narrow, twisting streets he followed were scarcely wide enough for a donkey cart. The tenement houses, three stories tall including the attics, leaned toward the street as if about to fall into it. There was not enough traffic to have worn away the packed, dirty snow heaped up against the walls of the houses on either side, and no incentive for the inhabitants to scrape it away, so there it would remain, accumulating over the course of the winter until it finally thawed and soaked into the dirt of the street, turning it to mud.

But that would not be for several moons yet. There was all of the winter to get through first. At least the cold kept down the smell—from backyard privies, chicken coops, pigeon houses, pig sties. The poor tried to eke out their meager food-stuffs any way they could. Pigeons were by far the most popular, since they could fly away by day to more prosperous parts of town and feed themselves at someone else's expense. There were clouds of them on every available perch, sitting as close together as possible for warmth, and whitening the broken slates and shingles of the rooftops with their droppings. Of course, with all the snow up there, the droppings were invisible in winter.

Skif was finally warm now, his breath puffing out whitely as he ran. He had no coat, of course, but no child in his neighborhood had a coat. There were three ways to get warm in the winter—work until you were warm, do something that kept you near enough to the fire that you weren't freezing, or—be as creative about finding warmth as Skif was.

After six turnings, he was in a slightly more respectable neighborhood. The streets were marginally wider, a half-hearted attempt to remove the snow had been made, and there were a few dark little shops on the first floors of the tenement houses. More chimneys sported thin streams of smoke, and at the end of this final street, just before it joined one of the main thoroughfares, was the Temple of Belden. It wasn't a large Temple as such things went; it had only four priests and a half-dozen novices. But the Order of Belden was a charitable

Order, which was just as well, since there wasn't much scope for anything but charity down here.

As such, one of the charitable acts performed here was to educate the poor children of the area. But Skif wasn't here because he had chosen the place, or even because Uncle Londer had picked it from a number of options. He was here because his second cousin, the middle son of his uncle's brood of three, was a novice here.

Cousin Beel had as little choice about his vocation as Skif did; Uncle Londer wished to impress his social superiors with his sense of charity, and so Beel became a novice. Beel seemed to like the life, though—or, he liked it as much as this curiously colorless young man could like anything. Beel was as forgettable as Kalchan was remarkable.

Skif pushed open a little side door in the chapter house next to the Temple. The door opened directly into a public room with several tables and benches in it; there were thirty or forty other children that took lessons there, and about half of them were already sitting on the benches, waiting for their meal. Skif slid in beside one of the smaller girls, a tiny big-eyed thing called Dolly. She smiled up at him in welcome; he was her protector and kept her from being harassed by any of the more aggressive children who would try to bully her outside of classes for anything that they thought they could get from her.

He took her cold little hands in his and held them until they warmed while they waited for the last of the children to straggle in. Skif heard her stomach growl while they waited; his answered hers, and she gave a little giggle.

Finally a small bell rang somewhere in the Temple marking the end of the First Service, and a door at the back of the room opened. Beel and one other novice entered, carrying baskets. The delicious aroma of bacon wafted gently to where Skif sat, trying not to fidget; every eye in the room was riveted on those baskets as Beel and the other novice left and returned with steaming pots of tea and thick clay mugs.

Cor! Can they move any *slower?*

It seemed an eternity before the last of the paraphernalia of breakfast finally was brought in and arranged to Beel's liking. Only then were the children permitted to come up to him, one at a time, and receive their rolls and mugs. By then, of course, the rolls were stone cold and the tea at best lukewarm.

It didn't matter. So long as the rolls weren't frozen hard as stones, so long as the tea wasn't a block of ice, there wasn't a child here that wouldn't devour every crumb and drink down every drop. Some of them began eating and drinking while they walked back to their places, but not Skif, and not Dolly either, for she followed his example. It wasn't for the sake of manners; Skif didn't have any, no more than any of the others. It was because he had figured out that if he ate over the table, he could catch every crumb, and he did. When they were done, he and Dolly licked their fingers and picked up the tiniest fragments from the wood.

Lukewarm as the tea was, it was still warmer than the room. The mug served double duty as a hand warmer until the tea was gone. They weren't allowed to linger over it, though, not with two novices standing over them.

Then Beel's fellow novice collected the empty mugs and vanished, leaving Beel to his teaching duties.

Skif should, in fact, not be here at all. He read and wrote as well as any of the children at these tables, and the law said only that children had to be able to read, write and figure to a certain level before their compulsory education was complete, not at what age a child could be released. Skif enjoyed reading and even took a certain aesthetic pleasure in writing; it would have been hard for him to feign being bad at either. Beel probably would have quickly caught on before long and sent him back to the tavern where he'd quickly be slaving for Kalchan—*and* doing without his breakfast. But figuring had never come easy to him, and it was boring besides. He still couldn't add two numbers of two figures each and come up with the same answer twice in a row, and in all likelihood neither answer would be the right one. Needless to say, although he pretended that he was trying, his progress was glacial. He had to make *some* progress, of course, or even Beel would suspect something, but he was going to put off the evil day when Beel would pronounce his education complete for as long as he could.

In the meantime, since he *was* so good at reading and writing, during those lessons Beel saw no reason why he should not take some of the workload off of his own shoulders, and Skif was put to tutoring the youngest children, including Dolly. He didn't mind; he was big enough to be able to bully those who weren't at all interested in learning things, and Beel had no objection to his delivering admonitory cuffs to the ear if it became necessary to keep discipline. That was the main thing that was hard about being the tutor; littles like Dolly who wanted to learn just needed some help over the rough spots.

It was turn and turn about then, and time for one of the other boys to tutor Skif—along with children three years his junior—in figures. For Skif, this was the worst part of the day, and not because he himself was a discipline problem; being anywhere other than the tavern was an improvement and he wasn't eager to get himself kicked out.

It was horribly cold in this room—there was a fire, but it didn't get things much above freezing and by now they were all suffering from icy hands and feet. He was bored. And breakfast had long since worn thin. Only in summer was this part of the day bearable, for as cold as the temple buildings were in winter, they made up for it by being pleasant in summer, and smelled of ancient incense rather than the reek of privies, of garbage, and of the muck of all of the animals hidden away in back courts.

There!

The heads of every child in the room, Skif's included, came up as the bell summoning the faithful to Midday Service rang from the top of the Temple. If they'd been a pack of dogs, their ears and tails would have quivered. Novice Beel sighed.

"All—" he began, and the children literally leaped from their seats and stampeded for the door before he could finish. "—right—" Skif heard faintly behind him as he scooped up Dolly and shoved his way with the rest through the open door with her held protectively in front of him.

Once outside, he broke away from the mob of children, bringing Dolly with him. The rest streamed in every direction, and Skif hadn't a clue what made them all so anxious to get where they were heading to do so at a run. Maybe it was the prospect of finding a little warmth somewhere. Without a word, he wrapped his arm around Dolly's thin shoulders and turned her in the direction of her home. Since a few days after her first appearance in the schoolroom, when he'd caught some of the older children teasing and tormenting her, he'd played her guardian. Her father brought her in the morning on the way to his work at the docks, but Skif was her escort home, where she would join the rest of the children in her family and her mother at their laundry. In winter, despite having to struggle with soaking, heavy fabric and harsh soap that irritated and chapped the skin, a laundry wasn't a bad place to work, since you could always warm up in the room where the washing coppers were kept hot over their fires. Dolly never lingered once they arrived; she only cast Skif a shy smile of thanks and scampered inside the building, where a cloud of steam poured out into the street from the momentarily open door.

His self-appointed duty complete, Skif was now free for as long as he could keep out of the way of his relatives.

Kalchan would work him until he dropped, not serving customers, since that was Maisie's job, but doing everything else but cooking—and "everything else" included some things that

made Skif feel sick just to think about. On the other hand, out
of sight was definitely out of mind with Kalchan, and so long
as Skif didn't claim meals, his eldest cousin probably thought
he was in lessons during the daylight hours. Fortunately Beel
had suffered enough under his older brother's fist as a child
that he didn't go out of his way to enlighten Kalchan as to
Skif's whereabouts out of school.

That did leave him some options. Sometimes he could find
someone with errands to run; sometimes he could shovel snow
or sweep crossings for a pennybit. There was refuse to haul off
for the rag-and-bone men if they came up short a man. But
none of that was to be counted on as a source of food or money
to buy it, and Skif had finally hit on something that *was*.

It took him far out of his own neighborhood, and into
places where his ragged, coatless state was very conspicuous.
That was the drawback; before he reached his goal, he might
be turned back a dozen times by suspicious folk who didn't
like the look of him in their clean and prosperous streets.

Eventually he left the tenements and crooked, foul streets
and penetrated into places where the streets were clean and
kept clean by people whose only job was to sweep them. The
transition was amazing to him, and even more amazing was
that there were single families that lived in buildings that
would serve to house a dozen or more families in *his* area. He
didn't even try to venture onto those streets; there were all
sorts of people there whose only job was to keep people like
him out.

Now he went to the alleys, slinking from bit of cover to bit
of cover. There was plenty of cover here; permanent rubbish
bins where ashes, broken crockery, bits of wood, scraps from
food preparation too small or too spoiled for anyone from
these houses to consider useful were left for the rubbish collectors. This was where the wood—and possibly some of the
foodstuffs—bought by Uncle Londer came from. Skif knew
better than to rummage in those bins; they "belonged" to the

rubbish collectors who guarded their territories jealously, with curses, kicks, and blows. But the rubbish collectors didn't care who they saw in their alleys so long as he left the bins alone, and they ignored Skif as if he was invisible. Sometimes there were other things left back here as well, usually weeds, bags of dead plants and leaves, sticks and trimmings from gardens. It all made places for a small boy like Skif to hide. These alleys were faced by blank walls that rose well above Skif's head, but not all of those walls were as impervious as they seemed.

He had skipped over three or four social strata now; he'd known better than to look for a mark among people like Dolly's parents or the small merchants. Such folk feared to lose what they'd built up and were as penurious in their way as his uncle; they didn't share what they had, and when they caught someone trying to get a bit for himself, punished him with fury. No, when Skif decided that he was going to help himself to the bounty of others, he knew he'd need to find someone who had so much that he couldn't keep track of it all, and so many servants that it wasn't possible even for them to do so.

The drawback was that in such a rich household, there were privileges that were jealously guarded, and as he knew very well, even those things that the owner thought were refuse had value. The cook and her staff all had the rights to such things as fat skimmed from the cooking, the burned or otherwise "spoiled" bits, and "broken meats"—which last were cooked leftover items that had been cut into or served from without actually having been on someone's plate. Depending on the household, unless such items were designated to go to the poor, the cook and helpers could sell such items from the back door, or give them to relatives who were less well-provided-for, or a combination of all of these things. "Scrapings"—the leftovers scraped from plates into a slop bucket by the dishwashers—belonged to the dishwashers in some households, or were fed to household animals in others, and again could be sold or carried off, if not fed to animals.

Stale bread and cake were the provenance of the pastry cook, sometimes a different entity from the head cook, who had the same options.

All these leftover items were jealously guarded from the time they became leftovers. But from the time they left the hands of the cooks until the moment that they were brought back to the kitchen, no one was paying any great amount of attention to the quantities on platters in a so-called "great" household.

And that was where Skif had found his little opportunity to exploit the situation.

He noted the first breach in the defenses by the cloud of sweet-scented steam rising over the wall; this was a huge household that had its own laundry. Making sure that he wouldn't be spotted, he kicked off his boots and hid them inside the wall, squeezing them in through a place where he'd found a loose brick. It had occurred to him more than once that he was probably using someone *else's* hiding place—bricks in well-tended walls like this one didn't just "come loose" by accident. He wouldn't be the least surprised to learn that someone (or several someones) in this great house had once used the place to store small articles purloined in the course of duties, to be retrieved and carried off later.

Now barefooted, he climbed nimbly over the top and into the open laundry yard, full of vats of hot water, bleaches, and soap in which household linens soaked before being pounded by a dozen laundresses, rinsed, and hung up to dry. Between the vats, sheets and towels were strung on lines crisscrossing the yard. The bleaches were so harsh that these vats were kept in the open, and away from the rest of the laundry where the clothing was cleaned, for a careless splash could ruin a colored tunic forever. The steam and the hanging linens gave him cover to get into the room where the livery for the pages was stored once it had been laundered, and on his way through, he grabbed a wet towel out of one of the vats to take with him.

The pages—there were at least twenty of them—went through a dozen sets of livery apiece in a week, for the servant who had charge over them insisted on absolute cleanliness.

This room—which they called a "closet" although it was as big as the Hollybush's common room—held only shelves that were stacked with tabbards, tunics, and trews for every possible size of boy. They didn't wear boots or shoes, perhaps because they were so young that they would probably outgrow boots or shoes too quickly; instead, they wore colored stockings with leather bottoms, which could fit a wide variety of feet. Hence, Skif's current barefoot status.

The rest of the livery was designed to be oversized on practically any child, so Skif would have no difficulty in fitting into whatever was clean. Within moments, his own clothing was hidden under piles of discarded but clean tabards too worn to be used for anything but really dirty jobs, but too good to be relegated to duty as rags. A quick wipe all over himself with the damp towel—a dirty boy would stand out dreadfully among the clean pages—and a quick change of clothing, and Skif was now a page.

Just in time for luncheon.

Now properly outfitted, and hence invisible to the rest of the staff, he dropped the filthy towel in a pile of others waiting to be cleaned, trotted out of the laundry just as if he was on an errand. He crossed a paved court to the kitchens, slipped inside the door, and joined the line of pages bringing common food into the lord's Great Hall. He made certain to take a platter heavily laden with a pile of what looked like boiled baby cabbages no bigger than his thumb; by the time it got to the table, two of them were in his pockets.

This Lord Orthallen must be a very important person. Every day he entertained a horde of people at his table, perhaps fifty or sixty of them, besides the dozen or so of his own immediate family. That was just *guests;* there was a small army of his own servants and retainers at still lower tables, but they had to serve themselves from great bowls and platters brought from the kitchen by one of their own number.

Skif and the other pages served only the guests, who got foods that were designed to be eaten with one's own knife and hands. After the tiny cabbages, he purloined a dainty little coin-sized meat pie, a soft roll of white bread, a cube of cheese, more cheese wrapped in pastry, a small boiled turnip, and an apple. That was all his pockets would hold. He made certain that he was in the procession of pages that got the platters going to those who sat below the lord's salt—he didn't have the manners to serve at the head table and he knew that he'd be recognized for an interloper. Those who sat lower were too busy eating, gossiping, and watching their betters to pay attention to the pages.

Once his pockets were full, Skif made certain to "accidentally" get some grease on the front of his tabard—an accident that occurred to at least three of the pages at every meal, since many of them were young and they were all rushing to and fro. As he expected, he was sent to the laundry to change.

Once there, he swiftly changed back into his own clothing, left the soiled uniform with others like it, and went back up— but not over the walls and into the alleys.

After all, why should he? He had nothing particular to do out there. His friends were all too busy working or on schemes of their own to get themselves fed to have any time for play— playing was what the fortunate children of the rich did. For the moment, he wanted a warm place to rest and eat, and there was one right here at hand.

There was an attic over the laundry, a loft area that was barely tall enough to allow him to walk hunched over, where old tubs and some of the laundry stores were kept. It got more than enough heat from the laundry below to be comfortably cozy and more than enough steam to keep down the dust. Here, Skif curled up inside an overturned wooden tub for extra concealment and dug into his purloined food.

He could, of course, have eaten three times what he'd sto-len—but it was twice what he'd get at the tavern, and not only entirely edible, but tasty to boot.

With his stomach relatively full, he curled up in the tub for a nap. Here, and not in his cubby at the Hollybush, was where he could sleep in comfort and security. And he did.

No matter how comfortable he was, Skif slept like a cat, with one eye open and one ear cocked, in case trouble stole upon him, thinking to catch him unaware. So even though he didn't know *what* woke him, when he woke, he came alert all at once, and instead of jumping to his feet, he stayed frozen in place, listening.

Wood creaked slightly, somewhere in the loft. Was it a footstep? The sound came again, a trifle nearer, then fabric brushed against something harder. There was someone up here with him.

Now, it wouldn't be one of the laundry servants on proper business; they came up the stair, clumping and talking loudly. It *might* be a servant or a page come up here to nap or escape work—if it was, although Skif would have a slight advantage in that the other wouldn't want to be caught, he had a profound disadvantage in that he didn't belong here himself, and the other could legitimately claim to have heard something overhead and gone to investigate. If that was the case, he'd be stuck under this tub until the other person left.

It might also be something and someone entirely different—a thief, who wouldn't want to be found any more than Skif did, who might flee, or might fight, depending on the circumstances, if Skif came out of hiding.

He didn't know enough yet; better to wait. It was highly unlikely that the other would choose Skif's particular tub to hide himself or anything else underneath. It was out of the way and smallish, and Skif had chosen it for precisely those reasons. Instead, he peered under the edge of it, as the surreptitious sounds moved closer, thanking his luck that it wasn't dusty up here. Now would be a bad time to sneeze.

It sounded, given the direction the sounds were coming from, as if the unknown had gotten into the loft the same way that Skif had, through the gable window at the end. Skif narrowed his eyes, waiting for something to come into his area of vision among the slats of the wooden tubs. The light was surprisingly good up here, but the sun was all wrong for Skif to see a shadow that might give him some notion of who the other intruder was. The creaking gave Skif a good idea that the fellow moved toward the stairs, which meant he was at least *thinking* of using them to descend into the laundry itself. That wasn't an option Skif would have chosen—unless, of course, the fellow was a thief, and was planning on purloining something from the laundry itself. There was plenty of stuff to steal in there; silk handkerchiefs and scarves, the embroidered ribbons that the young ladies of the household liked to use for their necks and hair and the young men liked to give them, the gossamer veils they wore in public—all light, easy to carry, presumably easy to sell. The only reason Skif hadn't helped himself before this was that he didn't know where to dispose of such things and was not about to share his loot with Kalchan.

A foot slid slowly into view; not a big foot, and most importantly of all, not a foot clad in the soled sock of a page or liveried indoor servant. This was a foot in a half-boot of very flexible black leather, laced tight to the ankle and calf, much worn and patched, not much larger than his own, attached to a leg in rusty black trews with worn places along the hem. This foot, and the person who wore those trews, did not belong here. No one in Lord Orthallen's service wore anything of the sort.

Skif made a quick decision, and struck. Before the other knew he was there, Skif's hand darted from under the tub, and Skif had the fellow's ankle held fast in a hand that was a lot stronger than it looked.

Skif had half expected a struggle, or at least an attempt to get free, but the owner of the ankle had more sense than that—or was more afraid of the attention that the sounds of a struggle would bring than anything Skif could do to him. So now, it was the other's turn to freeze.

Skif mentally applauded his decision. He thought he had a good idea of what was going through the other fellow's mind. Now, the arm that Skif had snaked out from beneath the tub was clad in a sleeve that was more patch than whole cloth. So Skif obviously didn't belong here either, and the two of them were at an equal advantage and disadvantage. For either to make noise or fuss would mean that both would be caught— and no point in trying to claim that one had seen the other sneak over the wall and followed to catch him either. An honest boy would have pounded on the back entrance to report the intruder, not climbed up after him. No, no—if one betrayed the other, both of them would be thrown to the City Guard.

So the other fellow did the prudent thing; he stayed in place once Skif let go of him so that Skif could slip out from under the tub. Like it or not, for the moment they were partners in crime. Skif, however, had a plan.

There was a moment when the other *could* have tried to knock Skif out and make a run for it, but he didn't. Such an action would have been noisy, of course, and he still might have been caught, but with one unconscious or semiconscious boy on the floor to distract those who would come clambering up here, he might have been able to get away. Skif breathed a sigh of relief when he was all the way out from under the tub and was able to kneel next to it, looking up at the interloper.

What he saw was a boy of about fifteen, but small for his age, so that he wasn't a great deal taller than Skif. His thin face, as closed and impassive as any statue's, gave away no hint of what he was thinking. His eyes narrowed when he got a good look at his captor, but there was no telling what emotion lay behind the eyes.

His clothing was better than Skif's—but then again, whose wasn't? Skif wore every shirt he owned—three, all ragged, all inexpertly patched by his own hands, all faded into an indeterminate brown—with a knitted tunic that was more hole than knit over the top of it all. His linen trews, patched as well, were under his woolen trews, which for a change, had been darned except for the seat which sported a huge patch made from an old canvas tent. This boy's clothing was at least all the same color and the patches were of the same sort of material as the original. In fact, unless you were as close as Skif was, you wouldn't notice the patches much.

He had long hair of a middling brown color, and a headband of dark braided string to keep it out of his eyes. His eyes matched his hair, and if he'd been fed as well as one of the page boys his face would have been round; as it was, the bones showed clearly, though not nearly as sharply defined as Skif's.

There were other signs of relative prosperity; the other boy's wrists weren't as thin as Skif's, and he showed no signs of the many illnesses that the poor were prone to in the winter. If he was a thief—and there was little doubt in Skif's mind that he was—this boy was a good enough thief to be doing well.

The two of them stared at each other for several moments. It was the older boy who finally broke the silence.

"Wot ye want?" he asked, in a harsh whisper.

Until that moment when he'd seized the other's ankle, Skif hadn't known what he wanted, but the moment his hand had touched leather, his plan had sprung up in his mind.

"Teach me," he whispered, and saw with satisfaction the boy's eyes widen with surprise, then his slow nod.

He squatted down beside Skif, who beckoned to him to follow. On hands and knees, Skif led him into the maze of tubs and empty packing crates until they were hidden from view against the wall, next to the chimney.

There they settled, screened by stacks of buckets needing repair. From below came the steady sounds of the laundry, which should cover any conversation of theirs.

"Ye ain't no page, an' ye ain't got no reason t'be in the wash house. Wot ye doin' here?" the boy asked, more curious than annoyed.

Skif shrugged. "Same as you, only not so good," he replied. He explained his ruse to get fed to the boy, whose lips twitched into a thin smile.

"Not bad done, fer a little," he acknowledged. "Noboddie never pays mind t'littles. Ye cud do better, though. Real work, not this pilferin' bits uv grub. I kin get through places a mun can't, an ye kin get where I can't. We might cud work t'gether."

"That's why I want ye t'teach me," Skif whispered back. "Can't keep runnin' this ferever. Won' look like no page much longer."

The boy snorted. "Won't need to. Here, shake on't." He held out his hand, a thin, hard, and strong hand, and Skif took it, cementing their bargain with a shake. "M'name's Deek," the boy said, releasing his hand.

Skif was happy to note that Deek hadn't tried to crush his hand in his grip or otherwise show signs of being a bully. "Call me Skif," he offered.

Deek grinned. "Good. Now, you stay here—I come back in a tick, an' we'll scoot out by th' back t'gether." He cocked his head down at the floor, and it was pretty clear that there wasn't anyone working down in the laundry anymore. It was probably time for supper; the laundresses and some of the other servants ate long before their betters, and went to bed soon after sundown, for their work started before sunrise.

Skif nodded; he saw no reason to doubt that Deek would play him false, since he was sitting on the only good route of escape. He and Deek made their way back to Skif's tub; Skif ducked back inside, and Deek crept down the stairs into the laundry.

Deek came back up quickly, and the quick peek of silk from the now slightly-bulging breast of his tunic told Skif all he needed to know. As he had expected, Deek had managed to slip downstairs, purloin small items of valuable silk, and get back up without anyone catching sight of him. As long as he took small things, items unlikely to be missed for a while, that weren't such rare dainties as to be too recognizable, it was quite likely that the owners themselves would assume they'd been mislaid. No specially embroidered handkerchiefs, for example, or unusual colors of veils. He beckoned to Skif, who followed him out over the roof, both of them lying as flat as stalking cats as they wiggled their way along the tiles, to minimize the chance of someone spotting them from below. From this position, they couldn't see much; just the lines of drying linens in the yard, the tops of bushes past the linens that marked the gardens, and the bulk of the magnificent mansion beyond. If anyone looked out of the windows of the mansion, they *would* be spotted.

Not likely though.

The pipe-clay tiles were infernally cold after the warm wash-house attic, and Skif clenched his teeth together to keep them from chattering. As he slid belly-down along them, they kept finding tears and rents to protrude through, right against his bare skin. The edges of the tiles caught on his rags, too; he had to move carefully, and make sure that nothing had snagged as he moved, to keep from dislodging one of them and sending it down with a betraying clatter. It seemed to be getting a little darker, although the sky was so overcast that Skif couldn't tell where the sun was. That was good; the closer it was to dusk, the less likely anyone would see them.

Already his bare feet ached with cold. The most risky part of this procedure was the moment that they got down from the roof onto the top of the wall. The roof actually overhung the wall, so that they had to dangle over the alley and feel with their toes for their support. And of course, this put them in clear view of anyone in the alley.

But as Skif already knew, it was too early for scrap collectors and too late for the rag-and-bone men, too late for tradesmen and too early for those delivering special items that Lord Orthallen's cooks did not have the expertise to prepare in time for an evening's feast. There was no one in the alley.

Deek went first; Skif followed. He slipped his legs over the edge of the roof and lowered himself down, hanging on grimly to the lead gutters, groping after the rough stone of the wall somewhere underneath the overhang with his benumbed toes.

When he finally got his feet on it and set them solidly, he eased himself down and under the overhang, his arms hurting with the strain. Deek crouched there, waiting for him with great patience, and he paused for just a moment to shake some feeling back into his fingers.

From the wall, they climbed down to the alleyway; Skif noted with concealed glee that Deek came down the same route that he himself used. "Wait a mo—" he said, as Deek made to move off, and retrieved his boots from the hidden nook.

Deek's mouth dropped open. "Cor! That be right handy, that do!" he whispered in amazement.

Skif just grinned, and shoved his boots on quickly. They

still couldn't afford to be caught here; someone might search them. Deek wasted no more time, but led Skif off in the opposite direction from which Skif had come. He didn't go that way for long, however; just far enough to get back into a more modest area. Then he cut back in the direction that Skif had expected. He didn't slow down, not for a moment, and Skif had to stretch his legs to keep up with him. For all that, he didn't look like a boy who was somewhere he shouldn't be; he strode with his head up, paying close attention to anything that stood out like a landmark, quite as if he had an errand he'd been sent on. Skif tried to emulate him.

As they worked their way back toward the south and east, Deek started to talk, quietly enough so that it wasn't likely they'd be overheard. " 'Sjest me an' a couple boys, an' Bazie," Deek said. "Bazie, he's the clever cuz what tells us how t'nobble. Cain't do it hisself; ain't got no legs. But 'e kin show us, an' he innerduced us t'the fence, so we gotta place t'sell the swag."

"He gonna have a prollem with me?" Skif wanted to know.

Deek shook his head. "Nah," he said decisively. "We bin one short since Larap tookt off on 'is own. No flop an' no feed, though," he added, casting a look aside at Skif. "Not lessen' ye bin wi' th'gang a sixmun."

"Gotta flop," Skif replied shortly. "An' I kin feed m'self. I kin wait."

But secretly, he was astonished at his good luck. That he even had a *chance* for a new place to sleep and meals—if he could just get out of Uncle Londer's clutches. Anything would be better than the Hollybush!

Deek laughed, and slapped Skif on the back, as they turned a corner and entered a working-class neighborhood where they could leave the alleys and take to the streets. This wasn't one anywhere near the Hollybush, and Skif wondered just how far they were from the tavern.

Far, I hope, he thought. *Don' want Kalchan catchin' wind uv this.*

Each turning that Deek made took them deeper into the kind of areas that Skif called home, though nothing looked familiar. The streets grew narrower, the buildings shabbier and in worse repair. Another corner turned, and they came unexpectedly into a little square, where there was a market going at full shout, with barrows and stalls everywhere. Deek ignored the noise, the hagglers, the confusion of people and barrows; he pushed in between a rag-and-bone man selling bundles of half-burned wood, and a barrow full of broken and cracked pottery, leading Skif into a narrow passage between two buildings not much bigger than his own slim shoulders.

Then, with an abrupt turn in the half dark, he darted into an opening in one wall and up a staircase. Skif followed, taking care where he put his feet, for there was plenty of debris on the rickety wooden stairs, some of it slippery. The stairs were steep, and switched back and forth, with landings on each floor that led to two or three closed doors.

At the top, however, there was only a single door, which Deek opened without knocking. Skif followed him inside, only to be confronted by a long hallway with more doors, lit from above by a single skylight with some translucent stuff in it that let in enough light to make out the doorways. Deek went straight to the end of the hall, much to Skif's bafflement. There was nothing there but the blank wall, an expanse of water-stained plaster with a couple of old, rusted hooks on it.

Deek paused at the end, and grinned back over his shoulder at Skif. "Figger it out, yet?" he taunted, then pulled on a hook.

A door separated itself from the cracked plaster, the lines of the door previously completely hidden in the cracks.

Deek motioned to Skif to go inside, and closed the door behind him. Now they went down a stair, more of a ladder than a staircase, one somehow sandwiched between the walls of buildings on all four sides; and in a moment, Skif realized

that this must be an air shaft, and at some point someone had
jury-rigged a stair inside it. There were windows looking into
the shaft, but most of them had shutters over them to keep out
the cold air. They climbed down and down until they passed
through the bottom of the shaft, and Skif knew that they were
below street level. If he hadn't already guessed that, the sudden increase in dampness would have given it away.

There was a door at the bottom of the stair; Deek knocked
on this one in a definite pattern that Skif didn't quite catch.
The door swung open, and Deek grabbed his arm and pulled
him inside.

Another boy, this one older than Deek, with hair of a mousy
blonde color, closed the door behind them. Skif stood at Deek's
side, and took it all in without saying a word.

It was warm down here, warm and humid. The source of
the warmth was a—

—copper wash boiler. Which was also the source of the
moisture. It sat in a brickwork oven in the far corner of the
stone-walled room, a chimney running up the corner behind
it, with a fine fire burning beneath it, and presumably, laundry
soaking in it. Hanging just below the ceiling were strings of
drying wash.

Silk objects hung there, expensive silk, mostly scarves and
handkerchiefs, a few veils, some lady's stockings and finely-
knit silk gloves—and a few perfectly ordinary shirts and tunics and trews, stockings, all darned and patched.

*Well, hey, if they're washin' the swag, they might's well
wash their own stuff, I guess.*

The fire beneath the cauldron, despite the name of "wash
boiler" was not hot enough to boil the water, only to keep it
warm. Next to the cauldron was a remarkable figure, seated
on a stack of flat cushions, busily darning the heel of a silk
stocking with fingers as fine and flexible as a woman's. He
was bald, shiny-pated in fact, with enormous shoulders and
chest muscles beneath a shabby tunic. The legs of his equally

patched trews were folded under at the knee, as Deek had implied. He didn't look up from his work.

There were two more boys in the room, one stirring the laundry with a stick, the other cracking and peeling hard-boiled eggs at an old table with one broken leg propped up and crudely nailed to an old keg. Skif tried not to look at the eggs; his pilfered lunch had long since worn thin. Besides the table and the stool the boy sat on, of furnishings there were none. There were boxes in various states of repair, old kegs, half-barrels, and a wide variety of cushions, quilts, and other linens. Anything that was made of fabric, unlike the rest of the contents of the room, was neatly patched and darned and in good repair—and clean, very clean. There was plenty of light here, from a motley assortment of lamps and candles. And there was definitely one thing missing—the usual smell of poverty, compounded of dirt, mildew, grease, mouse, and sweat.

The man finished his darning and, with a gusty sigh, tossed the stocking in with the rest of the laundry in the wash boiler. Only then did he look up. His eyes, a startling black, seemed to bore right into Skif's brain.

"Where ye get this'un?" he asked Deek, turning his gaze on Skif's companion.

If Deek had possessed such a thing as a cap, he'd probably have snatched it off and held it diffidently in front of him in both hands. As it was, he ducked his head. " 'E caught me, Bazie," Deek told the man. " 'E wuz in th' wash-house loft, an' 'e caught me cummin' in." Then, having gotten the difficult bit over with—admitting that he'd been caught by a mere child, he continued with more enthusiasm, describing Skif's own "lay" and his wish to be taught. The other two boys pretended not to listen, but Skif caught them watching him surreptitiously.

"Figgered 'e cud take Larap's place, mebbe, if'n 'e makes it past sixmun," Deek concluded, looking hopefully at his mentor.

Now Bazie transferred his unwavering gaze to Skif. "Ye livin' rough?" he asked, and Skif knew that he'd better tell the truth.

"At Hollybush," he replied shortly. "Kalchan's m'cuz, Londer's m'nuncle."

Evidently Bazie knew the Hollybush, since he didn't ask where or what it was. His gaze became even more piercing. "Bonded?"

With relief Skif shook his head. "Nuh-*uh!*" he denied vigorously. "Ma didn' bond me 'fore she croaked. Londer's pretty het 'bout it, but ain't nothin' 'e kin do now. An' 'e niver cud put me out, 'cuz 'e took me in, on th' rolls an all, reckonin' t' get me bonded."

A bonded child was just short of property; required to serve in whatever capacity his "guardian" chose until he was sixteen, for the privilege of being sheltered and fed. Skif's mother had neglected (perhaps on purpose) to bond her toddler to her brother when her man left her and she fell ill—she worsened and died before Londer could get the bond signed and sworn to. It was too late now; no notary would swear to a faked bond. Well—no notary would swear to a faked bond for the pittance of a bribe that was all that Londer would offer.

By the point when Skif's mother died, Londer was already on record with the same Temple Beel served at as the responsible party for his sister and nephew (hoping to get Skif's bond). As such, he was technically required by law to care for Skif until the age of twelve without any benefit. At twelve, which was no more than a couple of years away, he *could* turn Skif out, but he probably wouldn't. Skif was still supplying free labor at no real cost to him, and as long as that was going on, Londer would let sleeping dogs lie.

Now, the fact was that although Skif was under no obligation to serve at the Hollybush for his keep, the *only* thing he could coerce out of Kalchan and Londer was a place to sleep. The food they offered him—the leavings from customers' meals—a pig wouldn't touch. If he wanted to eat, he had to either find alternate ways of getting meals (as he had) or do even more work than he already was. And as long as he wanted to sleep at the Hollybush, which though wretched, was infinitely better and safer than trying to find a place on the street, he had to obey Kalchan's orders whenever he was around the tavern. There were a lot of things that could happen to a child on the street—"living rough"—and most of them were far worse than being beaten now and again by Kalchan, who had no taste for little boys or girls.

'Course, if 'e thunk 'e cud get away wit' it, 'e'd hev no prollem sellin' me. Kalchan would sell his own mother's services if he thought he wouldn't get caught. As it was, on the rare occasions when Skif got dragooned into "helping," he often had to endure the surreptitious caresses and whispered enticements of some of the customers who had wider ideas of pleasure than Kalchan did. As long as Kalchan didn't actually accept money in advance for the use of Skif's body, there was nothing that Skif could report to Temple or Guard.

And as long as Kalchan didn't take money in advance, the customers could only try to entice a boy; they wouldn't dare try to force him in public. The likelihood of one of them cornering Skif somewhere private was nonexistent. There wasn't a wall built he couldn't climb, and he knew every dirty-fighting trick there was for getting away from an adult.

After some time, during which Skif felt very uncomfortable, Bazie nodded. Now, at last, he showed a faint sign of satisfaction. " 'E might cud do," he said to Deek. "Give 'im a try."

Deek grinned, and elbowed him.

"Wouldn' mind puttin one i' th'eye uv that bastid Londer," Bazie continued, a gleam in his own black eyes. "Yew work out in one moon, yer in."

Deek sucked in his breath; he had told Skif it would be *six* moons, not one, before he'd be accepted into the gang. Skif was amazed himself, and tried hard not to grin, but failed.

Bazie raised an eyebrow. "Don' get cocky," he cautioned. " 'Tis as much t' put one i' the eye uv Londer."

Skif ducked his head. "Yessir," he said earnestly. "I unnerstan' sir." But he couldn't help feeling excited. "Ye'll be teachin' me, then?"

"Ye kin start now, at boiler," Bazie grunted, gesturing to the boy at the cauldron. "Ye take Lyle's stick."

Skif was not at all loath. For the second time today—the first had been when he was asleep in the wash-house loft—he was warm. Stirring a cauldron full of laundry was nowhere near as much work as toting rubbish for the rag-and-bone men.

Lyle was happy enough to give over the stick to Skif, who industriously stirred away at the simmering pot. Every so often, at Bazie's imperious gesture, he'd lift out a kerchief or some other piece of fabric on the stick. If Bazie approved, the second boy took it and hung it up to dry; if not, it went back in the pot.

Meanwhile Deek sorted his loot by color into baskets along the wall; Bazie, darning yet another silk stocking, noted Skif's incredulous stare as he did so, and snorted. "Ye think 'm gonna ruin goods w' dye runnin'? Think agin! We gets *twice* fer th' wipes 'cause they's clean an' mended, boy—thas a fair piece fer damn liddle work wi' no risk!"

Well, put that way—

Skif kept stirring.

Lyle began taking down kerchiefs that were dry; Bazie continued to mend, and Deek picked through one of the baskets, looking for more things that needed fixing. The third boy finished peeling the hard-boiled eggs, and stood up.

" 'M off, Bazie," he said. He was clearly the oldest, and Bazie looked up from his mending to level a measuring gaze at him.

"Ye mind, now," the man said, carefully. "Ye mind whut I said, Raf. Ye slip *one,* an' move on. No workin' a crowd on yer lone."

The boy Raf nodded impatiently with one hand on the doorknob. As soon as Bazie finished speaking, he was already out the door. Bazie shook his head.

"He don' lissen," the man said with gloom.

"Ah, he lissens," Deek assured their mentor. " 'E's jest inna hurry. They's a street fair a-goin' by Weavers, an' 'e wants t' get to't afore they pockets is empty."

Bazie didn't seem convinced, but said nothing to Deek. "Lemme see yer hands," he said to Skif instead, but shook his head sadly over the stubby paws that Skif presented for his inspection. "Ye'll not suit th' liftin' much," he decreed. " 'Least, ye'll nivver be a master. Ye got t'hev long finners fer the liftin'. Kin ye climb?"

Deek answered for him. "Like a squirrel, I seen 'im," the boy chimed in cheerfully. "An' look at 'is nose an' feet—'e ain't gonna get big for a good bit yet, maybe not fer years."

Bazie examined him carefully from top to toes. "I thin' yer right," he said after a moment. "Aye. Reckon ye got a matey, Deek."

"That'll do," Deek replied, with a grin, and turned to Skif. "We'll be learnin' ye th' roof walkin', then, wi' me. In an' out—winders, mostly."

"An' ye live t' see summer, ye'll be doin' the night walks," Bazie said with a little more cheer. "Won't be wipes yer bringin' 'ome then, nossir."

Deek snorted, and Skif felt his heart pounding with excitement. "Not likely!" Deek said with scorn. "Wipes? More like glimmers!"

"Ye bring 'ome the glimmers, and we'll be findin' new digs, me lads," Bazie promised, his eyes gleaming with avid greed. "Aye that, 'tis us'll be eatin' beef an' beer when we like, an' from cookshop!"

Lyle, however, looked worried, though he said nothing. Skif wondered why. It was clear from the wealth of kerchiefs—"wipes"—and other things here that Bazie was a good teacher. Skif saw no reason why that expertise shouldn't extend to second-story work and the theft of jewelry.

He'd never actually seen any jewelry that wasn't fake, all foiled glass and tin, but he could imagine it. He could imagine being able to eat all he liked of the kinds of food he served to Lord Orthallen's guests, too, and possessing fine clothing that wasn't all patches and tears—

" 'Nuff moon-calfin'," Bazie said sharply, recalling them all to the present. "Boy—Skif—be any more i' the pot?"

"Jes' this," Skif said, fishing out the last of the garments on the end of the stick. Bazie examined it, and grunted.

"That'll do," he decreed, and Lyle took it to hang it up. "Deek, next lot."

Deek brought over the next batch of wash, which was of mingled saffrons, tawnys and bright yellows, and dumped it in the cauldron. Lyle got up and took the stick from Skif without being prompted and began energetically thrusting the floating fabric under the water.

"Ye kin hev two eggs, Boy, an' then Deek'll get ye 'thin sight uv Hollybush," Bazie declared. "Eat 'em on th' way."

"Yessir!" Skif said, overjoyed, mouth watering at the idea of having two whole boiled eggs for himself. He picked a pair out of the bowl, tucking them in a pocket, and followed Deek out the door and up the rickety staircase.

Once down on the street he and Deek strolled along together like a pair of old friends, Deek putting in a laconic comment now and again, while Skif nibbled at his eggs, making them last. He'd had boiled eggs before this—they were a regular item at Lord Orthallen's table—but not so often that he didn't savor every tiny bite. Once Deek darted over to a vendor's wagon and came back with a pair of buns, paying for them (somewhat to Skif's surprise) and handing one to his new "mate."

"Why didn' ye nobble 'em?" he asked in a whisper.

Deek frowned. "Ye don' mess yer nest," he admonished. "Tha's Bazie's first rule. Ye don' take nuthin' from neighbors. Tha' way, they don' know what we does, an' 'f hue-an'-cry goes up, they ain't gonna he'p wi' lookin' fer us."

Well, that made sense. It had never occurred to Skif that if your neighbors knew you were a thief, you'd be the first one they looked for if something went missing. He ate his bun thoughtfully, as Deek pointed out landmarks he could use to find his way back tomorrow.

"I got lessons," Skif pointed out reluctantly, and Deek laughed.

"No worries," the boy replied. "Bazie won' be 'wake 'till midday. Ye cum then. Look—ye know this street?"

Skif looked closer at the street they had just turned onto, and realized that he did—he had just never come at it from this direction before. "Aye," he told Deek. "Hollybush be down there—" and pointed.

"G'wan—" Deek gave him a little push. "See ye midday."

The other boy turned on his heel and trotted back through the gloom of dusk along the way they'd come, and in a moment Skif couldn't make him out anymore.

With a sigh and a bowed head, he trudged toward his uncle's tavern and the cold welcome that awaited him. But, at least, tonight he had something to look forward to on the morrow.

K<small>ALCHAN</small> never asked him where he'd been, so long as he came back before dark. He just welcomed Skif back with a cuff to the ear, and shoved him into the kitchen. By now, the kitchen was full of smoke, and the cook coughed and wheezed while she worked. It wasn't just the fault of the chimney, which certainly could have used a cleaning—the cook routinely burned the bottom crust of the bread, burned what was on the bottom of the pot, dripped grease on the hearth, which burned and smoked.

Skif didn't have to be told what to do, since his duties were exactly the same thing every day. Poor half-witted Maisie, on the other hand, had to be told carefully how to go about her business even though it was all chores she'd done every day for the last however-many years. That was why, if Skif wasn't back by dark and the time when the big influx of customers came, he'd get more than a cuff on the ear. If you gave Maisie one thing to do, then interrupted her with something else, she became hysterical and botched everything.

First, the water barrel had to be filled again—not because anyone had used much of it in cleaning, but because like everything else in the Hollybush, it was old, used, and barely functional. It had a slow leak, and it cost nothing to have Skif refill it. To have it mended would have meant paying someone.

So back and forth Skif went, doing his best not to slosh the icy water on himself, particularly not down his boots. When the barrel was full, the next chore was to take the bundle of twigs on a stick that passed for a broom and sweep the water and whatever else was on the floor out into the courtyard, where the water promptly froze (in winter) or turned into mud (in summer). Since Skif was the one who went into and out of the courtyard most often, it behooved him to at least sweep it all to one side if he could.

Next was to bring wood in from the woodpile in the courtyard and mend the fire in the common room, which was also full of smoke, but not as bad as the kitchen. Then he collected the wooden plates left on tables, carried them to the kitchen and thriftily scraped the leavings back into the stew pot over the fire. It didn't matter what went in there, since it all blended into the anonymous, lumpy brown muck, well flavored with burned crud from the bottom, that was already there. A quick wipe with a rag, and the plates were "clean" and ready for the next customer.

Mugs were next; he'd figured that it was better to take plates in stacked and not try to mix mugs and plates, for if he tried, he'd drop something and get beaten for breaking it. These were crude clay mugs with thick bottoms to make the customer think he was getting more beer than he was. Those didn't even get a wipe with the rag, unless they'd been left in a plate and had greasy gravy all over them; they were just upended and stacked beside the plates. There was no tableware to bother collecting; Londer wouldn't have anything that could be so readily stolen. In this, however, he was exactly like every other tavern keeper around this area. Customers ate with their own wooden spoons, usually hung on the belts beside their money pouches. Some ate with their personal belt knives, although these useful implements were used less often. The food in cheap taverns was generally soup or stew, and didn't need to be cut up—nor was there often anything in the bowl or on the plate large enough to be speared on the point of a knife. Those who had no spoon shoveled the food into their mouths with improvised implements of heavy black bread. Black bread was all that was ever served at the Hollybush; made of flour that was mostly made of rye, buckwheat, and wheat chaff, like everything else associated with Uncle Londer, it was the cheapest possible bread to make. The strong taste covered a multitude of culinary sins, and since it was already black, it had the advantage of not showing how badly it was burned on the bottom.

When mugs and plates were collected, it was time to add to the stew in the cauldron. The cook put Skif to work "chopping vegetables" while she cut the meat scraps. The stew kept going day and night over the fire had been depleted by lunch and early dinner, and now had to be replenished. Londer's picks at the market were like everything else; more of what better inns and kitchens threw out. With a knife that had been sharpened so many times that it was now a most peculiar shape and as flexible as a whip, Skif chopped the tops and tails of turnips, carrots, whiteroots, and beets and flung them into the cauldron, along with the leftover crusts of burned bread too hard to serve even *their* customers. The cook added her meat scraps, and began stirring, directing him to deal with the bread she had removed from the bake oven built into the side of the chimney. There were only three rather lumpy loaves, but they wouldn't need more than that. The bread was used mostly as an implement, and secondarily to soak up the liquid part of the stew so that every drop paid for could be eaten.

Skif sawed at the bread—better bread would not have held up under the treatment he gave Kalchan's loaves, but this stuff was as heavy and dense as bricks and just about as edible. Every slice was thriftily measured out to the minimum that the customers would stand by means of two grooves cut in the tabletop, and once cut, was "buttered" with a smear of fat and stacked up waiting to be slapped onto a plate. No one ever complained that it was stale; Skif was not certain it would be possible to tell a stale slice from one freshly cut off of *these* loaves.

When the bread was done, it was time to go get plates again; business was picking up.

Skif could not imagine what brought all these customers to the Hollybush, unless it was that Kalchan's prices were cheaper than anyone else's. It certainly wasn't the food, which would have poisoned a maggot, or the drink, which would have gagged a goat. And Maisie was no draw, either; plain as a post, with her dirty hair straggling down her back and over her face, she skulked among the tables like a scared, skinny little starling, delivering full plates and empty mugs while Kalchan followed in her wake, collecting pennybits and filling the mugs from his pitcher. Only Kalchan dispensed drink; the one time that Skif had dared to do so in Kalchan's momentary absence, his cousin had left stripes on his back with his leather belt. No one actually ordered anything—there wasn't anything to order by way of choice. You sat down at a table and got beer, bread, and stew—or beer alone, by waving off Maisie's proffered plate or sitting at the fireside bench with the steady drinkers. When customers were done, Skif came around and collected their plates and mugs. If one wanted more, he waited until Maisie came around again and took another laden plate from her; if not, he took himself off. This way Kalchan never had to worry about a customer complaining he hadn't been served when he'd paid, or about a customer sneaking off without paying. The only exceptions to this rule were the folk occupying the two benches in front of the fireplace. They got beer, period, and signified they wanted refills by holding up their mugs to Kalchan. When they were done, they left their mugs on the floor—which were usually claimed by another bench warmer before Skif could collect them.

Skif made his rounds in an atmosphere thick with smoke and the fug of unwashed bodies, grease, stale beer, and burned food. Light came from tallow dips held in clamps on the wall, and from the fire in the fireplace. It wasn't much, and all the smoke dimmed the light still further. He couldn't have made out the faces of the customers if he'd wanted to. They were just an endless parade of dark-shrouded lumps who crammed food into their mouths and went their way without ever saying anything to him if he was lucky. Every so often one would fondle Maisie's thigh or breast, but if Kalchan caught him at it, he would have to pay an additional pennybit for the privilege.

There wasn't any entertainment in the Hollybush. Kalchan didn't encourage self-entertainment either, like singing or gaming. Most of the customers didn't know each other, or didn't care to, so conversation was at a minimum. As for fighting—it was wisest not even to consider it. Kalchan discouraged fighting by breaking the heads of those who fought with the iron-headed club he carried at his side, and dumped the unconscious combatants outside. The drunks here were generally morose and quiet, and either stumbled out of the door on their own two feet when their money ran out, or passed out and were unceremoniously dumped in the street to free up space for another customer. Once in the street, an unconscious, former customer had better hope that friends would take him home, or the cold would wake him up, because otherwise the thieves would strip him of everything of value and drop him in a gutter.

Difficult as it was to believe, customers kept coming in, all night long. The benches and tables were never empty until just before closing; Skif and Maisie never had a moment to rest. He'd tried once to reckon up how much money—in the tiniest of coins, the pennybit—Kalchan took in of a night. There were four pennybits to a penny; beer was two a mug, bread and stew were three for a plate. Just by way of comparison, a mug of good, clean water from something other than a pump in dubious proximity to a privy cost two pennybits (but it wouldn't get you drunk—and a mug of sweet spring water was three) and a bun like the one that Deek had bought him this afternoon was a full penny. So you could have something wholesome, though not much of it, for the same price as a full meal in the Hollybush. Evidently, bad as it was, there were enough people who felt they were getting value for their money to keep coming. The two fireside benches sat four each, and the four tables accommodated six eaters. Unless they planned a night to get drunk, the tables cleared pretty quickly. Skif figured that there were probably a couple hundred customers in here over the course of a day.

That was where Skif's grasp of numbers broke down—but he reckoned that the Hollybush brought in a couple hundred pennies in a night, and maybe a third of that during the day. Uncle Londer obviously had a good thing going here. His costs were low, buying cheap as he did, and the hire of his help was even lower. Maisie was a half-wit; Uncle Londer paid some relative of hers for her services. Whatever he paid, it wasn't much, and she never saw any of it; all she got was food and a place to sleep. Skif's labor was free, of course, and he seldom ate here. And the cook—

Well, he didn't know what the cook got. He never saw her getting paid, but she stayed, so she must have been getting something. It couldn't have been *that* much; even he could cook better than she did.

Maybe the attraction for her was the unlimited supply of beer. He never saw her without a mug somewhere nearby, and she had the yellowish color of someone who was drinking herself to death, although her shuffling footsteps were steady and she never seemed drunk.

The upshot was, this place was mostly profit for Londer, that much was for sure. Skif wasn't going to feel at all guilty about vanishing in a moon. Uncle Londer could just find himself another boy or do without.

What Kalchan was getting out of the situation was less clear; certainly he had Maisie's dubious charms to enjoy whenever he cared to, he did get real food rather than tavern swill, and he had his own special butt of drink that no one else touched, but what else was he getting? Every night after he locked the front door, he waddled down to his father's home with the night's takings, and came back empty-handed except for the box that held his own dinner. *He* slept in the common room on a greasy featherbed piled high with blankets that were stored during the day in the unused staircase. Was Londer splitting the profit with his son? If he was, what in Havens was Kalchan spending it on? It wasn't clothing, it wasn't women—not even the shabbiest streetwalker would touch Kalchan with a barge pole without a lot more up front than the penny or two Kalchan was likely to offer.

It had occurred to Skif lately that maybe Cousin Kalchan was just as stupid as he looked, and Uncle Londer gave him nothing in return for his labors at the Hollybush. If so, he didn't feel in the least sorry for him.

By the time that Kalchan dumped the last of the bench warmers outside and locked the front door, Skif was absolutely dead on his feet. Not tired—he'd had that nap in the wash house—but aching from neck to toes and longing for a chance to sit down.

Kalchan threw the bolt on the front door, and waddled out the back; when Skif heard the door slam shut behind him, he dropped down onto a bench to rest for a moment. The cook brought in three plates of stew and bread, and dropped them on the table. Skif took one look at the greasy, congealing mess, and pushed it toward Maisie, who had come to rest across from him and was already shoveling her food into her mouth as if she was afraid it was going to be taken from her at any moment. The cook had brought her own mug and picked up the beer pitcher that Kalchan had left on a table, shaking it experimentally. Finding there was still beer in it, she took it, her mug, and her plate to the fireside and settled down facing the remains of the flames, her back to her fellow workers.

Maisie finished her plate, picked up the platter in both hands and licked it, then went on to Skif's portion. She never said thank you, she never said anything. She never even acknowledged his presence.

Skif shuddered, got to his feet, and plodded into the now-deserted kitchen.

From his cubby, he took a tiny tin pot and a packet of chava leaves that he'd filched from Lord Orthallen's kitchen. Dipping water out of the barrel, he added the leaves and brewed himself a bedtime cup of bitter chava. The stuff was supposed to be good for you and make you feel relaxed and calm; at any rate, at this time of year it made a nice warm spot in his belly that let him get off to sleep.

He drank it quickly to get it down before Kalchan came back and then retreated to the cubby. The tin pot was shoved into the farthest corner where he kept a few other things that Kalchan didn't think worth taking—his own wooden spoon, a couple of pretty pebbles, some bird feathers, a spinning top he'd found. Then he wrapped himself up in his cast-off blankets, pillowed his head on his arms, and waited for Kalchan to get back, feigning sleep.

The only light in the kitchen came from the fire, and it was dying. It was the cook's job to bank it for the night, but she forgot more than half the time, which was why he had to start it again in the morning. When Kalchan came back, grunting and snorting, it was hardly more than a few flames over glowing coals. Kalchan pulled the door shut and dropped the bar over the inside, paying no attention to Skif.

Which meant that it had been a good night by Kalchan's

standards. If it hadn't been, he would either have hauled Skif out and knocked him around a bit before letting him get back to his bed, or he'd have bawled for the cook and had *her* lay into Skif.

Kalchan's return was the cook's signal to go on up to her loft. She shuffled in, dropped the curtain over the door, shoved ashes over the coals, and limped up the stairs. There was some sound of fumbling with cloth overhead, then silence.

Meanwhile, Kalchan settled down to his dinner, which he had brought back from his father's kitchen. In theory, half of that dinner was supposed to be Skif's, but in all the time he'd lived here, he'd never gotten a morsel of it. Kalchan "shared" it with Maisie—that is, he dropped tidbits to her as if she was a dog, in return for which—

Skif generally tried to be asleep by that time, the moment when Kalchan's bedding was arranged to his satisfaction beside the fireplace, and Maisie was arranged to his satisfaction in it. And tonight, both exhaustion and the unusual circumstance of having had three decent meals in a day conspired to grant him his wish for slumber.

He woke from the oddest dream that morning—a dream he couldn't quite fathom, unless it had come from yesterday's encounter with Bazie. He had been climbing like a spider along the ledge of a building, several stories up. It was the dead of a moonless night, and he was dressed all in black, including a black hood that covered everything except for a slit for his eyes. And he had the impression that there was a girl behind him, although he hadn't seen any girls at Bazie's.

It was an interesting dream, though, wherever it had come from.

He heard Kalchan snorting and moving around in the next room, slowly waking up; it must be morning, then. Somehow

Kalchan had the knack of being able to wake up at exactly the same time every morning, although it usually took him some time to go from sleep to full wakefulness. The one and only time that knack had failed him, he'd been dead drunk after swilling himself senseless on the free wine given out at some Guild Midwinter Feast three years ago. Not that Kalchan belonged to any Guilds, but he'd somehow managed to get himself invited or sneak in, and he'd certainly drunk far more than his share. He'd gotten back to the tavern on his own two feet, but had fallen straight onto the bedding that Skif and the cook had laid out in anticipation of his return, and he hadn't awakened until noon. Then, between anger at losing a whole morning's custom, and the temper caused by his hangover, he'd beaten Skif black and blue, blacked Maisie's eyes, and kept them all working and away from the Temple largesse of Midwinter Day. All taverns closed the afternoon of Midwinter Day—there was no point in remaining open, since there was a Feast laid on at the Temples for anyone who attended the Service beforehand. It was the one time of the year that Skif, Maisie, and the cook got a chance to stuff themselves sick on good, toothsome food, and Kalchan kept them from it, and beat them again the next day for good measure. That had marked the lowest point of Skif's life, and if he'd been bigger or older, he'd have run away and damn the consequences.

They never let him oversleep by that much again, not even though it meant a beating for awakening him. Not even broken bones would keep Skif from a Temple Midwinter Feast.

He was already up and waiting for Kalchan to unbar the kitchen door by the time his cousin waddled into the room. Kalchan looked at him with nothing other than his usual irritated glare, and performed that office, then turned and went back into the common room, leaving Skif to start the fire or go wait for the pony cart in the yard as he preferred.

For a wonder, when the cook had remembered to bank the fire, she'd actually done it right. There must not have been as much beer in the pitcher as she had thought. There was *one* coal left, not a lot, but enough to get some flames going with the help of lint, straw, and a little tallow. For once, Skif was done with his morning duties early, and he dashed out before Kalchan noticed.

That meant he was waiting at the Temple door long before any of the other pupils, and decided against his usual custom to go into the sanctuary and watch Beel and his fellow priests perform the service. Not that he cared one way or another about religion, but the sanctuary was a place to get out of the cold and to sit down.

For a service like this one, where no one was really expected to come join in the worship, there was no grand procession up the center of the Temple. Instead, a few priests came in from doors on either side of the altar, lit candles and incense, and began very quiet chanting. If you knew the chants and wished to join, you could—otherwise, you could observe and pray, according to your own nature.

He was the only person in the sanctuary other than the priests, and he had found a marginally warm place in the shadows of a pillar, so they probably didn't even notice him. They certainly didn't make any effort to pitch their voices to carry, and the distant murmur, combined with the fact that he could lean up against the pillar, allowed him to drop into a drowse again.

He drifted back into the dream of this morning; it seemed to be a continuation of the same story. This time he and the girl were crouched together in a closet, listening to something in the next room. The murmur of the priests at their devotions blended with the murmurs in the dream. Then the dream changed abruptly, as dreams tended to do, and he found himself incongruously staring deeply into a pair of large, deep blue eyes that filled his entire field of vision.

Blue eyes? *Whose* blue eyes? He didn't know anyone with blue eyes.

Abruptly, the bell signifying the end of the service rang, and he started awake.

Huh, he thought with bemusement. *Haven't dreamed this much in—can't 'member when. Must've been ev'thin' I et!*

He got to his feet when the priests were gone, sauntered out of the sanctuary, and joined the rest of the pupils now gathering for their lessons.

But today was going to be different. For the first time ever, he put real effort into his attempts to master numbers. If he was going to have a position with Bazie's gang, he *didn't* want the authorities looking for him to clap him back into lessons. There was always a chance that they would catch him. If that happened, his uncle would know exactly where to find him.

No, the moment that Bazie had a place for him, he wanted to be able to pass his test and get released from school. Then he could disappear, and Uncle Londer could fume all he wanted. At the moment, he couldn't see how hanging with Bazie's gang could be anything but an improvement over the Hollybush.

His determination communicated itself to his tutor, and the younger boy put more enthusiasm into the lesson than Skif had expected. By the end of it, he'd made more progress in that single morning than he had in the four years he'd been taking lessons.

When lessons were over and the bell rang, he got ready to shoot out the door with the rest, but before he could, he felt a heavy hand on his shoulder, holding him in his seat.

Beel. He must have noticed something was different. Skif's stomach knotted, and his heart sank. He was in trouble, he must be—and for once, he didn't know why, or for what reason. And that made it worse.

"You can all go—" said Beel, whose hand, indeed, it was—but Beel's hand kept Skif pinned where he was.

Only when the room had emptied did Beel remove his hand

from Skif's shoulder, and the young priest came around in front of him to stand looking down at him soberly.

"Skif—do you do work at the tavern in the afternoons?" Beel asked, a peculiarly strained expression on his face.

What?

Skif hesitated. If he told the truth, surely Beel would tell his father that Skif was a regular at playing truant from the Hollybush, and he would be in trouble. But if he didn't—Beel was a priest, and might be able to tell, and he would be in worse trouble.

But Beel didn't wait for him to make up his mind about his answer. "I want you to do something for me, Skif," he said urgently, his eyes full of some emotion Skif couldn't recognize. "I want you to promise me that today you *won't* go near the tavern from the time lessons let out until the time darkness falls."

The look Skif wore on his face must have been funny, since Beel smiled thinly. "I can't tell you why, Skif, but I hope that you can at least trust the priest if you can't trust your cousin. My father . . . is not as clever as he thinks he is. Someone is angry, angry at him, and angry at Kalchan. I think, unless he can be persuaded to curb his anger, that he is going to act this afternoon. You have nothing to do with all this, and you do not deserve to be caught in the middle."

And with those astonishing words, Beel turned and left, as he always did, as if nothing out of the ordinary had ever transpired between them.

After a moment, Skif shook off his astonishment and slowly left the building. Once out in the sunlight, he decided that whatever Beel was hinting at didn't really matter, because he had no notion of going back to the tavern during the day anyway. He was going to meet Deek, and get his first lessons in the fine art of thievery!

Deek wasn't lurking anywhere on the way to the building where Bazie's "laundry" was, but Skif remembered the way back to Bazie's, including the secret passages, perfectly. He suspected that this was his first test, and when he rapped on the door in an approximation of Deek's knock, it was Deek himself who opened it with a grin.

"I tol' ye 'e'd 'member!" Deek crowed, drawing Skif inside.

"An' I agreed wi' ye," Bazie said agreeably. "If 'e hadn', 'e wouldn' be much use, would'e?"

There was new laundry festooning the ceiling today— stockings and socks. Only Lyle was with Bazie and Deek; the third boy was nowhere to be seen.

" 'J'eet yet?" asked Lyle, as Deek drew him inside. At Skif's head shake, the other boy wordlessly gestured at the table, where half of a decent cottage loaf of brown bread waited, with some butter and a knife. Beside it was a pot of tea and mugs. Buttered bread, half eaten, sat on a wooden plate next to Bazie. All in all, it was the sort of luncheon that wouldn't disgrace the table of a retiring spinster of small means.

Not that Skif cared what it looked like—he'd been invited to eat, and eat he surely would. He fell on the food, cutting two nice thick slices of bread and buttered them generously, pouring himself a mug of tea. Bazie watched him with an oddly benevolent look on his face.

"Eat good, but don' eat *full* afore a job," he said, in a manner that told Skif this was a rule, and he'd better pay close attention to it. "Nivir touch stuff as makes ye gassy, an' nothin' that'll be on yer breath. Whut if ye has t' hide? Summun smells onions where no onions shud be, or wuss—" He blew a flatulent razz with his lips, and the other boys laughed. "Oh, laugh if ye like, but I heerd boys been caught that way! Aye, an' growed men as shoulda knowed better!"

Skif laughed, too, but he also nodded eagerly. Bazie was no fool; no matter that what his gang purloined was small beer compared with jewels and gold—it was obviously supplying them with a fair living, and at the moment, Skif wouldn't ask for more.

"Nah, good gillyflar tea, tha's the stuff afore a job," Bazie continued with satisfaction. "Makes ye keen, sharp. Tha's what ye need." He waited while Skif finished his bread and butter and drank a mug of the faintly acidic, but not unpleasant, tea. He knew gillyflower tea from the Temple, where it occasionally appeared with the morning bread, and it did seem to wake him up when he felt a little foggy or sleepy.

"Nah, t'day Deek, I don' want wipes," Bazie continued. "I got sum'thin' I been ast for, special. Mun wants *napkins.* Ye ken napkins?"

Deek shook his head, but Skif, who had, after all, been serving in Lord Orthallen's hall as an ersatz page, nodded. "Bits uv linen—'bout so big—" He measured out a square with his hands. "Thicker nor wipes, kinda towels, but fine, like. Them highborns use 'em t' meals, wipes their han's an' face on 'em so's they ain't all grease an' looks sweetly."

"Ha!" Bazie slapped his knee with his hand. "Good boy! Deek, where ye think ye kin find this stuff?"

Deek pondered the question for a moment, then suggested a few names that Skif didn't recognize. "We h'aint touched any on 'em for a while."

"Make a go," Bazie ordered. "I needs twa dozen, so don' get 'em all in one place, eh?"

"Right. Ye ready?" Deek asked, looking down at Skif, who jumped to his feet. "We're off."

"Not like *that* 'e ain't!" Lyle protested. "Glory, Deek, 'e cain't pass i' them rags!"

Bazie concurred with a decided nod. "Gi'e 'im summat on ourn. 'Ere, Lyle—i' the cubberd—"

Lyle went to the indicated alcove and rummaged around for a moment. " 'Ere, these're too small fer any on' us—"

The boy threw a set of trews and a knitted tunic at Skif who caught them. They were nearly identical to Deek's; the same neat and barely-visible patches, the same dark gray-brown color. Happy to be rid of his rags, Skif stripped off everything but his smallclothes and donned the new clothing.

Now Bazie and Lyle nodded their satisfaction together. "We'll boil up yer ol' thin's an' mend 'em a bit—ye kin 'ave 'em back when ye git back," Bazie said. "We don' wan' yer nuncle t' wonder where ye got new close."

"Yessir," Skif said, bobbing his head. "Thenkee, sir!"

Bazie laughed. "Jest get me napkins, imp."

Now properly clothed so that his ragged state wouldn't attract attention, Skif was permitted to follow Deek out into the streets.

They walked along as Skif had already learned to, as if, no matter how fine the neighborhood, they belonged there, that they were two boys who had been sent on an errand that needed to be discharged expeditiously, but not urgently.

Deek, however, knew every illicit way into the laundries and wash houses of the fine houses on these streets, and he led Skif over walls, up trees, and across rooftops. Together they waited for moments when the laundresses and washer-women were otherwise occupied, and dropped down into the rooms where soiled linens were sorted for washing.

It was Skif who picked out the napkins from among the rest—no more than two or three lightly soiled squares of linen at each place. He chose nothing that was so badly grease-stained that it was unlikely it could be cleaned, nor did he pick out items that were new.

Once retrieved, Deek did something very clever with them. He folded them flat, and stuffed them inside the legs of his trews and Skif's, so that there was no way to tell that the bits of fabric were there at all without forcing them to undress. When they had the full two dozen, with no close calls and only one minor alarm, Deek called a halt, and they strolled back to Bazie's.

Skif was tired, but very pleased with himself. He'd kept up with Deek, and *he'd* been the ones to pick out the loot Bazie wanted. Nothing new, nothing over-fine, nothing that would be missed unless and until a housekeeper made a full inventory. Not likely, that; not in the places that Deek had selected.

They made their way up, over, and down again, and back to Bazie's den. This time when Deek knocked, it was Bazie himself that opened the door for them, and Skif watched with covert amazement as he stumped back to his seat like some sort of bizarre four-legged creature, supporting himself on two wooden pegs strapped where his legs had been, and two crutches, one for each arm.

"Aaa—" Bazie said, in a note of pain, as he lowered himself down to his seat and quickly took off the wooden legs. "When ye brings back th' glimmers, young'un, I'll be gettin' proper-fittin' stumps, fust thing." He gestured in disgust at the crude wooden legs. "Them's no better nor a couple slats. How's it that a mun kin be sa good wi' needle an sa bad wi' whittlin'?"

He put the crutches aside, and looked at them expectantly.

"Here ye be, Bazie!" said Deek, taking the lead, and pulling napkins out of his trews the way a conjure mage at a fair pulled kerchiefs out of his hand. Skif did the same, until all two dozen were piled in front of their mentor.

"Hah! Good work!" Bazie told them. "Nah, young'un—ye look an ye tell me—wha's the big problem we got wi' these fer sellin' uv 'em?"

That was something Skif had worried about. Every single napkin they'd taken had been decorated with distinctive embroidered initials or pictures on the corners. "Them whatcha-calls in th' corners," Skif said promptly. "Dunno what they be, but they's all different."

"They's t' show what owns 'em, but ol' Bazie's gotta cure for that, eh, Deek?" Bazie positively beamed at both of them, and took out a box from a niche beside his seat. He opened it, and Skif leaned forward to see what was inside.

Sewing implements. Very fine, as fine as any great lady's. Tiny scissors, hooks, and things he couldn't even guess at.

His mouth dropped open, and Bazie laughed. "Ye watch, an ye learn, young'un," he said merrily. "An' nivir ye scorn till ye seen—"

Bazie took out the tiniest pair of scissors that Skif had ever seen, and a thing like a set of tongs, but no bigger than a pen, and several other implements Skif had no names for. Then he took up the first of the napkins and set to work on it.

Within moments, it was obvious what he was doing; he was unpicking the embroidery. But he was doing so with such care that when he was finally done, only a slightly whiter area and a hole or two showed where it had been, and the threads he had unpicked were still all in lengths that could be used.

"Nah, I'll be doin' that t' all uv them, then into th' bleach they goes, an' no sign where they come from!" Bazie rubbed his hands together with glee. "An' that'll mean a full five siller fer the lot from a feller what's got a business in these things, an' all fer a liddle bit uv easy work for ye an me! Nah, what sez ye t' that, young'un?"

Skif could only shake his head in admiration. "That—I'm mortal glad I grabbed fer Deek's ankle yesterday!"

And Bazie roared with laughter. "So'm we, boy!" he chuckled. "So'm we!"

SKIF did not go out again, nor did Deek. Instead, they emptied out the cauldron of its warm, soapy, green-gray water, pouring it down a drain hole in the center of the room, and refilled it with fresh. This was no mean feat, as it had to be done one bucketful at a time, from the common pump that everyone in the building shared—which was, predictably, in a well house attached to the side of the building to keep it from freezing. Bazie had special buckets, with lids that kept the water from slopping, but it still made for a lot of climbing.

No wonder Bazie was ready t' bring me in! Skif thought ruefully, as he poured his bucketful into what seemed to have become a wash cauldron without a bottom. His arms ached, and so did his back—this business of becoming a thief was more work than it looked!

"How often d'ye empty this'un?" he asked Bazie, who was mending a stocking as dexterously as he had unpicked the design on the napkins.

"Once't week," Bazie replied. "We saves all th' whites fer

54

then. Wouldna done it early, forbye th' *napkin* order's on haste, an' ye're here t' hep."

Skif sighed, and hefted the empty bucket to make another journey. This was like working at the Hollybush—

He had no doubt that he would be the chief cauldron filler until Bazie took on another boy, so he had this to look forward to, once a week, for the foreseeable future.

On the other hand, Bazie appeared to feed his boys well and treat them fairly. Skif had plenty of time to think about the situation, to contrast how Raf, Deek, and Lyle all acted around Bazie and how well-fed (if a bit shabby) they looked. So Bazie wasn't running a gang that was wearing silks and velvets and had servants to do their work. So he and the rest of the boys had to do a hauling now and then. They were eating, they were warm, and Bazie was a good master. What was a little hard work, set against that?

So he hauled and dumped, hauled and dumped, while his arms, back, and legs complained on every inward journey. When the cauldron was at last filled, Bazie let him rest for just long enough to drink another mug of tea. When the tea was gone, Bazie put him to building up the fire beneath the cauldron, then adding soap and a pungent liquid that he said would whiten the worst stains. When the water was actually boiling, at Bazie's direction he added the napkins, then other articles that *should* have been white. There wasn't a lot; pure white was a very difficult state to attain, so the boys didn't steal anything that should be white.

"Dunno how them Heralds does it," Bazie said, half in wonder and half in frustration. "Them Whites, 'sall they wears, an' how they nivir gets stains, I dunno."

"Magic," Deek opined cheekily, and Bazie laughed.

"Gimme stick," Deek told Skif. "Take a breather." Deek took over then, stirring while Skif lay back on a pile of straw-stuffed sacks that served as cushions, letting his aches settle.

Lyle arrived, tapping his code on the door, and Deek let him in. Raf was right behind him. Both boys began emptying their pockets and the fronts of their tunics as soon as they came in. Skif sat up to watch as Bazie supervised.

What came out of their clothing wasn't kerchiefs and other bits of silk this time, but metal spoons, knives, packets of pins and needles, fancy pottery disks with holes in the middle—

"Ah," Bazie said with satisfaction. "Wool Market good, then?"

"Aye," the boy named Raf said. "Crowd." This was the one that Skif hadn't seen much of yesterday, and if someone had asked him to point Raf out in a crowd he still wouldn't be able to. Raf was extraordinarily ordinary. There was nothing distinctive in his height (middling), his weight (average), his face (neither round nor square), his eyes and hair (brown), or his features (bland and perfectly ordinary). Even when he smiled at Skif, it was just an ordinary, polite smile, and did nothing; it seemed neither warm, nor false, and it certainly didn't light up his features.

Bazie watched him as he examined the other boy and mentally dismissed him—and Bazie grinned.

"So, young'un, wot ye think'o Raf?" he asked.

"Don' think much one way or 'tother," Skif said truthfully.

Bazie laughed, and so did Raf. "Na, ye don' see't, does ye?" Bazie said.

"Wall, he wouldn' see it now, would'e?" Raf put in. "If'n 'e *did,* that'd be bad!"

The others seemed to think this was a great joke, but it was one that Skif didn't get the point of. They all laughed heartily, leaving him sitting on the stuffed sacks looking from one to the other, perplexed, and growing irritated.

"Wha's the joke?" he asked loudly.

"Use yer noggin—" Lyle said, rubbing his knuckles in a quick gesture over Skif's scalp. "Raf's on the liftin' lay, dummy. So?"

"I dunno!" Skif retorted, his irritation growing. "Whazzat got ter do wi' wot I think uv 'im?"

"It ain't wot yer think uv 'im, 'tis 'is *looks,*" Deek said with arch significance, which made the other two boys go off in gales of laughter again, and Bazie to chuckle.

"Well, 'e ain't gonna ketch no gurls wi' 'em," Skif replied sullenly. " 'E don' look like nothin' special."

"And?" Deek prompted, then shook his head at Skif's failure to comprehend. "Wot's special 'bout *not* special?"

Finally, *finally,* it dawned on him, and his mouth dropped open in surprise. "Hoy!" he said. "Cain't give no beak no ways t' find 'im!"

A "beak," Skif knew, was one of the city watchmen who patrolled for thieves and robbers, took care of drunks and simple assault and other minor crimes. Anything major went to the Guard, and anything truly big went to one of the four City Heralds—not that Skif had ever seen one of these exalted personages. He'd never seen a Guard either, except at a distance. The Guards didn't bother with the neighborhoods like this one, not unless murder and mayhem had occurred.

Bazie nodded genially. "Thas' right. Ain't no better boy fer learnin' th' liftin' lay," he said with pride. "Even'f sommut sees him, 'ow they gonna tell beak wot 'e looks like if'n 'e don' look like nothin'?"

Now it was Skif's turn to shake his head, this time in admiration. What incredible luck to have been born so completely nondescript! Raf could pick pockets for the rest of his life on looks like his—he wouldn't even have to be particularly *good* at it so long as he took care that there was nothing that was ever particularly distinctive about him. How could a watchman ever pick him out of a crowd when the description his victim gave would match a hundred, a thousand other boys in the crowd?

" 'E's got 'nother liddle trick, too," Bazie continued. " 'Ere, Lyle—nobble 'im."

Not at all loath, Lyle puffed himself up and seized Raf's arm. "'Ere, you!" he boomed—or tried to, his voice was evidently breaking, and the words came out in a kind of cracked squeak. He tried again. "'Ere, you! You bin liftin'?"

Now Raf became distinctive. Somehow the eyes grew larger, innocent, and tearful; the lower lip quivered, and the entire face took on a kind of guileless stupidity mingled with frightened innocence. It was amazing. If Skif had caught Raf with his hand in Skif's pocket, he'd have believed it was all an accident.

"Whossir? Messir?" Raf quavered. "Nossir. I'm be gettin' packet'o pins fer me mum, sir. . . ." And he held out a paper stuck full of pins for Lyle's inspection, tears filling his eyes in a most pathetic fashion.

Bazie and Deek howled with laughter, as Lyle dropped Raf's arm and growled. "Gerron wi' ye."

As soon as the arm was dropped, Raf pretended to scuttle away with his head down and shoulders hunched, only to straighten up a few moments later and assume his bland guise again. He shrugged as Skif stared at him.

"Play actin'," he said dismissively.

"Damn *good* play actin'," Bazie retorted. "Dunno 'ow long ye kin work it, but whilst ye kin, serve ye better nor runnin' from beaks." He set his mending aside and rubbed his hands together. " 'Sall right, me boys. 'Oo wants t'fetch dinner?"

"Me," Raf said. "Don' wanta stir washin', an' don' wanta sort goods."

The other two seemed amenable to that arrangement, so Raf got a couple of coins from Bazie and took himself off. The napkins in the cauldron were finally white enough to suit Bazie, so Skif got the job of pulling the white things out and rinsing them in a bucket of fresh water, while Lyle hung them up and Deek sorted through the things that Lyle and Raf had brought back.

Presently he looked up. "Six spoons, two knifes, packet uv

needles, three uv pins, empty needlecase, four spinnin' bobs,"
he said. "Reckon thas 'nuf wi' wot we alriddy got?"

Bazie nodded. "Arter supper ye go out t' Clave. Ye kin take
napkins t' Dooly at same time. An' half th' wipes. Lyle, ye'll
take t' rest uv th' goods t' Jarmin."

"Kin do," Lyle replied genially, taking the last of the napkins from Skif. "Young'un, git that pile an' dunk in wash, eh?"

He pointed to a pile of dingy shirts and smallclothes in the
corner with his chin. "Thas ourn," he added by way of explanation. "Ye kin let fire die a bit, so's its cool 'nuf fer the silks
when ourn's done."

Skif had wondered—the stuff didn't seem to be of the same
quality as the goods that the boys brought back to Bazie. Obediently, he picked up the pile of laundry and plunged it into
the wash cauldron and began stirring.

"Ye moght be a wonderin' why we does all this washin' an
wimmin stuff," Bazie said conversationally. "I tell ye. Fust, I
tell m'boys allus t' nobble outa the dirty stuff—'cause thas
inna pile, an nobody ain't counted it yet. See?"

Skif nodded; he *did* see. It was like playing a page at Lord
Orthallen's meals. Food was checked before it became a dish
for a meal, it was checked for pilferage before it was taken to
the table, and it was checked when it came back to the kitchen
as leftovers. But there was that moment of opportunity while
it was in transition from kitchen to table when no one was
checking the contents. So, dirty clothing and linen probably
wasn't counted—why should it be? But if you stole something
off a wash line, or out of a pile of clean clothing intended for
a particular person, it would be missed.

"So, we gets stuff tha' way, but if's dirty, it ain't wuth so
much. 'F it were just th' odd wipe we git from liftin' lay,
wouldn' be wuth cleanin'—an' thas why most on liftin' lay
don' clean whut they nobble, 'cause they gotta get glim fer it
now so's they kin eat." Bazie peered at Skif to see if he was
following. "Us, we pass *straight* onta couple lads as has stalls

in market, 'cause what we got's clean an' got no markin's on't. Looks jest like wha' ye'd sell t' market stall an' yer ol' mum croaked an' ye're droppin' 'er goods. We spread it 'round t' several lads so's it don' look bad."

That made perfect sense. The used-clothing merchants buying the things had to know they were stolen, of course—either that, or they were idiots—but there was no other way to tell. And once Bazie's loot was mixed up with all the other things in a merchant's stall, it all looked perfectly ordinary. Servants often got worn, outgrown, or outmoded clothing from their masters as part of their wages or as a bonus, and most of that ended up with a used-clothing merchant. Then those who wished to appear well-to-do or seamstresses looking for usable fabric for better garments would find bargains among the bins. Pickpockets unlike Bazie's gang, who lifted used kerchiefs and the like—and outright muggers, who assaulted and stripped their victims bare—would have to sell their soiled goods to a rag man rather than directly to a stall holder.

"Me old mam made me learn th' sewin'," Bazie continued. " 'M a pretty dab 'and at un. Mended stuff's wuth more'n tore-up, an' unpickin' the pretties makes 'em plain—well, like napkins. All it costs's time—an' hellfires, I got time!"

"Smart," Skif said, meaning it. Bazie looked pleased.

"*Some* lads thinks as is sissy stuff, 'an' couldn' stick i' wi' us," Deek put in, scornfully. "*Some* lads, sayin' no names but as rhymes with *scare-up*, thinks is a waste uv time."

"*Some* lads'll end up under the beak inside a moon," Lyle said lazily. " 'Cause *some* lads kin ony think uv glim an' glimmers, an' don't go at thin's slow. I don' care, long's I gets m' dinner!"

Bazie laughed, as Skif nodded agreement vigorously. "Thas m' clever lads!" Bazie said approvingly. "Roof over t'head, full belly an' warm flop—thas' th' ticket. Glim an' glimmers kin wait on learnin t' be better nor good."

"Righto," Deek affirmed. "Takes a mort'o learnin'. They's

old thieves, an' they's bold thieves, but they ain't no old, bold thieves."

That seemed excellent advice to Skif, who stirred the cauldron with a will.

It wasn't until he began pulling garments out with the stick that Skif noticed his own clothing was in with the rest—and that Bazie had neatly mended and patched it while he was gone. He'd resewn Skif's clumsy work to much better effect, and Skif felt oddly touched by this considerate gesture.

Raf returned as he started on the next lot of purloined scarves, carrying a packet and another loaf of bread. "They's mort'o doin's over t' Hollybush," he said as he handed Bazie the packet.

Skif's head snapped around. "What doin's?" he asked sharply.

"Dunno fer certain-sure," Raf replied. "Summun sez a couple toughs come in an' wrecked t' place, summun sez no, 'twas a fight, an' ev'un sez summun's croaked, or near it. All I knows's theys beaks an' a Guard there now. Figgered ye shud know."

Bazie mulled that over, as Skif stood there, stunned, the wash stick still in his hands. "Reckon five fer supper," he said judiciously. "Huh."

"I cud go wi'im arter dark," Lyle offered. "We cud reck th' doin's."

Bazie shook his head. "Nay, no goin' near—Raf! Ye good fer goin' out agin? Hev a drink i' th' Arms?"

The grandly named "King's Arms" was the nearest rival to the Hollybush, and its owner had no love for Kalchan or Uncle Londer. One reason for the rivalry was economic—the Arms didn't serve the kind of swill that the Hollybush did, and charged accordingly. Many, many of the poorest customers opted for quantity over quality, and their custom went to Kalchan. If anything bad had happened to the Hollybush or its owner, the buzz would be all over the Arms.

"Oh, aye!" Raf laughed. "They don' know me there, an' leastwise ye kin drink th' beer 'thout bein' choked."

"Arms beer's nought so bad," Bazie said complacently. "Here—" he flipped a fivepenny coin at Raf. "Get a drink and fill me can, an' come on back."

Raf caught the coin right out of the air, picked up a covered quart beer pail, and saluted Bazie with two fingers. "I'm be back afore the bacon's fried," he promised.

Skif could only wonder what had happened—and how Beel had known that it would. And what if Beel *hadn't* given him that timely warning? He could have walked straight into a fight, or a trap, or who knew what trouble.

A shiver ran down his back—for his own near miss, and not for anything that might have happened to Kalchan. In fact, he sincerely hoped that Kalchan was at the very least cooling his heels in the gaol. Given all the rotten things that Kalchan had done—just the things that Skif knew about—he had a lot coming to him.

He shook his head and went back to his stirring. Bazie had been watching him closely, and seemed satisfied with what he saw. "Ye mot not hev a home," he ventured.

Skif shrugged. "Hell. Bargain's a bargain. Ye said, a moon, I'll not 'spect a flop afore that. 'F nobuddy's there, I kin sneak in t' sleep. I kin sleep on roof, or stairs, or summat." He managed a weak grin. "Or even Lord Orthallen's wash house."

Bazie now looked *very* satisfied; evidently Skif had struck exactly the right note with him. No pleading, no asking for special consideration—he'd got that already. Just matter-of-fact acceptance.

'Sides, 'tis only for a moon. That ain't long. Even in winter.

Actually, the wash house wasn't a bad idea. Skif had slept there once or twice before, when Kalchan had decided that in addition to a set of stripes with the belt, he didn't deserve a bed, and locked him out in the courtyard overnight. From dark until dawn the only people there would be the laundry maids, who slept there, and none of them would venture up to the storage loft after dark. The ones that weren't young and silly and afraid of spirits were old and too tired to do more than drop onto the pallets and snore. It would be cold, but no worse than the Hollybush.

The only difficulty would be getting in and out, since beaks and private guards were on the prowl after dark in force.

Well, he'd deal with the problems as they came up and not before. *Hard on me if I can't slip past a couple beaks.*

He didn't have very long to wait for his news; by the time the next batch of laundry was in the cauldron, Raf returned with Bazie's pail of beer and a mouth full of news.

"Well!" he said, as soon as Deek let him in. "Ol' Londer did hisself no good this time! What I heerd— 'e cheated a mun, sommun wi' some brass, an' th' mun got a judgment on 'im. So's the judgment sez the mun gets Hollybush. On'y nobuddy tol' yon Kalchan, or Kalchan figgered 'e weren't gonna gi'e up, or Londer tol' Kalchan t' keep mun out. So mun comes wi' bullyboys t'take over, an' Kalchan, 'e sez I don' think so, an lays inta 'em wi' iron poker!"

"Hoo!" Skif said, eyes wide with glee. "Wisht I'da been there!"

"Oh, nay ye don'—cuz it went bad-wrong," Raf corrected with relish. "Th' cook, she comes a-runnin' when she hears th' ruckus, lays in w' stick, an th' girl, she tries t' run fer it, an' slippet an starts t' scream, an' that brings beaks. So beaks get inta it, an' they don' love Kalchan no more nor anybuddy else, an' they commences t' breakin' heads. Well! When 'tis all cleared up, they's a mun dead wi' broke neck, an' Kalchan laid out like cold fish, t'cook ravin', an' t'girl—" Raf gloated, "—t'girl, she turn out t'be bare fifteen, no schoolin', an' pretty clear Kalchan's been atop 'er more'n once!"

"Fifteen!" Skif's eyes bulged. "I'da swore she was eighteen, sure! Sixteen, anyroad!"

Then again—he'd simply assumed she was. There wasn't

much of her, and she wasn't exactly talkative. She had breasts, and she was of middling height, but some girls developed early. Wasn't there a saying that those who were a bit behind in the brains department were generally ahead on the physical side?

"Thas' whut Londer, 'e tried t'say, but they got th' girl's tally from Temple an' she's no more'n bare fifteen an' that jest turned!" Raf practically danced in place. "So ol' Londer, he got it fer not schoolin' th' girl, an' puttin' er where Kalchan cud tup 'er, an not turnin' over Hollybush proper. Cook's hauled off someplace, still ravin'. Girl's taken t' Temple or summat. Kalchan, he's wust, *if* 'e wakes up, which Healers sez mebbe and mebbe not, 'e's up fer murder *an* fer tuppin' the girl afore she be sixteen."

Skif had to sit down. Kalchan and Uncle Londer had always come out on top of things before. He could scarcely believe that they weren't doing so now.

"Good thing ye weren' there," Bazie observed mildly. "Kalchan 'ud say t'was *you* was tuppin' girl."

"Me? Maisie?" Skif grimaced. "Gah, don' thin' so—ugh! Druther turn priest!"

"Well, wouldna' be call fer th' law if 'twas you. Couple kids foolin' 'round's a thing fer priests, not the law. Summun old's Kalchan, though, thas different, an' reckon 'f ol' Londer don' 'ang 'is boy out t' dry, he'll say 'twas you." Bazie rubbed his chin speculatively. "Don' 'magine girl 'ud conterdick 'im."

"Don' fergit, she's in Temple," Lyle piped up. "Dunno 'f they'd git 'er t'talk. Mebbe use Truth Spell."

"It don' matter," Skif decided. "I don' want nothin' t'do wi' em. I ain't goin' back."

Londer wouldn't know where he was, nor would Kalchan, who was, in any event, in no position to talk. The trouble was Beel knew he had stayed away. So would Beel send anyone looking for him? And should he tell Bazie about all of this?

Reluctantly, he decided that he had better.

"This's gettin' complisticatered," he said unhappily, and explained about Beel, and Beel's warning.

The others all sat silent for a moment, their eyes on him.

"This Beel, 'e knows nowt 'bout us?" Bazie asked, his head to one side, quizzically.

Skif shook his head. "'E ain't niver sed much t'me afore this," he replied. "I allus figgered 'e wuz jest Londer's eyes. Niver reckoned on 'im warnin' me." He considered the odd conversation a little further. "Must've known, an' didn' warn his Da neither. Niver reckoned on 'im stickin' t' th' law—an' ye kin bet Londer wouldn't. Huh. Turned on 'is own Da!"

Bazie nodded slowly. "Niver know wut bein' in Temple'll do wi' a mun," he said sagely. "Gets t'thinkin' 'bout 'is own soul, mebbe. Starts thinkin' 'is ol' man cud stan' bein' took down a peg, mebbe figgers th' ol' man cud stand t' get held 'countable. Figgers a kid don' need t' get mixed up in't."

"Point is, ain't nobuddy knows 'bout us," said Raf. He stared intently at Skif for a very long and uncomfortable moment. Finally, the older boy seemed to make up his mind. "Bazie, I sez we votes now. Young'un ain't behind wi' helpin', an' Deek sez 'e's good over roof. Bring 'un in."

Bazie looked at the other two as Skif blinked with bewilderment. What on earth was he getting at?

"Aye!" Deek exclaimed. "In by me!"

"Makes three," said Lyle lazily. " 'E's already done more'n a couple days than You Know did in a week."

Now Skif realized what they were saying, and his heart leaped as he looked to Bazie, the leader, the teacher—

"Oh, I'd already reckoned," Bazie said with a smile. " 'E might's well jump in. Lyle, ye take 'im wi' ye t' Jarmin, so's Jarmin gets t' know 'is face, an' 'e gets t' know th' proper pay fer th' goods."

He clapped Skif on the back. "Yer in, young 'un. They's room 'nuf an' a bed nobuddy got, an' plenty t' go 'round. Ye're well-come."

"Hey! Les' eat!" Deek exclaimed, before Skif could really get it fixed in his mind how his life had just been turned around, that he had just been fully accepted into the gang. That he never had to go back to Kalchan and the misery of the Hollybush again.

And no more lessons!

Bazie laughed, and distributed the labor. Skif was set to cutting the loaf and buttering the slices, Deek to frying slices of fat bacon over the fire beneath the cauldron, Lyle to get the plates and pot of mustard, Raf to pour small beer for all of them. Skif was a bit surprised by that last. Kalchan never shared beer with anyone—but Raf divided the quart equally among the five of them with Bazie's approval.

It was the first friendly meal that Skif had ever shared with anyone; the first time he had ever, within memory, eaten in a leisurely manner.

While they ate, Bazie decided what goods they would take to each buyer as soon as darkness fell. It would be better to take their bundles of goods out under the cover of night, just to be certain that no one in their building saw them toting around unusually bulky packages. Once they were out in the street, of course, they would just be three boys carrying out errands, but their neighbors in the building shouldn't be given the excuse to be nosy.

As soon as dinner was polished off and the last of the laundry hung up to dry, Skif and Lyle packed up the goods for Jarmin, the old clothes seller. Evidently Jarmin was a man who catered to those with a taste for finer things; almost all of the fancier goods were going to him. When everything had been selected, they each had a fairly bulky bundle wrapped in oilcloth. Bazie showed Skif how to use a piece of rope to make a crude backpack of it, to keep his hands free.

"Take a stick," he cautioned Skif; Lyle had already selected a stout cudgel from six or so leaning over in a corner near the door. "Plenty uv folk out there'll beat ye jest hopin' ye got summat they want."

Like I don't know that! Skif thought—but he didn't make any comments, he just selected a stick for himself.

The packs made negotiating the stairs a little awkward, but they got out all right, and Lyle strode down the street with the air of someone who had a place to get to in a hurry. Skif had to trot to keep up with him. For all that Lyle acted lazy back in the room, he could certainly put out some energy when he chose to!

He didn't waste any breath on talking either. What he *did* was to keep his eyes moving, up and down the street, peering at doorways, watching for trouble. Skif followed his example. Until now, he hadn't been out on the street much at night, and he was very conscious of how vulnerable two boys were. There wasn't much light. Nobody wasted much money on street-lamps around these neighborhoods. What little there was came from windows and a few open doors, and from the torches people carried with them.

They didn't have a torch, but Skif didn't really want one. Certainly having a torch or a lantern made it easier to see your way, but it also made it very clear how many people were in your group and whether or not you had anything that looked worth stealing. Plus you couldn't see past the circle of light cast by the torch, which made it easier for you to be ambushed.

The street was anything but deserted, despite the darkness. People came and went from cookshops and taverns, groups of young toughs strolled about looking for whatever they could get into, streetwalkers sauntered wherever there was a bit of illumination, with their keepers (if they had one) lurking just out of sight of potential customers. There were ordinary working men and women, too, coming home late from their jobs. For a bit it would only be a *little* more dangerous to be out on the street than it was during the day.

Skif had figured that this "Jarmin" would be somewhere

nearby, but apparently he was wrong. They must have gone a good ten blocks before Lyle made a turn into a dead-end street that was very nicely lit up indeed.

If the dim and sullen Hollybush had been at one extreme of the sorts of taverns frequented by the poor, this was at the other. The whole back of the cul-de-sac was taken up by a tavern blazing with tallow-dip lights; that had torches in holders right outside the door, and light spilling from parchment-covered windows. There was music, raucous laughter, the sounds of loud talk. A group of men were betting on a contest between two tomcats out in the street, and with them were three or four blowsy females of negotiable virtue, hanging on their arms and cheering on the two oblivious cats.

On either side of the tavern were shops, still open. Skif never got a chance to see what the one on the left sold, because they turned immediately into the one on the right.

This was their goal; an old-clothes shop that specialized in fancy goods of all sorts, but mostly for women. Skif had a shrewd idea where most of the females from the tavern spent their hard-earned coins.

Jarmin, a perfectly ordinary, clerkly sort of fellow, had an assistant to help him, and when he saw Lyle entering the front door, he left the customer he was attending to the assistant and ushered them both into the rear of the shop.

"Have you got sleeves?" Jarmin asked, as soon as he dropped the curtain separating front from back behind them. "I particularly need sleeves. And veils. But particularly sleeves. And I don't suppose you've got silk stockings—"

Lyle shrugged out of his pack, and Skif did the same. "Aye, Jarmin, all uv that. This's Skif; 'e's wi' us now. I'm be showin' 'im th' way uv things."

"Yes, yes." Jarmin dismissed Skif entirely, his attention focused on the packs. "You know, if you just have some good sleeves and stockings, I can sell a dozen pairs tonight, for some reason—"

"All or nowt, Jarmin. Ye know that. Ye takes all or nowt." Lyle had gone from lazy boy to shrewd salesman in the time it had taken to reach this place, and Skif marveled at him as he bargained sharply with the fretful shopkeeper. At length they arrived at a price that was mutually satisfactory, and Skif tried to look as indifferent as Lyle did. It was hard, though; he'd never seen so much money before in all his life.

Aye, but that's from how much work? A week, mebbe? An' there's five uv us t'feed.

Lyle divided the cash between them. "Just i'case," he said darkly, and showed Skif how to wrap it so that it didn't clink and tuck it inside his tunic where it wouldn't show. Only then did they ease out of the shop, where already Jarmin had frowsty girls crowding around the counter demanding shrilly to see the new goods.

If Lyle had set a brisk pace going out, he did better than that coming back. Only when they were safely in the building and heading up the stair did he finally slow down, with Skif panting behind.

"Sorry," he said apologetically. "Hate goin' out. Got caught oncet, 'fore I worked fer Bazie."

"No worries," Skif assured him. "I don' like it much, neither."

In fact, he didn't feel entirely comfortable until he was safely back in Bazie's room, where they pulled out their packets of coin and turned the lot over to a grinning Bazie.

"Good work," he told them both. "Fagged out?"

"'Bout ready t' drop," Skif admitted; now that they were back in the warmth and safety, the very long day, with all of its hard work and unexpected changes in his life suddenly caught up with him.

"Not me!" Lyle declared, and made a growling face. "Ready t' match ye at draughts, ol' man!"

Bazie chuckled. "Show th' young'un 'is cupbard, then, an' I'll get us set."

Lyle pulled on Skif's sleeve, and took him to the side of the room opposite the laundry cauldron, where he opened what Skif had taken to be shutters over a window. Shutters they were, but they opened up to a cubby long enough to lie down in, complete with a straw-stuffed pallet, blankets, and a straw-stuffed cushion. By Skif's standards, it was a bed of unparalleled luxury, and he climbed up into it without a moment of hesitation.

Lyle closed the shutters for him once he was settled, blocking out most of the light from the room beyond. Within moments, he was as cozy and warm as he had ever been in his life, and nothing was going to keep him awake. In fact, the sounds of laughter and dice rattling from the other room couldn't even penetrate into his most pleasant of dreams.

IF Skif thought he was going to get off easy by no longer attending lessons at the Temple, he got a rude awakening the next day.

He was used to getting up early, and he woke—or so he guessed—at or near his usual time. For a moment, he was confused by the total darkness, scent of clean laundry and the lack of *stench,* and most of all, by the fact that he was warm and comfortable. He had never awakened warm and comfortable before. Even in the middle of summer, he was generally stiff from sleeping on the dirt floor, and except in the very hottest days and nights, had usually had all the heat leeched from his body by the floor. Initially he thought he was still dreaming, and moaned a little at the thought that now he was going to have to awaken to Kalchan, cold, and misery.

Then he sat up, hit his forehead on the inside of the sleep cubby before he got more than halfway up, and remembered where he was. He lay back down—he hadn't hit his head that hard, since he hadn't tried to get up very fast.

I'm at Bazie's. Ol' Kalchan's in trouble, deep, 'n so's m'nuncle. An' I don't never have t' go back t' th' tavern!

He lay quietly on his back, stroking the woolen blanket with one hand, tracing the lines of each patch. It must have been patched and darned by Bazie; the seams were so neat and even. No one else was stirring, though, and for the first time he could remember, he lay back in his bed and just luxuriated in the freedom to lie abed as long as he cared to. Or as long as the others would let him—but it looked as if the rest were in no hurry to get about their business.

What was this new life going to be like? The other three boys seemed content and well-nourished, and he couldn't see how a legless man like Bazie could force them to stay if they didn't want to. There would be hard work, and a lot of it; he knew that much from yesterday, when he'd hauled water all afternoon. Danger, too. Despite the fact that the other boys had a cavalier attitude about being caught, there was a lot of danger involved in the life of even a petty thief, and the penalties were harsh. Plenty of people meted out their own punishments on those they nobbled, before the beaks were called, which generally meant a bad beating first, then being clapped in gaol, then any of a variety of punishments.

Official punishments were many and varied, none of them very appealing. *Which's the point, I s'pose.* A thief could be transported to work in someone's fields, could be sent to work as a general dogsbody for the Guard, could be left in gaol, could get lashes—it all depended on the judge. That was for the first time you got caught. After that, the punishments were harsher.

But he wouldn't think about that until after he'd been caught for the first time. If he was. If he was clever, fast, smart—he might never be. *Why not? I bin keepin' from gettin' caught 'till now, an' I'm just a young'un. Ye'd think I'd just get smarter as I get bigger.*

There would be a lot of learning time, though, a great many

menial chores as well, and he couldn't expect to share in the profits even his own hauls brought in for a while. That didn't matter; life here would be a paradise compared with what his life had been like at the tavern. In fact, he didn't much care if all he did was wash the stuff the others brought in for the next year! It wouldn't be any harder than working at the tavern, and he'd be full and warm all the time, with a bed like he'd never had before and clothing that wasn't more hole than fabric.

He lay in the darkness contemplating his future until he heard someone stirring, heard the shutters of another bed open, and the pad of feet on the floor. He turned on his side and saw a flicker of light through the cracks in the shutters of his cubby. He pushed them open cautiously, and looked out.

"Heyla, 'nother lark, eh?" Raf said genially. "Come gimme 'and, then."

Skif hopped out and shut the cubby doors behind him. Raf was bent over the fire under the wash cauldron, coaxing a flame from the banked coals. "Take yon tallow dip, take a light from here, an' light them lamps," he ordered, jerking his head at a tallow dip on the otherwise clean table behind him, barely visible in the dim and flickering light from the hand-sized fire. Skif picked it up, lit it at Raf's little fire, and went around the walls to relight the lamps he vaguely recalled hanging there. There were a lot of oil lamps—four!—and all of them were cobbler's lamps with globes of water-filled glass around the flame to magnify the light, the most expensive kind of oil lamp there was. Skif was impressed; he hadn't paid any attention before, other than to note absently that although this room didn't have any windows there was plenty of illumination. It was interesting; Bazie didn't spend money on luxuries, but in places where it counted—the good soap for the laundry, for instance, and the lighting, and decent fuel for the fireplace under the wash boiler, Bazie got the best.

When he was done, he blew out the tallow dip and put it

with the others in a broken cup above the firebox. By this time
the shutters of another cubby, one just above Skif's, had been
pushed open by a foot, and Deek's tousled head poked out.

"Eh, Bazie?" he called, yawning. "Yon ge'op? Me'n Raf'r
op. Young'un Skif, too."

"Aye," came a muffled reply, and the shutter to a third
eased open. This one was larger—taller, rather—and Bazie
was sitting up inside, peering out at them, the stumps of his
legs hidden under his blanket. Satisfied that the fire was well
started, Raf got up, and Deek swung himself out and down
onto the floor. The two of them went to Bazie's cubby and
linked hands. Bazie put an arm around each of their shoulders
and swung himself onto the "chair" made by their hands.

They carried him to a door beside the one that led outside—
one that Skif hadn't noticed before. Bazie let go of Raf's shoulder, which freed one of his hands, and opened it, and they
carried him inside. There was evidently another room there
that Skif had no notion existed.

The door swung open enough to see inside. The room was
a privy! Skif gaped, then averted his eyes to give Bazie a little
privacy—but it wasn't just *any* privy, it was a real water
closet, the kind only the rich had, and there was a basin in
there as well. The boys shut the door and left their leader in
there with the door closed until a little later, when a knock on
the door told he was finished. They carried him back to his
usual spot beside the fire, directly under one of the lamps.

"And mornin' t'ye, young'un," Bazie said genially.

"Mornin' Bazie," Skif replied, wondering with all his might
just how anyone had gotten a water closet built down here,
and where Bazie had gotten the money to do so. And why—

"Skif, ye're low mun now—'tis yer task t' fetch water fer
privy an' all," said Bazie, which answered at least the question
of where the water for flushing came from. "An' t'will be yer
task t' keep it full. Which—" he added pointedly, "—it needs
now."

"Yessir," Skif said obediently, and went for the buckets. Well, at least one thing hadn't changed—here he was, fetching water first thing in the morning!

It took about three trips to fill the tank above the privy and the pitcher at the basin, and another trip to fill the water butt that served for everything except the wash boiler. By that time all three boys were up and tidying the room at Bazie's direction. After a breakfast of hard-boiled eggs and tea, he ordered them all to strip down and wash off, using the soapy laundry water and old pieces of towel which were dropped back into the wash cauldron when they were done. Then, much to Skif's utter amazement, instead of putting their old clothing on, they all got *new,* clean clothing—smallclothes and all—from the same cupboard as his outfit from yesterday had come out of. Their old clothing went straight into the piles waiting to be washed.

"What's on yer mind, young'un?" Bazie asked as he tried to keep his eyes from bulging.

"D'we—get new duds *ev'ry* day?" he asked, hardly able to believe it.

"D'pends on how hard ye bin workin'," Bazie replied, "But aye, an' it'll be ev' third day at least. Ye're dirty, ye stan' out. Ye canna stan' out—an' mind wut I tol' ye 'bout *smell.*"

Skif minded very well, and he couldn't believe how thorough Bazie was; it was brilliant, really.

"Thas' why yon fancy privy—" Raf said with a chuckle.

"Heh. 'Twas coz *ye* didn' fancy carryin' me t' t'other, up an' down stair," Bazie countered, and they both laughed. "But aye, could'a had earth closet, or jest dropped privy down t'sewer 'thout it bein' water closet, but there'd be stink, ye ken, an' that'd be on us an' on t'goods we washed, eh? So we got mun t' put in water closet when' we took't this place."

Raf sighed. "Took a mort'o th' glim, it did," he said wistfully. "Didn' know ye'd saved tha' much, ye ol' skinflint."

"Kep't fer when we needed't," Bazie replied. "Yer wuz liddler nor th' young'un. Had Ames an' Jodri an' Willem then—an' we made 't up quick enow."

"Wut happened t' *them?*" Skif asked cautiously, fearing to uncover some old, bad news.

But Bazie laughed. "Ames's off! Took't up wi' some travelin' show, run's t' cup'n'ball lay, liftin' i' th' crowd. Jodri, 'e's on 'is own, took't t' sum place t'South. An' Willem made th' big 'un—got hisself th' big haul, an' smart 'nuff t' say, *thassit.* Bought hisself big 'ouse uv flats, like this'un, on'y in better part uv town, lives i' part an' rents out t'rest. Set fer life." Bazie chuckled, and Skif sighed with relief. If Bazie wasn't lying—and there was no reason to think that he was—then his "pupils" had done well for themselves.

And so should he.

It also spoke well that Bazie was perfectly pleased about their success and didn't begrudge them their independence.

"Nah, young'un, ye did good yestiddy, but 'tis in m'mind that mebbe ye shouldn' be seed fer a bit?" Bazie made a question out of it, and Skif was in total agreement with him.

"If th' Guard's got inta it—what wi' th' girl Maisie an' all—mebbe they lookin' fer me," Skif replied. "Ol' Kalchan, well, 'e got hisself in bad deep, an' Guard'll be lookin' fer witness t' whut 'e done. An' ol' Londer, *'e'll* be lookin' fer me t'shet me up."

"No doubt. Mebbe—permanent." Bazie lost that expression of pleasant affability that Skif had become accustomed to. "I know sumthin' uv ol' Londer, an'—mebbe *'e* wouldn' dirty 'is 'ands personal, but 'e knows plenty as would take a 'int 'bout gettin' ye quiet."

Skif shuddered. He had no doubt about that. " 'F I'm not 'bout, 'e'll let ol' Kalchan 'ang. Specially 'f Kalchan don' ever wake up. An' 'e'll say, 'e didn' know nothin' 'bout th' girl, an' no one t' say otherwise."

Londer had three sons, after all. He could afford to lose one.

Hellfires, 'e'll prolly get a girl and breed him a couple more, just t' be on th' safe side, Skif thought with disgust. He rather doubted that his uncle's long-dead spouse had enjoyed a love match with the man, for Londer never mentioned or even thought of her so far as he could tell. And Londer wouldn't have any trouble finding another bride either. All he had to do was go down to the neighborhood where the Hollybush had been or one like it, and he could buy himself a wife with a single gold piece. There were dozens of husbands who would sell him their own wives, or their daughters, brothers who would sell sisters, dozens of women who would sell him their own selves.

Well, that was hardly anything Skif could do something about.

"I think ye're gonna be m'laundry maid fer a fortn't or so, young'un," Bazie said. Skif was disappointed by that, of course, but there really wasn't any way around it. He had to agree, himself. *He* didn't want to get picked up by the Guard, and he surely didn't want his uncle looking to keep him quiet. There wasn't going to be any excitement in washing up scarves and veils—but he figured he might as well put a good face on it.

"Nawt s'bad," he replied, as cheerfully as he could. "Don' mind doin' laundry, 'specially bein' as it's pretty cold out there."

Raf, Lyle, and Deek looked pretty pleased over the situation, though. Well, they should be, since it got them out of hauling water, washing, and taking out whatever trash couldn't be burned.

"Cheer up," Raf said, clapping him on the back. "Bazie's nawt s'bad comp'ny, eh, Bazie? An' 'tis warm enuf in 'ere, real cozy-like. Better nor that there 'Ollybush, eh?"

"Oh, aye, an' 'e ain't 'eerd all me tales yet," Bazie laughed. "So I got an audience wut won' fall asleep on me!"

One by one, the other boys went out to prowl the streets

and see what they could filch, leaving Skif alone with Bazie. Little did Skif guess what lay ahead of him when he finished all the chores Bazie set him—including, to his utter shock, washing the stone floor!—and the last of what Bazie referred to as their "piece goods" were hung up on the lines crisscrossing the ceiling to dry.

Lunchtime had come and gone by then, and the boys had flitted in and out, leaving swag behind to be cleaned and mended, when Bazie said, "Right. Skif, fetch me th' book there—i' th' shelf next t' loaf."

Obediently, Skif went to the set of shelves that held their daily provisions—Bazie never kept much around, because of the rats and mice that couldn't be kept out of a room like this one—and found the book Bazie wanted. It wasn't difficult, since it was the *only* book there, a battered copy of a housewife's compendium of medicines, recipes, and advice lacking a back cover. He brought it over and started to hand it to the old man.

"Nay, nay—" Bazie said. "Sit ye down, 'ere, where light's best, an' read it. Out loud."

Puzzled, but obedient, Skif opened it to the first page and began to read. It was hardly the most fascinating stuff in the world, but Bazie followed his every word, frowning with concentration as he sounded out a few terms that were unfamiliar to him, and correcting him on the one or two occasions when he didn't say the words quite right.

"That'll do," Bazie said with satisfaction when he finished the chapter. "Ye read good 'nuff. Na, get ye bit uv charcoal from fire, an' copy out that fust receipt on table."

"On table?" Skif asked, flabbergasted. "That'll make right mess!"

"An' ye kin wash 't off, after," Bazie countered, in a tone that brooked no argument. So Skif fished out a burned bit of stick and did as he was told, with Bazie leaning as far forward as he could to see just how neat Skif's writing was.

"That'll do," he said again, when Skif finished. "Wash that, but don' drop th' charcoal. Ye're gonna do sums."

"Sums?" Skif squeaked, turning around to stare at the old man. *"Sums? Wut good're sums gonna do a thief?"*

"They're gonna make sure ye ain't cheated by fence, tha's wut," Bazie replied, as sternly—no, far *more* sternly—than ever Beel was. "Ye thin' I'm gonna let ye tak' th' swag t' fence if ye cain't even tell if's cheated ye? 'Ow ye think me other boys did so well, eh? 'Ow ye think Raf an' Lyle an' Deek knows wut's wut?"

"Aw, Bazie—" Skif wailed.

"An' none uv yer *'aw, Bazie.'* I ain't havin' no boys here wut cain't do th' bizness. Get th' coal in yer 'and an' sit ye down." The look in Bazie's eye warned Skif that if he argued, he might find himself out on the street, promises or no promises. With a groan, he bent over the scrubbed table, and prepared to reveal the depth of his ignorance.

And it was abysmal. It wasn't long before Bazie called a halt to the proceedings, with Skif wondering the whole time if Bazie wasn't going to reconsider, now that he knew what a dunce his "new boy" was.

"Skif, Skif, Skif," Bazie sighed, looking pained. "Oh, lad—tell me 'ow 'tis summun as smart as ye are got t' be so iggnerent."

"I didn' wan' miss me breakfust," Skif said humbly, head hanging in shame. "T' Queen sez ever' young'un whut's still takin' lessons gets breakfust. Niver did like sums, so's easy 'nuff not t' learn 'em."

Silence from Bazie for a moment, then, much to Skif's relief, a chuckle. "Well, 'tis 'onest 'nuff answer, an' nay so stupid a one," Bazie replied. "Well, young'un, ye're 'bout t' learn them sums, an' learn 'em t'hard way."

"The hard way," Skif soon learned, was to get them by rote. Bazie drilled him. And drilled him. And then, when he grew hoarse and Skif thought he *might* be done for the day, at least,

Bazie paused only long enough for a mug of hot tea to lubricate his throat and began the drill all over again. Only when Skif was mentally exhausted did Bazie give over, and at that point, Skif was only too pleased to haul water instead of reckoning his four-times table.

Shortly after that, Lyle returned with the makings of dinner and helped Skif put together a satisfying meal of bacon, day-old bread, and apples. As the bacon fried and the bread toasted, the other two appeared with a new lot of loot. Raf brought in more sleeves—this lot was a bit worn and threadbare about the hems, but Bazie examined them and gave it as his opinion that he could make a sort of trim out of some of them that would serve to cover the worn parts, making them look new.

Deek brought back only a couple of scarves and kerchiefs, but a great deal of news for Skif.

"Yer Nuncle Londer's 'angin' 'is boy Kalchan out t' twist on 'is own, which I guess we all figgered," he announced, as Skif and Lyle tucked thick slabs of bacon between two pieces of toasted bread and added mustard before handing them around. "It don' look like ol' Kalchan's gonna be much like hisself, though. Healers say 'is skull wuz fair cracked, an' they figger 'is brains is addled. They reckon 'e'll be good fer nowt but stone pickin' fer 'is life, an' I reckon they'll put 'im out wi' sum farmer or 'tother."

Skif snorted. "'E wuz no prize anyroad," he countered. "But if 'e's addled, reckon 'e cain't conterdick Nuncle Londer." But it was an odd thought. Kalchan, who never turned his hand to any physical labor if he could help it, eking out the rest of his life in the hard and tedious work of picking stones out of farm fields to make them easier to plow. Such work was endless, or so he'd heard; it seemed that no matter how many stones one dug out of a given field, there were always more working themselves to the surface.

Serves 'im right. It might not be a punishment that accurately fit the crime, but it suited Skif. His only regret was that,

once again, Uncle Londer was going to escape the consequences.

*But it don' bother me 'nuff that I wanta go talk t' Guard
about it.*

The new owner of the Hollybush had already moved his
own people in. The cook was gone, no one knew where, but
possibly still in Guard custody. The Hollybush was back in
business, but with slightly better food and drink and slightly
higher prices, or so Deek's sources had told him. The new people were a hard-faced woman who acted as cook, and her hen-
pecked husband who managed the drink, and their three
grown children. Rumor had it that the two daughters, who
acted as serving wenches, could be had for a modest price,
plying their trade in the curtained-off alcove that had served
Maisie as a sleeping cubby. Given that there were probably no
wages being paid to the children, plus the added income
brought in by the daughters, the place would probably remain
profitable despite higher prices that would drive some customers elsewhere.

What was important to Skif was that there was no point in
going back after his meager belongings; by now anyone who
was grasping enough to serve as madam to her own daughters
would have claimed everything usable for herself.

Well, they were welcome to it.

" 'F I nivir 'ear uv m'nuncle agin, 'twill be too soon," Skif
proclaimed loudly. "An' whoivir's got the 'Ollybush kin 'ave it,
much good may't do 'em. 'Eard awt uv Maisie, though?"

"Yer cuz Beel, wut's wi' th' Temple, took 'er, they sez,"
Deek told him. "Cleaned 'er up, 'ad 'Ealers wi' 'er. They sez
she's t'work i' Temple, i' kitchen, mebbe scrubbin' an'
cleanin'."

"She nivir did me 'arm," Skif observed slowly. "Nawt thet
she 'ad more'n a scatterin' uv wits t' begin wi'. Ol' Beel—'e
dun me a good turn, reckon 'e's dun wut 'e cud fer Maisie."

"Like I sed," Bazie put in, when comment seemed called

for, "Niver know wut a mon'll do, when 'e gets in Temple. I reckon ol' Londer ain' gonna be too pleased wi' yon Beel from 'ere on."

Skif smiled slowly. "Reckon yer right, Bazie."

The next several days passed much as the first had. Skif had originally been more than a little cautious around Bazie, especially when he found himself alone with the man. Crippled or not, Skif was in Bazie's control, and there was always the possibility that Bazie's interests in his boys went beyond the obvious. But Bazie never once showed anything but an honest friendliness that was both nurturing and practical. If Skif had ever known a real father, he would have recognized the odd feelings he was having now as being those of a son for a caring father—and he would have seen that Bazie's actions were like those of a caring father for his sons. He only knew that he liked Bazie enormously, and he trusted the man more and more with every moment. For his part, Bazie pretty much took care of his own needs, requiring only to be carried to and from the water closet. Skif was impressed by how calmly self-sufficient he was. He had guessed by now that Bazie was at least forty or fifty years old, and yet he never *seemed* old.

There was one thing, however, that Bazie always insisted on which seemed rather odd to Skif. One of his daily chores was to set a handful of wheat to soaking, and rinse the sprouting grains from previous days. When the sprouts got to a certain length, Bazie would eat them. He didn't seem to like them very much, but he doggedly munched them down.

" 'F ye don' like tha' muck, why'd ye eat it ev' day?" Skif finally asked.

" 'Cuz I like m' teeth," Bazie said shortly. " 'F I don' eat tha' muck, seein' as I niver sees th' sun, 'twon't be long 'fore I lose m'teeth an' gets sick. Tha's wut Healer tol' me fust time m' teeth started bleedin' an' I got sick. Mucky grass 's cheapest stuff 'round, so's tha's wut I eat in winter. Summer, 'course, they's good stuff i' market."

As the days passed, Skif finally grew bold enough to voice some of his curiosity about this most curious of situations. Besides, getting Bazie to talk made a welcome break from being drilled in sums as he scrubbed or stirred the laundry kettle.

At first, his questions were about commonplaces, but eventually he got up the courage to start asking more personal things. And, finally, he asked the most important of all.

"Bazie—wut 'appened t' yer legs?" he ventured, and waited, apprehensively, for a hurt or angry reply.

But Bazie voiced neither. Instead, he gazed at Skif for a moment. " 'Tis a long story, but 'tothers 'ave 'eard it, an' likely they'll figger it oughta be me 'as tells ye." He paused. "Ye ever 'ear uv th' Tedrel Wars?"

Skif shook his head.

"Thought not." Bazie sighed gustily. "Wuz back yon twenny yearn, easy, mebbe thutty. Well, I wuz in't. Tedrel mercs—tha's mercenaries, they's people wut fights wars fer money, fer them as don' figger on doin' the fightin' thesselves—they wuz paid t'come up from south, t' fight 'gainst Valdemar fer Karse. On'y 'twasn't t' be known thet they wuz doin' it fer Karse; they wuz a lot uv promises made 'bout Tedrels gettin' t' hev t'half uv Valdemar when they won." He shook his head. "Daft. 'Course, I didn' know thet. I wuz young 'n dumb, didn' think about nawt but loot an' wimmin."

"You wuz with 'em?" Skif asked, turning to look at him, mouth agape.

"Oh, aye. Stupid." He shook his head. "Furst fight, pract-ic'ly, got m' legs took off at knee. Didn' know then if 'twas good luck thet I lived, or bad. Got took up wi' rest uv prisoners, an' when war wuz over, didn' hev nowhere t' go. On'y I wuz in mercs cuz I wuz caught thievin' an' had t' 'ide, so me'n a couple other young fools decided we stick t'gether an' see 'f I cud teach 'em wut I knew 'bout thievin'. So we did, an' I did."

"Wut 'appened to 'em?" Skif asked.

Bazie shrugged. "Went back 'ome when they had th' glim, an' by then, I 'ad young Ames 'n Jodri, an' I reckoned I 'ad a good thing. I teach the young 'uns an' they share th' swag. Works out." He smiled—a little tightly. "Sorta like gettin' some uv th' loot I wuz promised. Heh. Mebbe I ain't got part uv Valdemar, but Valdemar's still feedin' me. An' I'm still alive, so I reckon I'm doin' all right."

Skif pondered all of that; it was kind of interesting. "So, how come ye take sech good care uv us, eh?" he asked.

Bazie laughed aloud. "An' ye'd do what if I didn'? Run off, right? 'Sides, I kinda like the comp'ny. 'Ad a good fam'ly an' I miss it. Me da wuz a good 'un, on'y 'e got 'urt, an' died, an' I 'ad t' do wut I culd fer me an' mum an' m' brothers—till they got sick an' died i' plague. Allus wished I'd 'ad family uv me own, on'y they's nuthin' but hoors wi' merc army, and wut wimmin 'ud hev a fam'ly wi' me now?" He shrugged. "So I reckon I make me own fam'ly, eh?"

"They sez, i' Temple," Skif ventured, "thet friends is th' fam'ly ye kin choose. I sure's *hellfires* wouldn' hev chose m' nuncle, nor Kalchan. Reckon this way's a bit better."

He was rewarded by a beaming smile from Bazie—and perhaps, just a hint of moisture in his eyes, hastily and covertly removed with a swipe of the hand. "Aye," Bazie agreed. "Reckon tha's right."

Skif quickly turned his questions to other topics, mostly about life as a mercenary, which Bazie readily answered.

"'Tis a life fer the young'n stupid, mostly, I'm thinkin'," he admitted. "Leastwise, wuz wi' Tedrels. Seems t' me, if yer gonna fight, mebbe ye shouldn' be fightin' fer things summun else thinks is 'portant. But 'twas lively. Did a mort'a travelin', though 'twas mostly on shank's mare. Got fed reg'lar. Seems t' me that lot uv lads joined thinkin' they wuz gonna get rich, an' I knew thet wouldn' 'appen. Reg'lar merc, 'e don' get rich, 'specially not Tedrels."

"Why?" Skif wanted to know.

Bazie laughed. "'Cause Tedrels wuzn't Guild mercs, tha's why! Tedrels, they sez, useta be in they own land, but got run out. So they took up fightin' fer people, th' whole lot uv 'em. By time I 'id out wi' em, Tedrels took wut nobuddy else would, cuz th' fights they took't weren't real smart. Ain't no Guild merc comp'ny wud fight 'gainst Valdemar! And ain't no Guild comp'ny wud fight *for* Karse. They's bunch uv fanatics, an' they ain't too good t'their own folk." He pondered for a moment. "Ye know, I kinda wondered 'f they figgered t' use us up, so's they wouldn' hev t' pay us. But I guess Cap'n wuz pretty desp'rate, so they took't th' job." He shook his head. "I'druther be'n 'onest thief. I figger'd t' make m'self scarce when th' coast wuz clear, on'y it niver wuz, an' they allus 'ad an eye lookin' fer deserters."

"Huh. So how come they ain't no problem gettin' folks fer Guard, 'f goin' t' fight's a dumb thing?" Skif wanted to know.

"Oh, th' Guard, thet's different," Bazie acknowledged. "They's got 'onor. When they ain't 'elpin' beaks, they's watchin' Border, cleanin' out bandits an' slavers." He shook his head. "Got no use fer bandits an' slavers. Us, we on'y take frum people kin afford a bit took't frum 'em. Tha's rule, right?"

Skif nodded; he'd already been given that rule numerous times. Here in the poorer part of town, the only legitimate targets, by Bazie's rules, were the people like Kalchan and Uncle Londer. Most thefts were out of the pockets and possessions of those who had the money to spare for luxury.

"Bandits an' slavers, they's hurtin' people nor better orf than us'n," Bazie declared. "So, bein' in Guard's 'onor'ble. An' Valdemar Guard takes care uv their own, so's not so daft t' join op."

This was getting altogether too confusing and complicated

for Skif, and evidently Bazie saw from his expression that he was sorely puzzled.

"Don' worry 'bout it fer now," he cautioned, "'Tis all complisticated, an' real 'ard t' 'splain. 'Ellfires, sometimes I cain't figger it out."

Skif pursed his lips, but decided that Bazie was probably right. There was just far too much in life that was altogether too complicated to try and work out. Like religion—if the Gods cared so much about people, why did they allow the Kalchans and the Londers—and worse—to go on doing what they did? Why wasn't everybody fed and warm and happy? Why were there rich people who had *piles* more things than they needed, and people like him who didn't have anything?

It was all far more than he could wrap his mind around, and eventually he just had to give up on it all.

Maybe someday he'd have some answers. For right now, he had food in his belly, a warm place to sleep, and friends.

And what more could anyone ask for, really? Gods and honor and all the rest of that stuff could go hang. He would put his loyalty with those who earned it.

SKIF was excited; finally, two weeks after he had officially joined the gang, something he had been hoping for all along happened. Bazie decided that when the boys returned from their own forays into the streets, although his talent probably lay in the area of burglary, he ought to have training in "the liftin' lay"—the art of the pickpocket.

All three of the boys were enthusiastic when Bazie put it to them. " 'E might's well as not!" Raf exclaimed. "Ain't no 'arm, an' 'e might 'ave th' touch arter all."

Deek nodded. " 'Sides, Bazie, any mun kin run shake'n'-snatch. An' fer that, we orter 'ave a new'un anyroad."

So Raf and Deek got out some bits and pieces from various cupboards, and began to put together a most peculiar object. When they were done, there was something like a headless man standing in the middle of their room, one hung all over with bells.

"There!" Bazie said, looking at their handiwork with plea-sure. "Mind, yon's not wut a mun wants t' 'ave in 'is place when beaks come callin'. Dead giveaway, that. But I do sez, I done good work wi' that lad. Ye'll no find a better 'un this side uv th' Border."

So Bazie had built this thing in the first place? It was very sturdy, in spite of being assembled from a lot of apparently disparate bits. In the mannequin's pockets were handkerchiefs, around his "neck" was a kerchief, and he had two belt pouches slung from his belt and a third tucked into the breast of his tunic.

Skif could not imagine how anyone could get at any of these tempting articles. Even the belt pouches were slung right under the mannequin's stuffed arm. But Raf, their expert, was about to show him.

"Watch close, young 'un," Bazie chuckled. "Yon Raf's slick."

He strolled up to stand beside the mannequin, looking from side to side as if he was observing the traffic in a street. Meanwhile—without ever so much as glancing at his quarry—his hand moved very, very slowly toward one of the handkerchiefs just barely hanging out of a pocket. Thread by thread, almost, he delicately removed it, and when it fell free of the mannequin's pocket, he whisked it into his own so quickly it seemed to vanish. As slowly as it had seemed to move, the whole business had not taken very long—certainly it was reasonable to think that a target would have remained standing beside the thief for that period of time, especially in a crowd or at the side of a busy street with a lot of traffic on it.

"Tha's th' 'ard way," Bazie told Skif, who watched with wide eyes. "Raf, 'e's th' best I ivir showed. 'E's got th' touch, fer certain-sure."

Now Raf sidled up to the other side of the mannequin, still casual and calm; he pretended to point at something, and while the target's attention was presumably distracted for a moment, out came a knife no bigger than a finger, and between one breath and the next, the strings of both belt pouches had been slit and knife and pouches were in Raf's pocket.

And all without jingling a single bell.

Now it was Lyle's turn, and he extracted the remaining handkerchief without difficulty, although he was not as smooth as Raf. "I'm not near that good," Deek said, "So I'm got t' do th' shake'n'snatch. Tha' takes two."

He got up, and he and Lyle advanced on the mannequin together. Then Lyle pretended to stumble and fell against it, setting all the bells jingling; as it fell into him, Deek grabbed for it. " 'Ey there, lad!" he exclaimed. "Steady on! An' you—watch where yer goin', you! Mussin' up a gennelmun like that!"

Skif would have expected Deek to pretend to brush the mannequin off, and get hold of his goods that way, but Deek did nothing of the sort. He simply set it straight. They both moved off, but now the mannequin no longer had the kerchief around its neck, and Deek held up both the kerchief and the pouch that had been tucked inside its tunic triumphantly.

"Tha's th' easy road, but riskier," Bazie noted. "Chance is, if mun figgers 'e's been lifted, 'e'll send beaks lookin' fer th' shaker—tha's Lyle."

"An' I'm be clean," Lyle pointed out. "Ain't nothin' on me, an' beak'll let me go."

"But if 'e knows th' liftin' lay, it'll be Deek 'e'll set beak on, an' Deek ain't clean. Or mun might even be sharp 'nuff t' figger 'twas both on 'em," Bazie cautioned. "Ye run th' shake'n'-snatch, ye pick yer cony careful. Gotta be one as is wuth it, got 'nuf glim t' take th' risk, but one as ain't too smart, ye ken? An' do't when's a mort uv crowd, but not so's ye cain't get slipput away."

Skif nodded solemnly.

"Na, 'tis yer turn. Jest wipes, fer now."

Skif then spent a humbling evening, trying to extract hand-kerchiefs from the mannequin's pocket without setting off the bells. Try as he might, with sweat matting his hair from the strain, he could not manage to set off less than two. And here he'd thought that he'd been working hard, hauling water and doing laundry, or going over walls and roofs with Deek! That had been a joke compared with this!

At length, Bazie took pity on him. "That'll be 'nuff, lad," he said, as Skif sagged with mingled weariness and defeat. "Ye done not bad, fer th' fust time. Ye'll get better, ye ken. Put yon dummy i't' corner, an' leave 'im fer now. Time fer a bit uv supper."

Skif was glad to do so. It was beginning to occur to him that the life of a thief was not as easy as most people believed, and most thieves pretended. The amount of skill it took was amazing; the amount of work to acquire that skill more than he had imagined. Not that he was going to give up!

I'll get this if't kills me.

"So, wha's news, m'lads?" Bazie asked, deftly slicing paper-thin wafers of sweet onion. This was going to be a good supper tonight, and they were all looking forward to it. Deek and Skif had done well for the little gang.

Lyle sliced bread and spread it with butter that Skif had gotten right out of a fancy inn's kitchen that very morning. He and Deek had been down in the part of town where the best inns and taverns were, actually just passing through, when one of those strokes of luck occurred that could never have been planned for.

The inn next to the one they had been passing had caught fire—they never found out why, only saw the flames go roaring up and heard the hue and cry. Everyone in the untouched place they'd stopped beside, staff and customers alike, had gone rushing out—either to help or to gawk—and he and Deek had slipped inside in the confusion.

Somehow, without having a plan, they'd gotten in, snatched the right things, and gotten out within moments. For one thing, they had gone straight to the kitchen as the best bet. Taking money was out of the question; they didn't know where the till was. There was no time to search for valuable property left behind in the confusion. Without discussion, they had gone for what they needed, where they knew they would find something worth taking.

The kitchen.

Like the rest of the inn, it was deserted—when the chief cook left, everyone else had taken the excuse to run out, too. There must have been a big delivery not long before, since the kitchen was full of unwrapped and partially unwrapped parcels of food.

It was like being turned loose in the best market in town. Skif had grabbed a wrapped block of butter, a cone of sugar, and a ham, and a handful of the brown paper the stuff had come wrapped in. Deek had gone for a whole big dry-cured hard sausage, a string of smaller ones, and half a wheel of cheese. Then out the back and over the wall they went, into an alley that was full of smoke and hid them beautifully. As soon as they were in the smoke, Skif and Deek pulled out the string bags they always brought with them just in case something in the nature of foodstuffs presented itself. Quickly wrapping up the articles in paper under cover of the smoke, they stuffed their booty into the bags, then came running out of the smoke into the crowd, coughing and wheezing far more than was necessary, acting like innocents who'd gone shopping for their mums and been caught in the alley. No one paid them any mind—they were all too busy ogling the fire and the bucket brigade or craning their necks to see if the fire brigade had gotten to the burning inn yet. Skif and Deek had strolled homeward openly, carrying enough food to last them all for weeks. All of it luxury stuff, too—not the sort of thing they got to taste more than once in a while. They had eggs a lot, since they were pretty cheap, with just about anyone who had a bit of space keeping pigeons or chickens, even in the city.

Bread was at every meal; bread was the staple of even the poorest diets.

Roots like tatties and neeps were cheap enough, too, and cabbage, and onions—even old Kalchan had those at the inn. Dried pease and beans made a good soup, and Kalchan had those, too, though more often than not they were moldy.

Skif had eaten better with Bazie than he ever had in his life, even allowing for what he'd snitched from Lord Orthallen's kitchen. Good butter, though—butter that was all cream and not mixed half-and-half with lard—they didn't see much of that. Deek's cheese wasn't the cheap stuff that they generally got, made after the cream had been skimmed from the milk. And as for ham and sausages—sausages where you didn't have to think twice about what might have gone into them— well, those were food for the rich. And sugar—

Skif had never tasted sugar until he started snitching at Lord Orthallen's table. Bazie had a little screw of paper with some, and once in a while they all got a bit in their tea. Now they'd be able to sweeten their tea at every meal.

Each of them had a slice of bread well-buttered, with a thin slice of onion atop, and a slice of hard sausage atop that. The aroma of sage and savory from the sausage made Skif's mouth water. Bazie had put some of his sprouting beans on his slice, and had taken a second slice of buttered bread to hold it all together. Skif hoped the sprouts wouldn't taste bad with all that good stuff in and around it. They were going to eat like kings for a while.

"Kalchan croaked." That was from Lyle, with his mouth full. "They sez. Nobuddy sez nothin' 'bout Londer. I ast 'round 'bout Skif. Don' seem nobuddy's lookin' fer 'im now. Reckon they figger 'e saw t'set-to an' run off."

"Huh." Skif shrugged. "Tol' ye about th' fire. Tha's all we saw." Deek nodded agreement, but his mouth was full, so he added nothing.

"White shirt's sniffin' 'round Little Puddin' Lane," said Raf. "Dunno why; askin' a mort'uv questions, they sez."

Huh. Wonder what Herald wants down there? There wasn't anything down in that part of town that a Herald should have been interested in; Little Pudding Lane was just a short step above the neighborhood of the Hollybush so far as poverty went.

"Stay clear uv them for now," Bazie advised. "They got ways'uv tellin who's lyin'."

"No fear there!" Raf promised. "Ain't gonna mess wi' no witchy white shirt!"

Be stupid to, Skif reflected. Not that he'd ever actually seen a Herald, except once, passing at a distance. Even then, he wasn't sure it had been a Herald. It could just have been a pale-colored horse.

Bazie shrugged. "Dunno they be witchy, jest sharpish. Ah, like's not, 'tis summat got nawt t'do wi' likes uv us. When any'un seed a white shirt down *here,* eh?"

"Not so's I kin 'member," Raf, the oldest, said at last. Skif and Deek both shook their heads.

"Saw 'un oncet, passin' through," Lyle offered, and grinned. "Passin' fast, too! Reckon had burr under 'is saddle!"

"White shirt's don' bother wi' us," Bazie said with certainty, and finished the last bite of his supper with great satisfaction. "Slavers, raiders, aye. Big gang'uv bandits, aye. E'en summat highwayman, e'en footpad, 'f 'e's stupid 'nuff to murder along'uv robbin'. But us? A bit'uv cheese here, a wipe there? Nothin' fer them. 'Tis th' beaks we gotta watch for. But all th' same—" he finished, brow wrinkling, "steer clear'uv 'em. They nivir done me no 'arm, e'en wi' me an' the' rest fightin' 'em, but they nivir done me no favors either, an' Karsites allus said they was uncanny." He laughed. "Well, *demons* is wut they said, but figger the source!"

When Skif went to bed that night, though, he wondered what would have brought a "white shirt"—a Herald—down as close to their territory as Little Pudding Lane. It had to be something important, for as Bazie said, the Heralds didn't bother themselves about petty thieves as long as it was only a crime against property and not against a person.

Bazie had strict rules about *that,* too—not the least because if by some horrible accident someone *was* hurt, it could be a hanging offense. It made no sense to court that kind of trouble all for the sake of some loot you could get another time. Better to drop everything and run if it all went bad. Even if you were one of a team, there was no point in coming to the rescue when *that* would only mean that two of you would be caught instead of one.

The worst that would happen to any of them would be some time in gaol, and perhaps a beating administered by the victim; only Raf had a previous offense against him, and he would take care to give another name if he was caught. Bazie had coached Skif on this with great care. The very best ploy was to get rid of anything you had on you, so you'd be clean. If you couldn't do that, the next best was to act scared, and cry and carry on and say that you were starving, had no job, and couldn't get one, then produce a convincing cough as if you were very sick. None of them were so well-fed that they looked prosperous, though none of them ever went hungry either, and they could probably carry the story off as long as the beaks didn't get involved. Lyle, with his innocent face and ability to make his eyes seem twice their size, had gotten away with that more than once.

Wish I could, Skif thought with envy. But—Lyle was another on the liftin' lay, and it was easier to get away with that when you were caught out on the street than it was when you were caught in someone's house.

Raf was sitting up with Bazie, although Deek and Lyle had already gone to bed. Their voices came easily through the shutters of his bed. "Lissen, Bazie, Midwinter Fair's a-comin', an' I'm thinkin' we should be workin' it in twos," Raf said quietly. "One liftin', an' one t'carry. Mebbe I'm bein' nervy, but I don' like t'idea uv yon white shirt sniffin' round."

"You reckon?" Bazie sounded interested. "Hadn' tried that afore, hev we?"

"Ain't's risky. Reckon I take's the young'un, Lyle take Deek. An *ev'ry* time we gets a lift, we takes it t' carrier. Carrier brings it here. Then no matter how wrong 't all goes, ain't no'un caught wi' more'n one lift on'im." Raf sounded very sure of himself, and truth to tell, Skif agreed with him. It would be a lot more work that way for the carrier, who would have to run back and forth between wherever the Fair they were working was being held, and here, but Raf was right. No matter what happened, no matter what went wrong, no one would be caught with more loot than a single kerchief or pouch.

"Som'thin' got ye spooked?" Bazie asked shrewdly. Skif could imagine Raf's shrug. "Can't 'magine white shirts lookin' fer lifters."

"Mebbe. Somethin' i' th' air. Not like white shirts t' be i' this t' th' chancy parts'uv town. Somethin's up. An'—" Raf paused. "Lots'uv forners pretendin' not t'be forners lurkin' about, i'taverns, askin' questions, little too casual-like."

"Na, ye stay clear'uv *them,* boy!" There was real alarm in Bazie's voice. "Tha's stuff fer th' highborns! Ain't no call t'get mixed up wi' them!"

"Eh." Raf agreed, but he still sounded worried. "Bazie, ye gotta wonder—how long afore *their* bizness gets down amongst us? Ye know whut they sez—rotten apple falls fastest and futhest."

"On'y thin' you an' me an' the likes'uv us got t' 'ave t'do wi' *them* is t' get out uv way when they falls."

And that seemed to be the end of that. Skif was asleep before Raf helped Bazie into bed.

When the Midwinter Fairs began, the first thing they had to do was try and figure out which ones they would work, because every other thief and pickpocket in Haven would be doing the same. Bazie had a shrewd way of eliminating them, based on the number of beaks assigned to each, the general level of prosperity, and the number of drunks by midafternoon. He wanted a moderate number of beaks, a slightly-better-than-middle level of prosperity, and a high level of drunks. So, not too surprisingly, he decided that they should work the Fair associated with the Brewers Guild. He also picked one very large Fair held just outside the city, where there were going to be a large number of tent taverns because it was playing host to a series of contests among performers. Not Bards; in fact, Bards were excluded. These were to be contests among ordinary musicians with no Gifts.

He chose a third Fair for no reason that Skif could tell, but Raf and Deek grinned over it so broadly that he figured he'd get the joke when he saw it.

The last chosen was the first Fair of the seven days of Midwinter Festival; Lyle went out with Deek early in the afternoon, with Skif and Raf following about a candlemark later.

It was an overcast day, the still air with a soft feeling about it, and humid. The clouds hung low, so low they looked about to touch the roofs of the buildings to either side of the narrow street. Skif kept looking up as they walked down the streets, heading for the square where the Fair had been set up. Weather like this meant snow, the kind that packed together easily.

He wasn't disappointed; it came drifting down shortly after they got on their way, big, fat, fluffy flakes of it.

"Is snow good or bad fer bizness?" Skif asked anxiously. Midwinter had never been more than a date to him before this; he'd avoided the Fairs, since he hadn't any money to spend and kids as ragged as he'd been back in the bad Kalchan days were generally chased away by stall holders and beaks. Why bother to linger about the edges of a place you wouldn't be allowed into? So he hadn't any idea what to expect, or whether weather would make any difference in the number of people crowding the aisles between the stalls.

Raf cast a glance upwards and smiled. "*This* kinda snow's good," he opined. "Gets people playful, belike. Gets 'em thinkin' 'bout fun, an' not 'bout keepin' an eye out. Na, snow wit' a nasty wind, tha's diff'rent. Or colder, tha's diff'rent, too. This's near-perfek. Perfek 'ud be sun, right arter this kinda snow." He scratched his head speculatively. "This weather 'olds, reckon there'll be drink stalls an 'ot food stalls down t'river, too, an' aside summa th' ponds i' fancy parks. People'll be skatin', makin' snow stachoos an' forts, 'avin' snowball fights."

"Kids?" Skif asked. "Littles?"

Raf laughed. "Na, growed people, too! Graybeards, even! I seed 'em!"

Skif could only shake his head at the notion of full-grown adults having the leisure to pursue snow sports.

They heard the Fair long before they saw it, a jangle of instruments, laughter, loud voices, echoing down the narrow street. And when they saw it, it was just a patch of color at the end of the street. Only as they approached it did the patch resolve into people, waving banners, and a couple of tents bedecked with painted signs on canvas.

Obviously, there was far more to it than that to account for all the noise, but that was all they could see at the end of the street.

This was usually the cattle market, where larger livestock was bought and sold once every fortnight. Part of the market— the part where really *fine* horses and stud bulls and prize milch cows were sold—was actually underneath a building on ten tall stone pillars. It was like a fine house where the ground floor had been reserved for stalls for beasts. Skif didn't know what went on in the building atop those pillars, but it was probably some sort of commerce. The rest of the place was just an open square, which on market days had rough wooden pens set up for the more plebeian stock; sheep, goats, donkeys, mules, and those cattle and horses without aristocratic lineage.

As they came to the end of the street, the Fair filled that square and even edged onto the walkways around the perimeter. And the first thing that met Skif's astonished eyes was a woman, in a flounced dress so short he could see her legs up to the thigh, balancing along a rope strung from the eaves of a shop to the staircase of the stone cattle stalls.

"Na, young'un," Raf said in his ear, "Iff'n ye kin do *that,* ye kin call yersel' a roof walker, eh?"

Skif shut his open mouth and followed Raf into the aisles of the Fair. Within a very short time, it became perfectly obvious to him why Bazie had picked *this* Fair for them to prowl. There were next to no women among the patrons, and very little besides food and drink for sale. The drink was *all* alcoholic; mulled ales, wines, and ciders, cold beer, cold wine, and cold spirits of wine, which Skif had only heard of, never seen. The food was all hot, spicy, or salty. The rest of the stalls were uniformly for either entertainment or games of chance. And there were more entertainers in this place than Skif had ever seen in his lifetime. Jugglers, acrobats, musicians—that was only the start of it. There were trick riders, most of them women and attired very like the girl on the rope overhead—a man who did the most astonishing things with a loop of rope—a fire-eater—a sword swallower. And girl dancers, whose costumes were even more abbreviated than the riders! Which was probably why most of the patrons here were men and boys. . . .

The dancers, of which there were two different troupes, and a set of raree shows promising to display the most amazing oddities, held pride of place in the stone cattle stalls. They'd used their tents to fashion canvas-walled rooms beneath the roof, firmly anchored to the stone sides of the stalls, making it impossible to lift the corner for a free look, to the acute disappointment of the boys swarming the place. The rest of the entertainers had to make do with their tents.

Raf found a good place for him to stand out of the way, just beside the stone staircase, where he also had a fine view of the ropedancers. He disappeared into the crowd.

Wake up now, he told himself sternly. *Ye're here t'work, not gawk.*

It was hard, though—so many distractions, what with the dancers going across the rope when the crowd tossed enough in their dish to make it worth their while, with the glimpses of men on stilts at the farther edge of the Fair, the music coming from the dancers' stalls, and the enthusiastic bawling of the tent men, each proclaiming that nothing had ever been seen like the wonders in *his* tent.

Well, certainly Skif had never seen anything like this.

Just as he was starting to get cold, Raf reappeared with a cunningly-made paper cone full of hot chestnuts, which they shared—and under cover of which, Raf passed Skif a fat belt pouch. After Skif had peeled and eaten enough nuts to warm hands and stomach, Raf took back the half-empty cone and loudly told him to run on home.

After a brief whining plaint, Skif trotted off, exactly like a younger brother chased off by an elder. And once away from the Fair, he broke into a loping run. In no time at all he had left the pouch with Bazie to be examined and counted, and he was on his way back, more than warmed up by his exertions.

It took longer for Raf to return the second time; Skif hoped that this meant he was being very careful. He also hoped that by the time he brought back Raf's second or third lift, Bazie would tell him that they'd collected enough for the day. Although this Fair was exciting and completely fascinating, Skif couldn't help being nervous about the composition of the crowd—mostly male, and mostly drinking. It wouldn't take much for an ugly situation to develop.

The ropedancers didn't seem to mind his being there, though, which was a plus; he'd been afraid they might chivvy him off. While he waited for Raf to appear again, he watched them closely, trying to figure out how they did it. There were four of them; two girls, a young man, and a little boy; the latter didn't walk the rope himself, he seemed to be there mostly to balance on the shoulders of the young man.

Reckon since ye cain't see up his skirt fer an extra thrill, they figger they gotta have th' little'un there t' make it more dangerous.

Of the two girls, the youngest was the most skilled; while the older one just walked the rope, stopping midway for some one-footed poses, the younger one had an entire repertoire of tricks. So far Skif had seen her balance on one foot while she drew the other up with her hands to touch her heel against the back of her head, dance a little jig in the middlemost part of the rope, jump up and come down on the rope again, and make three skips with a jump rope out there. It was even-up between her and the older one for the dancers called out most often— the older one was, well, *older,* and had breasts and all, but the younger one was more daring.

It soon became obvious to Skif that the young man and the little boy were there to draw the crowd—they were the ones that went out for free. The girls didn't dance unless there was enough money collected in the tin bucket hung at the side of the stone staircase—and there was an older man with them who emptied it every time one of them went out. Skif thought there was a distinct family resemblance there with all of them.

Just then, Raf came up again, this time with a pair of waxed paper cones full of hot mulled cider. He handed one to Skif.

"Be kerful drinkin'," he cautioned, in a lowered voice. "They's summut in bottom."

"Seen Lyle?" Skif asked in a normal tone. "'E sed 'e'd be 'ere, didn' 'e?"

"Oh, aye, an' 'is mum's gonna be right riled," Raf said cheerfully, as Skif sipped the hot, spicy liquid, fragrant with apples. " 'E's 'ad a pair uv beers an' 'e's a-workin' a third."

Lyle's gotten two lifts and Raf saw him working a third? That was good news. By this point Skif understood why Raf had warned him. There was something hard and heavy at the bottom of the cone, heavy enough that if he didn't finish the cider quickly and carefully, the cone might start to disintegrate and leak. "I'm gonna go 'ome an' see'f Mum'll be lettin' us stay past dark," he offered.

Raf gave him a nod. "I be over t'orse dancers," he said, and wandered away as Skif trotted off again.

He continued to sip at the hot cider until he could actually see what was in the bottom. It looked like jewelry—chain, with a seal attached. And from the taste now in the cider, it was silver. He ducked into a blind alley and fished the thing out, dumped the last of the cider and then, thinking, put it back into the paper cone. Nobody as poor as he was would waste waxed paper by throwing it away—it was too useful as a spill for starting fires. So he screwed the thing up into a spill shape with the chain and seal inside, and went on his way again.

Bazie was pleased with the lift, but gave no hint that he was ready for them to stop, so back Skif went again.

Raf had warned him that he might be noticed—by the rope-dancers themselves, if no one else—if he went to the same spot a third time. The new meeting point was the tiny corral holding the trick riders; Raf had pointed out a good place the first time they'd gone past, where a farm cart full of hay was pushed up against the corral fence. That was where Skif went, propping hands and chin on the lower railing as he watched one of the riders riding—standing—on the back of a remarkably placid horse.

A heavy hand gripped his shoulder.

Skif jumped—or tried to; with that hand on his shoulder, he couldn't do more than start. Heart racing, he turned his head, expecting a beak. *I'm clean!* he thought, thanking his luck that he was. *I'm clean! 'E cain't do more'n tell me t' get out!*

But it wasn't a beak that held his shoulder. It was his cousin Beel.

"Beel!" he squeaked.

"I'm pleased you recall one family member, Skif," Beel said gravely. "I'd like to know where you have been."

Skif thought quickly. "Wuz runnin' errand, came back, an saw t'fight," he said, trying to look absolutely innocent. "Saw beaks in't, an— well, 'ad t'spook, Beel. Couldn' do nothin', so I 'ad t'spook."

Beel nodded. "But then where have you been? Why didn't you come to—"

Skif took a chance and interrupted. "Beel—I *cain't* go back t' Nuncle Londer," he whispered. "Them beaks, they want me t'tell 'em stuff 'bout Maisie—but ye *know* tha's stuff Nuncle don' want me t'tell!"

The corners of Beel's mouth turned down, but he took his hand from Skif's shoulder. "It would be wrong of me to—put temptation in the path of anyone, let alone my own father," he said reluctantly. He didn't say what temptation, but they both knew what it was. "Just tell me—no, don't tell me where you are and what you're doing—but are you continuing with your lessons, at least?"

Skif groaned, and Beel smiled reluctantly. "Am I! They's wus'n you! Set me a sum, I dare ye!"

"Twelve plus fifteen," Beel asked instantly, knowing that Skif couldn't have added that when he'd run.

"Twenny—" Skif screwed his eyes shut and concentrated. "Twenny-se'en!" He looked up at his cousin triumphantly. Beel lifted his hands, conceding defeat.

"But what should I say if my father asks if I've seen you?" the priest wondered out loud, worriedly. "Lying—"

Skif clambered up into the hay. "Tell 'im ye seed me i' cattle market, then ina farm cart frum t'country," he suggested pertly. "An 'twon't e'en be a fib!"

Now Beel smiled ruefully, and shook his head. "You're too quick and facile for your own good, Skif," he said. "You worry me. But all right—if Uncle Londer thinks you've gone and hired yourself out as farm labor, he's not going to bother trying to find you." He rested one hand on Skif's head—in a blessing?—and moved off into the crowd.

Fortunately no one else seemed to have been paying any attention to this interchange. Skif clambered down out of the cart—reluctantly, for the hay had been soft and warm—before anyone from the trick riders' group could scold him for being up there.

He was still sweating, just a little. That had been a narrow escape. How could he ever have guessed that Beel of all people would show up here? This was *not* the sort of atmosphere he'd expect a priest to seek out!

He looked anxiously for Raf, hoping the older boy hadn't been caught. After much too long a wait, he spotted Raf working his way through the crowd coming toward him. The relief was enough to make him feel light-headed.

"Time t' go," Raf said as soon as the two of them were together. "Wut I got now'll gi' Bazie 'nuff, an' I sore yer cuz 'ere."

"I did more'n see 'im," Skif said, as they worked their way out to the street together. He explained what had happened as they walked together toward home.

"Aw, hellfires!" Raf responded, making a motion of wiping his forehead. "Tha's a close'un!"

"Too close," Skif agreed. "I took't chance on Beel bein' a good'un—ye ken 'e warned me, afore th' to-do. An' 'e is, I guess."

"Well, I saw 'im doin' some beggin' fer Temple; guess tha's 'ut brung 'im there," Raf said. "I'd made lift, an' I nipped off t' look fer ye."

It had been far too close a call and Skif's heart was still beating hard. But at least they'd made some good lifts today, and no harm done.

Skif had managed—by luck and a glib tongue—to squeak out of danger again.

It was a good, dark night—not quite moonless, but it had been a day moon, shining in the blue sky half the afternoon, and it would be down before Skif was done with tonight's job. Right now, the shadows were perfect for getting into his target. Skif sniffed the air appreciatively, but silently; it was crisp and cold, with a hint of wood smoke, but not as much as there would have been if all of the fireplaces in his target house were running. With a dry autumn this year, there was no treacherous ice on the roof or tops of the walls. In the fall the first bit of cold kept people off the street at night and tucked up in a cozy tavern, instead of wandering about, taking a chance of getting run off by the Watch for the fun of gawking at the show homes of the rich. All except for the rich themselves, of course, who were making the rounds of their estates—if they had them—or their friends' estates. It was hunting season, and no one who was anyone would be caught dead in Haven at this time of year, not when they could go out to the country and use the slaughter of wild game as an excuse to have house parties.

It was very strange. Granted, wild game was a luxury, and featured prominently in the menus of the rich. But surely their foresters and servants could do a better job of going after it than people who didn't hunt for a living.

Still, all to the good. A smart lad with the wit to go and hold horses outside the Great Houses always knew who was having a country-house party and who was going to it. When the master was away, the servants left behind took their own sort of holiday, and getting into and out of a place was child's play.

Well, it was if the "child" was Skif.

Hidden in a join of two walls, where one stuck out a little farther than the other and left a vertical slot of dark shadow, Skif waited until the Watch passed. There was always the Nightwatch to reckon with, in the fine neighborhoods. When he'd worked by day, snatching things out of the laundries of many of the fancy houses he now robbed, he hadn't had to worry about the Nightwatch.

Not that he worried too much about them now—so long as he knew the schedule. He kept his head turned away as they passed with their lantern to keep from having his night vision ruined, then nicked across the top of Jesolon's wall to the top of Kalink's.

The home of the arrogant "new money" grain merchant Kalink was his goal tonight. The irony was that *this* Kalink wasn't even the one who made the money—that had been the work of the old man, who according to gossip had been perfectly content to live quietly, if comfortably, in the country until he died. Not the son, though. Gossip grudgingly admitted he had as good a head for business as the old man, maybe better, but *he* wasn't going to molder in the countryside, not he! He got himself a show-wife, long on looks and short on wits, and had this brand new manor house built right up

against Jesolon's, first tearing down the smaller place that had
been there. He hadn't been content to simply add on—no,
nothing was good enough for him but brand new, nor would
he hear any advice on the subject. It didn't matter to *him* that
having walls run right up to the side of a house just made a
road for a thief to walk on—hadn't he the very latest in locks
and catches and other theft-foiling hardware? Hadn't he ornamental ironwork on all the windows?

*Hasn't he left enough room between them bars to put a don-
key through?* Skif snickered to himself, as he slipped over the
roof of the stable to the uneven triangle of shadow just against
the wall of the house that the moon wouldn't reach at this
time of night. He managed it all without a hint of sound, not
the rattle of a stone, not the slip of a slate. In his all-black
"sneak suit," with hands in black gloves and face wrapped in
a black scarf, smeared with charcoal where the scarf didn't
reach, the only part of him visible was his eyes.

Oh, yes, indeed, Kalink was "new money" in Haven and
proud of it. Proud enough to have halved the space where his
garden had been in order to put in a stable for a single horse,
the fool! True enough, a horse was a very expensive, very conspicuous luxury in the city, but *one* horse would only pull a
cart (which there was no room for) or a tiny, two-wheeled,
half-carriage called a "gig," that would only carry two people
at a time (and which barely fit in the stable with the horse).
Your servants couldn't use it for real shopping, it was fair use-
less for transporting anything large or heavy, if you had a
country estate or summer home as Kalink did, you still had to
hire a wagon to carry your baggage when you went back for
hunting season or summer. You had to drive it yourself, for
there wasn't room for a driver. It was good for two things—for
arriving at a fancy "do" with the wife, and for the wife or a
daughter to go off with a servant to drive to make her daytime
social calls. If wife or daughter couldn't drive, the only way

your women could use it for *their* shopping was if they arranged for whatever they bought to be delivered.

Which was, of course, what Kalink's brainless bit of a show-wife always did, though she did have wit enough to be able to drive herself, so she took her personal maid instead of a manservant. Skif's lip curled in contempt. *Very* nice.

And in exchange for this ostentatious bit of status-flaunting merchandise, you lost half your garden, and had to have an extra boy around to drive and to tend the creature from dusk to dawn, just to keep the beast from stinking up the neighborhood and drawing flies.

The show-wife had a weakness for jewelry, and brainless though she might be, she had a true expert's eye for picking out the best. And a boy who volunteered to hold m'lady's horse while she browsed through the goldsmiths' row in search of more of the stuff heard a lot.

Especially when m'lady was discussing with her new maid what to do with her purchases. And since m'lady was in a hurry to go on her social calls as well as brainless, and the maid was new and didn't know where the concealed cupboard for the valuables was, m'lady told her all about it right then and there instead of waiting until she was back home and showing her.

Now came the only tricky part. Skif wasn't going to take his eyes off the garden below, or the garden next door, so he had to reach up over his head and feel for the ledge of the gabled window there, then pull himself up onto the windowsill by the help of the bars there and the strength of his arms alone. Quietly. Smoothly. So that no movement of a shadow-within-a-shadow would draw the attention of someone he hadn't spotted.

The Nightwatch had some good, sharp men on it—not many, but some. That was why Skif took no chances by turning his back. And when he'd finished with Kalink, he'd never hit this neighborhood again, no matter how juicy it seemed.

With hands wrapped around the bars on the window, he drew himself up into the enclosure; like the work of the rope-dancers, it looked smooth and easy, but it was hard work. Hard enough to make his arms scream as he pulled himself up, braced himself, pulled himself farther up, braced, then finally got himself up onto the windowsill. He wedged his thin body between two of the bars, and waited. Watching, listening, for any sign of another shadow down below, now slipping out of cover to go and fetch his fellow thief catchers.

Nothing.

Just for good measure, he waited until fingers and toes were chilled, but not numb and clumsy, and only then did he slip the special, paper-thin, flexible knife blade from the sheath strapped to his ankle and slip the catches—for there were two, which was Kalink's idea of being clever—of the window beside him. He didn't open the window, though. Not yet.

From out of the breast of his tunic came a tiny bladder full of lamp oil, which he used on the bottom edge of the window to ease its passage; this was no time to have it stick. Then he squirted the last of it on the hinges—no time to have them groan either! Only then did he push the two halves of the window open, shove his body sideways between the bars, and feel with his foot for the floor, all of it moving as slowly as a tortoise. When he was certain that his footing was secure, he put all of his weight on it, brought the other leg in through the window—and closed it, putting on one of the catches to hold it shut. There were plenty of jobs that had been ruined because the thief forgot to close the window behind himself on a cold night, and some servant felt a draft.

Skif knew where he was; the room used by the show-wife's maid. He'd watched over the course of several nights when Kalink and his wife were at some party or other, knowing that the girl would have to stay up to help her mistress undress. The windows of the master's bedroom might have fancy locks on them, but the maid's cubby wouldn't, and it was a guarantee that the maid's room would give off right onto the master's bedroom. That was one of Bazie's first lessons when Skif began doing *real* work—the layout of the fancy houses.

The weak point in a house was always the personal maid's room, or the manservant's, but the maid was the easiest target. The personal maid—she had special status, because she had to be able to do more than just run errands. Fine sewing and embroidery, hairdressing, getting her mistress into and out of her fancy clothes and doing it unobtrusively—that was just the start of her duties. She might have to cook sweet and soothing dainties if her mistress was indisposed and the cook had gone to bed, she certainly had to be able to do a bit of nursing if her mistress was ill, pregnant, or elderly. Depending on where her loyalties were, she might be the master's spy on his wife—or run discreet messages and make assignations with her mistress' lovers. She had to know how to make and apply beauty treatments, even cosmetics. And she had to be available day or night, except when the mistress was out of the house and hadn't taken her along.

All that required a room of her own, adjoining the master's bedroom—or the mistress's, if husband and wife didn't share a bed. And since the last thing the mistress would tolerate was the ability of her maid to go sneaking off without the mistress knowing about it, the maid generally had to go through the master's bedroom to get to the rest of the house. That prevented the maid from entertaining men in her own room, and greatly curtailed her ability to slip off and be entertained by them elsewhere. A good lady's maid was something no woman wanted to lose, so it was worth the effort to keep her from the lure of masculine company.

After all, she might get married, or pregnant, or both. Then what would her mistress do?

Dismiss her, of course, and go on the hunt for another; this was a quest more fraught with hazard and emotional turmoil than the search for a new cook. One could train a new maid, of course, but then one would have to be willing to put up with a great deal while the girl was in training.

Skif remained crouched on the floor and waited while his eyes adjusted to the deeper darkness in this tiny room. He reached out cautiously and encountered the rough wool of a blanket to his right.

So—the bed was there. He moved carefully to avoid making the floorboards creak, and edged over to the bed. Making sure not to lean on it, he located the head and the foot, then eased down to the foot and felt for the wall.

From the wall, he found the door, and eased it open, creeping through it practically on hands and knees.

His nose told him that he was in the bedroom, and that the room was the exclusive domain of the mistress, for the aroma of perfume and scent in here was far heavier than most men would tolerate. So—the mistress and master slept separately. He'd rather expected that; the show-wife, whether she knew it or not, shared her husband's attentions with a lady of— earthier qualities. Kalink kept her in a nice little set of rooms near the cattle market, where she had once been a barmaid. The show-wife was just that; a trophy to be displayed before other men and eventually got with an heir.

Well, this was his goal. He grinned to himself. Old Kalink thought he was being so clever! Most hiding places for valuables were in concealed wall cupboards, but according to the wife, Kalink had the brilliant notion to put *his* in the floor, under the bed. Well, *Kalink* thought it was a brilliant idea. Skif would not only be able to get at it with ease, he'd be hidden while he went through the goods at his leisure.

The bed was easy enough to see, even in the dim light from the three unshuttered windows, for the curtains hadn't been drawn since the mistress wasn't home. There was plenty of moonlight in this enormous room, which faced south and west—poor little maid, she had her window on the east side, where the sun would smack her right in the eyes if she hadn't gotten up by dawn. Skif kept his head down, though, and still moved cautiously, traveling crabwise below the level of the windows. The bed was one of those fashionable, tall affairs that you needed a set of steps to get into—

—so that you could get to the safe-cupboard *under* it, of course—

—and Skif slid beneath it with plenty of room to spare.

Now, for the first time, he drew an easy breath. If he found what he thought he was going to find, this one haul of loot would keep him and the two new boys Bazie had taken in, and do so in fine style for a year or more.

Which we need. They ain't liftin' enough t'keep us in old bread.

He slipped off one glove, and felt along the floorboards for the tell-tale crack that would show him where the edge of the lid was, and whatever sort of mechanism there was to lock it shut.

He was the last of the old lot; Deek had undergone an unexpected growth spurt that turned him into a young giant and made his intended occupation of house thief entirely impractical. He served as a guard for a traveling gem merchant now— who better to watch for thieves than a former pickpocket? Last Skif had heard, he was on his way to Kata'shin'a'in.

Raf had gotten caught, and was currently serving out his sentence on the Border with Karse, for he'd made the mistake of getting caught with his hand on the pouch of a Great Lord.

Lyle had given up thievery altogether, but only because he'd fallen in love instead. He'd gone head over heels with a farmer's daughter one Fair Day in the cattle market, and she with him, and over the course of six weeks had managed to charm her old father into consenting to marriage. Lyle had taken to country life as if he'd been born to it, which amazed all of them, Lyle himself not the least.

Bazie had gotten two new boys just before Lyle fell to the love-god's arrows, and it was left to him and Skif to train them up. That was why Skif was going for a big stake *now;* the boys weren't up to the lifting lay yet, and only one was adequate at swiping things out of laundries. Skif had the feeling that Bazie had taken them more out of pity than anything else; Lyle had brought them in after finding them scouring the riverbanks—mudlarking—for anything they could salvage. Thin, malnourished, and as ignorant as a couple of savages, even Bazie wasn't about to try and pound reading, writing, and reckoning lessons into them. *That* fell on the head of some poor priest at the nearest Temple.

Skif traced the last line of the lid of the safe-cupboard and found the keyhole easily enough. No one had made any effort to hide it, and he slid his lock pick out of a slit pocket in his belt and went to work by touch.

Before very long, he knew for a fact that Kalink had been cheated, for this was the *cheapest* lock he had ever come across in a fancy house. It wasn't the work of more than a few moments to tickle it open, and ease the lid of the safe-cupboard open.

With the lid resting safely on the floor, Skif reached into the cupboard and began lifting out heavy little jewel cases, placing them on the floor until he had emptied the cupboard. What he wanted was gold and silver.

Gold was soft; with a hammer and a stone, Skif could pound chains and settings into an amorphous lump, which any goldsmith would buy without a second thought and at a reasonable price. Silver wasn't bad to have; you could cut it up with a chisel and render the bits unidentifiable. He'd rather not have gemstones; you couldn't just take them to a goldsmith, and you wouldn't get more than a fraction of their worth.

So he opened each box and examined its contents by feel; rejecting out-of-hand all gem-studded rings, earrings, and brooches. He selected chains, bracelets, pendants, anything that was mostly or completely made of metal. The emptied boxes went into the bottom of the cupboard, with the rest stacked on top. With luck, the theft wouldn't even be uncovered for days after Kalink and his wife returned. By then, of course, everything would have been disposed of, melted down—it might even become part of whatever baubles the mistress picked to replace what was lost!

Each piece he selected, he wrapped in one of Bazie's purloined silk handkerchiefs to cut down on sound and stored in one of the many pockets of his "sneak suit." It didn't do a thief a great deal of good to be chiming and chinking when he moved!

He hesitated once or twice, but in the end, opted to be conservative in what he chose. He had no way of getting rid of that triple rope of pearls, for instance, nor the brooch that featured a huge carven cabochon. And when his fingers told him that the piece he was holding was of finely-detailed enamel, he couldn't bear the idea of destroying something that so much work and creativity had gone into. The same, for the wreath of fragile leaves and flowerlets—a clever way of getting around the fact that a commoner couldn't wear a coronet. But the rest of what he chose was common enough, mere show of gleaming metal, without much artistry in it.

He replaced the last box and eased the lid back down on the cupboard. Now came the fun part: getting out.

He didn't want the maid to get into trouble; that was hardly fair. If he left the window in her room with the catches undone, she'd be the first to be blamed. So after he slid out from under the bed, he crept across the mistress' room to try the next door over.

It was a bathing room, and he laughed silently. *Good old Kalink! Nothing but the best for him for certain-sure. Nothing but the latest!* There was an indoor privy, everything flushed away with water after you'd done, and a boiler to heat bath water, all served from a cistern on the roof. Good place to leave open.

He opened the catch on the window and pushed open the shutters that served this room instead of ironwork. Let Kalink presume that this was how his thief got in, and wonder how on earth he came up the wall from the yard, or down the wall from the steeply-pitched roof.

Now he returned to the maid's room. He'd go out the way he came, but he had a trick to use on the kind of simple bar catches on that window. A loop of string on each of them let him pull them closed again once he'd closed the window behind him.

By now the moon was down, and there wasn't a chance anyone could see him. In moments, he was down in the alley, running like a cat, heading for his next destination. He didn't dare be caught in *this* outfit! There would be no doubt in anyone's mind that of what his business was!

But there was a remedy for that, too. Two streets over was that wonderfully handy cavity in Lord Orthallen's wall, and that was where he'd left a set of breeches and a tunic. In the safety of the utter blackness, he pulled the bricks loose and extracted them. The hood of his shirt became a high collar, the scarf around his face and throat went around his waist beneath the tunic. He wiped the charcoal from his face with the inside of the tunic, and in very little time, a perfectly respectable young lad was strolling down the street with a bundle under his arm. He could be anyone's page boy or young servant on any of a dozen errands, and he even passed patrols of the Nightwatch twice without any of them stopping or even looking at him.

If they had, they'd have found nothing worse than a bundle of gentleman's underthings. And if he was asked, he'd mumble and hide his face and say he couldn't *rightly* say, but his mistress had told him to take them quietly to a certain gentleman and there wasn't anything else he could tell them.

The Watch would, of course, assume that the gentleman in question had been forced to make a hasty exit from a bedroom

where he'd had no business being and had left the least important of his clothing behind. As it was no business of the Watch
to oversee the morals of anyone, Skif would be sent on his
way, perhaps with a laugh.

The closer he got to his destination, the more relaxed he
felt. Already he was planning where to take the metal, how
to show the two boys to pound the gold and silver into flat,
indistinguishable sheets.

Hunger caught up with him then; he hadn't eaten much,
following Bazie's dictum that a full stomach made for a slow
thief. Bazie wasn't actually expecting him for some time yet,
since it was always his habit to go home by as circuitous a
route as possible. A thief might be expected to hurry back to
his den to hide his loot—and so a thief who feared pursuit
would do. But no one knew that Skif carried a small fortune
about his person, nor did any sign of it show. No one knew
that the Kalink household had been robbed this night. There
was no pursuit.

So why hurry back? *A thief runs when no one chases him,*
was another of Bazie's dictums, and he was right. If Skif
looked guilty, acted guilty, the Watch *might* detain and search
him, just on principle.

So, as soon as he reached a street of inns and taverns—the
same one, in fact, where he had robbed the kitchen of a burning tavern so very long ago—he drifted to the busiest, a hos-
telry called the "White Rider" with a sign of a Herald and his
Companion.

The place was packed full, with not one, but two musicians,
one at each fireplace, holding forth. It was, of course, impossible to hear either of them in the middle of the room. Skif found
a place on a bench next to a weary woman and her brood of
four children, got the attention of a serving girl by grabbing
her apron as she went by, and ordered food. He tried ordering
wine—he always did—and the girl smirked. When she came

back with his meat pie and drink, the drink was cider. He sighed and paid her.

While the wealthy were *out* of the city, the common folk came in. A great deal of business happened here in the fall, before the snows made it hard to travel. Skif picked out half a dozen different accents just from where he was sitting.

There could not have been a more vivid contrast to Skif's old home, too cold three seasons of the year, full of sullen silences, always in semi-darkness. Here it was cozy, and the air vibrated with talk and sound. There were plenty of lights, and there was no problem seeing what you were eating. The tabletop got regularly wiped down with clean rags, and although the floor was collecting a fair bit of debris over the course of the evening, Skif had no doubt it would start out the next day being swept clean enough to eat off of. The cooking aromas were all tempting, and there was no reek of stale beer and wine. If the customers themselves were a bit whiffy, well, it had been a hard day for some of them.

Skif relaxed further, his belly full of good food and cider. The woman gathered up her herd and left, to be replaced by a couple of equally weary fellows who could have been any sort of craftsman or farmer. Or possibly skilled laborers, come for one of the hiring fairs.

They both seemed rather concerned, huddling together to murmur at each other, and finally the one nearest Skif asked him politely what the least expensive meal was.

Skif gave them a friendly grin, and his recommendation.

They's a right couple 'uv conies! he thought, wondering which of the lads who worked this inn on the liftin' lay would lighten their pockets before they found work. Not that it was inevitable of course, but it was likely. You had choices in the liftin' lay; you could work half a dozen of easy marks like these two, or you could go for one big score who'd be cannier, better guarded. In either case there was about the same amount of risk, for each time you worked a mark in a crowd, you increased the risk of getting caught.

Well, that wasn't his outlook. He didn't work the liftin' lay anymore, and the two lads back with Bazie were too ham-handed for it right now. He finished the last of his cider, shoved the pottery mug to the middle of the table, and extracted himself from the bench, taking his bundle with him.

From here on, his story—if he was caught by the Watch—would change. Now he was bringing his father's clothing home from the pawnshop. It wasn't at all unusual for a family to have articles of clothing in and out of pawn all the time, and in some families, in more often than out.

And as he stepped out into the street, sure enough, a Watchman across the street caught sight of him, frowned, and pointed his truncheon at him.

"You! Boy!" he barked. "Halt there!"

Obediently, and with an ingratiating, cringing smile, Skif obeyed.

"What've ye got there?" the Watchman asked, crossing the street. Skif held out his bundle, hunching his shoulders, and the Watchman poked it with his truncheon. "Well? Speak up!"

" 'S m' Dad's shirt 'n' smalls, m'lor'," Skif sniveled. "Jest got 'em f'om Go'den Ball, m'lor'." With the fall hiring fairs going on all over Haven, the set of good linen smallclothes that had been in pawn all summer *would* come out again, for someone who was going to a hiring fair would be dressed in his best.

Then they'd go right back in again, if the job was only until winter and the end of hunting season.

"Open it," the Watch demanded. Skif complied; no one paid any attention to them as he did so, firstly because you didn't interfere with the Watch, and secondly because you didn't want the Watch's attention brought down on you.

The Watchman's eyes narrowed suspiciously. "If yer Dad's

smalls 've been in the nick, what're ye doin' eatin' at yon Rider?'' he demanded.

A stab of alarm mixed with chagrin pierced Skif, but he didn't show it. Even as he opened his mouth, he had his answer. After all, this was Quarter-Day, or near it—servants and laborers with year-round jobs got paid four times a year. " 'Tis out'a me *own* wages, m'lor!" he said with a touch of indignation. "M'Dad got a busted arm an' m'Ma didn' say nothin' till now, when I got me Quarter-Days!" Now he let his tone turn grumbling. "Reckon a lad kin hev a bit uv dinner when 'e's missed 'is own so's 'e kin help out 'is own fambly on 'is own half-day!"

There; just enough story to let the Watchman fill in the rest on his own—a son in service, a father injured and out of work, neither parent saying anything until the boy had the money to retrieve the belongings they'd put in pawn to see them over the lean time. Common servants got a half a day off—which usually began well into the afternoon and was seldom truly a "half-day"—once every fortnight or so. Servants as young as Skif usually didn't leave their employer's houses except on the half-day off after they'd gotten paid. Servants like Skif pretended to be wouldn't have gone out during dinner time either, which was probably why the Watchman had been suspicious, for why would a common servant spend his wages on food he could have gotten for free at his master's table? Or if he was visiting his parents, why hadn't *they* fed him?

But—Skif's story had him visiting his parents, discovering the situation, and going out after the pawned clothing. Presumably there was nothing in the house to eat, his job wouldn't include the benefit of "broken meats" to take home to his relatives, and as a result, he was missing a meal to do his duty to his parents. Skif was rather proud of his fabrication.

The Watchman grunted. "Wrap it up, then, boy, and keep moving," was all he said. Skif ducked his head and tied up the bundle again, then scuttled away.

The back of his neck was damp with sweat. That had been a close one! He made a mental note not to use that story or that inn again any time soon.

But with the haul he'd just made, he shouldn't have to.

Better be careful. Be just my luck now t' get hit with some'un pullin' a smash'n'grab. That was the crudest version of the liftin' lay, a couple of boys careening at full speed down the street, one after the other. One would knock a mark over, while the other came in behind and scooped up whatever he dropped. If that happened to Skif, while the Watchman's eye was still on him, the Watchman would be suspicious all over again if Skif didn't pursue his attackers, or refused to swear out charges against them. And at the moment, he couldn't afford the suspicions that might lead to being searched!

So he clutched his bundle tightly and raised his eyes to look up and down the street for the little eddies of activity that would mark a couple of smashers on a run.

And that was when he saw the red glow above the rooftops.

Fire.

He picked up his pace.

A *big* fire.

And from the look of it—somewhere near home. There would be a crowd, a mob—and a mob meant opportunity, even in a neighborhood as poor as his, for fire drew spectators from all over. He might not be an expert at the liftin' lay, but he was good enough to add to his take in the kind of crowd drawn by a big fire.

He moved into a trot. Get home, empty out his pockets, then go out in the mob—

He joined a stream of running, shouting spectators and would-be helpers, all streaming toward the fire like so many moths attracted to the light. Now he could see the lick of flames above the rooftops. He was jostled on all sides and had to concentrate to keep hold of the bundle and keep his own head cool while everyone around him was caught up in the fever of the moment.

And he couldn't help notice that he was getting nearer and nearer to his own home. Excitement began to take on a tinge of alarm. *Hellfires! It's close! Wonder who—*

He turned the corner with the rest of the mob—and stopped dead.

His building. *His* home. Now nothing but flames.

8

THIS was no place for a Herald. But then Herald Alberich was no ordinary Herald.

He hunched over his drink and rubbed at eyes that watered from the smoke filling the room, his ears filled with the droning of drunks, his nose wrinkling at the stench of too many unwashed bodies, burned food, and spilled beer. He had been in this part of Haven to meet an informant in a disgusting little hole of a tavern called "The Broken Arms"—an obvious and unsubtle reference to what would happen to a patron who displeased the owner. The sign above the door, crudely and graphically painted, enforced that—human arms do not normally bend in four places.

The informant had never showed his face, which didn't really surprise Alberich. He'd never reckoned the odds to be better than even at best. The man might have gotten cold feet; or he might even be entirely cold at this point—cold and dead. If so, it was fifty-fifty whether Alberich would ever find out what had happened to him. Bodies didn't always turn up. Even when the river was frozen over, there were plenty of ways in which a corpse could vanish without a trace. The people Alberich suspected of intrigue against the Queen were powerful, and had a very great deal to lose if they were unmasked. They had the ways and means to insure that more than one petty informant vanished without a trace if they cared to make it so.

The Herald sipped his stale beer, and watched the rest of the customers from beneath lowered eyelids. In the back of his mind, he felt his Companion fretting at the situation, and soothed him wordlessly. He knew that no one was going to recognize him, no matter what Kantor thought. Alberich did not stand out in this crowd of ne'er-do-wells, pickpockets, and petty thieves.

He probably wouldn't had he not bothered to disguise himself; he never *would* wear the traditional uniform of Herald's Whites even when presiding over the classes of Heraldic Trainees in his capacity as the Collegium Weaponsmaster, preferring instead a leather uniform of a slightly darker gray than the color used by the Trainees.

Herald's Whites—let those with fewer sins on their souls wear the Whites. He'd have worn black, if the Queen hadn't expressly forbidden it.

"Bad enough that you look like a storm cloud," she'd told him. *"I won't have them calling you 'Herald Death.' You stand out quite enough as it is from the rest of the Heraldic Circle."* He didn't point out to her that they might as well call him "Herald Death," that his business *was* Death, the ways and means of dealing it out. He simply bowed and let her have her way. She was the Queen, after all.

But at the moment, he was not on official duty, and he wore nothing like a uniform; his clothing was as drably nocolored, as tattered and patched as that of any man around him. His unfashionably short hair was concealed beneath an ancient knitted cap of indeterminate shape and origin. Only his sword and knives—themselves both disguised beneath plain, worn leather sheaths—would have told a different story about him.

Or perhaps not; to a slum-dwelling bullyboy, his sword was his life, and many of them bore weapons of superior make. A blade that bent or snapped, or wouldn't hold an edge, wasn't the sort of tool to risk your life on. Alberich was supposed to be that sort of sell-sword, a man whose blade went to the man with the price of it, with no questions asked on either side.

In the absence of his informant, Alberich was going to have to pretend he was here for the same reason as everyone else; to get drunk. He would probably have to use this tavern again, and he definitely needed to keep in character; he didn't dare break this carefully constructed persona. It had taken too long to build.

Most of the beer was going to hit the floor, though. Like many of the patrons here, he had his own mug, a leather-jack, tarred on the inside to make it waterproof and kept tied to his waist when not in use. Only, unlike theirs, his had a hole in the bottom; he seldom took an actual sip when the mug went to his lips. He relied on the slow but steady leak and the crack in the table he sat at to conceal where the rest of it got to. No one in this place was going to notice beer on the floor under the layer of rushes that hadn't been changed for a year or more. Only when his mouth dried or he needed something to wash the stench of the place from his tongue did he actually drink. The beer, stale and flat, was still preferable to the taste left behind in breathing the miasma of this miserable tavern.

Impatience made his head throb, and he forced himself to look bored instead of pained. He was wondering just how many more mugs of the noxious stuff he'd have to down before he pretended to stagger out, when the street outside erupted into what sounded like a riot.

Shouts—*screams!* His heart rose into his throat, and his pulse hammered in his ears as every nerve in his body reacted to the alarm.

He—and virtually everyone else in the tavern—jumped to their feet and ran for the door. He wasn't slow to react, but there were still plenty of people who were between him and it. He ran right into a wall of jostling bodies.

He told himself that this was a good diversion to get out and back to the Collegium, but he couldn't help himself. The noise out there was of panic and fear, and he *had* to respond. For the rest, of course, any disturbance held a potential for profit. . . .

Sweat stink mingled with a different kind of smoke—this was coming from the street outside. The noise now was like nothing he'd heard off a battlefield. He shoved his way through the crush at the door ruthlessly, elbowing one man in the ribs and brutally kicking another in the knee to get them out of the way. Both men swore and turned on him; both shrank out of the way when they saw who it was. He had a formidable reputation here; another reason why he was reluctant to sacrifice this persona. He could virtually come and go as he liked unmolested, and it had taken him no few knife fights to build that reputation. He had yet to draw his sword in here, which was a mercy, though his opponents only thought he was showing his contempt for them by meeting their swords with his knives. The poor fools had no idea that he was saving them from almost certain death at his hands if he pulled the longer blade. It wasn't his skill he was worried about, it was theirs; he'd seen drunken brawls end fatally when one idiot slipped and rammed himself onto another's sword. It had happened while he watched far too often to want to see that happen with him holding the blade. And it wasn't because he liked them that he spared their wretched lives, it was because if he killed a man, even by accident, the Watch would come, and there would be questions, and there would go his hard work in establishing Rokassan among the bully-boys.

That was why it was Alberich here, and not another Herald.
He was . . . practical.

He delivered another elbow blow to a set of ribs, this time
with enough force to it to make the man in his way *whuff*,
curse, and bend over, and Alberich was out into the not-so-
open street.

It should have been dark and relatively empty. It wasn't. It
was filled wall-to-wall with a churning mass of spectators and
a growing number of those who actually were doing something. A lurid red glow reflected off their filthy, upturned faces
as the wretched denizens of this neighborhood organized
themselves into lines of hands that passed buckets of water
away toward Alberich's right.

The source of the glow was as hellish as any Sunpriest sacrificial fire Alberich had ever seen in Karse.

An inferno that had once been a building raged madly
against the black of the night sky. It was one of the nearby
tenement blocks, and it was a solid sheet of flame from its
foundation to its roof. It couldn't have been more fully involved, and Alberich was struck motionless for a moment at
the sight, for he couldn't imagine how it had *gotten* that way
so quickly—short of a Red-Robe Priest's demon calling. For
one horrible moment he wondered wildly if a Red-Robe *had*
infiltrated the capital of Selenay's Kingdom—

But then an acrid whiff told him the real reason the building was so thoroughly engulfed.

Tar. Someone had been painting the sides of the building
with tar. The heavy black smoke roiling over the tips of the
highest flames confirmed it. A sudden wind drove it down into
the street, and screams turned to coughs and gasps.

Now, that wasn't uncommon in this part of the city. Landlords didn't care to spend more than they had to on mainte-
nance of these old buildings, and when they got word that an
inspection was in the offing, they frequently created a new and
draftless facade by tarring and papering the exterior with any

of a number of cheap substitutes for real wooden siding. The work could be done in a day or less, and when finished, presented a less ramshackle appearance that generally fooled overworked inspectors into thinking that the building was in better shape than it actually was. With so many buildings to inspect and so little time, the inspector could easily convince himself that *this* one didn't need to be looked at any closer, and move on. The work would hold for a while, but soon the paper would disintegrate, the tar soak into wood left unpainted for so long that it soaked up anything, and the place would revert to its former state. A little darker, perhaps, and for a while the tar would fill in the cracks that let in the winter winds, but nothing more.

Still . . . it seemed odd to Alberich that the thing should be blazing with such fiendish enthusiasm. Slum landlords were as stingy with their tar and paper as they were with everything else, and to burn like this, someone must have laid the stuff on with a trowel—

"Stop him! Stop that boy!"

Alberich sensed, rather than saw, the swirl in the crowd that marked someone small and nimble bouncing off the legs of those around him. Then a wiry, hard body careened into his hip.

He was running *to* the fire. Somehow, Alberich knew that—and his ForeSight showed him what would happen if the boy made it through the crowd.

A small body writhing in the flames, screaming, dying— An echo of the sacrificial fires of Karse. His gorge rose.

Automatically he reached out and snared the tunic collar of the boy before he could get any farther.

The boy turned on him, a spinning, swirling fury. "Let me go!" he screamed. *"Let me go!"* He spat out a stream of invective that rivaled anything Alberich had *ever* heard, and flailed at Alberich's arm with hard little fists. "I gotta get in there, ye bastid! *I gotta!*"

Screaming and writhing in the flames. . . .

Alberich didn't bother arguing with the brat, who was red-faced and hysterical, and he didn't have time to calm him. No doubt his family was in there—

Gods. He pulled the boy off his feet, and the brat still fought.

Well, if they were, they were all dead, or they were somewhere out in the street, sobbing over the loss of their few possessions. Nothing could survive that inferno, but there was no reasoning that point. Alberich couldn't let the boy go—

But there was work here; he might not be dressed in Whites, but he knew his duty, which was to help to save the buildings around the doomed one. He couldn't do that if he was playing nursemaid. With a grimace of pity, Alberich pulled his dagger as the boy continued to struggle toward the blaze, and tapped him behind the ear with the pommel nut the first moment the target presented itself.

The boy went limp. Alberich was still near enough to the door of the tavern to struggle back and drop him just inside, as far out of harm as possible in this neighborhood. Then he joined one of the many bucket brigades coalescing out of the mob. Until the Guard and the pumps and hoses arrived, they had to help convey water to soak down the buildings to either side of the fire to keep it from spreading. Already Kantor was raising the alarm for him, and help could not be more than a few moments away.

But he felt a moment of pleasure at the way people around him were responding to the emergency. So they weren't *all* villains, even though that was all he'd met since he began frequenting The Broken Arms. Even in this neighborhood, people could work together.

With one accord, the water throwers wisely concentrated their efforts on the buildings that were merely in danger and let the blazing tenement burn itself out. Anything and everything that could hold water was being pressed into service, with men and strong women sending the heavy, laden vessels toward the fire and smaller women and children passing the empties back to be filled again. Alberich's concentration narrowed to a few, vital tasks. Breathing. Taking the bucket. Passing it on with a minimum of spillage. Turning back for another.

Before he lost track of anything but the pain in back, shoulders, and arms and the cold that soon penetrated his soaking wet hands, legs, and feet, Alberich saw buckets, pots, pans, and even a chamberpot making the circuit up and back, up and back, while people shouted incoherent directions, and the flames laughed at their efforts.

Skif woke stiff and cold, with his head aching so much it hurt to open his eyes. He would just as soon have rolled over and gone back to sleep, but the pounding pain behind one ear and the cold prevented him from doing so—as did the sudden and electrifying realization that he wasn't in his bed.

He sat up abruptly, despite a stab of agony that made him yelp.

The cold, gray light of the street coming in at an open door next to where he sat completely disoriented him. Where was he?

This isn't home—

Then it all came back, in a rush. The triumph of the successful run.

The fire.

The man who'd grabbed him, keeping him from—from—

With an inarticulate howl of grief, he scrambled to his feet and staggered out into the street.

He coughed in the miasma of fog and stale smoke that met him like a wall. He fought through it, staggered a few paces—and stared, unbelieving, at the absolute ruin of his home.

Gone. All gone. A few blackened timbers stuck up out of the wreckage, marking where the staircase had been. The rest—was an unidentifiable pile of charred wood and still-smoldering wreckage.

The vultures were already hauling away whatever they could claw out, for in this place, even charcoal could serve to help eke out firewood and grant a few more hours of warmth. They had baskets, barrows—their clothing and faces black with soot.

Somewhere under there was his home—Bazie—and the boys.

Another howl tore itself out of his throat, and he hurled himself at the burned-out building, scrambling over what was left of the wall to the corner where the secret stair should have opened to Bazie's little den. It was underground—surely it was safe, surely *they* were safe—

They have to be safe!

But he couldn't help thinking . . . how long it took them to get Bazie out on the rare occasions when he emerged from the room. What a struggle it was to get him to the latrine, much less up the stairs. And that was on a bright spring day, not amid choking smoke and flames—

He began to dig, frantically, first with his bare hands, then with a piece of board until that broke, then with the blade of a shovel he found, still hot enough to blister. His throat closed, his gut clenched. He welcomed the pain in his hands—he should have been there! If he'd been there—if only—

He dug, with his eyes streaming tears and his heart breaking, dug and dug and dug until finally he was too exhausted to dig anymore.

He collapsed among the wreckage, and wept, leaning against a broken beam, until his sides ached and his eyes burned, and still he could not weep himself free of the pain.

Gone. All gone . . . I should have been here. All gone . . . it's my fault. All gone, all gone. . . .

Around him, people continued to scavenge, oblivious to his grief, or ignoring it. His grief turned to anger, then, and he stood up and tried to scream at them for the plundering ghouls that they were—but his throat was raw and his brain wouldn't work and all he could do was moan.

In the end, it was Jarmin, unlikely Jarmin, clerkly proprietor of the shop who bought their plundered silks, who found him there, whimpering like a whipped dog. Jarmin, who stepped mincingly into the wreckage, looked him up and down and asked, without any expression at all, "Got swag?"

Skif, shocked out of his grief for a moment by the sheer callousness of the query, began to shake his head. Then, suddenly remembering that triumph that seemed to have happened a hundred years ago, nodded.

Jarmin took him by the elbow and hauled him to his feet. Shock sealed his mouth and made him docile, though his aching eyes still streamed tears, his gut ached, and deep inside he wanted to strike out at whatever was nearest.

To strike out at himself.

Gone, all gone!

They picked their way to the street, with Jarmin still holding tightly to Skif's elbow, and once there, Jarmin headed determinedly toward his own shop. Skif just went along, too heartbroken to think, too full of bottomless mourning to care if Jarmin was about to lead him off somewhere to kill him for his loot.

Let him. I deserve it. I wasn't there.

They entered the shop, all of its tawdriness only too apparent by day. The girls were nowhere to be seen as Jarmin shoved Skif before him, past the counter, through a flap of hanging cloth, then up a narrow staircase that ended in a room just under the roof. A single dirty window covered with oiled parchment let in enough light to see by. There was a pallet there, and blankets, and some storage boxes; nothing else. Jarmin had to stoop to fit under the rooftree, and he shoved Skif roughly down onto the pallet, and gestured impatiently at his tunic.

Skif read the gesture for the demand that it was, and slowly undid his clothing to pull out the jewelry he'd taken last night. He laid it out on the pallet. Jarmin squatted down beside him and examined it piece by piece, grunting a little, but otherwise saying nothing.

Now he's gonna kill me. Skif could form the thought, but couldn't muster anything beyond the grief to care what happened to him. Care? No, that wasn't true. He cared. He deserved death. If he'd gotten back sooner, if he hadn't been so determined to bring back every damned piece that couldn't be traced—

I'd have been there. I'd have noticed in time. I'd have gotten them out.

Gone. All gone.

He just sat where he was, staring at his own hands, while Jarmin turned the jewelry over and over in his hands.

Finally the fence pulled the kerchief off his own neck and bundled it all up. He shoved the ends under his belt and knotted them, got up slowly and painfully, then descended the staircase. It looked from where Skif sat as if he was sinking into the floor. . . .

Tears began again, burning his eyes and his raw cheeks, and Skif didn't even bother to wipe them away. His nose closed up, his gut spasmed, and his thoughts ran around and around in a tight little spiral, like a mouse in a trap. *Gone. My fault. I should have been there.*

A moment later Jarmin was back again, a bundle of cloth under one arm, a jug in his hand.

"Here," he said gruffly. "These ought to fit you." He dropped the clothing down next to Skif, who stared at it without comprehension. "Even swap; the swag for these, food, and this room for three moons. After that, you get another place or start paying." As Skif stared at him as if he was speaking in a foreign tongue, he glanced at the jug in his hand as if he was surprised by its presence. "Oh, aye. And you get this."

He shoved it at Skif until Skif took it from him perforce.

"Go on. Pop the cork and drink it," Jarmin said fiercely.

Numbly, Skif obeyed. The cork came out with difficulty; the liquid inside tasted of cherries and burned like fire, burned him from his tongue to his gut, all the way down.

He knew as soon as he tasted it what it was, though he had never done more than sip a bit before this, the dregs left in some rich man's glass; spirits-of-wine, and worth its weight in silver. He gasped at the fire in it, but didn't spill a drop; it would bring blessed oblivion, which now he wanted more than he'd ever wanted anything. It went to the head quickly; in a few swallows, he was dizzy. A few swallows more, and he had trouble holding the jug. Jarmin, his eyes gleaming fiercely in the half light, steadied it for him and helped him lift it to his mouth.

"Keep drinking, boy," he heard, as from a far distant land. " 'Twon't take the hurt away, but it'll numb it for a while."

Numb . . . Numb was good. Maybe if he was numb, he wouldn't keep seeing Bazie and the boys . . . and the flames.

He swallowed again, the stuff burning its way down into his belly. Now he was more than dizzy; the room swam around him and tilted disconcertingly. Jarmin took the jug, corked it, and set it aside as he sagged down onto the pallet.

The room was definitely moving, but he didn't care. He just didn't want to have to watch it, so he closed his eyes. "Best thing for you, boy," he heard, then footsteps on the stair.

He didn't actually pass out; he hadn't drunk quite enough for that. But every time the numbness and the dizziness started to wear off, he heaved himself up onto his elbow and took another long pull at the jug until it came back again. Now and again he tired of simply feeling the room circling him and opened his eyes to watch the ceiling rotate. When the light started to fade, Jarmin appeared again with a lantern and bread and sops, a chamberpot, and a big jug of water. He made Skif eat and drink all of the water before he took the lantern and the plates away. Skif took some more pulls on the jug, then, and as shrill voices and the cajolery of the girls drifted in through the window, he let the liquor take him away to a place where nothing mattered anymore.

Jarmin told him later that he'd stayed drunk for a week. Sometimes he cried, but only when he was alone. Sometimes he heard someone moaning, and dimly realized that it was himself. All he knew was that the jug was, temporarily, his best friend. Jarmin kept it full, but insisted on his eating and drinking water, an annoyance he put up with because it meant that Jarmin would top off the jug.

He retained enough of sense and the cleanliness Bazie had drummed into him to make proper use of the chamberpot. It never seemed to stink, so Jarmin must have kept it clean as well.

Jarmin also came up to talk to him now and again. For a while, he ignored the words and the man because he didn't want to go to the place where words meant something. For a while, that is, until something Jarmin said jarred him back into *thinking.*

"Word is," Jarmin said, into Skif's rosy fog, "That fire was *set.*"

Set? Skif opened his eyes with an effort. "Wha?" he managed, mouth tasting of old leather and liquor.

Jarmin didn't look at him, and his tone was casual. "Word is that the landlord got a surprise inspection, and was going to have to fix the place. Or get fined. Going to cost him dearly, either way. So he burned it instead, and is calling it a terrible accident."

Understanding—and anger—stirred sluggishly. "He— *burned* it?"

Jarmin shrugged, as if it all mattered not a whit to him. "Word is, that's the case. Don't who the landlord is—was," he corrected. "*You* know how it is. Probably some high-necked merchant, or even highborn. Couldn't possibly be connected with us, nor where we live. Couldn't soil himself by openly owning the place, but takes our copper right enough. So long as no one knows where he got it. But he wouldn't want to have to spend good coin either, not when burning it costs him less and allows him to sell the lot afterward."

Anger burned away the fumes of the liquor—hot as the flames that had destroyed his only family. "He burned it?" Skif repeated, sitting up, fists clenching.

"Word is that. *Who*ever he is." Jarmin shrugged, then with a sly look, pushed the jug toward Skif.

Skif pushed it back, still dizzy, but head getting clearer by the moment.

He burned it. Or ordered it burned, whoever he is.

"No warning, of course," Jarmin continued casually. "Because that would tip off the inspectors that he didn't mean to fix it. And the highborn don't care how many of us burn, so long as an inconvenient building is gotten rid of. That is how it is."

There was light in the window and relative quiet on the street. It must be day, and the girls were asleep. Skif was still drunk, and he knew it, but he was getting sober, more so with every breath, as his anger rose and rose, burning like the flames that had taken his family. He looked down at himself, and saw that he was still wearing the filthy clothing he'd been brought here in. The pile of clean stuff still lay at the foot of the pallet. "Wanta bath, Jarmin."

"Comes with the room," Jarmin said indifferently. "I'll tell madam. Get yourself downstairs when you can."

He descended the stairs, and Skif waited until he could stand without too much wavering. Then he picked up a shirt, trews, and socks, and followed.

Jarmin was behind the counter tending to a customer, but waved him out the door. Skif tottered out, blinking owlishly at the daylight, and the door of the brothel next to Jarmin's shop opened. An oily-looking fellow beckoned to him, and Skif went in.

He wasn't given any time to look around the shabby-luxurious "parlor" where customers came to choose from the girls if they hadn't already picked one. The oily fellow hustled him into the back where there was—

A laundry.

Only the remains of the liquor and the firmest of controls kept Skif from breaking down right there and then. The urge to wail was so great he practically choked.

There were several tubs, two of which had girls in them, three of which had laundry. Before he could lose his head and bawl, a burly woman with work-reddened hands and a tight, angry mouth stripped him before he could open his mouth and shoved him into the last of the tubs. She didn't give him a chance to wash himself either; she used the same brush and lye soap that she used on the linen on *his* hide, with the same lack of gentleness.

The bristles lacerated his skin, his scalp. He didn't let out a single sound as she scrubbed as if she intended to take his skin off, then made him stand, rinsed him with a bucket of water cold enough to make him gasp, and bundled him in a sheet. His own clothing went into one of the tubs with laundry in it, and she handed him the plain trews, socks, and shirt he brought with him, leaving him to clothe himself as she turned back to her work. He noticed that the girls didn't get the same ungentle treatment. They were allowed to bathe themselves and did so lazily, completely ignoring his presence.

Well, that was all right. He didn't want any stupid whores fussing over him like he was some sort of animate doll. He didn't want *their* sympathy. He didn't want anyone's pity.

Hard. I gotta be hard. That's what I gotta do.

He dried himself off—the laundress snatched the sheet away from him before he could lay it down and popped it back into a tub—and got the clothing on. It was rather too big, but that hardly mattered. All he had left now were his own boots, which he pulled on, and left without a backward glance.

His head was clear enough now, and while the laundress had scrubbed him, his grief had somehow changed, shrunk, condensed down into a hard, cold little gem that formed the core of a terrible anger that seemed almost too large to contain in so small a compass as his heart.

Revenge. That was what he wanted, more than anything in the world. And he wasn't going to rest until he got it.

He walked into Jarmin's shop, and the old man gave him a sharp glance, then a nod of satisfaction. "You'll do," was all he said, and tossed him a pouch.

It clinked. Skif opened it and found a little money; mostly copper, a bit of silver. He tucked it inside his shirt. It was little enough. Jarmin was cheating him, of course. The room, the food, the clothing, the baths—none of that was worth a fraction of what he'd stolen. Jarmin wasn't *giving* him anything.

And Skif didn't want anything but this—the expected cheating, the usual grifting. No more kindness. No more generosity. He could move on from here without looking back or regretting anything. This was a business transaction for Jarmin. Save one of the best thieves he knew and ensure a steady supply of goods for his shop—as simple as that.

So he didn't thank the man for the money; he just nodded curtly and went back out into the street. He knew what the money was for—tongues weren't loose without money. And Skif was going to have to find a lot of tongues to loosen. It was going to take a long time, he already knew that. That was fine, too. When revenge came, it would come out of nowhere. The enemy would never know who it was that hit him, or why.

Just as disaster had come upon him, and with equal destruction in its claws. When he was finished, whoever had killed Bazie would be left with nothing, contemplating the wreckage of what had been his life, with everything he valued and loved gone in an instant.

Just like Skif.

Skif smiled at the thought. It was the last smile he would wear for a very long time.

9

SMOKE drifted over the heads of the customers; it wasn't from the fireplace, but from the tallow dips set in crude clay holders on the tables and wedged into spaces between the bricks around the room. Skif sat as far from the door as it was possible to be, in the "odd" corner of The Broken Arms, a kind of rectangular alcove just before the walls met, into which someone had wedged a broken-legged stool, making a seat hemmed in on three sides with brick. The brick was newer here, so this might be an old entrance; gone now, since the next building over was built right up against this one. Or maybe it had been a window slit; you couldn't have used it as a door, not really. It was too short and too narrow. Maybe a former fireplace, before the big one was put in, before this room became a tavern. No, it wasn't big enough for a man to be comfortable sitting here, but it was perfect for him. Here he could spend hours unnoticed, the wenches had gotten so used to it being empty.

Before things got so crowded, he'd bought himself a jack of

small beer and a piece of bread and dripping, so his stomach was full but not full enough to make him drowsy. Meanwhile the number of customers rose, and the place got warmer. This nook was a good place to tuck himself into when he wanted to eavesdrop on conversations. Eavesdropping was almost as good as paying for information, and it cost nothing. He'd become adept at being able to sort one set of voices from all of the babble and concentrate on them. Once in a while one of the wenches would notice that he was there, and like this afternoon, he'd buy a mugful of small beer and a piece of bread so that they'd leave him alone, but that was only when the place was less than half full. When it was crammed tight, as it was now, he'd be overlooked all night.

He'd already wedged himself up onto the seat, knees just under his chin and his arms wrapped around them, so not even his feet were in anyone's way. Every bench and stool at every table was full; not a surprise with rain coming down in barrel loads outside. Not a good night for "business," except within walls.

Not that anyone in the Arms was going to do any business. That sign over the door wasn't there for a joke. That was what made and kept the Arms so popular; when you walked in here, you knew you'd come out with your purse no lighter than the cost of your food and drink. The women wouldn't try and get you drunk so they could talk you into paying for wine for them either. The wenches here weren't hired for their looks, gods knew—absolute harridans, most of 'em. They'd been hired because they knew the liftin' lay, and how to spot someone at business. One whistle from one of them, and the miscreant would find himself on the street with his own arms looking just like the ones on the sign. It was a good dodge for the wenches, for certain-sure; a young thing, plain though she might be, would still have an excuse to come sidling alongside of a fellow with a bit of an invitation. An old hag wouldn't; and though her fingers might still be wise, they weren't as nimble as a young thing's, so if she tried the old dodge of stumbling into a fellow, the odds were that he'd be clapping his hand to his belt pouch before she could get into it. *And* if he didn't, and she got it, her feet wouldn't carry her as far or as fast anymore. The older you got in the trade, the likelier it was you'd be caught that fatal third time, and unless she got herself a gaggle of littles to teach the trade to—taking everything they lifted, of course—there wasn't much an aging woman could do to turn a penny. There weren't a lot of women who learned the high roads or the ketchin' lay, professions that could keep you going for a long time, so long as you were limber enough to climb or bold enough to cosh.

Not that Skif held with the ketchin' lay. Bazie'd turned up his nose at it; didn't take a mort of skill nor brains to take a cosh to a fellow's head and make off with his goods. And the Watch and the Guards didn't give a third or even second chance to anyone caught at *that* trade; caught once, you saw ten years of hard labor for the Guard.

The women Skif knew didn't hold with the ketchin' lay either, though he wasn't sure what the difference was between laying a fellow out with a cosh and taking his goods when he was drunk dead asleep. Whatever, *that* was still another trade, and an old hag couldn't ply it either.

So it was good business all around for "Pappa" Serens. He had the reputation now, and always had himself a full complement of cheap serving wenches, seeing as he gave them all bed space, drink, board, and a couple of coppers now and again. They got free access to the cheapest beer after closing, as much as they cared to drink, and to the dregs of every barrel and mug of whatever price during the hours of custom, so long as they didn't get drunk. Every one of Serens' four "girls" had her own pottery pitcher back in the kitchen, and no mug belonging to the tavern ever went back out to the custom without being drained—every drop—into one of those pitchers. Since by this point in their lives what they were mostly interested in was a warm bed and enough drink to knock them out every night, nobody was complaining about the low wages. The drinking killed them off, of course, but the moment that one was carried out the door on a board, another came in on her own two feet to replace her.

Serens supplied a unique commodity for this part of the city. You could go to a dozen taverns to lift skirts, to a dozen more for a cheaper drunk than you got here, even to a couple for a bigger meal at the same price. The Arms, however, was the only place Skif knew of where you could set yourself down without worrying about fingers at your belt pouch, have beer that wouldn't choke you and a meal that wouldn't sicken you, and talk *about* anything *to* anyone, unmolested. The wenches were ugly, but they kept their mouths shut, and their eyes on their own business. There were occasional fights, but it was generally some young bullyboy trying to prove something, it usually went outside, and the older, wiser sell-sword he'd picked would settle him down quick enough. And if it didn't go outside and racketed among the benches, Seren himself, big as a bull and quick as a stag, would settle it, and The Broken Arms would have another gutterside advertisement of how the proprietor treated those who broke the rules.

Tonight, with waterfalls pouring from the clouds outside and the wind in the right direction so that the chimney drew properly instead of sending smoke into the room, there wouldn't be any disturbances. Everyone was too comfortable to want to find himself out in the dark and rain. Skif could stay here tucked up until closing. And he would; right now his doss was a stable garret, cheap enough and cool enough even by day, now it was summer, but boring. Worse, with the rain pouring down; it'd lull him to sleep and mess him up. He slept by day, not by night, and he didn't need to find himself starting to nod in the middle of a job because he'd let his sleeping and waking patterns get messed up.

Besides, if he wasn't going to be able to work tonight, he might as well see if he couldn't pick up something interesting.

In the months since the fire, he'd made some progress finding out who was responsible—not anywhere near as fast as he'd have liked, but not so little that he was disappointed. He'd traced the money and responsibility up the line from the immediate "landlord" to whom they'd paid their rent, through two middlemen, both of whom were worse off for the loss of the building and neither of whom actually owned it. There, he'd come to a dead-end, but *someone* had given orders it be burned and *someone* had carried out those orders, and there weren't too many who were in the business of burning down buildings. Skif had, he thought, identified them all.

He had no intention of going up to any of them and confronting them about it. In the first place, there was nothing he could offer in the way of a bribe or a threat to get them to talk. In the second place, doing so would likely get him dead, not get him answers. So he was taking the slow and careful path, much though it irked and chafed him; coming here as often as he could to listen to their talk. For here was where all dubious business was conducted, and here was where the one who was really responsible might come to commission another such job.

In point of fact, as luck would have it, one of Skif's targets sat not a foot away from him tonight, making it absurdly easy to pick out his words from amidst the babble all around him.

So far it had been nothing but idle talk of bets won and lost, boasting about women, tall tales of drinking bouts of the past. On the other hand, the man hadn't been talking to anyone but his cronies. He was a professional, and well enough off by the standards around here; he didn't *have* to spend his evening in the Arms. He could get himself a woman, have a boy deliver a good tavern meal to his room, or find a better class of place to drink in. So maybe, just maybe, he'd come here tonight to make a contact, or even a deal.

When he got up to ask someone at one of the two-person

tables if he'd move to the seat *he* had just vacated—for a monetary consideration—and take his comrade with him, Skif felt a thrill of anticipation and apprehension. He *was* meeting someone!

The door at the front of the tavern opened and closed, and there was a subtle movement in the crowd. It wasn't that the tavern patrons actually moved away from the newcomer, but they *did* make room for him to pass. They hadn't done *that* for anyone since Skif had been sitting there, which meant that whoever had come in was respected, but not feared. So he wasn't one of those half-crazed bullies, he wasn't someone that people feared could be set off into a rage. But they gave him room. You earned that here.

When the man made his way to Skif's part of the tavern, Skif knew why people gave him room. He didn't know the man's name, but he knew the face—closed, craggy, hard. The man was a sell-sword; he didn't start quarrels, but those that others started with him, he finished, and he was so good he never actually drew his sword when fights were picked with him. After the third bullyboy to go outside with him wound up in the dust, finished off by a man with two knives against their swords, no one picked another fight with him. Defeat was one thing; anyone could have a bad day and get beaten in a fight. Humiliation was another thing altogether. You could live down a bad day; you lived with humiliation forever, if only inside your own head.

So nobody bothered *this* man anymore.

He took his seat at the little table across from Skif's target with an attitude that said—quite calmly—that he had expected that the seat would be free and would be *kept* free for him.

But to Skif's disappointment, even though he strained his ears as hard as he could, he couldn't make out anything more than an occasional word, and none of them had anything to do with the fire.

"Rethwellan" was one word. "Vatean" was another. The first was a country somewhere outside of Valdemar; the second he recognized as a merchant—a very wealthy merchant—and a friend of the great Lord Orthallen. Skif still filched food from Lord Orthallen on a regular basis; he'd gone back to it in the wake of the fire, after his three moons had run out. It was hard to go back to the roof road, and the liftin' lay didn't pay enough for him to have a room, buy drinks to loosen tongues, and eat, too. So all this winter past, he'd lifted silks and fenced them, lived in a little box of a garret room tucked into the side of the chimney of a bakehouse—wonderfully warm through the rest of the winter, that was—and went back to mingling with the servants in Lord Orthallen's household to get his food. Only now he knew far, far more. Now he knew how to slip in and out of the household, knew how to conceal more and *what* to conceal. He knew what delicacies to filch and trade for entire meals of more mundane foodstuffs. That, perhaps, was the best dodge.

With educated eyes, he soon learned how to get into and out of the storage rooms without being caught. The easiest way was to bribe one of the delivery boys to let *him* take what had been ordered to Lord Orthallen's manse. Now these days he no longer bothered to disguise himself as a page. While the cook or the butler was tallying what had come in on his pony cart, he would carry foodstuffs into the storage room and leave a window unlocked. Then he would come back once the frantic work of preparing a meal had begun, slip in, help himself to whatever he wanted, and slip out again. He wasn't buying a lot of food anymore.

When the bakehouse room became unendurable in late spring, he packed up his few possessions and found his new room over a stable that supplied goats and donkeys for delivery carts. Cheap enough, with windows on both sides, it caught a good breeze that kept it cool during the day while he was sleeping. The animals went out each day at dawn—when he got back from his work—and came back at sunset, by which time he was ready to leave. The goats and donkeys took their pungent smells and noise with them, and by the time he had finished eating and was ready to sleep, there was nothing but the sound of the single stableboy cleaning pens and very little smell. It was a good arrangement all around, and if his landlord never asked what he did all night, well, he never asked why on nights of moon-dark a certain string of remarkably quiet donkeys with leather wrapped around their hooves went out when he did and arrived back by dawn.

By spring he had gone back to roof work, although he kept his thefts modest and more a matter of opportunity than planning. What he did mostly was *listen,* for it was remarkable what information could be gleaned at open windows now that the weather was warm. Some of that, he sold to others, who trafficked in such information. Why should *he* care who paid to keep a secret love affair *secret,* or who paid to avoid tales of bribery or cheating or other chicanery quiet? It was all incidental to his hunt for Bazie's murderer, but if he could profit by it, then why not? When a valuable trinket was left carelessly on a table in plain sight, though, it usually found its way into his pocket, and then to a fence. His own needs were modest enough that these occasional thefts, combined with his information sales and garden-variety raids on laundry rooms, kept him in ready coin.

The beauty of it all was that the three activities were so disparate that no one who knew one of them was likely to connect him with the other two. If it became too dangerous to filch silks, he could step up his roof work. If he somehow managed to get hold of some information that proved dangerous, he could stop selling it, and filch more laundry. And if rumors of a clever sneak thief sent the Watch around on heightened alert, he could stop going for the trinkets and confine himself to listening at chimneys, which sent up no smoke in this lovely weather, but did provide wonderful listening posts.

Unfortunately, although he had cultivated acute hearing, it wasn't good enough to enable him to hear what it was that the dour sell-sword was saying.

However, it did seem as if the man was *buying,* not selling, information. When the surreptitious motion that marked the passing of coins from hand to hand finally took place, it was the sell-sword who passed the coins to Skif's target, and not the other way around.

Might could be I could sell 'im a bit, if's Lord Orthallen he's wantin' t' hear about, Skif thought speculatively. He decided to investigate chimneys at the manse at the next moon-dark. They might prove to be useful.

"Fire," he heard then, which brought him alert again, and he closed his eyes and put his head down, the better to concentrate.

"Bad enough," the sell-sword grunted. "Ye'd'a seen me a-passin' buckets that night."

Skif's target, who Skif knew as "Taln Kelken," but who the sell-sword addressed as "Jass," laughed shortly. "Could'a bin rainin' like 'tis now, an' ye'd nawt hev got it out," he replied, with a knowing tone. "Reckon when a mun hev more'n twenny barrels uv earth tar an' wax painted on mun's buildin', take more'n bucket lines t'douse it."

Earth tar! Skif had heard rumors that the reason the fire had caught and taken off so quickly was because it had been tarred—but this was the first he'd heard of earth tar and *wax!* Ordinary pine tar, or *pitch,* as it was also called, was flammable enough—but the rarer earth tar, which bubbled up from pits, was much more flammable. And to combine it with wax made no sense—the concoction would have been hideously expensive.

Unless the point was to turn the building into a giant candle.

Only one person could know that about the fire. The man who'd set it.

Now Skif had that part of the equation, and it took every-thing he had to stay right where he was and pretend he had dropped into a doze with his forehead on his knees. Anger boiled up in him, no matter that he had pledged he would not do anything until he knew the real hand behind the fire. The bullyboy sounded proud of himself, smug, and not the least troubled that whole families had died in that fire, and others been made bereft, parentless, childless, partnerless.

And my family—-gone. All gone.

"And just how would you know that?" the sell-sword asked. His tone was casual . . . but there was anger under it as deep, and as controlled as Skif's. The bullyboy didn't hear it, so full of himself he was; maybe only someone with match-ing anger would have. It shocked Skif and kept him immobile, as mere caution could not have.

"That'd be tellin', wouldn' it?" the bullyboy chuckled. "An' that'd be tellin' more'n I care to. 'Less ye've got more'v what brung ye here."

The sell-sword just grunted. "Curious, is all," he said, as if he had lost interest. "Don' 'magine th'lad as ordered that painted on 'is buildin' would be too popular 'round here."

"What? A mun cain't hev a coat've sumthin' *good* put on 'is property 'thout folks takin' it amiss?" the man known as both Jass and Taln said with feigned amazement. "Why man, tha's what's painted on ships t'make 'em watertight! Mun got word inspectors weren't happy, 'e puts the best they is on yon buildin'! Is't *his* fault some damnfool woman kicks over a cookstove an' sets the thing ablaze afore he kin get th' right surface on't, proper?"

"You tell me," the sell-sword sneered. Evidently he didn't care much for the man he faced. Maybe Taln-Jass couldn't tell it, but there was thick-laid contempt in the sell-sword's voice.

The bullyboy laughed, and Skif seethed. "That'd be tellin'. An' I'm too dry t'be tellin'."

Skif thought that this was a hint for the sell-sword to buy

his informant a drink, but a scrape of stools told a different story. "This rain ain't liftin' afore dawn," the arsonist said. "I'm off."

"Sweet dreams," the sell-sword said, his tone full of bitter irony that wished the opposite.

Laughter was his only answer. Skif opened his eyes to see his target turn and shove his way out through the crowd to the door. The sell-sword remained seated, brooding.

Then his back tensed. He stood up, slowly and deliberately, and for a moment Skif thought he was going to turn around to look behind him to see who might have been listening to the conversation.

Skif shrank back into his alcove as far as he could go, and tried to look sleepy and disinterested. Somehow he did not want this man to know that *he* had heard every bit of the last several moments.

But evidently the sell-sword trusted in the unwritten rules of the Arms. He did not turn. He only stood up, and stalked back out through the crowd, out the door, and into the rain.

Two tenants of a nearby, more crowded table took immediate occupation of the little table. And Skif breathed a sigh of relief, before he settled back into his smoldering anger. Because now that he knew who the tool was—that tool would pay. Perhaps not immediately, but he *would* pay.

When the rain died, Skif left; there was still a drizzle going, but not enough to keep him in the Arms any longer. His mind buzzed; his anger had gone from hot to cold, in which state he was able to think, and think clearly.

Somehow, he had to find the next link in the chain—the man who had paid for the arson. But how?

Loosen the bastard's tongue, that's what I gotta do. As Skif dodged spills out of waterspouts and kept when he could to the shadows, he went over his options.

No point tryin' to threaten 'im. Alone, in his stable loft, he could indulge himself in fantasies of slipping in at a window and taking the man all unaware—of waking the scum with the cold touch of a knife at his throat. But they were fantasies, and Skif knew it. Knives or no, unaware or not, the bullyboy was hard and tough and bigger than Skif. Much bigger.

So what were his real options? Drink? Drugs?

Not viable, neither of them. He couldn't afford enough of the latter to do any good, and as for the former—well, he'd seen that particular lad drink two men under the table and stagger out with his secrets still kept behind his teeth. The closest he ever got to boasting was what he'd done tonight.

Just stick on 'im like a burr, Skif decided, and ground his teeth. It wasn't the solution he craved. *Watch 'im, an stick to 'im. If he takes up summat to 'is rooms, I gotta figger out which chimbley leads t' his, or—*

Suddenly, an idea struck him that was so brilliant he staggered.

I don' need all that dosh fer shakin' loose words loose no more! He *knew* who had set the fire! So the money he had been using to pay bribes could be used for—

For a room in th' bastard's own place!

Above, below, or to either side, it didn't matter. So long as Skif had an adjoining surface, he could rig the means to hear what was going on no matter how quiet the conversation was. Bribes weren't all he'd been paying for—he'd been getting lessons at spycraft. How to follow someone and not be detected. How to overhear what he needed to. In fact, so long as Skif had a room *anywhere* in the arsonist's boarding house, he'd be able to eavesdrop on the man. It would just take a little more work, that was all.

He lifted his face to the drizzle and licked the cool rain from his lips, feeling that no wine could have a sweeter taste. *I'm gonna get you now,* he thought with glee. *An' once I know what you know—*

Well.

Knives weren't the only weapons. And poisons were a sight cheaper than tongue-loosening drugs.

"I don' need a lot've room," Skif said to the arsonist's scrawny, ill-kempt landlord, who looked down at him with disinterest in his watery blue eyes. "No cook space, neither. Mebbe a chimbley an' a winder, but mostly just 'nuff room t' flop."

"I mebbe got somethin'," the landlord said at last. Skif nodded eagerly, and did not betray in the slightest that he already *knew* the landlord had exactly what *he* wanted, because Skif had bribed the tenant of the highly-desirable room right next to his target to find lodgings elsewhere. Young Lonar hadn't taken a lot of bribing—he was sweet on a cookshop girl, and wanted some pretties to charm her out of her skirts and into his bed. Skif simply lifted a handful of jingling silver bangles from a dressing-table placed too near an open window; they were worth a hundred times to Lonar what Skif would have gotten for them fenced.

It had taken him time to work this out, time in which his anger kept ice water flowing in his veins and sparked his brain to clever schemes. First, finding out the arsonist's exact room. Next, casing the place, and discovering who his neighbors were. Then picking the most bribable, and finally, the bribe itself.

Lonar had one room—Skif had even been in it several times already. It was ideally suited for Skif's purposes; the back of the arsonist's own fireplace and chimney formed part of one of the inner walls. From the look of the bricked-up back and the boarded-up door in the same wall, the room and the arsonist's had once been part of a larger suite, and the fireplace had been open between the two rooms, giving each a common hearth.

"Ten copper a fortnight," the landlord said tersely. "No coo-kin', no fires. Chimbley oughter be enough t'keep ye warm'o nights."

In answer, Skif handed over enough in copper and silver to pay for the next six moons, and the man nodded in terse satisfaction. This wasn't unusual behavior, especially out of someone who had no regular—or obvious—job. When you were flush, you paid up your doss for as long as you could afford. When you weren't, you tried to sweet-talk the landlord as long as possible, then fled before he locked up your room and took your stuff.

Probably he expected that Skif would be gone by the end of those six moons.

Be nice, but I ain't countin' on it.

The landlord handed over a crude chit with an "M"—for Midwinter Moon—on it. That was how long Skif had; if the landlord tried to cheat him by claiming he'd paid for less time, he could show it to a court to prove how long his tenancy was supposed to be. There was, of course, no key to be handed over, not in a place like this one. Tenants were expected to find their own ways of safeguarding their belongings. Some were more interesting than others.

Skif pocketed his chit, picked up his pack and bag, and ran up the narrow stairs to the second-floor landing. Three doors faced it; his own was in the middle. His room wasn't much bigger than a closet between the two sets of two rooms each on either side. The door was slightly ajar, and Skif slipped inside quickly, closing it behind him and dropping a bar across it. The room itself wasn't much wider than the door.

Lonar hadn't left anything behind but dirt. The walls, floor, and ceiling were a uniform grime color. Impossible to tell if there was paint under the dirt. Closed shutters in the far wall marked the window. From the amount of light leaking in around them, it didn't look as if they were very weathertight. Not that it mattered. Skif wasn't here for the decor. He was, however, here for the walls.

Never mind how well the shutters fit, it was the window itself that featured prominently in Skif's plans.

He flung open the shutters to let air in, and unrolled his pallet of blankets on the floor, adding his spare clothing beneath as extra padding, and untied the kerchief in which he had bundled the rest of his few belongings. Including the one, very special object that he had gone to a lot of trouble to filch.

A glass. A *real* glass.

He set it in the corner out of harm's way, and laid himself down on his pallet, closing his eyes and opening his ears, taking stock of his surroundings. Bazie would have been proud of him.

Not a lot of street noise; this house was on a dead-end, and most of the other places on the street also supplied rooms to let. Skif identified the few sounds coming from outside and ignored them, one by one.

Above him, footsteps. Four, perhaps five children of varying ages, all barefoot. A woman, also barefoot. That would be Widder Koil, who made artificial flowers with paper and fabric. Presumably the children helped as well; otherwise, he couldn't imagine how she alone would earn enough to feed them all. The voices drifted down from above, edgy with hunger, but not loud.

Below, nothing. The first-floor tenant was still asleep; he was a night carter, one of the few tenants here with a respectable and relatively well-paying job.

To the left, the wall with no fireplace, four shrill female voices. Whores, four sisters sharing two rooms; relatively prosperous and without a protector. They didn't need one; the arsonist slept with at least two of them on a regular basis, and no one wanted to chance his anger.

And to the right . . .

Snores. The chimney echoed with them.

Not surprising; like Skif, the arsonist worked at night. The question was, which of the two rooms was the man's bedroom?

Skif's hope was that it was not the one with the fireplace, but there was no way of telling if the man was snoring very loudly in the next room, or not quite as loudly in the fireplace room.

At least I can hear him.

Well, there was nothing more to do now. He let his concentration lapse, and consciously relaxed the muscles of his face and jaw as he had learned to do when he wanted to sleep. He would be able to learn more in a few candlemarks. And when his target went out tonight, so would he.

He woke all at once, and knew why. The window above his head showed a dark-blue sky with a single star, his room was shrouded in shadows, and next door, the snoring had stopped.

Jass-Taln was awake.

He sat up quickly and felt in the corner for his precious glass. He put it up against the wall and put his ear against the bottom of it.

The man moved like a cat; Skif had to give him that much grudging credit. He made very little noise as he walked around his rooms, and unlike some people, he didn't talk to himself. No coughing, no sneezing, no spitting; how ironic that a cold-blooded murderer made such an ideal neighbor.

Ideal. Unless, of course, you actually wanted to hear what he was up to.

Now there was some noise in the fireplace! Skif frowned in concentration, isolating the sounds.

Whittling. Shavings hitting the bricks. The sound of a hand scraping the shavings together, then putting them in the grate.

Then the rattling and scratching of a handful of twigs. A log coming down atop them.

A metallic *clunk* startled him, though he should have expected it. Taln-Jass had just slapped a pan down onto the grill over his cooking fire.

A while later; the sound of something scraping and rattling in the pan. Eating sounds. Frequent belches.

All of which were sweeter than any Bard's music to Skif's ears. The trick with the glass worked, just as his teacher had claimed it would! And it sounded as if the room with the fireplace was the arsonist's "public" room, for all of these noises were nearer than the snores had been. Which meant that when the man brought clients here for private discussions, it would be the room nearest Skif where those discussions would take place.

A fierce elation thrilled through him, and he grinned with clenched teeth. Who needed drink, drugs, or even threats when you could listen to your target at will, unnoticed?

Now all he needed was time and patience, and both were, at last, on his side.

A̲LTHOUGH Skif's patience was taxed to the uttermost by
the lack of any concrete progress in his quest, he at least was
collecting a great deal of personal information on his "neighbor," Jass. The arsonist, it soon developed, had as many
names as there were moons in the calendar.

Not only was he known by the two Skif knew, but he was
addressed variously as "Hodak" by his landlord, "Derial" by
the whores, and various nicknames derived from the slight
squint of one eye when he was thinking, his ability to move
silently, the fact that a small piece was missing from his ear,
and some not-very-clever but thoroughly obscene epithets that
passed for humor among his acquaintances.

Skif decided on "Jass." Easy to remember, it had no associations for him other than his target. But he was careful never
to personally address the man at all, much less by name, since
he wasn't actually supposed to know any of his names. The
few times they met on the stairs or the landing, Skif ducked
his head subserviently and crammed himself to the wall to let

the arsonist pass. Let Jass think that Skif was afraid of him—all that meant was that Jass had never yet gotten a look at anything other than the top of Skif's head.

A man of many trades was Jass. Over the course of three fortnights, Skif listened in to his conversations when he had someone with him in his rooms—pillow talk and business talk, and boasts when deep in his cups. He wasn't "just" an arsonist. If he had been, he'd have gone short more often than not, as that wasn't a trade that he was called on to practice nearly often enough to make a living at it. Together with all four of the whores he practiced a variation on the ketchin' lay where one of the girls would lure an unsuspecting customer into Jass' clutches where the would-be lecher soon found himself hit over the head and robbed.

He was also known for setting fires, of course—though, so far since Skif had moved in, they were all minor acts of outrage, designed to frighten shopkeepers into paying for "protection" from one of the three gangs he worked for, or to punish those who had refused to do so. On rare occasions, he sold information, most of which Skif didn't understand, but seemed to have to do with intrigues among some of the city's wealthier folk. Where he got these tidbits was a mystery to Skif, although there was a direct connection with the darker side of Haven, in that the information generally was about who among Jass's cronies had been hired by one of the upright citizens, and for what dirty job.

The craggy-faced sell-sword was not the only one interested in Jass' information. There were at least three other takers to Skif's knowledge, two of whom transacted their business only within the four walls of Jass's fireplace room.

But to Skif's growing impatience, not once had Jass been commissioned by the same person who had put him to igniting the tenement house.

Skif might have learned more—this summer brought a rash of tiny, "mysterious" fires to blight the streets of Haven—but he had to eat, too. Frustratingly, he would sometimes return to his room after a night of roof walking only to hear the tail end of a conversation that *could* have been interesting, or to hear Jass himself come in after a long night of—what? Skif seldom knew; that was the frustrating part. He might learn the next day of a fire that Jass *could* have been responsible for, or the discovery of a feckless fool lying coshed in an alley, who had trusted in the blandishments of a face that drink made desirable that *might* belong to one of Jass' girls. But unless Jass boasted, and boasted specifically, there was no way of telling what could be laid at his door and not someone else's.

Midsummer came and passed, remarkable only for Midsummer Fairs and the fine pickings to be had at them, and Skif was no closer to uncovering the real culprit behind the fire. Day after day he would come awake in the damp heat of midday with a jolt the moment that the snoring in the other room stopped, and lie on his pallet, *listening.* Sweat prickled his scalp, and he spread himself out like a starfish in a vain hope of finding a hint of cooler air. He longed for the breezes of his stable loft, but still he lay in the heat, waiting for a word, a clue, a sign.

He had thought that he knew how to be patient. As days became weeks, and weeks tuned to moons, he discovered he knew nothing at all about patience. There were times when his temper snapped, when he *wanted* to curse, rail at fate and at the man who was so obstinately concealing his secrets, to pound the floor and walls with his fists. That he did none of these things was not a measure of his patience, but rather that he did not *dare* to reveal himself to Jass by an overheard gaffe of his own.

The more time passed, the more his hatred grew.

But at least he was not alone in hating and despising Jass. The sell-sword was no friend to the arsonist either, not if Skif was any judge. Twice he had caught the man glaring at Jass' back with an expression that had made Skif's blood turn cold.

Twice only—no more than that, but the second time had been enough to convince Skif that the first was no fluke. Whatever he had done to earn the sell-sword's enmity, Skif was certain that only the fact that Jass was, and remained, useful to the man that kept Jass alive and unharmed.

One stifling day, Skif lay on the bare boards of his room dressed in nothing more than a singlet, eyes closed and a wet cloth lying across them in an attempt to bring some coolness to his aching head. He could only breathe in the furnacelike air, and reflect absently on how odd it was that this part of town actually stank less than some better-off neighborhoods. But that was simply because here, where there was nothing, *everything* had a value. Even nightsoil was saved and collected—tannery 'prentices came 'round to collect urine every morning, paying two clipped-pennybits a pot, and the rest went straight into back-garden compost heaps. People who had birds or pigs collected their leavings for their gardens, and as for the dung from horses and donkeys—well, it was considered so valuable that it barely left the beast's bum before someone scuttled out to the street and scooped it up. Nothing went to waste here, no matter how rotten food was, it went into *something's* belly. As a consequence, the only stench coming off these streets and alleys was of sweat and grime and stale beer, but nothing worse than that. Why, Skif could hardly bear to walk in the alley of a merchants' neighborhood in this weather!

Jass' snores still echoed up the chimney; how could the man sleep in heat like this?

The faintest breath of air moved across the floor, drifting from the open window to crawl under the crack beneath the door. Drops of sweat trickled down Skif's neck and crept along his scalp without cooling him appreciably.

A fly droned somewhere near the ceiling, circling around and around and bumping against the grime-streaked paint in a mindless effort to get beyond it. It could have flown out the window, of course, but it was determined to find a way through to the next story of the house, no matter how unlikely a prospect that seemed.

Skif felt a curious kinship with the fly. At the moment, his own quest seemed just about as futile.

And he was just as stupidly, bullheadedly determined not to give it up.

He wondered if perhaps—just perhaps—he ought to start spending the day somewhere other than here. Somewhere in a cellar perhaps, where he would be able to doze in blessed coolness. So long as he managed to awaken before Jass did, and get back here. . . .

But as sure as he did *that,* Jass would change his habits and start sleeping, at least in part, by night, so that he could conduct some of his business by daylight.

At least I'm savin' money on eats, he thought wryly. In this heat he had no appetite to speak of, and spent most of his food money on peppermint tea. It was easy enough to make without a fire; just put a pot full of water and herb packets on the windowsill in the sun, and leave it to brew all day. And it cooled the mouth and throat, if not the body.

Skif found himself thinking longingly of rain. A good thunderstorm would cool the city down and wash the heaviness out of the air. Rain was his enemy—he wouldn't, couldn't work in the rain—but it would be worth not working for one night.

In weather like this, anyone who could afford to went off into the country anyway. Houses were shut up, furniture swathed in sheets, valuables taken away with the rest of the household goods. Only those few whose duties kept them here remained; Lord Orthallen, for one—he was on the Council, and couldn't leave. Which was just as well for Skif's sake, since his larder was supplying Skif's peppermint and the sugar to sweeten it.

Next door, the snoring stopped. Jass was awake at last.

No sounds of cooking this past fortnight; Jass was eating

out of cookshops rather than add to the heat in his rooms by lighting a fire.

Within moments Skif knew that there was no point in lingering around this afternoon; Jass would be going out and probably not returning until after nightfall, if then.

No point in Skif staying inside either. He wasn't going to sleep, not here. He might as well see if there was somewhere, anywhere in the city where there was a breath of cooler air.

In loose breeches, barefoot, and with his shirtsleeves rolled up, he was soon out into the street, where virtually everyone looked just as uncomfortable and listless as he. For once, the narrow streets proved a blessing; not much sun got past the buildings to bake the pounded dirt and add to the misery.

It occurred to him that Temples, constructed of thick stone, just might harbor some lingering coolness in their walls. In fact—the Temples over in wealthier parts of Haven usually had crypts beneath them, which would *certainly* be as cool as any wine cellar, and a deal quieter.

Aye, but then I get preached at, or I get asked what I want. They find me i' the crypt, they run me out, sure as sure. Them Priests is like ants, always where ye don' want 'em. Wisht I could find me a Temple crypt wi' nawt about.

Well . . . maybe he could; there were plenty of the highborn who had their own chapels, and private crypts, too, in the city cemeteries. There, he'd run little risk of being disturbed.

Some might have second thoughts about seeking a nap among the dead, but Skif wasn't one of them.

A candlemark later, Skif slipped down the stairs of a private chapel in one of the cemeteries reserved for the highborn. The chapel was above, where those who were queasy about *any* actual contact with the dead could pray; Skif headed down into the family crypts. Said lordling was gone, the house shut up, with only a couple of maids and an old dragon of a housekeeper. So there wouldn't be any impromptu visits by the family. The chapel had been locked, but that was hardly going to stop Skif.

He'd picked this place in particular because the family was known for piety and familial pride—and because there *hadn't* been a death in more than a year. Napping among the dead was one thing; napping among the recently-interred was another. And family pride, Skif hoped, would have seen to it that the crypt was kept clean and swept. He didn't mind the dead, but spiders were something else and gave him the real horrors.

It was darker than the inside of a pocket down here, but his hunch had been right. It was blessedly cool, and he pressed his overheated body up against the cold marble walls with relief while he waited for his eyes to adjust. Some light did filter down the staircase from the chapel windows above, and eventually Skif was able to make out the dim shape of a stone altar, laden with withered flowers, against the back wall. He sniffed the air carefully, and his nose was assaulted by nothing worse than dust and the ghosts of roses.

There were two rows of tombs, each bearing the name and station of its occupant graven atop it. No statues here; this family wasn't *quite* lofty enough for marble images of its dead adorning the tombs.

Skif yawned, and felt his way to the stone table at the back of the chapel, meant for flower offerings. Just in case someone came down here, he planned to take his nap in the shadows beneath it.

Stone didn't make a particularly yielding bed, but he'd slept on stone plenty of times before this; it would be no worse than sleeping on the floor of his uncle's tavern, and a lot quieter.

He was very pleased to note that his hunch had paid off; even beneath the table there wasn't much dust. He laid himself out in the deep shadow with his back pressed against the wall and his head pillowed on his arm. The stone practically sucked the heat right out of his body, and in moments, for the first time in days, he fell into a deep and dreamless sleep.

It seemed only heartbeats later that something jolted him awake.

He froze, his eyes snapping open, and saw the wavering light of a single candle illuminating the staircase he had only just crept down.

"Yer certain-sure there ain't gonna be nobody here?"

That's Jass! Skif thought in shock. *What's he doing here?*

Surely not grave robbing—the amount of work it would take to get into one of these tombs was *far* beyond anything the Jass that Skif knew would be willing to do! Even supposing there was anything of value interred there. . . .

"I'm quite sure," said a smooth and cultured voice. "Rovenar and his family are at his country estate, and none of his father's friends are still alive to pay him a graveside visit. Besides, it would hardly matter if anyone *did* come. I have the key; Rovenar trusts me to see that no one gets in here to work any mischief in his absence. If anyone should appear, I am simply doing him that favor, and you, my servant, have accompanied me."

"Servant?" Jass growled. It was amazing how well the stairs worked to funnel sound down here; Skif would have thought they were in the same room with him.

The voice laughed. "Bodyguard, then." The voice was clearly amused at Jass' attitude toward being taken as a servant.

It occurred to Skif that if he was seeing the light of a candle up there, it must be later than he'd thought when he was initially startled awake. It must have been the turning of the key in the lock on the chapel door that woke him, and he blessed the owner who had put in a door that locked itself on closing.

Whatever brought Jass and the unknown gentleman here, it had to be something out of the ordinary.

"What'd ye want t' meet *here* for?" Jass grumbled. "Place fair gives me th' creeps."

"It is cool, it is private, and we stand no chance of being overheard," the voice replied. "And because I have no mind to pay a call on *you*. I pay you; you can accommodate yourself to me."

Skif winced. Nothing could have been clearer than the contempt in those words.

But either Jass was inured to it, or he was oblivious to it.

Mebbe he just don't care. Anyone who'd been entrusted with the key to a lordling's chapel had to have money, at least, and the song of that money must ring in Jass's ears, deafening him to anything else.

"So wut's th' job *this* time that you don' want ears about?" Jass asked bluntly. "It better pay better nor last time."

"It will," the voice said coolly. "Not that you weren't paid exactly what the last job was worth—and I suspect you made somewhat more, afterward. I'm given to understand that you are considered something of an information broker."

"Ye never give me enuff fer quiet," Jass said sullenly.

Skif felt as if he'd been struck by lightning. *Bloody 'ell! This's where Jass gets 'is stuff about th' highborns!*

"I don't pay for what I don't require," the voice countered. "Just remember that. And remember that when I *do* pay for silence, I expect it. Don't disappoint me, Jass. You'll find I'm a different man when I've been disappointed."

A shiver ran down Skif's back at the deadly menace of that voice, and he was astonished that Jass didn't seem to hear it himself. Jass was either oblivious or arrogant, and neither suggested he'd be enjoying life for very much longer unless he realized he was treading on perilous ground. "Th' job," he simply prompted impatiently, quite as if *he* was the one in charge and not his client.

"Simple enough," the smooth, cultured voice replied. "Another fire, like the one I commissioned last winter. But this time, I don't want any cleverness on your part. No earth tar, no pine tar, no oil or mineral spirits; *nothing* to encourage the blaze. The warehouse will be left open for you, so start it from the inside."

Skif froze; he couldn't have moved to save his life. There it was—everything he'd been looking for. Except that he couldn't see who Jass was talking to, and he'd never heard that voice before.

Jass growled. "Ain't gonna burn good," he complained. "Might even save it, if—"

"Nonsense," the voice replied firmly. "In this heat and as dry as it's been? It'll go up like chaff. People were suspicious the last time, Jass. There were enquiries. I had a great deal of covering up to do. It was exceedingly inconvenient for me, a considerable amount of totally unexpected work. What's more, some of that work went to saving *your* neck. Some of the tenants didn't get out—and if the fire had been traced back to you, they'd have hanged you for murder."

Jass actually laughed, but it had a nasty sound to it. "Well, they didn't, did they? Tha's cuz there weren't no witnesses. I seen t' that. Tha's why people didn' all get out. 'Cause I quieted 'em."

Skif's heart turned to ice.

"And that is supposed to show me how clever you are?" The man snorted. "You're very good at what you do, Jass, and my lord Orthallen gave you high recommendations, but you've become arrogant and careless. Stick to what you're told to do. Don't try to be clever. And if you get caught, I'll wash my hands of you, don't think I won't."

"Jest gimme th' job," Jass growled, and the voice related details and instructions.

Jass thinks if 'e's caught, 'e kin turn 'is coat an' tell on milord, there, savin' 'is own neck. But Skif was *listening,* as Jass was not, and he knew that if Jass was ever caught, his life wasn't worth a bent pin. If there was even the *chance* that the

Watch was on to Jass, his employer would ensure his silence in the most effective way possible.

It wouldn't take much—just another interview in an out-of-the-way place like this one. Only Jass would not be meeting "milord," and there would be an extra corpse in the cemetery.

There was a metallic chink as money passed from one hand to another, and Jass counted it.

"Remember what I said," the voice warned. One set of footsteps marked the owner's transit to the door of the chapel, and Jass got up to follow. "Don't get creative. Just set the fire, and get out."

"Awright, awright," Jass sneered. *"My lord."*

The light vanished; the candle must have been put out. The door swung quietly open on well-oiled hinges, with only a faint sigh of displaced air to mark it opening. Then it shut again with a hollow sound, and the key rattled in the lock.

'E's gettin' away! I dunno 'oo 'e is, an 'e's gettin' away!

Skif practically flew up the stairs, no longer caring if he was discovered, so long as he could see who that voice belonged to!

Too late. Not only were they gone, he couldn't even hear footsteps. He flung himself at the windows—hopeless; not only was it dark outside, but the windows didn't open and they were made of colored glass as well. There was no way he could see *anything* through them—except for one single blob of light, a lantern, perhaps, receding into the darkness. He returned to the door, but you couldn't just *open* it from within once you got inside, it had to be unlocked from the inside as well as from the outside. Cursing under his breath, he got out his lock picks again, knowing that this would cost him yet more time, in the dark and fumbling in his hurry.

He cursed his clumsy fingers and the lock picks that suddenly turned traitor on him; at last he heard the *click* of the tumblers and wrenched the wretched door open.

There wasn't a single light to be seen within the four walls of the cemetery. They'd gotten far enough away that they were out of sight among the tombs, and by now Jass and his employer would have gone their separate ways, with nothing to show the connection between them, nothing to prove that "milord" *wasn't* just paying a sentimental or pious visit on the anniversary of someone's death.

No! Skif wasn't going to give up that easily.

From here there was only a single path winding among the chapels, crypts, and trees, and Skif tore up it. There were only two entrances, and he thought he knew which one "milord" would take. He had to catch the man before he left the cemetery—he had to! He had to *know*—

With his heart pounding and his eyes burning with rage, he abandoned everything but the chase. At a point where two private chapels faced one another across the path, where he might have slowed, just in case there was someone lurking in the shadows, he only sped up.

And at the last moment as he passed between them, too late to avoid the ambush, he sprung a trap on himself.

A trap that took the form of a cord stretched at knee-height along the path.

Skif hit it, and went flying face-first into the turf. The impact knocked the breath out of him and left him stunned just long enough for the ambusher to get on top of him and pin him down.

He fought—but his opponent was twice his size and had probably forgotten more dirty tricks than Skif knew. Ruthless, methodical, he made short work of one young boy. Before he could catch the breath that had been knocked out of him by the fall, Skif found himself gagged, his hands tied behind his back, pulled to his feet, and shoved into one of those two chapels.

The door shut with an ominous brazen *clang*. Skif's feet were kicked out from beneath him before he could lash out at his captor, and he went to the floor like a sack of meal.

There was a rattle of metal, and the shutter of a dark lantern opened. Skif blinked, eyes watering at the light, as the craggy sell-sword who had bought so much information from Jass peered down at him

"Well, well. A trap for a fox I set, and I catch a rabbit," the man said, looking down at Skif with no humor in his face whatsoever. He wasn't talking like one of the denizens of Haven's rough streets anymore; he had an accent that Skif couldn't place. "Now, why is it, I wonder, that wherever I find Jass, also you I find?"

Skif glared at him over the gag, daring him to try something. Not that he had the slightest idea of what he was going to do if the man made a move. . . .

But the man only stooped swiftly, and seized one of Skif's ankles. Kick as hard as he could, Skif could do nothing against the man's greater strength; at the cost of a bump on the head that made him see stars, he gained nothing and found himself with both ankles trussed and tied to his wrists, which were in turn tied behind his back. Only then did the man take off the gag, taking care not to let his hands get within range to be bitten.

He squatted easily beside Skif, sitting on his heels. "I believe it's time speech we have, you and I," he said, frowning. "And it is that I hope for your sake that you *aren't* Jass' errand boy."

He stared hard at Skif for a long time; Skif worked his jaw silently, and continued to glare at him, although he was beginning to feel a little—odd. As if there was something messing about inside his head.

So if 'e wants ter talk, why don't 'e get on wi' it? he thought furiously. And at that exact moment, the man smiled grimly, and nodded to himself.

"What were you doing here?" the sell-sword asked as soon as Skif's mouth was clear of the threads the cloth had left on his tongue.

"Sleepin'!" Skif spat, and snarled in impotent fury. If it hadn't been for this bastard, he'd have found out who Jass' employer was! He made up his mind not to tell the man one word more than he had to.

"In a cemetery?" The man raised one eyebrow.

Skif found angry words tumbling out of his mouth, despite his resolution not to talk. "Wha's it matter t'*you*? Or *them*? They's not gonna care—an' it's a damn sight cooler an' quieter here than anywheres else! Them highborns is all playin' out i'country, *they* ain't gonna know 'f I wuz here!"

"You have a point," the man conceded, then his face hardened again. "But why is it that you just *happen* sleeping to be in the same place where Jass goes to have a little chat?"

"How shud *I* know?" Skif all but wailed. "I drops off, next thing I knows, he's up there yappin' t' summun an' *I* wanta know who!"

If he'd had his hands free, he'd have clapped both of them over his mouth in horror. His tongue didn't seem to be under his control—what was happening to him?

"Oh, really?" The man's other eyebrow arched toward his hairline. "And why is that?"

"Becuz Jass' the bastid what set th' big fire an' burned me out—an' the mun whut was with 'im wuz th' mun what *paid* 'im t' do it!" Skif heard himself saying frantically. "I know'd it, cuz I 'eerd 'im say so! 'Is boss set 'im another fire t' start right whiles I was listenin'! An' I wanta know who *he* is cuz I'm gonna get *'im*, an' then I'm gonna get Jass, an—"

"Enough." The man held up a sword-callused palm, and Skif found his flood of angry words cut off again. Just in time, too; there had been tears burning in his eyes, and he didn't want the man to see *them.* He blinked hard to drive them away, but he couldn't do much about the lump in his throat that threatened to choke him.

Wut in hell *is happenin' t' me?*

But the man darted out a hand, quick as a snake, and

grabbed Skif's shoulder and shook it. That hand crushed muscle and bone and *hurt*—

"Now, to me you listen, boy, and engrave my words on your heart you will—" the man said, leaning forward until all Skif could see were his hawk-sharp, hawk-fierce eyes. "You playing are in deeper waters than you know, and *believe* me, to swim in them you cannot hope. Your nose out of this you keep, or likely someone is to fish you out of the Terilee, with a rock around your ankles tied, *if* find you at all they do."

Skif shuddered convulsively, and an involuntary sob fought its way out of his throat. The man sat back on his heels again, satisfied.

"Jass will to worry about shortly, much more than the setting of fires have," the man said darkly. "And he *will* answer for the many things he has responsible been for."

"But—"

"That is all you need to know," the man said forcefully, and the words froze in Skif's throat.

The sell-sword pulled out a knife, and for one horrible moment, Skif thought that he was dead.

But the man laid it on the floor, just out of reach, and stood up. "Too clever you are, by half," he said, with a grim little smile. "Now, about my business I will be. The moment I leave, getting yourself loose you can be about. Manage you will, quite sure I am."

He dropped the shield over the dark lantern, plunging the chapel into complete blackness. In the next moment, although Skif hadn't heard him move, the door opened, a tall, lean shadow slipped through it, and it closed again.

Skif lost no time in wriggling over the stone floor to the place where the man had left the knife. When he was right on top of it, he wriggled around until he could grab it. As soon as he got it into his hands, he sawed through the cord binding his wrists to his ankles. Not easy—but not impossible. The man had left him enough slack in his ropes to do just that.

Once that was cut, he managed to contort his body enough to get his arms back over to the front of himself and then sawed through the bindings at ankle and wrist. It was a good knife; sharp, and well cared for. If it didn't cut through the cords holding him as if they were butter, he wasn't forced to hack at them for candlemarks either.

But all the time his hands were working, his mind was, too.

Who—and *what*—was that man? How had he managed to get Skif to tell him everything he knew? Why did he want to know so much about Jass?

Why'd 'e lemme go? Why'd 'e warn me off?

Not that Skif had any intention of being warned off. *Oo's 'e think 'e is, anyroad? Oo's 'e think 'e was talkin' to?* If there was one thing that Skif was certain of, it was his own expertise in his own neighborhood. However clever this man thought he was, he wasn't living right next door to his target, now, was he? He hadn't even known that Jass was the one who'd set that fire—Skif had seen a flicker of surprise when his own traitorous mouth had blurted *that* information out. He might think himself clever, but he wasn't as good as all that.

But 'ow'd 'e make me talk? More to the point, could he do it again if he got Skif in his hands?

Best not to find out.

'E won' catch me a second time, Skif resolved fiercely, as he cut through the last of the cords on his wrists and shook his hands free.

He stood up, sticking the knife in his belt. No point in wasting a good blade, after all. His anger still roiled in his gut; by now Jass was far off, and his employer probably safe in his fancy home.

I'll know 'is voice, though, if I ever hear it agin. Small consolation, but the best he had.

He slipped out the door of the chapel and closed it behind himself, not caring if he left this one unlocked or not. Around him the dead kept their silence, with nothing to show that there had ever been anyone here. Crickets sang, and honeysuckle sent a heavy perfume across the carefully manicured lawn. Jass had picked a good night for a clandestine meeting; the moon was no bigger than a fingernail paring.

Skif made his way to the spot where the wall was overhung by an ancient goldenoak—he hadn't come in by a gate, and he didn't intend to leave by one either. All the while his mind kept gnawing angrily on the puzzle of the sell-sword. *Bastid. Oo's 'e t' be so high i' th' nose? Man sells anythin' 'e's got t' whosever gots the coin!* Hadn't he already proved that by buying information from Jass? *An' wut's 'e gonna do, anyroad? Where's 'e get off, tellin' me Jass's gonna go down fer the fire? Why shud 'e care?*

Unless—*he* had a wealthy patron himself. Maybe someone who had lost money when the fire gutted Skif's building?

Or maybe Jass' own employer was playing a double game—covering his bets and his own back, hiring someone to "find out who set the fire" so that *if* Jass got caught, the rich man could prove that he had gone far out of his way to try and catch the arsonist. Then no matter what Jass said, who would believe him?

The thought didn't stop Skif in his tracks, but it only roiled his gut further. The bastards! They were all alike, those highborns and rich men *and* their hirelings! They didn't care who paid, so long as *their* pockets were well-lined!

Skif swarmed up the tree by feel, edged along the branch that hung over the opposite side, and dropped down quietly to the ground, his heart on fire with anger.

Revenge. That's what he wanted. And he knew the best way to get it, too. If he didn't have a specific target, he could certainly make all of them suffer, at least a little. Just wait until they all came back from their fancy country estates! Wait until they returned—and came back, not just to things gone missing, but to cisterns and sewers plugged up, wells and chimneys blocked, linens spoiled, moths in the woolens, mice in the pantry and rats in the cellar! He'd cut sash cords, block windows so they wouldn't close right, drill holes in rooftops and in water pipes. It would be a long job, but he had all summer, and when he got through with them, the highborn of Valdemar would be dead certain that they'd been cursed by an entire tribe of malevolent spirits.

No time like right now, neither, he thought, with smoldering satisfaction as he fingered the sharp edge of his new knife.

So what if he didn't have a specific target. They were all alike anyway. So he'd make it his business to make them all pay, if it took him the rest of his life.

SKIF had every intention of beginning his campaign of sabotage that very night, but when he tried to get near the district where the homes of the great and powerful were, he found the Watch was unaccountably active. There were patrols on nearly every street, and they weren't sauntering along either. *Something* had them alerted, and after the third time of having to take cover to avoid being stopped and questioned, he gave it up as hopeless and headed back to his room with an ill grace.

He got some slight revenge, though; as he turned a corner, a party of well-dressed, and very drunk young men came bursting out of a tavern with a very angry innkeeper shouting curses right on their heels. They practically ran him over, but in the scuffle and ensuing confusion, he lifted not one, but three purses. Making impotent threats and shouting curses of his own at them (which had all the more force because of his personal frustrations), he turned on his heel and stalked off in an entirely different direction.

Once out of sight, he ducked into a shadow, emptied the

purses of their coins into his own pouch, and left the purses where he dropped them, tucking his pouch into the breast of his tunic. Then he strolled away in still another direction. After a block or two, there was nothing to connect him with the men he'd robbed. That was a mistake that many pickpockets made; they hung onto the purses they'd lifted. Granted, such objects were often valuable in themselves—certainly the three he'd taken had been—but they also gave the law a direct link between robber and robbed.

As he walked back toward his room, he managed to get himself back under control. Taking the purses had helped; it was a very small strike against the rich and arrogant bastards, but a strike nevertheless. *Just wait till they get to a bawdy house, an' they've gotta pay—he* thought, with grim satisfaction. *They better 'ope their friends is willin' t' part with th' glim!* Skif had seen the wrath of plenty of madams and whoremasters whose customers had declined to pay, and they didn't take the situation lightly—nor did they accept promissory notes. They also employed very large men to help enforce the house rules and tariffs. When young men came into a place in a group, *no one* was allowed to leave until everyone's score had been paid. Those who still had purses would find them emptied before the night was over.

The thought improved his humor, and that restored his appetite. Now much fatter in the pocket than he had been this afternoon, he decided to follow his nose and see where it led him.

It took him to a cookshop that stood on the very border of his neighborhood, halfway between the semirespectable district of entertainers, artists, musicians (not Bards, of course), peddlers, and decorative craftsmen and their 'prentices, and his own less respectable part of town.

I've earned a meal, he decided; taking care not to expose how much he had, he fished out one of the larger coins from his loot and dropped the pouch back into his tunic. Best to get rid of the most incriminating of the coins.

He eased on in; it was full, but not overcrowded, and he soon found space at the counter to put in his order. With a bowl of soup and a chunk of bread in one hand, and a mug of tea in the other, he made his way back outside to the benches in the open air where there were others eating, talking, or playing at dice or cards. Hot as it was, there were more folk eating under the sky than under the roof.

As was his habit, he took an out-of-the-way spot and kept his head down and his ears open. He was very soon rewarded; the place was abuzz with the rumor that *someone* had broken into the home of the wealthy merchant, Trenor Severik, and had stolen most of his priceless collection of miniature silver figurines. Severik had literally come home in time to see the thief vanishing out the window. Hence, the Watch; every man had been called out, the neighborhood had been sealed off, and anyone who couldn't account for himself was being arrested and taken off to gaol. It seemed that one of those arrested was an acquaintance of several of those sitting near Skif.

"Hard luck for poor Korwain," one of the artists said, with a snicker. "He couldn't say where he'd been—*of course.*"

His friends nearly choked on their meals. "I told him that woman was trouble," said another, whose dusty beard and hair bedecked with stone chips proclaimed him to be a sculptor. "Two sittings, and she's got me backed into a corner, tryin' to undo m'britches!" He shuddered, and the rest laughed. "*Patron of arts*, she calls herself! My eye!"

"Heyla, we tried to warn you, so don't say we didn't!" called a fellow with a lute case slung over his back. "Korwain knew it, so he's only got himself to blame!"

"That's what happens when you let greed decide your commissions for you," put in another, whose mouth looked like a miser's purse and whose eyes gloated at a fellow artist's misfortune. "I'd rather live on bread in a garret and serve the Temples than feast on marchpane and capon and—"

"Your paintings are so stiff they wouldn't please *anyone* but a priest, so don't go all over pious on us, Penchal!" cat-called the first artist.

That set off an argument on artistic merit and morality that Skif had no interest in. He applied himself to his soup, and left the bowl and mug on the table while the insults were still coming thick and fast, and rapidly building to the point where it would be fists, and not words, that would be flying.

At least now he knew why the Watch was up, and he wouldn't dare try anything for days, even a fortnight. Why would anyone bother to steal the collection of silver miniatures, anyway? They were unique and irreplaceable, yes, but you'd never be able to sell them anywhere, they were too recognizable, and you wouldn't get a fraction of their value if you melted them down. Oh, a thief could hold them for ransom, Skif supposed, but he'd certainly be found out and caught.

The only way the theft made sense was if someone had gotten a specific commission to take them. It was an interesting thought. Whoever had made the commission would have to be from outside Haven; what was the use of having something like that if you couldn't show it off? Anyone in Haven would know the collection as soon as it was displayed. The client could even be outside Valdemar altogether. So the thief, too, might be from outside Valdemar. . . .

Huh. That'd be somethin', he thought, keeping an eye out for trouble as he made his way back home. *Have'ta be some kinda Master Thief, I guess. Somebody with all kinds uv tricks. Wonder if they's 'prentices fer that kinda work?* He'd never heard of a Master Thief, much less one that took on protégés, but maybe that sort of thing happened outside of Valdemar. *Like mebbe they's a whole Guild fer Thieves. Wouldn' that be somethin'!*

He amused himself with this notion as he worked his way

homeward. He never, even when he had no reason to believe
that he was being followed, went back home directly. He always doubled back, ducked down odd side passages, even cut
over fences and across back gardens—though in the summer,
that could be hazardous. In *his* neighborhood, no one had a
back garden for pleasure. People used every bit of open ground
to grow food in, and often kept chickens, pigeons, or a pig as
well. And they assumed anyone coming over the fence was
there to steal some of that precious food. Those that didn't
have yards, but did have balconies, grew their vegetables in
pots. Those that had nothing more than a window, had window boxes. Even Skif had a window box where he grew beans,
trailing them around his window on a frame made of pieces of
string. It was just common sense to augment what you could
buy with what you could grow, but that did make it a bit more
difficult to take the roundabout path until after the growing
season was over.

It wasn't as late as he'd thought; lots of people were still
up and about, making it doubly hazardous to go jumping in
and out of yards. The front steps of buildings held impromptu
gatherings of folks back from their jobs, eating late dinners
and exchanging gossip. Most of the inns and cookshops had
put benches out onto the street, so people could eat outside
where it was cooler. It was annoying; Skif couldn't take his
usual shortcuts. On the other hand, so many people out here
meant more opportunities to confuse a possible follower.

With that in mind, he stopped at another cookshop for
more tea and a fruit pie. More crust than fruit, be it added, but
he didn't usually indulge in anything so frivolous, and the
treat improved his temper a bit more. Not so much that he
forgot his anger—and the burning need to find out who Jass'
boss was—but enough so that he was able to look as though
nothing in his life had changed in the last few candlemarks.

He paid close attention to those who sat down to eat after
him, but saw no one that had also been at the previous cook-

shop. That was a good sign, and he quickly finished his tea and took the shortest way home.

Jass wasn't back yet. Neither were his girls—which meant that Jass probably wasn't going to set his fire tonight. Skif watered his beans and stripped for bed, lighting a stub of a candle long enough to actually count his takings.

His eyes nearly popped out of his head, and he counted it twice more before he believed it.

Gold. Five gold crowns, more than he'd ever had in his life! He'd thought the tiny coins were copperbits, not gold, and he'd paid for his meal and his treat with larger silver royals so as to get rid of two of the most conspicuous coins in his loot. He'd never dreamed the men could have been carrying gold.

Gold. Gold meant—everything. With gold, he suddenly had the means to concentrate *entirely* on finding Bazie's murderer. He wouldn't have to work the entire summer. With gold, he had the means to offer the kind of bribe that would loosen even the most reluctant of tongues.

With gold—he could follow up on the only real clue he had that wasn't connected to Jass.

"*. . . my lord Orthallen gave you high recommendations . . .*"

Gold could actually buy Skif a way into Orthallen's household—you didn't just turn up at a Great Lord's doorstep and expect to be hired. You had to grease palms before you got a place where you could expect to have privileges, maybe even collect tips for exemplary service. Gold would purchase forged letters of commendation—very rarely did anyone ever bother to check on those, especially if they were from a household inconveniently deep into the countryside. Those letters could get Skif into, say, a position as an undergroom, or a footman. A place where he'd be in contact with Lord Orthallen's guests, friends, and associates. *Where he could hear their voices.*

This one encounter changed everything. . . .

Maybe.

It was one plan. There were others, that would allow Skif

to hang onto the unexpected windfall. Jass wouldn't have been paid for the job entirely in advance—he'd have to collect the rest, and maybe Skif could catch him at it. There were other places where Skif could go to listen for that familiar, smooth and pitiless voice.

But the idea of insinuating himself into a noble household was the kind of plan that the craggy-faced sell-sword would not be able to anticipate. If he knew anything at all about Skif, he'd know that in the normal course of things, pigs would fly before someone like Skif would get his hands on enough money to buy his way into Lord Orthallen's household.

So Skif carefully folded the five gold coins into a strip of linen and packed them with his larger silver coins in the money belt that never left his waist. Then he blew out his candle, laid himself down, and began his nightly vigil of listening for Jass and Jass' business.

Because while gold might add to his options, if Bazie had taught him anything at all, it was to never, ever *abandon* an option just because a new one opened up.

But Jass didn't come back that night, nor the next day. Skif fell asleep waiting to hear his footsteps on the stairs, and woke the next morning to the unaccustomed sound of silence next door. He waited all day, wondering, with increasing urgency, what was keeping the man from his own rooms.

By nightfall, though, he knew why.

At dusk, a three-man team of the Watch came for Jass' two girls, *escorting* them off, rather than taking them off under guard, so it wasn't that they were arrested or under suspicion. Skif was at his window when they showed up, and he knew before they ever came in view that *something* was wrong, for the whole street went quiet. People whisked themselves indoors, or around corners, anything to get out of sight, and even the littles went silent and shrank back against their buildings, stopping dead in the middle of their games, and staring with round eyes at the three men in their blue-and-gray tunics and trews. The Watch never came to *this* part of town unless there was something wrong—or someone was in a lot of trouble.

Skif ducked back out of sight as soon as they came into view, and when he heard the unmistakable sound of boots on the staircase, huddled against the wall next to the door so that no one peering underneath it would see his feet.

What're they here for? For me? Did that feller turn me in? Did summun figger I lifted them purses? His mind raced, reckoning the odds of getting out via his emergency route through the window if they'd come for *him*, wondering if that sellsword had somehow put the Watch onto him. And if he had—*why?*

The footsteps stopped at his landing, and his heart was in his mouth—his blood pounding in his ears—every muscle tensed to spring for the window.

But it wasn't his door they knocked on—and they knocked, politely, rather than pounding on it and demanding entrance. It was the girls' door, and when one of them timidly answered, an embarrassed voice asked if "Trana and Desi Farane" would be so kind as to come down to the Watch-station and answer a few questions.

Skif sagged down onto the floor, limp with relief. Whatever it was, it had nothing to do with him.

Now, everyone knew that if the Watch had *anything* on you, they didn't come and politely invite you to the Watch Station. When someone came with that particular request, it meant that you weren't in trouble, though someone else probably was. But if you were asked to come answer questions and you refused, well . . . you could pretty much reckon that from then on, you were marked. And any time one of the Watch saw you, they'd be keeping a hard eye on you, and they'd be likely to arrest and fine you for the least little thing. So after a nervous-sounding, unintelligible twitter of a conversation among all four of the sisters, Trana and Desi emerged and five sets of footsteps went back down the staircase.

Now he had to see what was up! When Skif peeked out around the edge of the window, he saw that two of the Watch were carrying lit lanterns, making it very clear that the two girls weren't being manhandled, or even touched. And he could see that the two girls had taken long enough to lace their bodices tight, pull up their blouses, and drop their skirts where they were usually kirtled up to show their ankles. They were definitely putting on a show of respectability, which only made sense. That was the last he saw of them until just before dark.

They returned alone, but gabble in the street marked their arrival, waking Skif from a partial doze.

Their sisters must have been watching from the window; they flew down the stairs to meet them, and half the neighborhood converged on them. Skif took his time going downstairs, and by then the block was abuzz with the news that Jass had been found dead in a warehouse that afternoon, and the girls had been brought in to identify the body. There was no question but that he was the victim of foul play; he'd been neatly garroted, and his body hidden under an empty crate. He might not even have been found except that someone needed the crate and came to fetch it, uncovering this body.

Damn. . . . Skif couldn't quite believe it, couldn't quite take it in. *Dead? But—*

By the time Skif drifted to the edge of the crowd to absorb the news, Trana and Desi were sobbing hysterically, though how much of their sorrow was genuine was anyone's guess. Skif had the shrewd notion that they were carrying on more for effect than out of real feeling. Their sisters, with just as much reason to be upset, looked more disgruntled at all of the attention that Trana and Desi were getting than anything else.

Skif huddled on the edge of the crowd, trying to overhear

the details. There weren't many; he felt numb, as if he'd been hit by something but hadn't yet felt the blow. Before a quarter candlemark had passed, the landlord appeared.

He had tools and his dimwitted helper; he pushed past the crowd and ran up the stair. The sounds of hammering showed he was securing the door of Jass' room with a large padlock and hasp. An entire parade, led by the girls, followed him up there where he was standing, lantern in one hand, snapping the padlock closed. "There may be inquiries," he said officiously when Desi objected, claiming that she'd left personal belongings in Jass' rooms. "If the Watch or the Guard wants to inspect this place, I'll be in trouble if I let anyone take anything out."

There wouldn't be any inquiries, and they all knew it; this was just the landlord's way of securing anything of value in there for himself.

But if they knew what I knew—Skif thought, as he closed and bolted his own door, and put his back to it.

He began to shake.

Of all the people who could have wanted Jass dead, the only one with the money to get the job done *quietly* was the smooth-voiced man in the cemetery. What had the sell-sword said? *"You're in deeper waters than you can swim—"* or something like that. Deep waters—his knees went weak at how close he'd come last night to joining Jass under that crate. If he'd been caught down in that crypt—

Skif sat down on his bedroll and went cold all over. There was at least one person in Haven who knew that there was a connection between Skif and Jass. And that craggy-faced sell-sword just might come looking for him, to find out exactly what, and how much, Skif knew.

I got to get out of here. Now!

The thought galvanized him. It didn't take him long to bundle up his few belongings. More and more people were showing up to hear the news directly from the girls, and the more people there were moving around, the better his odds were of getting away without anyone noticing. He watched for his chance, and when a group of their fellow lightskirts descended on Desi and Trana and carried them off to the nearest tavern, the better to "console" them, he used the swirl of girls and the clatter they generated to his advantage. He slipped out behind them, stayed with them as far as the tavern, and then got moving in the opposite direction as quickly as he could.

He didn't really have any ideas of where he was going, but at the moment, that was all to the good. If *he* didn't know where he was going, no one else would be able to predict it either.

The first place that anyone would look for him would be *here*, of course, but as Skif trudged down the street, looking as small and harmless as he could manage, he put his mind to work at figuring out a place where someone on his track was *not* likely to look. What was the *most* out of character for him?

Well—a Temple. But I don' think I'm gonna go lookin' t' take vows— was his automatic thought. But then, suddenly, that didn't seem so outlandish a notion. Not taking vows, of course—but—

Abruptly, he altered his path. This was going to be a long walk, but he had the notion that in the end, it was going to be worth it.

Skif made his eyes as big and scared as he could, and twisted his cap in his hands as he waited for someone to answer his knock at the Temple gate. This Temple was not the one where his cousin Beel was now a full priest; it wasn't even devoted to the same god, much less the same Order. This was the Temple and Priory of Thenoth, the Lord of the Beasts, and this Order took it on themselves to succor and care for injured, sick, and aged animals, from sparrows and pigeons to broken-down carthorses.

It existed on charity, and as such, was one of the poorest Temples in Haven. And one thing it could always use was willing hands. Not everyone who worked here in the service of Thenoth was a priest or a novice; plenty of ordinary people volunteered a few candlemarks in a week for the blessing of the God.

Now, what Skif was hoping was that he could hide here for the sake of his labor. He hoped he had a convincing enough story.

The door creaked open, and a long-nosed Priest in a patched and dusty brown robe looked down at him, lamp in one hand. "If you be seekin' charity, lad, this be'nt the place for ye," he said, wearily, but not unkindly. "Ye should try the—"

"Not charity, sor," Skif said, putting on his best country accent. "I be a norphan, sor, mine nuncle turn me out of the far-um, and I come here t'city a-lookin' for horse-work, but I got no character. I be good with horses, sor, an' donkeys, an' belike, but no mun gi' me work withouten a character."

The Priest opened the door a little wider, and frowned thoughtfully. "A character, is't? Would ye bide in yon loft, tend the beasts, and eat with the Brethren for—say—six moon, an' we give ye a good letter?"

Skif bobbed his head eagerly. "Ye'd gi' me a good character, then? Summut I can take fer t'work fer stable?"

He's taken it! he thought with exultation.

"If ye've earned it." The priest opened the gate wide, and Skif stepped into the dusty courtyard. "Come try your paces. Enter freely, and walk in peace."

Skif felt his fear slide off him and vanish. No one would look for him here—and even if they did, no one would dare the wrath of a God to try and take him out. So what if his story wasn't quite the truth?

I don' mind a bit'uv hard work. God can't take exception t'that.

The priest closed the gate behind them, and led Skif into and through the very simple Temple, out into another courtyard, and across to a stabling area.

As he followed in the priest's wake, Skif was struck forcibly by two things. The first was the incredible poverty of this place. The second was an aura of peace that descended on him the moment he crossed the threshold.

It was *so* powerful, it seemed to smother every bad feeling he had. Suddenly he wasn't afraid at all—not of the sellsword, not of the bastard that had arranged for Bazie's building to burn—

Somehow, he knew, he *knew,* that nothing bad could come inside these walls. Somehow, he knew that as long as he kept the peace here, he would not ever have to fear the outside world coming in to get him.

That should have frightened him . . . and it didn't.

But he didn't have any leisure to contemplate it either, once they entered the stable. Skif had ample cause now to be grateful for the time he'd spent living in that loft above the donkey stable where he'd gotten acquainted with beast tending— because it was quite clear that the Order was badly shorthanded. One poor old man was *still* tottering around by the light of several lamps, feeding and watering the motley assortment of hoof stock in this stable.

Skif didn't even hesitate for a moment; this, if ever, was the moment to prove his concocted story, and a real stableboy wouldn't have hesitated either. He dropped his bedroll and belongings just inside the stable door, and went straight for the buckets; reckoning that water was going to be harder for the old fellow to carry than grain or hay. And after all, he'd had more than his share of water carrying when he'd been living with Bazie. . . .

The old man cast him a look of such gratitude that Skif almost felt ashamed of the ruse he was running on these people. Except that it wasn't exactly a ruse . . . he *was* going to do the work, he just wasn't planning on sticking around for the next six moons. And, of course, he was going to be doing some other things on the side that they would never know about.

As he watered each animal in its stall, he took a cursory look at them. For the most part, the only thing wrong with them was that they were old—not a bad thing, since it meant that none of them possessed enough energy or initiative to try more than a halfhearted, weary nip at him, much less a kick.

Poor old things, he thought, venturing to pat one ancient donkey who nuzzled him with something like tentative affection as he filled its watering trough. And these were the lucky ones—beasts whose owners felt they deserved an honorable retirement after years of endless labor. The unlucky ones became stew and meat pies in the cookshops and taverns that served Haven's poor.

"Bless ye, my son," said the old priest gratefully, as they passed one another. "We be perilous shorthanded for the hoof stock."

"Just in stable?" Skif asked, carefully keeping to his country accent.

The priest nodded, patting a dusty rump as he moved to fill another manger. "With the wee beasts, the hurt ones, there's Healer Trainees that coom t'help, an' there's folks that don't mind turnin' a hand with cleanin' and feedin'. But this—"

Skif laughed softly. "Aye, granther, this be work, eh?"

The old priest laughed himself. " 'Struth. They say there's a pair of novices coming up, come winter, but till then—"

" 'Till then, I'll be takin' the heavy work, granther," Skif heard himself promise.

When the last of the beasts were watered and fed, the old man showed him his place in the loft, and left him with a lantern, trudging back to the Chapter House. Like his last bed above a stable, this was in a gable end with a window supplied with storm shutters, piled high with hay, that looked out over the courtyard. He spread out his bedroll, stowed his few possessions in the rafters, blew out the lantern, and lay down to watch the moon rise over the roofs of Haven.

This's been—about th' strangest day of m'life, he thought, hands tucked behind his head. What was just about the strangest part of it was that he had literally gone from a state of fearing for his very life, to—this.

There was such an aura of peace and serenity within these walls! What might have seemed foolish trust under any other circumstances—after all, he was just some stranger who'd shown up on their doorstep, and at night, yet—was perfectly understandable now that Skif could see the poverty of the place himself. There literally was nothing to steal. If he didn't do the work he'd promised, he wouldn't be fed, and he'd be turned out. There was no reason for the Brethren not to trust him.

He should have been feeling very smug, and very clever. He'd found the perfect hiding place, and it was well within striking distance of the manors of the high and mighty.

Instead, all he could think was that, as workworn and weary as both the priests had seemed, there had also been something about them that made his cleverness seem not quite as clever as he'd thought it was. As if they had seen through his ruse, and *didn't care.* And that didn't make any sense at all.

I've got to think this through— he told himself, fighting the soporific scent of cured hay, the drowsy breathing of the animals in their stalls beneath him, and the physical and emotional exhaustion of the last day and night.

It was a battle he was doomed to lose from the start. Before the moon rose more than a hand's breadth above the houses, he was as fast asleep as the animals below.

Skif started awake, both hands clutching hay, as a mellow bell rang out directly above his head. For a moment he was utterly confused—he couldn't remember where he was, much less why he'd been awakened by a bell in the pitch-dark.

Then it all came back, just as someone came across the courtyard bearing a lit lantern.

Hellfires! he thought, a little crossly, yet a little amused. *I shoulda known this lot'd be up afore dawn! Mebbe I ain't been so smart after all!*

"Heyla, laddie!" called the aged voice of last night from below. "Be ye awake?"

"Oh, aye, granther," Skif replied, stifling a groan. "I be a-coomin' down."

He brought last night's lantern down with him, and he and the old man made the morning rounds of the stable in an oddly companionable silence. The old man didn't ask his name—and didn't seem to care that Skif didn't offer it. What he *did* do was give Skif the name and history of every old horse, donkey, mule, and goat in the stable, treating each of them like the old friend it probably was.

When they finished feeding and watering, the old man led Skif into the Chapter House, straight to a room where others of the Order had stripped to the waist and were washing up. Not wanting to sit down to breakfast smelling of horse and goat, Skif was perfectly willing to follow their example. From there they all went to breakfast, which was also eaten in silence—oat porridge, bread, butter and milk. Skif was not the only person who wasn't wearing the robes of the Order, but the other two secular helpers were almost as old as the priest who tended the stable. There *were* younger priests, but they all had some sort of deformity or injury that hadn't healed right.

One and all, either through age or defect, they seemed to be outcasts, people for whom there was no comfortable niche in a family, nor a place in the society of other humans. Maybe

that was why they came here, and devoted themselves to animals. . . .

Yet they all seemed remarkably content, even happy.

After breakfast, it was back to the stable, where Skif
mucked out the stalls while the old priest groomed his
charges. Even the goats were brushed until their coats
shone—as much as the coat of an aged goat could. Then it
was time for the noon meal, with more washing-up first, then
the old man had him take the couple of horses that were still
able to do a little work out to help carry a few loads about the
compound. He and his charges hauled firewood to the kitchen,
feed grains to bird coops, rubbish out to be sorted, muck to
bins where muck collectors would come to buy it.

The place was larger than he'd thought. There were mews
for aging or permanently injured hawks and falcons, a loft for
similarly injured doves and pigeons, kennels for dogs, a cat-
tery, a chicken yard that supplied the Order with eggs, a small
dairy herd of goats, and a place for injured wildlife. It was here
that Skif caught sight of a couple of youngsters not much older
than he, wearing robes of a pale green, and he realized with a
start that these must be the Healer Trainees he'd heard about.
It was, quite literally, the first time he had ever seen a Healer
of any rank or station, and he couldn't help but gawp at them
like the country bumpkin he was pretending to be.

Then it was time for the evening meal—all meals were very
plain, with the noon and evening meal consisting of bread,
eggs, cheese, and vegetables, with the addition of soup at the
noon meal and fruit at the dinner meal. Then came the same
feeding and watering chores he'd had last night, and with a
start, he realized that the entire day had flowed past him like
a tranquil stream, and he hadn't given a single thought to anything outside the four walls of the Order.

And realized with an even greater start that he didn't care,
or at least, he hadn't up until that time.

And he felt a very different sort of fear, then. The place was changing him. And unless he started to fight it, there was a good chance that it wouldn't be long until no one recognized him. And possibly even more frightening, he had to wonder how long it would be before he wouldn't even recognize himself.

SKIF decided that no matter how tired he was, he was not going to put off the start of his vendetta any longer. And he wasn't going to let the deep peace of this place wash away his anger either.

When he finished watering the animals for the night and the old priest tottered back to the Chapter House, he blew out his lantern, but perched himself in the loft window to keep an eye on the rest of the Priory.

One by one, lights winked out across the courtyard. Skif set his jaw as a drowsy peace settled over the scene, and hovered heavily all around him. He knew what it was, now—this was the Peace of the God, and it kept everyone who set foot here happy and contented.

Granted, that wasn't bad for those who lived here; there were no fights among the animals, and there was accord among those who cared for them. But this peace was a trap for Skif; it would be all too easy to be lulled by it until he forgot the need for revenge—forgot what he was. He didn't want to forget what he was, and he didn't want to become what this place wanted him to be.

When the last light winked out, he waited a little longer, marking the time by how far above the horizon a single bright star rose. And when he figured that everyone would surely be asleep, he moved.

For someone like Skif, there was no challenge in getting over the walls, silently as any shadow. He knew where to go first, too. If he could not strike at his foe directly, he could at least strike at someone who was near to his real target. Serve the rich bastard right, for trusting someone who would murder innocent people just because they were in his way. Besides, all those rich bastards were alike. Even if this one hadn't actually murdered poor folks, he probably wouldn't care that his friend *had*.

And my Lord Rovenar was oh, so conveniently away on his family estate in the country.

Lord Rovenar's roof was fashionably paved in slate. It was with great glee that Skif proceeded to riddle the entire roof with cracks and gaps. The next time it rained, the roof would leak like a sieve.

There was also a cistern up here, a modern convenience that permitted my lord and his family to enjoy the benefits of running water throughout the mansion. Skif hastened the ruin of the upper reaches of the building by piercing the pipes leading downward, creating a slow leak that would empty the cistern directly into the attics, and from there into the rest of the house.

Besides rainwater, the cistern could be filled by pumping water up from the mansion's own well. But by the time Skif was finished, any water pumped up would only drain into the attics with the rest of it.

So much for vandalism on the exterior. Skif worked his way over to an attic window, which wasn't locked. After all, the servants never expected anyone to be up on the roof, and certainly wouldn't expect that anyone who *did* get up on the roof would dangle himself over the edge, push open the shutters with his feet, and let himself inside.

His night had only just begun.

When he let himself out again, this time from a cellar window, his pockets were full of small, valuable objects and the trail of ruin had continued, though most of it would take days and weeks before it was discovered. Skif had left food in beds to attract insects and mice, and had ensured that those pests would invade by laying further trails of diluted honey and crumbs all over the house around the baseboards where it was unlikely that the maids—slacking work in the master's absence—would notice. He left windows cracked open—left shutters ajar. Insects would soon be in the rooms, and starlings and pigeons colonizing the attic. The skeleton staff that had been left here would not discover any of this, for his depredations took place in rooms that had been closed up, the furnishings swathed in sheets. My lord would return to a house in shambles, and it would take a great deal of money and effort to make it livable again.

He ghosted his way across the kitchen garden and over the wall, using a trellis as a ladder. But once on the other side, he laid a trail of a different sort—all of those valuable trinkets he'd filled his pockets with. He scattered them in his wake, and trusted to greed to see to it that they never found their way back to their true owner again. He took nothing for himself, if for no other reason than that it would prevent anyone from connecting *him* with the trail of damage.

He slipped easily back over the Temple walls and got into his bed in the loft in plenty of time for a nap. When the bell sounded and woke him, if he wasn't fully rested, at least he didn't look so exhausted that anyone commented on it.

Although the meals he'd shared with the Brethren yesterday had been shared in silence, evidently there was no actual *rule* of silence, for the noon meal brought a flurry of gossip from the outside world.

"The Master Thief struck again last night," said one of the younger priests to the rest of the table. "The streets are full of talk."

"And he must be from somewhere outside Haven, so they say," added another with a shake of his head. "Singularly careless, he was; he left a trail of dropped objects behind him, I heard. I can vouch that there are so many people scouring the alleys for bits of treasure that some of the highborn have asked the Guard to drive them back to the slums."

"I hope," said the Prior, with great dignity, "that the Guard declined. The alleys are public thoroughfares; they do not belong to the highborn. Neither is the Guard answerable to those with noble titles who are discomfited by the poor outside their walls. There cannot be any justification for such a request."

"Since there are still treasure hunters looking in every nook and cranny, I suspect they did decline," the young priest said cheerfully. He seemed highly amused, and Skif wondered why.

The Prior shook his head sadly. "I know that you have little sympathy when rich men are despoiled of their goods, Brother Halcom."

"If the gods choose the hand of a thief to chastise those who are themselves thieves, I find it ironic, but appropriate, sir," Brother Halcom replied evenly. "This Master Thief has so far robbed two men who have greatly oppressed others. You know this to be true."

"Nevertheless, the thief himself commits a moral error and incurs harm to his soul with his actions," the Prior chided him gently. "You should spend less time gloating over the misfortune of the mighty and more in praying that this miscreant realizes his errors and repents."

Brother Halcom made a wry face, but the Prior didn't see it. Skif did, however, and he noted when the young priest rose from the table that his leg ended in a dreadful club foot. The priest had spoken in the accents of someone who was highly educated, and Skif had to wonder how much Brother Halcom knew *personally* about the two who had "officially" been robbed.

And whether he knew anything about the one that Skif had despoiled. . . .

For one moment, he wondered if the young man had really meant what he said. He'd sounded sympathetic.

Fah. He'll have no time fer the likes of me, no doubt, he thought, hardening his heart. *Well, look who's stuck muckin' out the stalls, an who's playin' with the broke-winged birds! Push comes t' shove, money an' rank stands together 'gainst the rest of us what always does the dirty work anyroad.*

He finished his meal and went back out to clean kennels.

With the Master Thief out last night—and everybody and his dog hunting for the goodies that Skif had let fall—the last thing Skif was going to do was to go out again tonight. No, things would have to cool down a bit before he ran the rooftops again. It gave him a great deal of pleasure, though, to lie back in the sweet-smelling hay and contemplate last night's work. The only thing that spoiled his pleasure was the thought that this unknown Master Thief was going to get all of the credit for *his* work.

On the other hand, it would probably anger the Master Thief to be saddled with the eventual blame for all of the vandalizing Skif had done.

And at the moment, no one would be looking for a mere boy; they'd be trying to catch a man. This Master Thief was proving rather useful to Skif's campaign.

I s'pose I oughta be grateful to 'im, Skif thought, but he didn't feel grateful.

In fact, after a while, he realized that he wasn't as satisfied with last night's work as he thought he should be. It just wasn't enough, somehow. He was thrashing around at random, blindly trying to hit the one he *truly* wanted to hurt and hoping that somehow in the chaos he'd connect with a blow. And even then—how did putting holes in someone's roof measure up to burning down a building and committing cold-blooded murder in the process?

It didn't, and that was that. *I want him,* Skif thought angrily. *I want the bastard what ordered it!*

Nothing more—but nothing less. And right now, he was settling for less.

Still, that Brother Halcom had a point, too. He'd seemed to think that the two highborn nobles that had been robbed had pretty much deserved it and probably Lord Rovenar had done a dirty deed or two in his life, and Skif had been nothing more than the instrument of payback. That wasn't a bad thought.

Brother Halcom knew the highborn. . . .

Brother Halcom *might* know enough to give Skif a clue or two to the identity of the one highborn that Skif really wanted. So maybe Skif ought to see if he could get Brother Halcom to talk.

Finding someone to hurt that he *knew* deserved it might feel better than this random lashing out.

And maybe, just maybe, Brother Halcom would know who the smooth-voiced highborn was.

Skif watched Brother Halcom from a distance for a full week before making a tentative approach. He learned two things in that time; Brother Halcom was from a highborn family, and he was here because he wanted to be. Not that his family hadn't tried to get their "deformed" offspring out of sight, but they'd chosen a much more comfortable—and secluded—Temple for him to enter. Halcom had stood up to them, and threatened to make a scene if he wasn't allowed *his* choice.

That gave Skif a bit more respect for the man, and Halcom's value rose again in his eyes when he realized that Halcom didn't shirk the dirty work after all. He just did the small things, rather than the large. He did his share of cleaning— usually cleaning up after the Healer Trainees when they'd finished treating a sick or injured animal. When there was a beast that needed to be tended all night, it was Halcom, like as not, who stood the vigil. And when an animal was dying, it was Halcom who stayed with it, comforting it as best he could.

Finally, Skif found a moment to make a cautious overture to the young priest. Halcom had hobbled out to the stable to assist, not a Healer Trainee, but a farrier who often donated his time and expertise, and Skif was also called on to help. The injury was a split and overgrown hoof on a lamed cart- horse; Halcom was asked to hold the horse's head, since he, more than anyone else, was able to keep animals calm during treatment. And Skif was there to hold the hoof while the farrier trimmed it and fastened a special shoe to help the hoof heal.

When the farrier had left, and Skif had taken the horse back to its stall, Halcom seemed disinclined to leave. "You've been doing good work here, friend," Halcom said, looking around at the rest of the stable without getting up from the hay bale he was sitting on. "I'm glad you came here. Poor old Brother Absel just isn't up to the heavy work anymore."

"Thankee, sor," Skif said, keeping to his persona of coun- try bumpkin, and bobbing his head subserviently. "Would ye might be a-givin' me a character, too? That be what'm here for."

"I could probably do better than that, if what you want is stable work," Halcom admitted, but with a raised eyebrow. "I've no doubt I could recommend you to several people for that. Is that what you want?"

"Oh, aye, sor," Skif replied, feigning eagerness.

"Balderdash," Halcom countered, startling Skif. "You're better than that. You don't *really* want to be a lowly stable-hand for the rest of your life, do you?" His eyes gleamed with speculation. "You are much too intelligent for that. What are you aiming at? Master of Horse? Chief Coachman?"

"Ah—" Skif stammered, before he got his wits together. "But I've got no training, sor. Dunno much but burthen beasts, and never learnt to drive."

Halcom waved that aside as of no consequence. "Nor have most boys your age when they go into service. As small as you are, though—learning to handle the reins could be problematic. I'm not sure you could control a team."

"I be stronger nor I look, sor," Skif said, stung.

Halcom laughed, but it didn't have that sly, mean sound to it that Skif had half expected. "Oh, you'd make a fine smart little footman, sitting up beside your master on a fashionable chariot, but I'll tell you the truth, lad, there is not a single highborn or man of means and fashion that I'd feel comfortable sending you to in that capacity. The good men have all the loyal footmen they need—and the others—" he shook his head. "I won't send you to a bad master."

"Ye might tell me who they be, sor?" Skif offered tentatively. "If I didna know it, I might take a place I was offered—"

"So you can avoid them?" Halcom nodded thoughtfully. "That's no bad idea. Clever of you to think of it." And he proceeded, with forthright candor, to outline the character of every man he thought Skif ought not to take service with. He was so candid that Skif was, frankly, shocked. Not at the litany of faults and even vices—his upbringing in the worst part of Haven had exposed him to far worse than Halcom revealed. No, it was that Halcom was not at all reticent about unrolling the listing of faults of his "own kind."

As Halcom spoke, Skif found himself at war within himself. He *wanted* to trust Halcom, and he had sworn never to trust anyone. More than that, he wanted to *like* Halcom. It seemed to him that Halcom could easily become a friend.

And he did *not* want any more friends.

"That leaves plenty of good masters to take service with, mind," Halcom pointed out when he was finished, and smiled. "And for all my differences with my own family, I can quite cheerfully recommend you to take service with them. They're quite good to those who serve them well."

Huh. It's only their own flesh'n'blood that they muck about with, eh? Skif thought. *Guess you'n'me have more in common than I thought.*

"It was your own uncle that turned you out, wasn't it?" Halcom said suddenly, startling Skif again with his knowledge of Skif's "background." Halcom laughed at his expression, wryly. "I suppose we have more in common than either of us would have suspected."

" 'Twas your nuncle sent ye off?" Skif ventured.

Halcom nodded, and his face shadowed. "My existence was an embarrassment," he admitted sourly. "My uncle feared that my presence in his household would cast a shadow over some pending betrothal arrangements he was negotiating. My father—his younger brother—has no backbone to speak of, and agreed that I ought to be persuaded to a vocation."

"What?" Skif asked indignantly. "They figger you'd scare the bride?"

"My uncle suggested that the prospective bride's father might rethink his offer if he thought that deformity ran in my family," Halcom said bluntly, his mouth twisting in a frown. "Since my parents are dependent on his generosity for a place, I suppose I can't blame them. . . ." He sighed deeply, and his expression lightened. "In the end, really, I'm rather glad it happened. I had very little to do with myself, I'm really not much of a scholar, and— well, needless to say, I'm not cut out for Court life either. I've always loved animals, and neither they, nor my fellow Brothers, care about this wretched leg of mine. And I *did* manage to shame my uncle into making a generous donation when he dumped me here."

Skif nodded his head, concealing as best he could that he

was racked by an internal struggle. He really, truly *wanted* to be Halcom's friend. And he really, truly, did not want to make another friend that he knew he would only lose.

I ain't stayin' here forever, he told himself sternly. *He wouldn' be so nice if he knew what I was. Hellfires, he'd turn me straight over to th' Watch if he knew what I was!*

But he could almost hear the place whispering to him. It wanted him to stay. He could have a friend again. No one here would care what he had been, only what he was now, and what he might become. Oh, he'd never be rich—but he'd never starve either.

He steeled himself against the seductive whispers of peace. Him? Bide in a place like this? Not when he had a debt to repay! Not when there was someone out there that was so ruthless he would do anything to anyone who stood in his way!

Besides, this place would put him to sleep in a season. He'd turn into a sheep inside of a year. And if there was one thing that Skif had no desire to become, it was a sheep.

"Well, I imagine you've heard more than enough to send you to sleep about *me,*" Halcom said, hauling himself to his feet again. "And I still have my charges to attend to. I won't keep you from your own duties any more, lad—but do remember what I've told you, and that if you want a second letter of commendation to go with the Prior's when you leave, I will be happy to write one for you."

That last, said as Halcom turned to go, had the sound of a formal dismissal, superior to inferior.

There, you see? he taunted that seductive whisper. *I ain't a friend to the likes of a highborn, even if his people did cast 'im off. A mouse might's well ask a hawk t'be his friend. Hawk might even say yes—till he got hungry.*

Another week passed, and the city was struck with a heat wave that was so oppressive people and animals actually began dying.

The Queen closed the Court and sent everyone but her Privy Council out of the city. But there was nowhere for the poor and the working classes to go, and even if there had been, how could ordinary people just pack up and leave? How would they make a living, pay their bills, feed their children? Life in Haven went on as best it could. As many folk as could changed their hours, rising before dawn, working until the heat grew intolerable, enduring as best they could until late afternoon, then taking up their tasks again in the evening. The Prior knew a clever trick or two, though, and the Brethren began going through the poorer neighborhoods, teaching people what the Prior had taught them—for although it was the Lord of the Beasts that the Brethren served, nevertheless, Man was brother to the Beasts.

Water-soaked pads of straw in windows somehow cooled the air that blew through them, so long as there was a breeze. And if there wasn't, the cheapest, more porous terra-cotta jars filled with water and placed about a room also helped to cool the air as the water evaporated from them. Stretching a piece of heavy paper over a frame, then fastening that frame by one side to the ceiling and attaching a cord to a corner created a huge fan that would create a breeze when the winds themselves didn't oblige; there were always children to pull the cord, and they didn't mind doing so when the breeze cooled *them* as well. And the same cheap terra cotta that was used for those jars could be made into tiles to be soaked with water and laid on the floor—also cooling a room or the overheated person who lay down on them. It helped; all of it helped.

People were encouraged to sleep on flat rooftops or in their gardens or even in parks by night, and in cellars by day.

But there was always someone greedy enough to want to make a profit from the misfortune of others. Suddenly the dank and dark basement rooms that had been the cheapest to rent became the most expensive. Not all landlords raised the rents on their cellars, but many did, and if it hadn't been so stiflingly hot, there might have been altercations over it.

But it was just too hot. No one could seem to get the energy even to protest.

Skif was terribly frustrated; it was nearly impossible to move around the city by night without being seen! And yet, with all of the wealthy and highborn gone, it should have been child's play to continue his vendetta! Why, the huge manors and mansions were so deserted that the Master Thief must have been looting them with impunity, knowing that no one would discover his depredations until the heat wave broke and people returned to Haven.

Hellfires, Skif thought grumblingly, as he returned from an errand to the market, through streets that the noon heat had left deserted. *It'd be easier to make a run by day than by—*

Then it hit him. *Of course!* Why not make his raids by day? He was supposed to be resting, like everyone and everything, during the heat of the day. No one would miss him at the Priory, and there would be no one around to see him in the deserted mansions, not with the skeleton staffs spending their time in the cool of the wine cellars, most of them asleep if they had any sense!

That's pro'lly what the Master Thief's doing! he thought with glee. He was delighted to have thought of it, and enjoyed a moment of mental preening over his own cleverness.

Well, he certainly would *not* be wearing his black "sneak suit" for these jobs. His best bet was to look perfectly ordinary. The fact was, he probably wouldn't even need to get in via the rooftops; the doors and windows would all be unlocked. After all, who would ever expect a thief to walk in the kitchen door in broad daylight?

He brought the bag of flour and the basket of other sundries he'd been sent for to the kitchen and left it on the table.

The Brother who acted as cook had changed the routine because of the heat. A great many things were being served cold; boiled eggs, cheese, vegetables and so forth. Actual *cooking* was done at night and in ovens and on brick stoves erected in the kitchen courtyard. The biggest meal of the day was now breakfast; the noon meal was no longer a meal, but consisted of whatever anyone was able to eat (given the heat, which killed appetites), picked up as one got hungry, in the kitchen. Big bowls of cleaned, sliced vegetables submerged in water lined the counters, loaves of bread resided under cheesecloth, boiled eggs in a smaller bowl beside them. There was butter and cheese in the cold larder if anyone wanted it, which hardly anyone did.

Skif helped himself to carrot strips and celery and a piece of bread; he ate the bread plain, because he couldn't bear the thought of butter either. The place might just as well have been deserted; the only sign that there *had* been anyone in the kitchen was the lumps of bread dough left to rise under cloths along their shelf.

Skif wasn't all that hungry either, but he ate and drank deeply of the cooled water from yet another terra-cotta jar. Then he went straight back out, as if he had been sent on a second errand. Not that there was anyone about to notice.

He sauntered along the streets, watching the heat haze hovering above the pavement, keeping to the shade, and noting that there still were a few folk out. They paid no attention to him, and he gave them no more than a cursory glance.

There was not so much as a hint of the Watch. No surprise there; what was there for them to do? There would be no fights, and it was too hot for petty theft, even if there was anything open at noon to steal from.

Where to hit? That was the question. He had no clear target in mind, and he wasn't as familiar with who belonged to which great mansion as he would have liked. Finally he decided, for lack of any other ideas, to bestow his attentions on one Thomlan Vel Cerican, a charming fellow who had amassed a great deal of wealth by squeezing his poor tenants and giving them as little in the way of decent housing as he could get away with. He was one of the landlords who had responded to the current heat wave by evicting tenants from the newly-desirable basement rooms and charging a premium rate for them—sending the evicted to live in the attics.

It seemed as good a reason as any to wreak as much havoc as humanly possible on him. If he hadn't burned his own buildings to avoid having to make repairs, it was only because he had balked at actually destroying anything he owned.

So Skif's steps took him in the direction of the great homes of those who aspired to be counted among the highborn, not those who had actually gotten to that position.

There was still no sign of Watch, Guards, or anyone else. He strolled along the street, not the alley, and nothing met his interested gaze but shuttered and curtained windows behind the gates. These houses, while imposing, did not boast the grounds and gardens of those of the true nobility. Land was at a premium within the second set of city walls.

There were three sets of walls, in fact—four, if you counted the ones surrounding the Palace and the three Collegia. Each time that the city of Haven had outgrown its walls, a new set had been built. When that happened, land within the previous walls became highly desirable. Now, between the first set and the Palace walls, only the highborn, those with old titles, had their mansions (and indeed, manors), which had enormous gardens and landscaped grounds. Between the second and first, those who had newer titles, most less than a generation old, and the wealthy but not ennobled kept their state. Lesser dwellings had been bought up and razed to make way for these newer mansions. There were gardens, but they were a fraction of the size of those of the Great Lords of State. But there were parks here, places where one could ride or stroll and be observed. Between the third walls and the second lived most of the rest of the city, although the populace had already begun to spill outside the walls, and many of those whose wealth was very recent had taken to building mansions that aped those of the Great Lords of State, but outside the walls altogether, where land was cheaper.

Eventually, Skif supposed, another set of walls would be built, and then it would be his neighborhood that would be razed to make way for the mansions of the wealthy.

Skif passed one of the parks, and decided to take a rest near a lily-covered pond. It was deserted, the air shimmering with heat above the scorched lawns between the trees. His target was on the other side of this park, and it occurred to him that it wouldn't be a bad idea to observe it from the comfort of the park while he cooled off a little.

Even though he had sauntered along in slothful fashion, he was still sweating. He pulled his linen shirt away from his body and threw himself down in the shade of a huge oak tree beside the pond. The ground was marginally cooler than the air or his body, but there were no signs that anyone was actually sleeping here at night, despite the suggestions of the authorities.

Skif wasn't surprised. The Watch probably *was* discouraging the poor from moving into the parks in this section of the city, even though there were more of them here than between the second and third walls. The Watch was answerable directly to the wealthy folk living here—as opposed to the Guard, which was answerable to the Crown. Even though *they* were not here to witness the poor camping out of a night in "their" park, not one of the moneyed lot who lived around here even wanted to consider the prospect. The local Watch probably had orders to clear out campers as fast as they arrived.

Skif turned his head to peer between bushes nearby, thinking he heard something. Some zealous Watchman, perhaps? If so, he'd better be prepared with a story about why he was here.

He had heard something, but it wasn't a member of the Watch.

There was a horse wandering loose around the park, taking nibbles out of the grass, sampling the flowers. It was a handsome creature, white as snow, and still wore a saddle and bridle. Reins dangled from the bridle—no, it was a bitless hackamore, he saw. No one would leave reins dangling like that—your horse could all too easily catch a leg in them, stumble, fall and perhaps break a leg.

But if you didn't tie the reins off properly when you left a horse waiting, the horse could jerk them loose and wander off, leaving them dangling just like these were.

For one wild moment, Skif thought—*Is that a Companion?*

But no—if it had been a Companion, there would certainly be a Herald somewhere about. And besides, the saddle and hackamore were old, very plain, well-worn. Everyone knew that Companions went about in elaborate blue-and-silver tack, with silver bridle bells and embroidered barding. There were plenty of white horses around that weren't Companions. It was something of an affectation in some fashionable sets to ride white horses, or have a carriage drawn by matched teams of them.

No, some idiot hadn't tied his horse properly. Or, far more likely given the worn state of the tack, some groom had taken his master's mare out for some exercise and had combined the chore with some errand of his own. He hadn't tied the horse up, and she'd pulled her reins loose and wandered away. That groom would be in a lot of trouble—but since there wasn't anyone combing the park looking for this beast, evidently he hadn't missed her yet.

Well, his loss was Skif's gain.

Working at the Priory had given him a *lot* more familiarity with horses than he'd had before. He'd even learned to ride. And faced with this opportunity for profit on four legs, he grinned broadly.

You're mine! he told the grazing mare. *Lessee; horse fair's runnin' over on the east side. Or I kin take her out of the walls altogether an' sell her. Or I kin take her t'Priory an' collect th' reward when she shows up missin'. . . .*

The last option wasn't a bad notion, though the first was the real money maker.

The horse moved around the bushes and out of his sight; knowing that she was probably some high-strung well-bred beast, he got up slowly and began to stalk her. If he, a stranger, was going to catch her rather than spooking her, he'd have to catch her by surprise.

When she actually moved between two thick, untrimmed hedges, he could hardly believe his good luck. She couldn't have gotten into a better situation for him to corner her!

Knowing that a horse is averse to backing up, he ran around to the front of the hedges, and struck.

Making a dash out of cover, he grabbed for the reins and the saddle in the same movement, hauling himself into the saddle before she had time to do more than snort. And somehow, before he realized it, he was in the saddle and in control!

For just about a heartbeat.

Because in the next moment, the horse tossed her head, jerking the reins out of his hand, and set off at a gallop, and all he could do was cling desperately to the pommel of the saddle.

13

Aʟʟ Skif could do was hold on, with every aching finger, with knees and thighs, wrists and ankles. If he could have held on with his teeth, he would have. If he could have tied his *hair* to the saddle, he would have.

He'd lost the stirrups almost at once, shortly after he lost the reins. That didn't give him a lot of options; either cling on like a burr, or try to jump off. But the mare was going so fast, he knew if he jumped, he'd get hurt.

Badly, *badly* hurt—

And that was if he was lucky. He'd seen someone who'd been thrown from a galloping horse, once. The poor fool had his back broken. Healers could fix that, he'd been told, if the Healer got to you quickly enough, if you were important enough to *see* a Healer. He'd seen countless people thrown from runaway wagons, and they always ended up with broken arms and legs. That was bad enough.

She was at the gallop, head down, charging along as if she'd gone mad, pounding down the paved streets, the occasional bystander gawking at them as they tore past. No one tried to stop the runaway horse, and all that Skif could do was hang on tight and trust to the fact that as hot as it was, she'd tire soon. She'd have to tire soon. She was only a horse, just a fancy horse, she couldn't run forever—

He closed his eyes and crouched over the saddle, gripping her with his thighs and holding onto the pommel of the saddle with all his might. Her mane whipped at his face, it was like being beaten with a fly whisk, and he gasped with every driving blow of her hooves that drove the pommel into his gut. She'd be slowing any moment now.

Any moment now . . .

Oh, please—

He cracked his eye open, and closed it again.

She wasn't slowing. If anything, she was running faster. People, shops, pavement blurred past so fast he was getting sick. His eyes watered as some of her mane lashed across them.

How was that possible?

Hellfires! I stole a racehorse! Of all the stupid, idiot things to have done—

He opened his eyes again, just in time to see a wagon pull across the street in front of them and stop.

She's got to stop now—

She raised her head a little, and her ears cocked forward.

She's not gonna stop!

The driver stared at them, then abruptly dove off the seat. The mare increased her pace; he felt her muscles bunch up under his legs.

She's gonna jump it!

She shoved off, her forequarters rising; he clawed desperately at the saddle as his weight shifted backward. He screamed in terror, *knowing* he was going to fall, then the wagonbed was underneath him—

She landed; he was flung forward, his nose and right eye

slamming into her neck. He saw stars, and his head exploded with pain. Somehow, some way, he managed to hang on. The thought of falling off terrified him more than staying on.

She didn't even break stride as she continued her run and careened around a corner; sweat flew off her, and she didn't even seem to notice. She was off around another corner, pounding through a half-empty market, then toward the last of the city walls.

No—

But she wasn't listening to what he wanted.

She plunged into the tunnel beneath the walls, and for a moment her hooves echoed in the darkness, sounding like an entire herd of horses was in here with him.

There were Guards on the wall! Surely, surely they would stop her— Then she was out, with no sign of a Guardsman.

Skif dared another glance, out of the eye that wasn't swelling. Through his tears all he could see was a road stretching ahead of them, the road leading away from Haven. He couldn't even tell *which* road; all he knew for certain was that they were flying down a roadway, and people were scattering out of their way, shouting curses after them.

The mare wove her way in and out of the traffic with the agility of a dancer. He actually felt the touch on his ankle as they brushed by other riders, the whiplike cut of a horse's tail as it shied out of the way. And somehow, she was getting faster.

He knew if he tried to throw himself off now, he'd die. It was just that simple. No one, not even an experienced rider, could slip off a horse at speeds like this and live. He wouldn't just break bones, he'd break his neck or his skull and die instantly. All he could do was what he had been doing; hang on, try not to get thrown, and hope that when she stopped, he'd be able to get off of her without her killing him.

He gritted his teeth together, hissing with the pain of his

eye and nose, so full of fear there was no room in his head for anything else.

The sounds of shouting and cursing were gone. He dared another glance. There were no more buildings beside the road now, nothing but fields with tiny farmhouses off in the distance. The road still had plenty of traffic, though, and the mare wove her way in and out of it with a nonchalance that made the hair on the back of his head stand up. People weren't shouting and cursing at them because they were too busy trying to get out of the way.

He had never been so terrified in his entire life.

He squeezed his eyes tight shut again, and for the first time in his life, began to pray.

Skif was limp with exhaustion, dripping with sweat and aching so much that he wasn't sure he even cared what happened to him now.

He also had no idea where he was. The mare had gotten off the main road and was still running, though not at the headlong pace she'd held through the city. This was a normal gallop—if anything this mare did was normal!

This was a country road, rutted dirt, with trees on both sides that met over his head, forming a tunnel of green. If his eye and nose hadn't hurt so much—and if he hadn't been so terrified—he'd never been anywhere like this before in his life.

He had no idea how far they were from Haven. A long way; that was about all he could tell. So in addition to the rest of it, he was hopelessly lost, and completely outside familiar territory.

And the sun was setting.

He wanted to cry.

He *did* cry; tears leaking silently out from the corners of his eyes. His nose felt as if it was the size of a cabbage, and it throbbed.

The mare suddenly changed direction again, darting into a mere break in the trees, down a path so seldom used that there weren't even any cart tracks in it. She slowed again, to a trot.

Now he could hear what was going on around him; birds, the wind in the trees, the dull thud of the mare's hooves on the turf. So this was what people meant by "peaceful countryside"? Well, they could *have* it. He'd have given an arm for his loft room right now.

He could probably have gotten off her back at this point— but for what? He didn't even know where he was! Here they were in the middle of a complete wilderness, with no shelter, nothing to eat, and no people, so where would he go? Somehow he had to convince this devil beast to get him back home—

Now she slowed to a walk, and all he could do was slump over her neck, as the light coming through the trees took on an amber cast. She was sweating, but no more than one of the horses he was familiar would have been after a moderately hard job. She should have been foaming with sweat. Foaming? She should be collapsed on the ground by now!

Head bobbing with each step, she ambled down the path, and then, with no more warning than when she'd started this run, she stopped.

Skif looked up through eyes blurring with exhaustion and tears of frustration and fear.

Now what?

They stood in a tiny clearing, in front of the smallest building he had ever seen. They were completely surrounded by trees, and the only other object in the clearing was a pump next to the building with a big stone trough beneath it. He couldn't hear anything but birds and the wind. If there were any humans anywhere around, there was no sign of them. For the first time in his life, Skif was completely alone.

He'd have given anything to see a single human being. Even a Watchman. If the Watch had showed up, he'd have

flung himself into their arms and begged them to take him to
gaol.

Every muscle, every bone, every inch of Skif's body was in
pain. His nose and eye hurt worst, but everything hurt. He sat
in the saddle, blinking, his bad eye watering, and choked back
a sob. Then he slowly pried his fingers, one at a time, away
from the pommel of the saddle.

He looked down at the ground, which seemed furlongs
away, and realized that he couldn't dismount.

It wasn't that he didn't *want* to, it was that he couldn't. He
couldn't make his cramped legs move. And even if he could,
he was afraid to fall.

Then the mare solved his problem by abruptly shying sideways.

He didn't so much slide off the saddle as it was that the
horse and her saddle slid out from underneath him. He made
a grab for the pommel again, but it was too late.

He tumbled to the ground and just barely managed to catch
himself so that he landed on his rump instead of his face, in a
huge pile of drifted leaves.

It hurt. Not as badly as, say, hitting hard pavement would
have, but it still hurt.

And it knocked what was left of his breath out of him for a
moment and made him see stars again.

When his eyes cleared, he looked around. He sat in the middle of the pile of old, damp leaves, dazed and bewildered at
finding himself on the ground again. "Ow," he said, after a
moment of consideration.

The mare turned, stepping lightly and carefully, and shoved
him with her nose in the middle of his chest.

He shoved back, finally roused to some sensation other
than confusion. "You get away from me, you!" he said angrily.
" 'f it wasn't for *you*, I—"

She shoved at him again, and without meaning to, he

looked straight into her eyes. They were blue, and deep as the sky, and he fell into them.

:Hello, Skif,: he heard, from somewhere far, far away. *:My name is Cymry, and I Choose you.:*

And he dropped into a place where he would never be alone or friendless again.

When he came back to himself, the first thing he did was stagger to his feet and back away from the Companion. Never mind the wonderful dream he'd been in—it *was* a dream. It couldn't be real. Something was terribly wrong.

His Companion Cymry looked at him and he felt her amusement.

His Companion. And that was just not possible.

"Are you outa your *mind?*" he croaked, staring at her.

:No,: she said, and shook her head. *:I Choose you. You're a Herald—well, you will be after you go through the Collegium and get your Whites. Right now, you're just a Trainee.:*

"Like hell!" he retorted feelingly. "You are crazy! Or—I am—" It occurred to him then that all this might just be some horrible dream. Maybe when he'd jumped onto the horse, it had thrown him, and he was lying on his back in that park, knocked out cold and hallucinating. Maybe he hadn't even seen the horse, the heat had knocked him over and he was raving. None of this was happening—that must be it—

:Don't be stupid,: Cymry replied, shoving at him with her nose. *:Be sensible! Do you ever have black eyes and a broken nose in a dream? It's not a dream, you're not unconscious, and you are Chosen. And you're going to be a Herald.:*

"I don't bloody well think so!" he said, trying to back further away from her and coming up against the wall of the little building. "If you think I am, *you're* crazy. Don' you know what I *am?*"

How could this be happening? He didn't *want* to be a Herald! Oh, even Bazie had spoken about them with admiration, but no Heralds were ever plucked out of a gutter, not even in a tale!

:Of course I do,: she replied calmly. *:You're a thief. A rather good one for your age, too—:*

"Well, then I can't be a Herald, can I?" He groped for words to try and convince her how mad, how impossible this was. Even though, deep inside, something cried out that he didn't want it to be impossible. "Heralds are—well, they're all noble an' highborn—"

She snorted with amusement at his ignorance. *:No they aren't. Not more than a quarter of them at most, anyway. Heralds are just ordinary people; farmers, craftsmen, fisherfolk—ordinary people.:*

"Well, they're heroes—"

:And none of them started out that way,: she countered. *:Most of them started out as ordinary younglings, being Chosen by a Companion. There wasn't anything special about them until then—not visibly, anyway.:*

"They're *good!*"

She considered that for a moment, head to one side. *:That rather depends on your definition of "good," actually. Granted, they are supposed to uphold the law,:* she continued thoughtfully, *:But in the course of their duties, plenty of them break the law as much as they uphold it, if you want to be technical about it.:*

"But—but—" he spluttered, as the last light pierced through the tree trunks and turned everything a rosy red, including Cymry. "But—Heralds are—they do—"

:Heralds are what they have to be. They do what the Queen and the country need,: Cymry said, supremely calm and confident. *:We Choose those who are best suited to do those things and supply those needs. And what makes you think that the Queen and country might not need the skills of a thief?:*

Well, there was just no possible answer to that, and even though his mouth opened and closed several times, he couldn't make any sounds come out of it.

She paced close to him, and once again he was caught—though not nearly so deeply—in those sparkling sapphire eyes. *:Now look—I'm tired and hungry and sweaty. So are you.:*

"But—" They were in the middle of nowhere! Where was he—? How was he—?

:This is a Way Station, and as a Herald Trainee—don't argue!—you're entitled to anything in it.: She whickered softly. *:I promise, there's food and bedding and just about anything you might need in there. There's also a bucket of water inside to prime the pump with. I suggest that before it gets too horribly dark, you pump up some water, clean both of us up, and get us both some of the food that's waiting. You are hungry, aren't you? You can eat and rest here for the night, and we can talk about all of this.:*

She cocked both of her ears at him, and added, *:And while you're at it, it wouldn't hurt to make a poultice for that black eye you're getting. It's becoming rather spectacular.:*

Herald Alberich, Weaponsmaster to Heralds' Collegium and sometime intelligence agent for Queen Selenay, put down the brush he'd been using on Kantor's mane and stared at his Companion in complete and utter shock.

Companions didn't lie—but what Kantor had just told him was impossible.

"You must be joking!" he said aloud, in his native tongue.

Kantor turned his head to look at his Chosen. *:As you well know,:* he said, with mock solemnity, *:I have no sense of humor.:*

"In a pig's eye," Alberich muttered, thinking of all of the

tricks his Companion had authored over the years—including the one of smuggling himself past the Karsite Border to Choose and abduct one Captain Alberich of the Karsite Army.

:But I assure you, I am not joking. Cymry has managed to Choose that young scamp you've caught eavesdropping on you over the past couple of months. He is a thief, and she'll probably be delivering him to the Collegium some time tomorrow. So I suggest you prepare your fellow Heralds. He promises to make things interesting around here.: Kantor arched his neck. *:But before you do that, you might take that brush along my crest; it still itches.:*

"What in the name of Vkandis Sunlord are we supposed to do with a thief?" Alberich demanded, not obliging Kantor with the brush.

:What you always do with the newly Chosen. You'll train him, of course.: Kantor turned his head again and regarded his Chosen with a very blue eye. *:Hasn't it occurred to you that a skilled thief would be extremely useful in the current situation that you and the Queen have found yourselves in? Scratch a thief, you'll find a spy. Set a thief to take a thief, and you have been losing state secrets.:*

"Well—"

:Of course it has. All you have to do is appeal to the lad's better instincts and bring them to the fore. I assure you, he has plenty of better instincts. After all, he's been Chosen, and we don't make mistakes about the characters of those we Choose. Do we?: Kantor didn't have any eyebrows to arch, but the sidelong look he bestowed on Alberich was certainly very similar.

"Well—"

:So there you are. About that brush in your hand—:

Belatedly, Alberich brought the brush up and began vigorously using it along Kantor's crest. The Companion sighed in blissful pleasure, and closed his eyes.

And Alberich began to consider just how he was going to

break the news about this newest trainee to Dean Elcarth and the rest.

Assuming, of course, they weren't already having similar conversations with *their* Companions.

It was a good thing that Bazie had taught him how to cook. Yes, there was food here, but it wasn't the sort of thing the ordinary city-bred boy would have recognized as such.

:I'd have told you what to do,: Cymry said, her head sticking in the door, watching him, as he baked currant-filled oatcakes on a stone on the hearth. He'd also put together a nice bean soup from the dried beans and spices he'd found, but he didn't think it would be done any time soon, and he was hungry now. *:I wouldn't let you starve. I'm perfectly capable of telling you how to use just about anything in this Way Station.:*

"Somehow I ain't s'prised," he replied, turning the cakes deftly once one side was brown. "Is there anything ye *can't* do?"

:I'm a bit handicapped by the lack of hands,: she admitted cheerfully.

She—and he—were both much cleaner at this point. Beside the pump, there had been a generous trough, easily filled and easily emptied. After she'd drunk her fill, and he had washed and brushed her down as she asked, he'd had a bath in it. Then he emptied it out and refilled it for her drinking. The cold bath had felt wonderful; it was the first time in a week that he'd been able to cool down. He'd also washed up his clothing; it was hanging on a bush just outside. It was a lot more comfortable to sit around in his singlet, since there wasn't anyone but Cymry to see him anyway.

She'd told him which herbs to make into a poultice that did a lot to ease the ache of his eye and nose, and more to make into a tea that did something about his throbbing head. She already knew, evidently, that he could cook, and had left him alone while he readied his dinner over the tiny hearth in the Way Station. Now he couldn't imagine why he hadn't figured out she was a Companion immediately.

Unless it was just that the idea of a Companion wandering around in an old worn set of tack was so preposterous, and the idea of a Companion deciding to make a Herald out of a thief was still more so.

:*I told them to tack me up in the oldest kit in the stables that would fit me,*: she offered, as he scooped the oatcakes off their stone and juggled one from hand to hand, waiting for it to cool enough to eat. He gave her a curious stare.

"Ye—ye *kidnapped* me!" he accused.

:*Well, would you have come with me if I'd walked up to you and Chosen you?*: she asked, her head cocked to one side. :*I am sorry about your nose, but that was an accident.*:

"But—"

:*I've known for several weeks that you were my Chosen,*: she said, as if it was so matter-of-fact that he shouldn't even be considering any other possibility. :*I've just been waiting for the opportunity to get you alone where I could explain things to you.*:

"But—"

:*You've already lost this argument, you know,*: she pointed out. :*Three times, in fact.*:

He gave up. Besides, the cake was cool enough to eat. And he was hungry enough by this point to eat the oats raw, much less in the cakes he'd just made.

He put a second poultice on his eye and nose and lay back in the boxbed that filled most of the Way Station. It had a thick layer of fresh hay in it, covered over with a coarse canvas sheet; it was just as comfortable as his bed in the Priory, and although he wasn't sleepy yet, he didn't really want to venture out into the alien environment outside his door. He heard things out there; all manner of unfamiliar sounds enlivened the darkness, and he didn't much care for them. There were wild animals out there, owls and bats and who knew what else. There could be bears. . . .

:You don't for one moment think that I would let anything *hurt you, do you?:* The unexpected fierceness of that question made him open his good eye and turn his head to look at her, where she lay half-in, half-out of the doorway.

"I don' know anything 'bout you," he admitted, slowly. "Nothin' at all 'bout Companions."

:Well, I wouldn't.: She sighed. *:And you're about to learn a great deal about Companions.:*

"No, I ain't. They're gonna take one look at me an' throw me out," he replied, stubbornly.

:No, they aren't. They already know who you are, what you are, and that I'm bringing you in tomorrow.:

"What?" he yelped, sitting up straight, keeping the poultice clapped to his eye with one hand.

:Well, not everybody, just the people who need to. The Dean of the Collegium—that's the Herald who's in charge of the whole of Heralds' Collegium. Herald Alberich, the Weapons-master. The Queen's Own and the Queen. A couple of the other teachers. They all know, and they aren't going to throw you out.: She was so matter-of-fact about it—as if it shouldn't even occur to him to doubt her. *:As to how they know, I told them, of course. Actually I told them through their Companions, but it amounts to the same thing.:*

He flopped back down in the bed, head spinning. This was all going much too fast for him. Much, *much* too fast. "Now what am I gonna do?" he moaned, mostly to himself. "I can't ever go back—th' Watch'd hev me afore I took a step—"

:You couldn't go back anyway.: Cymry replied.

"But—"

:Skif—do you really, really *want me to leave you?:* The voice in his mind was no more than a whisper, but it was a

whisper that woke the echoes of that unforgettable moment when he felt an empty place inside him fill with something he had wanted for so long, so very, very long—

"No," he whispered back, and to his profound embarrassment, felt his throat swelling with a sob at the very thought.

:I didn't think so. Because I couldn't bear to lose you.: Her thoughts took on a firmer tone. *:And I won't. No one tries to separate a Companion and her Chosen. That would be— unthinkable.:*

He lay in the firelit darkness for a long time, listening to the strange night sounds in the woods outside, the beating of his own heart, and his own thoughts.

Then he sighed heavily. "I guess I gotta be a Herald," he said reluctantly. "But I still think there's gonna be trouble."

:Then we'll face it together. Because I am never, ever going to let anyone separate us.:

In the morning, gingerly probing of his nose and the area around his eye—and the fact that he could actually open that eye again—proved that the poultice had done its work. He cleaned himself up in the cold water, and donned his shirt and trews—wrinkled and a little damp, but they'd have to do. They both ate, he cleaned the things he'd used and shut the Way Station up again. He'd been stiff and sore when he woke up, but he knew from experience that only moving around would make that kind of soreness go away. Besides, at the moment, he couldn't wait to get back to the city where he belonged. Whatever people saw in "the country" was invisible to him. The silence alone would drive him crazy in a day.

There was just one problem, of course—and that was that he wasn't going *home,* he was going to this Collegium place. As he mounted Cymry's well-worn saddle—with a great deal more decorum this time—he shook his head slightly. "I still think there's gonna be trouble," he predicted glumly.

:Skif, there will always *be trouble where you are,:* she replied mischievously. *:We'll just have to try to keep it from getting out of hand!:*

Without a backward glance, she started up the forest trail, going in a few paces from a walk to a trot to an easy lope. It was very strange, riding her, now that he knew what she was. For one thing, she wasn't a horse—he didn't have control over her, and that was the way it was *supposed* to be, not an accident. But as they moved out of the woods and onto roads that had a bit of morning traffic, he began to notice something else.

Now that they weren't charging down the road in a manner threatening to life and limb, people *paid attention* to Cymry, they clearly knew what she was, and they looked at her, and by extension her rider, with *respect.*

Or at least they did until they saw his black eye.

But even then, they looked at him with respect only leavened with sympathy. And since they weren't galloping at a headlong pace, but rather moving in and out of the traffic at a respectable, but easy trot, some people actually began to call greetings to him and her.

"New-Chosen, aye, lad?" said a farmer, perched so high on the seat of his wagon that he was eye-to-eye with Skif. And without waiting for an answer, added, "Here, catch!" and tossed him a ripe pear.

Startled, he caught it neatly, and the second one that the same man tossed to him, before Cymry found another opening in the traffic and moved smoothly ahead.

:If you'd cut that up into quarters, I'd like some.:

He was only too pleased to oblige, since he had the feeling that was what the farmer intended anyway. The little eating knife he always kept in his belt was accessible enough, and since he didn't have to use the reins, he didn't have to try and cut the pears up one-handed. She reached around and took each quarter daintily from his hand as he leaned over her neck to hand it to her.

Everywhere he looked, he met smiles and nods. It was a remarkable sensation, not only to be noticed, but to elicit that reaction in total strangers.

He did feel rather—naked, though. He wasn't at all comfortable with all of this *noticing.*

:Don't worry. You'll blend in once you're in your Grays. You'll be just another Trainee.:

He was getting used to her talking in his head—*Mindspeech,* she called it—and he was starting to get vague pictures and other associations along with the words. When she talked about being "in his Grays," he knew at once that what she meant was the uniform of the Heraldic Trainees, modeled after the Heralds' own uniforms, but gray in color.

:That's so people don't expect you to know what you're doing yet,: she told him, looking back over her shoulder at him with one eye. *:And by the way, you don't have to actually talk to me for me to hear and understand you.:*

So she knew what he was thinking. That wasn't exactly a comforting thought. A man liked to have a little privacy—

:And when you're a man, I'll give it to you.:

"Hey!" he said, staring at her ears indignantly, and garnering the curious glances of a couple driving a donkey cart next to him.

:Oh, don't be so oversensitive! I won't eavesdrop! You'll just have to learn not to "shout" all your thoughts.:

Great, now he would have to watch, not only what he did and said, but what he thought. . . . This Herald business was getting more unpleasant all the time.

:It's not like that, Skif,: she said coaxingly. *:Really it isn't. I was just teasing you.:*

He found a smile starting, no matter how he tried to fight it down. How could he possibly stay angry with her? How could he even get angry with her? And maybe that was the point.

He wasn't sure how long it had taken them to get from

the park where he'd found her to the Way Station where they stopped, but it took them most of the morning to get back to Haven. The Guards on the walls paid absolutely no attention to him, although they had to have seen him careening down the road yesterday. Cymry didn't volunteer any information as he craned his neck up to look at them, then bestowed a measuring glance at the two on either side of the passage beneath the wall. He wondered what they were thinking, and what they might have said or done yesterday.

They sure didn't try to stop us, anyway. Not that it was likely that they'd have had much luck—not with only two Guards on the ground and Cymry able to leap a farm wagon without thinking about it. Maybe it was just as well they hadn't tried. He might have ended up with both eyes blackened.

Once they got inside the city walls, though, people stopped paying as much attention to them. Well, that wasn't such a surprise, people saw Heralds coming and going all the time in Haven. On the whole, he felt a bit more comfortable without so many eyes on him.

Their progress took him through some areas he wasn't at all familiar with as they wound their way toward the Palace and the Collegia. He didn't exactly have a lot to do with craftsmen and shopkeepers—his forte was roof walking and the liftin' lay, not taking things from shops. That had always seemed vaguely wrong to him anyway; those people worked hard to make or get their goods, and taking anything from them was taking bread off their tables. Helping himself to the property of those who already had so much they couldn't keep track of it, now, that was one thing—but taking a pair of shoes from a cobbler who'd worked hard to make them just because he took a fancy to them was something else again.

Once they got in among the homes of the wealthy, though, it was a different story. He eyed some of those places, all close-kept behind their shuttered windows, with a knowing gaze. At one point or another he had checked out a great many of them, and he knew some of them very, very well indeed. The owner of *that* one had not one, but two mistresses that his wife knew nothing about—and they didn't know about each other. He treated them all well, though, so to Skif's mind none of them should have much to complain about. Sometimes he wondered, however, where the man was getting all the money he spent on them. . . .

:*He's honest enough, but there are others,*: Cymry put in. :*You see what I mean by needing your skills?*:

He furrowed his brow and concentrated on *thinking* what he wanted to say instead of saying it out loud. :*I suppose—*: he said dubiously.

But they were soon past the second wall, out of the homes of the merely wealthy, and in among the manses of the great. And Skif had to snicker a little as they passed Lord Orthallen's imposing estate. It was the first time he'd come at it from the front, but he couldn't mistake those pale stone walls for any other. How many times had he feasted at m'lord's table, and him all unaware?

They passed Lord Orthallen's home, passed others that Skif had not dared approach, so guarded around were they by the owner's own retainers. And finally there was nothing on his right but the final wall, blank and forbidding, that marked the Palace itself.

His apprehension returned, and he unconsciously hunched his head down, trying to appear inconspicuous, even though there was no one to see him.

No—there was someone.

The next turning brought them within sight of a single Guardsman in dark blue, who manned a small gate. Cymry trotted up to him quite as if she passed in and out of that gate all the time, and the man nodded as if he recognized her.

"This would be Cymry," he said aloud, casting a jaundiced eye up at Skif, who shrank within himself. "They're expecting you," he continued, opening the gate for them to pass through, although he didn't say who *they* were.

Cymry walked through, all dignity, and began to climb the graveled road that led toward an entire complex of buildings. Skif tensed. *Now I'm in for it,* he thought, and felt his heart drop down into his boots.

Hᴇ sat in Cymry's saddle like a sack of grain, and waited for doom to fall on him. She had taken him up the path, through what looked like a heavily-wooded park, past one enormous wing of a building so huge it *had* to be the Palace. Eventually they came to a long wooden building beside the river in the middle of a huge fenced field—he'd have called it a stable, except that there weren't any doors on the stalls. . . .

Then again, if this was where Companions stayed, there wouldn't be any need for doors on the stalls, would there?

It had a pounded-dirt floor covered ankle-deep in clean straw, and there was a second door on the opposite side, also open. These gave the only light. Cymry walked inside, quite at home.

The building was oddly deserted except—

Except—

For three people who were very clearly waiting for him just inside the door. One was an odd, birdlike man, slight and trim, hardly taller than Skif, with a cap of dark gray hair and an

228

intelligent, though worried, expression. The second was taller, with a fairly friendly face which at the moment also bore a distinctly worried expression. Both of them wore the white uniform only a Herald was allowed to wear.

His "welcoming committee," evidently.

He couldn't see the third one very well, since he was standing carefully back in the shadows. The third person wasn't wearing the white uniform though; his clothing was dark enough to blend in with the shadows.

Could be sommut from the Guard, he thought gloomily. *Gonna haul me off t' gaol soon's the other two get done with me.*

:He's not, and you're not going to gaol,: said Cymry. But that was all she said. He couldn't find it in himself to feel less than uneasy about the shadowy lurker.

She stopped a few paces away from the two men, and Skif gingerly dismounted, turning to face them with his hands clasped behind his back. A moment later, he dropped his eyes. Whatever was coming, he didn't want to meet their faces and see their disgust.

"So," said the smaller one, "you seem to be the young person that Companion Cymry has Chosen."

"Yessir," Skif replied, gazing at his ill-shod toes.

"And we're given to understand that you—ah—your profession—you—" The man fumbled for words, and Skif decided to get the agony over with all at once.

" 'M a thief, sir," he said, half defiantly. "Tha's what I do." He thought about adding any number of qualifying statements—that it had been a better choice than working for his uncle, that no one had offered him any *other* sort of employment and he had to eat; even that if Bazie hadn't been around to take him in and train him, he'd probably be dead now and not Chosen. But he kept all of those things to himself. For some reason, the clever retorts he had didn't seem all that clever at the moment.

The shorter man sighed. "I suppose you're expecting me to give you an ineffective and stuffy lecture about how you are supposed to be a new person and you can't go on doing that sort of thing anymore now that you're a Trainee."

Skif stopped looking at his toes and instead glanced up, startled, at the speaker. "Uh—you're not?"

"*You* are not stupid," the man said, and smiled faintly, though his tone sounded weary. "If you've already played over that particular lecture in your mind, then I will skip it and get to the point. I am Dean Elcarth. I am in charge of Herald's Collegium. The moment you entered the gate here, so far as we are concerned, whatever you were or did before you arrived here became irrelevant. You were Chosen. The Companions don't make mistakes. There must be the makings of a Herald in you. Therefore you are welcome. But when you get in trouble, and you will, because sooner or later at least half of our Trainees get in trouble, please remember that what you do reflects on the rest of us as well, and Heralds are not universally beloved among a certain faction of the highborn. The others will give you the details as they see fit, but the sum of what I have to say is that you are *supposed* to be part of a solution, not part of a problem, and I hope we can show you why in such a way that you actually feel that in your deepest heart."

During this rather remarkable speech, Skif had felt his jaw sagging slowly. It was *not* what he had expected to hear. His shock must have been written clearly on his face, because the Dean smiled a little again. "This is Herald Teren," he continued, gesturing to the other man, who although friendlier, was looking distinctly worried. "He is, technically, in charge of you, since he is in charge of all of the newly Chosen. You'll be getting your first lessons from him, and he will show you to your new quarters and help get you set up. Under normal circumstances, he would have picked out a mentor for you among the older students—but these are not normal circumstances. So although one of the older students will be assigned as a mentor, in actuality you will have a very different, though altogether *unofficial* mentor."

"That," said a grating voice that put chills up Skif's back, "myself would be."

He knew that voice, and that accent—though when he'd heard it before, it hadn't been nearly so thick.

And when the third figure stepped out of the shadows, arms folded over his chest, scar-seamed face smiling sardonically, he stepped back a pace without thinking about it. Skif had never seen the hair before—stark black with thick streaks of white running through it—because it had been hidden under a hood or a hat. But there was no mistaking that saturnine face or those cold, agate-gray eyes. This was the sellsword who'd spoken with (and spied on?) Jass, who had threatened Skif in the cemetery.

"*You!*" he blurted.

"This is Herald Alberich, the Collegium Weaponsmaster," said the Dean, "And I will leave you with him and Teren."

"But you can't b–b–be a Herald—" Skif stammered. "Where's yer, yer white—"

"Herald Alberich has special dispensation from Her Majesty herself not to wear the uniform of Heraldic Whites," Herald Teren interrupted, as Alberich's expression changed only in that he raised his right eyebrow slightly.

And now, suddenly, an explanation for Skif's own rather extraordinary behavior in the cemetery hit him, and he stared at the Herald in the dark gray leather tunic and tight trews with something like accusation. "You *Truth Spelled* me!"

Now that he knew Alberich was a Herald, there was no doubt in his mind why he had found himself telling the man what he knew that night in the cemetery. Everyone knew about Heralds and their Truth Spell, though Skif was the first person in his own circle of acquaintances who'd actually undergone it, much less seen it.

The two Heralds exchanged a glance. "Elcarth's right," said Teren. "He's very quick."

"Survive long he would not, were he not," Alberich replied, and fastened his hawklike eyes on Skif, who shrank back, just as he had that night. "I did. Because there was need. Think on this—had you by any other been caught, it would *not* have been Truth Spell, but a knife."

Skif shivered convulsively, despite the baking heat. The man was right. He gulped.

Alberich took another couple of steps forward, so that Skif was forced to look up at him. "Now, since there is still need, *without* Truth Spell, what you were about in following that scum, you will tell me. And *fully*, you will tell it."

There was something very important going on here; he didn't have nearly enough information to know what, or why, but it was a lot more than just the fact that Jass had been killed, though that surely had a part in it. But Skif raised his chin, stiffened his spine, and glared back. "T'you. Not t'*im*. I know you. I don' know 'im."

The Heralds exchanged another glance. "Fair enough," Teren said easily. "I'll be outside when you're ready for me to take him over."

Herald Teren turned and strode out the door on the other side of the stable. Skif didn't take his eyes off Alberich, whose gaze, if anything, became more penetrating.

"Heard you have, of the man Jass, and his ending." It was a statement, not a question, but Skif nodded anyway. "And? You followed him for moons. Why?"

" 'E burned down th' place where m'mates lived." Skif made it a flat statement in return, and kept his face absolutely dead of expression. "They died. I heard 'im say 'xactly that with m'own ears, an' 'e didn't care, all 'e cared about was 'e didn' want t' get caught. Fact, 'e said 'e *got rid* of some witnesses afore 'e set th' fire. Might even've been them."

Alberich nodded. "He was not nearly so free with me."

Skif tightened his jaw. "Honest—I was in the cem'tery by accident, but I was where I could 'ear real good. An' I 'eard 'im *an' th' bastid what hired 'im* talkin' 'bout a new job, an' talkin' 'bout the old one. I already figgered I was gonna take 'im down somehow—but only *after* I foun' out 'oo 'twas what give 'im th' order."

A swift intake of breath was all the reaction that Alberich showed—and a very slight nod. "Which was why you followed him." A pause. "He was more than that—more than just a petty arson maker, more even than a murderer. As his master was—is. Which was why I followed him."

Skif only shook his head. Alberich's concerns meant nothing to him—

—except—

"You *know* 'oo 'e is!" he shot out, feeling himself flush with anger. "The boss! You *know!*" He held himself as still as a statue, although he would cheerfully have leaped on the man at that moment, and tried to beat the knowledge out of him.

But Alberich shook his head, and it was with a regret and a disappointment that went so deeply into the tragic that it froze Skif where he stood. "I do not," he admitted. "Hope, I had, you did."

At that moment, instead of simply glaring at him, Alberich actually *looked* at him, caught his eyes, and stared deeply into them, and Skif felt a sensation like he had never before experienced. It was as if he literally stood on the edge of an abyss, staring down into it, and it wasn't that if he made a wrong move he'd fall, it was the sudden understanding that *this* was what Alberich had meant when he'd said that these were waters too deep for Skif to swim in. There were deep matters swirling all around him that Skif was only a very tiny part of, and yet—he had the chance to be a pivotal part of it.

If he dared. If he cared enough to see past his own loss and sorrows, and see greater tragedy and need and be willing to lay himself on the line to fix it.

:Chosen—please. This is real. This is what I meant when I said that we needed you.:

He gazed into that abyss, and thought back at Cymry as hard as he could— *:Is that the only reason you Chose me?:*

Because if it was—

—if it was, and all of the love and belonging that had filled his heart and soul when he first looked into her eyes was a lie, a ruse to catch someone with his particular "set of skills"—

:Are you out of your mind?: she snapped indignantly, shaken right out of her solemnity by the question. *:Can't you* feel *why I Chose you?:*

That answer, unrehearsed, unfeigned, reassured him as no speech could have. And something in him shifted, straining against a barrier he hadn't realized was there until that moment.

But he still had questions that needed answering. "An' if ye find this 'master,' no matter how highborn 'e is," he asked slowly, "ye'll do *what?*"

"Bring him to justice," Alberich replied instantly, and held up a hand, to forgo any interruptions. "For murder. Of your friends, if no other can be proved, although—"

"There are others?" Skif asked—not in amazement, no, for if the bastard, whoever he was, had been coldhearted enough to burn down a building full of people, he surely had other deaths on his conscience.

Now, for the first time, Alberich's face darkened with an anger Skif was very glad was not aimed at him. "Three of which I know, and perhaps more. And there is that which is worse than murder, which only kills the body. Slaving, for workers, but worse, to make pleasure slaves. Behind it, he is. In small—in the selling of children, here, even from the streets of Haven. *And* in large, *very* large, wherein whole families are reaved from their homes and sold OutKingdom."

Skif heard himself gasp. There had always been rumors of

that in the streets, and Bazie had hinted at it—but even his uncle hadn't stooped that low.

Worse than murder? Well—yes. He closed his eyes a moment, and thought about those rumors a moment. If the rumors were more than that, and the children—orphans or the unwanted—who vanished from Haven's streets ended up in the place where Bazie had intimated they went—

—and if there really were entire villages full of people who were snatched up and sold OutKingdom—

"Worse," he heard himself agreeing.

"And one answer there is, for such evil." Alberich's stone-like expression gave away nothing, but Skif wasn't looking for anything there. He already had his answer; forget anything else, he and this iron-spined man had a common cause.

And somewhere inside him, the barrier strained and broke.

"I'm in," was all he said. "I'm with ye." Alberich's eyes flickered briefly, then he nodded.

"More, we will speak, and at length. Now—"

There were a great many things Alberich could have said. *If you want revenge, you'd better keep your nose clean,* for instance, or *if you get yourself thrown out of here for messing up, neither one of us will get what he wants.* Or *you'll have to work hard at being respectable, because it's going to take someone who looks respectable to trap this bastard.*

He said none of those things. He let another of those penetrating looks analyze Skif and say something else. Something—that had warning in it, but against danger and not mere misbehavior. Something that had acceptance in it as well, and an acknowledgment that Skif had the right to be in this fight. And Skif nodded, quite as if he had heard every bit of it in words.

Alberich smiled. It was the sort of smile that said, *I see we understand one another.* That was all, but that was all that was needed.

A moment later, the sound of boots on the straw-covered

floor marked Herald Teren's return. "Later speech, we will have," Alberich promised, as Teren reached them. "For now— other things."

The other things were not what Skif had expected. Not that he'd really had any inkling of what to expect, but not even his vaguest intuitions measured up to his introduction to the Collegium and his first candlemarks as a Trainee.

"If you're all right, then, follow me," Herald Teren said, and started off, quite as if he assumed Skif would follow and not bolt. Which Skif did, of course; it seemed that he was "in for it" after all, but not in the way he'd thought. His emotions were mixed, to say the least.

On top of it all was excitement and some apprehension still. Just beneath that was a bewildered sort of wonder and the certainty that at any moment they would realize they'd made a mistake—or that fearsome Alberich would call the Guards. He'd lived with what he was for so long. . . .

Beneath *that,* though—was something still of the new image of the world and his place in it that he'd gotten during that encounter with Alberich. That—granted, the world *stank,* and a lot of people in it were rotten, and horrible things happened—but that *he,* little old Skif, petty thief, had a chance that wasn't given to many people, to help make things better. Not right; the job of making everything *right* was too big for one person, for a group of people like the Heralds, even—but *better.*

And under all of *that,* slowly and implacably filling in places he hadn't known were empty, was a feeling he couldn't even put a name to. It was big, that feeling, and it had been the thing that had broken through his barriers back there, when Cymry reaffirmed her bond with him. It was compounded of a lot of things; release, relief, those were certainly in there. But with the release came a sense that he was now irrevocably bound to something—something good. And *accepted* by that "something." A feeling that he belonged, at last, to something he'd been searching for without ever realizing that he'd been looking. And there was an emotion connected with Cymry in there that, if he had to put a name to it, he might have said (with some embarrassment) was love. It was scary, having something that *big* sweep him up in itself. And if he had to think about it, he knew he'd be absolutely paralyzed—

So he didn't think about it. He just let it do whatever it was going to do, turning a blind eye to it. But he couldn't help but feel a little more cheerful, a little more at ease here, with every heartbeat that passed.

And there was plenty to keep him distracted from anything going on inside him, anyway.

Teren led him away from the stable and toward a building that absolutely dwarfed every other structure he had ever seen. And if he was impressed, he hated to think how all those farmboys and fisherfolk Cymry had talked about must have felt when they first saw it.

The building was huge, three-and-a-half stories of gray stone with a four-story double tower at the joining of two of the walls just ahead of them. "This is Herald's Collegium and the Palace," Teren said, waving his hand in an arc that took in everything. "You can't actually see the New Palace part of the structure from here; it's blocked by this wing next to us, which is where all the Kingdom's Heralds have rooms."

"But most uv 'em don't live here, at least, not most of th' time," Skif stated, on a little firmer ground. "Right?"

Teren nodded. "That's right. The only Heralds in *permanent* residence are the teachers at the Collegium and the Lord Marshal's Herald, the Seneschal's Herald, and the Queen's Own Herald. Have you any idea who *they* are?"

Skif shook his head, not particularly caring that he didn't

know. This new feeling, whatever it was, had a very slightly intoxicating effect. "Not a clue," he said. "I figger ye'll tell me in them lessons. Right?"

"Right, we'll leave that to Basic Orientation; it isn't something you need to understand this moment." Teren seemed relieved at his answer. "Now, straight ahead of us is Herald's Collegium, which is attached to the residence wing, both for the convenience of the teachers and—" he cast a jaundiced eye on Skif "—to *try* and keep the Trainees out of mischief."

Skif laughed; it was very clear from Teren's tone and body language that he meant all Trainees, not just Skif. He couldn't help but cast an envious glance at the wing beside them, though; he couldn't help but think that as a Trainee, he'd probably be packed in among all the other Trainees with very little privacy.

"Healer's Collegium and Bardic are also on the grounds, on the other side of Heralds,' " Teren continued, waving his hand at the three-and-a-half story wing ahead of them. "You'll share some of your classes with students from there. Healer Trainees wear pale green, Bardic Trainees wear a rust red rather than a true red. There will also be students who wear a pale blue which is similar to, but darker than, the pages' uniforms. Those are a mixed bag. Some of them are highborn whose parents choose to have them tutored here rather than have private teachers, but most are talented commoners who are going to be Artificers."

"What's an Artificer?" Skif wanted to know.

"People who build things. Bridges, buildings, contrivances that do work like mills, pumps," Teren said absently. "People who dig mines and come up with the things that crush the ore, people who make machines, like clocks, printing presses, looms. It takes a lot of knowing how things work and mathematics, which is why they are here."

"Keep that away from me!" Skif said with a shudder. "Sums! I had just about enough of sums!"

"Well, if you don't come up to a particular standard, you'll be getting more of them, I'm afraid," Teren said, and smiled at Skif's crestfallen face. "Don't worry, you won't be the only one who's less than thrilled about undertaking more lessons in reckoning. You'll need it; some day, *you* may have to figure out how to rig a broken bridge or fix a wall."

They entered in at a door right in the tower that stood at the angle where the Herald's Wing met the Collegium. There was a spiraling staircase paneled in dark wood there, lit by windows at each landing. Skif expected them to go up, but instead, they went down.

"First, Housekeeping and Stores," Teren informed him. "The kitchen is down here, too. Now, besides taking lessons, you'll be assigned chores here in the Collegium. All three Collegia do this with their Trainees. The only thing that the Trainees don't do for themselves is the actual cooking and building repair work."

Skif made a face, but then something occurred to him. "Highborn, too?" he asked.

"Highborn, too," Teren confirmed. "It makes everyone equal—and we never want a Herald in the field to be anything other than self-sufficient. That means knowing how to clean and mend and cook, if need be. That way you don't owe anyone anything—because we don't want you to have anything going on that might be an outside influence on your judgment."

"Huh." By now, they had reached the lowest landing and the half cellar—which wasn't really a cellar as Skif would have recognized one, since it wasn't at all damp, and just a little cooler than the staircase. Teren went straight through the door at the bottom of the staircase, and Skif followed.

They entered a narrow, whitewashed room containing only a desk and a middle-aged woman who didn't look much different from any ordinary craftsman's wife that Skif had ever seen. She had pale-brown hair neatly braided and wrapped around her head, and wore a sober, dark-blue gown with a spotless white apron. "New one, Gaytha," said Teren, as she looked up.

She gave him a different sort of penetrating look than Alberich had; this one looked at everything on the *surface*, and nothing underneath. "You'll be a ten, I think," she said, and stood up, pushing away from her desk. Exiting through a side doorway, she returned a moment later with a pile of neatly folded clothing, all in a silver-gray color, and a lumpy bag. "Here's your uniforms—now let me see your shoes."

When Skif didn't move, she gestured impatiently. "Go ahead, put your foot on the edge of the desk, there's a lad," she said. With a shrug, Skif did as he was told, and she *tsked* at his shoes.

"Well, *those* won't do. Teren, measure him for boots, there's a dear, while I get some temporaries." She whisked back out again while Teren had Skif pull off his shoes, made tracings of his feet, then measured each leg at ankle, calf and knee, noting the measurements in the middle of the tracing of left or right. By the time he was finished, the Housekeeper was back with a pair of boots and a pair of soft shoes. Both had laces and straps to turn an approximate fit into a slightly better one.

"These will do until I get boots made that are fitted to you," she said briskly. "Now, my lad, I want you to know that there are very strict rules about washing around here." This time the look she gave him was the daggerlike glare of a woman who has seen too many pairs of "washed hands and arms" that were dirty down to the wristbone. "A full bath every night, and a *thorough* washup before meals—or before you *help* with the meal, if you're a server or a Cook's helper. If you don't measure up, it's back to the bathing room until you do, even if all that's left to eat when you're done is dry crusts and water. Do you understand?"

"Yes'm," Skif replied. He wasn't going to point out to this

woman that a dirty thief is very soon a thief in the gaol. That was just something she didn't need to know.

"Good." She took him at his word—for now. He had no doubt he'd be inspected at every meal until they figured out he knew what "clean" meant. "Now, I don't suppose you have *any* experience at household chores—"

"Laundry an' mendin' is what I'd druther do; dishes, floor washin', an' scrubbin' is what I can do, but druther have laundry an' mendin'," he said immediately. "Can boil an egg, an' cut bread'n'butter, but nought else worth eatin'."

"Laundry and mending?" The Housekeeper's eyebrows rose. "Well, if that's what you're good at—we have more boys here than girls, so we tend not to have as many hands as I'd like that are actually *good* at those chores."

Her expression said quite clearly that she would very much like to know how it was that he was apt at those tasks. But she didn't ask, and Skif was hardly likely to tell her.

"This boy is Skif, Chosen by Cymry," Teren said, as Gaytha got out a big piece of paper divided up into large squares, each square with several names in it.

"I've got you down for laundry and mending for the next five days," Gaytha said. "Teren will schedule that around your classes and meals. We'll see how you do."

"Off we go, then." Teren said, and loaded Skif's arms with his new possessions.

Back up the steps they went, pausing just long enough at the first floor for Teren to open the door and Skif to look through it. "This is where the classrooms are," Teren told him, and he took a quick glance down the long hall lined with doors. "We're on Midsummer holiday right now, so all but two of the Trainees are gone on visits home. It's just as well; with this heat, no one would be able to study."

"Do what they's does in th' City," Skif advised, voice muffled behind the pile of clothing. "*They* ain't gettin' no holidays.

Work from dawn till it gets too hot, then go back to't when it's cooled off a bit."

"We're ahead of you there," Teren told him. "It's already arranged. Follow me up to the second floor."

Teren went on ahead, and Skif found him holding open the door on the next landing. He stepped into another corridor, this one lined with still more doors. But it ended in a wall, and seemed less than half the length of the one on the first floor. It was a bit difficult to tell, because the light here was very dim. There were openings above each door that presumably let the light from the room beyond pass through, and that was it for illumination.

"You *won't* be living on this side of the common room," Teren told him. "This is the girls' side. The common room where you take all meals is between the boys' and girls' side. Come along, and you'll see."

He led the way down the corridor, opened a door, and Skif preceded him into the common room. There were windows and fireplaces on both sides, and the place was full of long tables and benches, rather like an inn. Skif made a quick reckoning, and guessed it could hold seventy-five people at a time—a hundred, if they squeezed in together. "How many of them Trainees you got?" he asked, as Teren held the door in the opposite wall open for him.

"Forty-one. Twenty-six boys, fifteen girls." Teren turned to catch his grimace. "That does make for some stiff competition among the ladies—or are you not interested in girls yet?"

"Never thought 'bout it," he said truthfully. "Where I come from—"

Where I come from, you don' get no girl 'less you pays for 'er, an' I got better things t'spend m' glim on, he thought. But no point in shocking this man. He'd probably go white at the thought.

"And this is your room," Teren said, interrupting his

thoughts, opening one of the doors. Eager now to put down his burdens, Skif hurried through the door.

He was very pleasantly surprised. There was a good bed, a desk and chair, a bookcase, and a wardrobe. It had its own little fireplace—no hoping to get warmth from the back of someone else's chimney!—and a window that stood open to whatever breeze might come in. All of it, from the wooden floor to the furniture to the walls, was clean and polished and in good condition, though obviously much-used. When Skif set his clothing down on the bed, he was startled to realize that it was a *real* mattress, properly made and stuffed with wool and goose down, not the canvas-covered straw he'd taken as a matter of course.

He had never, not once, slept on a real mattress. He'd only seen such things in the homes of the wealthy that he'd robbed.

"Grab a uniform and I'll take you to the bathing room," Teren told him, before he could do more than marvel. "You need to get cleaned up and I'll take you down to the kitchen for something to eat. Then I'll take you to Dean Elcarth, and he can determine what classes you'll need to take."

It didn't seem that Herald Teren had any intention of leaving Skif alone.

With a stifled sigh, Skif picked out smallclothes, a shirt, tunic, trews, and stockings, debated between the boots and the shoes and finally decided on the latter as probably being more comfortable, With an eye long used to assessing fabric, he decided that the trews and tunic must be a linen canvas, the shirt was of a finer linen, the boots of a heavier canvas with leather soles and wooden heels. Interesting that the temporary boots were of canvas rather than leather—they'd be quicker to make up, and a lot more forgiving to feet that weren't used to boots. Or even shoes—some of the farmboys who came in to the markets went barefoot even in the city, right up until the snow fell.

Trailing behind the Herald, wondering if the man considered himself to be guide or guard, Skif left his room.

The bathing room was a shock. Copper boilers to heat the water, one with a fire under it already, pumps to fill them, pipes carrying cold and hot water to enormous tubs and commodious basins, boxes of soft, sage-scented soap and piles of towels *everywhere*—

Skif forgot Teren's presence entirely. No matter how hot it was, he reveled in a bath like no one he knew had ever enjoyed. He soaked and soaked until the aches of that horrible ride with Cymry were considerably eased and he felt cleaner than he ever had in his whole life.

In fact, it was only after he'd dried off (using a towel softer than any blanket he'd ever owned) and was half dressed in the new clothing that Teren spoke, waking him to the Herald's presence.

"Mop up your drips with the towel you used, and wipe out the tub, then drop the towel down that chute over there. Send your old clothing after it." Teren nodded toward a square opening in the wall between two basins, and Skif finished dressing, then obeyed him. How long had he been there? Had he left while Skif was filling the tub? It bothered him that he couldn't remember.

I always know where people are. Am I losing my edge?

Teren waited for him by the door, but held out a hand to stop him before he went back through it. "Hold still a moment, would you?" he asked, and put a single finger under Skif's chin, turning his face back into the light from the windows. "I thought most of that was dirt," he said contritely. "I beg your pardon, Skif. Before I take you to Elcarth, I'd like you to see a Healer for that nose and eye."

Another moment of mixed reaction—a little resentment that the man would think he was so slovenly that he'd have *that* much dirt on his face, and small wonder that the Housekeeper had been so abrupt! But that was mingled with more astonishment. A *Healer?* For a *broken nose?*

But within moments, he found himself sitting across from a green-clad Healer, a fairly nondescript fellow, who examined him briskly, said "This will only hurt for a moment," and grabbed his nose and pulled.

It certainly *did* hurt, quite as much as when he'd hit Cymry's neck in the first place. It hurt badly enough he couldn't even gasp. But the Healer had spoken the truth; it only hurt for a moment, and in the very next moment, it not only stopped hurting, *it stopped hurting.*

He opened his eyes—and both of them opened properly now—and stared into the Healer's grin. "You'll still look like a masked ferret," the fellow said cheerfully, "but you should be fine now."

"How *did* you do that anyway?" Teren asked, as they made their way back to Herald's Collegium and Skif's interview with Herald Elcarth.

"Cymry jumped a wagon, an' I hit 'er neck with my face," he replied ruefully, and found himself describing the entire wild ride in some detail as they walked.

"She made you think you'd *stolen* her?" Teren said at last, smothering laughter. "Forgive me, but—"

"Oh, it's pretty funny—now," Skif admitted. "An' I s'ppose it'll be funnier in a moon, or a season, or a year. Last night, I c'n tell you, it weren't funny at all."

"I can well imagine—" By this time, they were back down the stairs into the half basement in the Collegium again. "It'll be funnier still when you've got yourself on the outside of some lunch. Here's the kitchen—" Teren opened a door identical to the one that led to the Housekeeper's room, but this one opened onto an enormous kitchen, silent and empty. "I haven't had anything since breakfast either." He gave Skif a conspiratorial wink. "Let's raid the pantry."

15

"USUALLY, our cook, Mero, is down in the kitchen," Teren told him as they cleaned up what little mess they'd made. "Now listen, I am not telling you this because I think you're going to filch food, I'm telling you this because all boys your age are always hungry, and after the last couple of centuries running the Collegium, we've figured that out. When Mero is here, you can ask him for whatever you want to eat and if he isn't knee-deep in chaos, he'll be delighted to get it for you. When he's *not* here—and I know very well from my own experience how badly you can need a midnight snack—only take food from the pantry we just used. The reason for that is that Mero plans his meals very carefully—he has to, with so many inexpert hands working with him—and if you take something he needs, it'll make difficulties for him."

Skif thought fleetingly of the number of times he'd taken food from Lord Orthallen's pantry—and hoped it hadn't made difficulties for that cook.

Odd. He wouldn't have spared a thought for that yesterday.

"Now. Healed, fed, and ready for Dean Elcarth?" Teren didn't wait for an answer, but strode off, heading for the stairs.

This time they walked through the corridor that held all the classrooms; again, it was lit by means of windows over each classroom door. From the spacing, the rooms were probably twice the size of the one they'd given Skif.

Why so many and so much room?

Maybe in case it was needed. Just because they only had forty-six Trainees now didn't mean they couldn't have more at some other time. And Teren had said that the classes were shared with Bardic and Healer Trainees—and those others. That would be interesting.

They passed through the double doors that marked the boundary between Collegium and Herald's Wing, and Teren turned immediately to a door on the left. "This is where I'll leave you for now. I will see you tomorrow, and we'll start Basic Orientation. And a couple of the other introductory classes. That way, when everyone gets back and Collegium classes start again, you'll be able to join right up."

He tapped on the door; a muffled sound answered, and Teren opened it, and putting a hand just between Skif's shoulder blades, gently propelled Skif inside before he got a chance to hesitate.

The door shut behind him.

Skif found himself in a cluttered room, a very small room, but one that, from the open door to the side, must be part of a larger suite. There were four things in this room, besides Dean Elcarth; books, papers, chairs, and a desk. There were bookshelves built into the wall that were crammed full of books; books and papers were piled on every available surface. Elcarth motioned to Skif to come in and take the only chair that wasn't holding more books, one with a deep seat and leather padding that was cracked and crazed with age.

He sat in it gingerly, since it didn't look either sturdy or comfortable. He should have known better; nothing bad that he'd assumed about the Heralds ever turned out to be right. The chair proved to be both sturdy and comfortable, and it fit him as if it had been intended for him.

Herald Elcarth folded his hands under his chin, and regarded Skif with a mild gaze. "You," he said at last, "are a puzzle. I must say that Myste and I have searched through every Chronicle of the Collegium, and I cannot find a single instance of a thief being Chosen. We've had several attempted suicides, three murderers—which, I will grant, were all self-defense, and one of them was Lavan Firestorm, but nevertheless, they were murderers. We've had a carnival trickster, a horse sharper, and a girl who pretended to be a witch, told fortunes which turned out to be correct ForeSight, but also took money for curses she never performed, relying instead on the fact that she'd be long gone before anyone noticed that nothing bad had happened to the person she cursed. We've had a *former* assassin. We've even had a spy. But we've never had a thief."

Skif tried to read his expression, and didn't get any clues from it. Elcarth merely seemed interested.

"So, I have to ask myself, Skif. Why you? What is it about you that is so different that a Companion would Choose you?" He tilted his head to the side, looking even more birdlike. "Alberich, by the way, has told me nothing of why he recognized you. In fact, he didn't say much at all about you, except that he knew who you were, but until Kantor told him, he had not known you were specifically a thief."

"What d'ye wanta know?" Skif asked. The best way to limit the damage might be to get Elcarth to ask questions, so that he could carefully tailor his answers.

"More to the point, what do *you* want to tell me?" Elcarth countered. "Usually—not always, but usually—the Chosen sitting where you are start pouring out their life stories to me. Are you going to be any different?"

"I ain't the kind t'pour out m'life story to anybody," Skif replied, trying not to sound sullen, wondering just how much he was going to have to say to satisfy the Dean's curiosity. "I dunno. I ain't never *hurt* nobody. I stick t'the liftin' lay an' roof work. . . ."

He hadn't given a second thought to whether Elcarth would understand the cant, but Elcarth nodded. "Picking pockets and house theft. Which explains why you were in *that* park in broad daylight. Taking advantage of the fact that no one was about in the heat, hmm?"

Skif blinked. How had—

"Your trail out of the city was shatteringly obvious," Elcarth pointed out. "Not to mention hazardous. From the moment Cymry left the park with you, there were witnesses, many of them members of the City Guard. But that only tells me what you do, not what you are—and it's what you *are* that is what I need to know." At Skif's silence, he prodded a little more. "Your parents?"

"Dead," he answered shortly. But try as he might, he couldn't stand firm in the face of Elcarth's gentle, but ruthless and relentless questioning. Before very long, Elcarth knew something of his Uncle Londer, of Beel, and of Bazie and Bazie's collection of "boys"—and he knew what had happened to all of them. Especially Bazie. And he knew about the fire.

He managed to keep most of the details to himself, though; at least he *thought* he did. The last thing he wanted was to start unloading his rage on Elcarth. It was a handle to Skif's character that Skif didn't want the Dean to have.

But he didn't manage to keep back as much as he would have liked, though, and just talking about it made his chest go tight, his back tense, and his stomach churn with unspoken emotion. Part of him wanted to tell this gentle man everything—but that was the "new" part of him. The old part did not want him to be talking at all, and was going mad trying to keep him from opening his mouth any more than he had.

Fortunately at that point, Elcarth changed the subject entirely, quizzing him on reading, figuring, writing, and other subjects. That was what he had expected, although he didn't care for it, and his stomach soon settled again. It took longer for the tension to leave his back and chest, but that was all right. The tension reminded him that he needed to be careful.

Outside the office, the day moved on, and the heat wave hadn't broken. Thick as these stone walls were, the heat still got into Elcarth's office and both of them were fanning themselves with stray papers before the interview was over. "I think I can place you, now," Elcarth said, by late afternoon. "But I'm going to be putting you in one class you probably aren't going to appreciate."

"Figuring!" Skif groaned.

"Actually—no. Not immediately. I'm going to ask Gaytha to teach you how to speak properly." Elcarth sat back and waited for Skif's reaction.

If he'd expected Skif to show resentment, he got a surprise himself. "Huh. I s'pose I can see that—though you shoulda 'eard—*heard*—me afore—*before*—Bazie got hold of me." Actually he wasn't at all displeased. You didn't get to be a *good* thief by being unobservant, and Skif had known very well that his speech patterns would mark him out in any crowd as coming from the "bad part of town" near Exile's Gate. If he was going to consort with the highborn and be taken seriously, he'd better stop dropping his "h's".

Among other things.

And he might as well start being careful about how he spoke now. "Is that all you want with me?" he asked, watching every syllable, adding as an afterthought, "sir."

"For now." Elcarth studied him, and Skif forced himself not to squirm uncomfortably under that unwavering gaze. "I hope eventually you'll feel freer to talk to me, Skif." He looked for a moment as if he was about to say more, then changed his mind. "I believe you have another interview before you—"

"I—" Skif began, but a tap on the door interrupted him.

"Come!" called Elcarth, and the door was opened by Herald Alberich. Who was, of course, the very last person that Skif wanted to see at this moment, when Elcarth had him feeling so unbalanced and unsettled.

Alberich looked at him for a moment, but not with the gaze of a hawk with prey in sight, but with a more measuring, even stare. "Come, I have, to take our new one off, Elcarth," he said simply. "Companion's Field, I think. Cooler it will be there."

"Well, I'm satisfied with him, so he's all yours," Elcarth replied, making Skif wince a little. But Alberich smiled, ever so slightly.

"Your Cymry is anxious to see the work of the Healer," he said to Skif. "And it is that I have evaluation of my own to make. Please—come."

He reached out and beckoned with one hand, and Skif got reluctantly to his feet.

Unlike Teren, Alberich did not seem inclined to *lead* Skif anywhere. Instead, he paced gravely beside Skif, hands clasped behind his back, indicating direction with a jerk of his chin. They left the Herald's Wing by the same door through which they'd first entered the Collegium; Skif recognized the spot immediately. There were plenty of trees here, and Skif was glad of the shade. And glad of the light color of the Trainee uniform. He hated to think what it would have been like if the outfit had been black.

"To the riverbank, I think," Alberich said, with one of those chin jerks. "You are puzzled by my accent."

"Well—aye," Skif admitted. "Never heard naught like it."

"Nor will you. It is from Karse that I am. A Captain I was, in the service of Vkandis Sunlord." With a glance at Skif's startled face, Alberich then turned his face up toward the cloudless sky. "We have something in common, I think. Or *will* have. The thief and the traitor—neither to be trusted. *Outside* the Heraldic Circle, that is."

Skif swallowed hard. A Karsite. A Karsite *officer*. From the army of Valdemar's most implacable enemy.

"But—why—"

"That is what I—*we,* for Kantor suggested this—wish to be telling you," Alberich said gravely as they approached the riverbank. His face cleared, then, as they rounded a section of topiary bushes and the river appeared, dazzling in the sun. "Ah, there they are!"

Two Companions waited for them, and Skif knew Cymry from the other immediately, though *how,* he couldn't have said. He rushed to greet her, and as he touched her, he felt enveloped in that same wonderful feeling that had been creeping in all afternoon, past doubts, past fears, past every obstacle. He pulled her head down to his chest and ran his hands along her cheeks, while she breathed into his tunic and made little contented sounds. He could have stayed that way for the rest of the afternoon. . . .

But Alberich cleared his throat politely after a time, and Skif pulled away from her with great reluctance. "A grotto there is, in the riverbank. Cool as a cellar in this heat, and our Companions will enjoy it as well."

Cymry seemed to know exactly where they were going, so Skif let her lead him. Skif kept one hand on her neck and followed along. She led him down a steeply-sloped, grassy bank to the edge of the river itself, and there, partly out of sight from the lawn above, was a kind of ornamental cave carved into the bank, just as Alberich had said. It was just about tall enough to stand up inside, and held three curved, stone benches at the back. Nicely paved, ceilinged, and walled with flagstone, it was wonderfully cool in there, and the two Companions took up positions just inside, switching their tails idly, as Alberich and Skif took seats on built-in benches at the back.

This wasn't so bad. Without the Herald looming over him, without actually having to look him in the eyes, Skif felt more comfortable. And in the dim coolness, the Herald seemed a bit more relaxed. Alberich cleared his throat again, as soon as they settled. "So. It is you who have been telling tales for the most of today. Let someone else, for a candlemark."

"Suits," Skif said shortly, and leaned back into the curved stone bench.

"Karse," Alberich began, meditatively. "I left my land, and to an extent, my God. They call me traitor there. Think you—it is odd, that I love them both, still?"

"I dunno," Skif replied honestly. "Dunno much 'bout Gods, an'—truth t'tell, I never thought overmuch 'bout anythin' like a whole *country*. Mostly didn' think 'bout much past m'own streets."

Alberich nodded a little, his gaze fixed on the river flowing outside the grotto. "No reason there was, why you should."

Skif shrugged. " Ol' Bazie, he didn' think much of Karse, an' I reckon he thought pretty well of Valdemar, when it comes down t'cases. Least—" Skif thought hard for a moment, back to those memories that he hadn't wanted to think about at all for a very long time now. "Huh. When he lost 'is legs, 'twasn't Karse as saw 'im Healed, nor the Tedrels. 'Twas Valdemar. An' he 'ad some good things t'say 'bout Heralds."

"Tell me," Alberich urged mildly, and Skif did. It was surprising, when he came to think about it, how much good Bazie had said about Valdemar and its Heralds, especially considering that he'd fought against both.

Alberich sighed. "I love my land and my God," he said, when Skif was through. "But—both have been—are *being*—ill served. And that is neither the fault of the land, nor the God."

He told his story concisely, using as few words as possible, but Skif got a vivid impression of what the younger Alberich must have been like. And when he described being trapped in a building that was deliberately set afire to execute him, Skif found himself transposing that horror to what Bazie and the boys must have felt.

But there had been no Companion leaping through the flames to save them. There had been no happy ending for Bazie.

"It was the King's Own and another Herald who came at Kantor's call," Alberich said meditatively. "Which was, for my sake, a good thing. Few would question Talamir's word, fewer dared to do so aloud. So I was Healed, and I learned—yes," he said, after he glanced at Skif. "Oh, smile you may, that into Grays I went, and back to schooling at that age! A sight, I surely was!" He shook his head.

"Why?" Skif asked. "Why didn' you just tell 'em t' make you a Herald straight off?"

"And knowing nothing of Heralds or Valdemar? Stubborn I am often, stupid, never. Much I had to unlearn. More did others have to learn of me. Selenay, after Talamir, was my friend and advocate—after them, others. More than enough work there was here, to keep me at the Collegium, replacing the aged Weaponsmaster. More than enough reason to stay, that others have me beneath their eye, and so feel control over me in their hands." He smiled sardonically. "Did they know what I learn for the Queen *here,* it is that they would send me out to the farthest Border ere I could take breath thrice."

Since Skif had seen him at work, he snickered. Alberich bestowed a surprisingly mild glance on him.

"Now, your turn, it is, for answering questions," he said, and Skif steeled himself. "But first of all, because I would know—why choose to be a thief?"

An odd question, and as unexpected as one of Alberich's rare smiles. Skif shrugged. " 'Twas that—or slave for m'nuncle Londer. Wasn't much else goin'—an' Bazie was all right."

His heart contracted at that. *All right!* What a niggardly thing to say about a man who had been friend, teacher, and in no small part, savior! Yet—if he said more, he put his heart within reach of this Herald, this Alberich, who had already said in so many words that he would use anything to safeguard Valdemar, the Queen, and the Heralds. . . .

And that's bad, how? whispered that new side of him.

Shut up! replied the old.

Skif became aware that a moment of silence had lengthened into something that Alberich might use to put a question. He filled it, quickly. "Bazie was pretty good t'us, actually." He paused. "You gonna Truth Spell me again?"

Alberich shook his head. "What I did was done in need and haste. Much there is I would learn of you, but most of it will wait. And what I would know, I think you will tell freely for the sake of your friends."

So now, for a second time, Alberich asked questions about Jass and Jass' master, this time helping Skif to pry out the least and littlest morsel of information in his memory. This time, though, the questions came thoughtfully, as slow as the heat-heavy air drifting above the riverbank and cloaking it in shimmer, each question considered and answered with the same care. Alberich was right about this much. In this case, Alberich's goals and Skif's were one, and the two voices inside him were at peace with one another.

The light had turned golden as they spoke, and the heat shimmer faded. There had been a long time since the last question, and Skif slowly became aware that lunch was wearing thin. As his stomach growled, Alberich glanced over at him again, with a half-smile.

"You know your way about, I think," the Weaponsmaster said. "Tomorrow we will meet, and you will begin your training with me, and with others."

Then, with no other word of farewell, Alberich rose and stalked out, his Companion falling in at his side like a well-trained drill partner.

"You've been mighty quiet," Skif said to Cymry in the silence.

:You were doing perfectly well without me,: she replied, with a saucy switch of her tail. *:Well. Here you are, left perfectly alone on the Palace grounds. You can go and do whatever you want; no keeper, no guardian. You could go climb to the Palace roof if you wanted to, bearing in mind the Queen's Guard might catch you. Or hasn't that occurred to you yet?:*

It hadn't, and the revelation hit him like a bucket of cold water.

"You *sure*?" he gasped.

:As sure as I'm standing here.: She switched her tail again, but this time with impatience. *:They trust you. Isn't it time you started to trust them? Just start, that's all.:*

An odd, heavy feeling came into his throat. Once again, the sense that something portentous had happened, something that he didn't understand, came over him.

It was more than uncomfortable, it was unsettling, in the sense of feeling the world he knew suddenly shift into something he no longer recognized.

"I'm hungry," he announced, hastily shunting it all aside. "An' I reckon I saw some ham an' bacon in that pantry."

Cymry whickered; it sounded like a chuckle. *:I reckon you saw more than that. Go on, come back and meet me here once you've stuffed yourself.:*

Skif got up, and now that he was moving again, he felt every single bruise and strain from yesterday's ride.

Was it only yesterday? It felt like a lifetime ago. . . .

As he got up, he actually staggered a little with stiffness. Cymry moved quickly to give him a shoulder to catch himself on, and after he'd steadied himself, he gave her a self-conscious little kiss on her forehead.

:Go on,: she said playfully, giving him a shove with her nose. *:Just don't eat until you're sick.:*

You didn't become a successful thief without learning the layout of a place on the first time through it. Nevertheless, Skif couldn't help but feeling a little self-conscious as he made his way across the grass, overshadowed by the silent building. And he couldn't help looking for those who might be looking for *him*. But there were no watchers; Cymry had been right. And when he left the heat of the outdoors for the cool of the great kitchen, he discovered it just as deserted as it had been when Teren brought him.

He opened the pantry doors and stood amid the plenitude, gazing at the laden shelves and full of indecision. Bacon or ham? White bread, or brown? It was too hot to eat anything cooked-up fresh, besides being far too much trouble, but there was an abundance of good things that could be eaten cold. His mouth watered at the sight of a row of ceramic jars labeled "Pikld Beets," but the discovery of a keg of large sour cucumber pickles made him change his mind about the beets. There were so many things here that he had only tasted once or twice, and so many more he'd seen, but never tasted—

But although Cymry had warned him playfully about eating himself sick, he was mindful of that very consideration. Too many times he'd seen people in his own streets do just that, when encountering unexpected abundance. After all, none of this was going to disappear tomorrow, or even later tonight (unless he ate it) and he wasn't going to have his access to it removed, either.

When this Cook gets back t'work— Oh, there was a thought! If there was so much here ready for snacking, what wonderful things must the Cook prepare every day? Visions of the kinds of things he'd seen in the best inns passed through his mind— minced-meat pasties, stews with thick, rich gravy, egg pie and oh, the sweets. . . .

Eventually he made his selections, and put a plate together. He ate neatly and with great enjoyment, savoring every bite, finishing with a tart apple and a piece of sharp cheese. Then, as he had when he had eaten earlier with Teren, he cleaned up after himself and put everything away.

A glance through the windows above the great sink as he was washing up showed him that the sky had gone to red as the sun set. There would be plenty of time to spend with Cymry, and at that moment, there was nothing in the world that he would rather have been doing.

Back up and out he went, under a sky filled with red-edged, purple clouds, passing trees just beginning to whisper in an evening breeze, through the quietude that seemed so strange to him after the constant noise of the city proper. Cymry waited for him where he had last seen her, watching the sun set and turn the river to a flat ribbon of fire.

He put an arm over her shoulder, and they watched it together. How many times had he watched the sun rise or set above the roofs of the city? Too many to count, certainly, but he'd never had as much time as he would have liked to enjoy the sight, even when it was a truly glorious one like tonight.

Come to that, there had never been anyone with him who understood that it was a glorious sight until tonight. Bazie would have—but Bazie had spent most of his time in the cellar room, and there was never the time or leisure for his boys to bring him up for a sunset.

They stood together until the last vestige of rose faded from the clouds, and only then did they realize that they were not alone.

Behind them were another Herald and Companion, who must have come up behind them so quietly that not even Skif's instincts were alerted—and that took some skill.

Skif didn't even know they were there until Cymry reacted, with a sudden glance over her shoulder, a start and a little jump.

Then he looked behind, and saw the strangers.

He turned quickly, sure that they were somewhere they shouldn't have been, but the tall, elderly man standing with one arm around his Companion's shoulders (even as Skif had stood with Cymry) smiled and forestalled any apology.

"I beg your pardon, youngling, for startling you," the man said, his voice surprisingly deep for one as thin as he was. "We often come here to admire the sunset, and didn't see any reason to disturb your enjoyment. Rolan tells me that you are Skif and Cymry."

The man's uniform was a touch above the ones that Herald Teren and Dean Elcarth had worn; there was a lot of silver embroidery on the white deerskin tunic, and Skif would have been willing to bet anything he had that the trews and shirt this Herald wore were silk.

The Companion was something special as well; he was just a little glossier, just a little taller, and had just a touch more of an indefinable dignity than any of the others Skif had seen thus far did.

:*This is the Queen's Own Herald Talamir and Rolan, the Grove-Born,*: Cymry said hastily in his mind, in a tone that told Skif (even though he had no idea what the titles meant) that these two were somehow very, very special, even by the standards of Heralds.

"Yessir, Herald Talamir," Skif said, with an awkward bob of his head. It was a very odd thing. He had seen any number of highborn, and never felt any reason to respect them. He *did* respect the Heralds he'd met so far—but this man, without doing more than simply stand there, somehow *commanded* respect. But at the same time, there was an aura of what Beel might have called *mortality* and what others might have called *fey* that hung about him.

The Herald's smile widened. "And I see that you and Cymry Mindspeak. That is excellent, especially in so early a bond." Talamir stepped forward and extended his hand to Skif, and when Skif tentatively offered his own, took it, and shook it firmly but gently. "Welcome, Skif," was all he said, but the words were a true greeting, and not a hollow courtesy.

"Thankee, sir," Skif replied, feeling an unaccountable shyness, a shyness that evidently was shared by Cymry, who kept glancing at the other Companion with mingled awe and admiration. Talamir seemed to expect something more from him, and he groped for something to say. "This's—all kinda new t'me."

"So I'm told." Mild amusement, no more. No sign that Talamir had been told anything of Skif's antecedents. "Well, if you feel overwhelmed, remember that when I first arrived here, I was straight out of a horse-trading family, I'd never spent a night in my life under anything but canvas, and the largest city I ever saw was a quarter of the size of Haven. My first night in my room was unbearable; I thought I was going to smother, and I kept feeling the walls pressing in on me. Eventually, I took my blankets outside and slept on the lawn. Very few of us are ready for this when we arrive here, and—" he chuckled softly, the merest ghost of a laugh, "—sometimes *here* is even less ready for us. But we adapt, the Trainee to the Collegium and the Collegium to the Trainee. Even if it means pitching a tent in the garden for a Trainee to live in for the first six months."

Skif gaped, totally unable to imagine this elegant gentleman living in a tent, but quickly shut his mouth. "Yessir," he replied, his usually quick wits failing him.

He had no idea how to end this conversation, but the Herald solved his dilemma for him. "Have a good evening, youngling," Talamir said, and he and his Companion turned and drifted off through the dusk like a pair of spirits, making no sound whatsoever as they moved over the grass. The moon, three-quarters now, had just begun to rise, and its light silvered them with an eldritch glow.

"Is't just me," Skif asked, when he was pretty sure they were out of earshot, "Or are they *spooky?*"

:*They're spooky,*: Cymry affirmed, with an all-over shiver of her coat. :*Rolan is Talamir's second Companion. Taver was killed in the Tedrel Wars, when Talamir and Jadus were trying to rescue the King. They say that everyone thought Talamir was going to follow Taver and King Sendar until Rolan came and pulled him back. Ever since then, Talamir's been— otherworldly. Half his heart and soul are here, and half's in the Havens, they say.:*

Skif shook his head. All this was too deep for him.

:Still!: Cymry continued, shaking off her mood. *:His mind is all here, and Talamir's mind is better than four of anyone else's! Would you like to see Companion's Field?:*

"I thought this was Companion's Field," Skif replied confusedly.

She made a chuckling sound. *:This is only the smallest corner of it. Most of it is across the river. Think you can get on my back without a boost?:*

"Please. I can pull m'self up a gutter on t'roof without usin' legs," he retorted. "I oughta be able t' get on your back!"

She stood rock still for him, and after a moment of awkwardness, he managed to clamber onto her bare back. Stepping out into the twilight at a brisk pace, she took him across the river on a little stone bridge, and they spent a candlemark or two exploring Companion's Field.

Finally the long day caught up with him, and Skif found himself yawning and nodding, catching himself before he actually dozed off and fell off Cymry's back. Cymry brought him right back to the place where they'd met, and from there, he stumbled up to his room.

Someone had come along and lit the lanterns set up along the walls, so at least he wasn't stumbling because he couldn't see. When he got to the door of his room, he discovered that someone had also slipped a card into a holder there that had his name on it.

A sound in the corridor made him turn; his eyes met the brilliant blue ones of an older boy—hair soaking wet and wrapped in a light sleeping robe, on his way out of the bathing room. The other boy smiled tentatively.

"Hullo!" he greeted Skif. "I'm Kris; you must be the new one, Skif. It's me and Jeri here over Midsummer."

"Uh—hullo," He eyed Kris carefully; definitely highborn, with that accent and those manners. But not one with his nose in the air. "Jeri a girl or a boy?"

"Girl. She'll be your year-mate; got Chosen six moons ago. Oh, I made sure I left enough hot water for a good bath."

"Thanks." That decided him. Maybe he'd already had one bath today, but he was still stiff and sore, and another wouldn't hurt.

Kris was still looking at him quizzically. "I hope you don't mind my asking—but how did you get that black eye? It's a glory! If you haven't seen it, it's gone all green and purple around the edges, and black as black at your nose."

"Smacked it inta Cymry's neck," Skif admitted ruefully. "Ain't never jumped on a horse afore."

Kris winced in sympathy. "Ouch. Better go soak. Good night!"

"Night," Skif replied, and got a robe of his own to take the boy's advice.

When he got back to his room and started putting his new belongings away to clear his bed so he could sleep, he found one last surprise.

On the desk were all of his things. Every possible object he owned *except* the most ragged of his clothing from both his room next to Jass', and the Priory. Including his purse, with every groat still in it.

Startled, he tried to *think* at his Companion. *:Cymry!:* he "called" her, hoping she'd answer.

:What do you need?: she asked sleepily, and he explained what he'd found.

:Who did that? And how come?: he finished. It worried him. . . .

:Oh. That would be Alberich's doing, I expect,: she replied. *:Usually they go send someone to tell families that the Cho-*

sen's arrived safely, and to get their belongings, if they didn't bring anything with them. Don't you want your things?:

Well, of course he wanted his things. *:I just—:*

The fact was, he worried. Who went there. What they'd said. And how they'd known where he came from. . . .

:Kantor says it was all Alberich's doing, at least getting your things from your room.: Well, that was one worry off his mind. Alberich would have gone as the sell-sword, and intimidated his way in. Good enough. *:He sent off the usual Guardsman to the Priory. They'll have told the Priory you were Chosen, and the Guardsman would have brought someone hired to take your place, so the Priory won't go shorthanded. Kantor says Alberich didn't tell your old landlord anything. Is that all right?:*

Since it was exactly what he would have wanted had he been asked, he could only agree. *:Aye. That's fine, I reckon.:* In fact, he couldn't think of anything else he could possibly want.

:Get some sleep,: she told him. *:It'll be a long day tomorrow.:*

A longer one than *today?* With a sigh, he climbed into bed, feeling very strange to be in such a bed, and even stranger not hearing the usual noises of the city beyond his walls.

But not so strange that he was awake for much longer than it took to find a comfortable position and think about closing the curtains he'd left open to let in every bit of breeze. About the time he decided it didn't matter, he was asleep.

A SCANT week later, Skif was just about ready to face all the returning Trainees. He knew what the Heralds of Valdemar were about now—at least, he knew where they'd come from and what they did. And he was starting to get his mind wrapped around why they did it. If he didn't understand it, well, there were a great many things in the world that he didn't understand, and that didn't keep him from going on with his life.

Something had happened to him over the course of that week, and he didn't understand any of it. The things he had always thought were the only truths in the world weren't, not here anyway. He was going to have to watch these Heralds carefully. They might be hiding something behind all this ac-ceptance and welcome.

But since a lot of what was going on with him had to do with feelings, he came to the unsatisfactory and vague conclu-sion that maybe it wasn't going to be possible to *understand* it. He was caught up like a leaf in the wind, and the leaf didn't have a lot of choice in where the wind took it. If it hadn't been that Cymry was a big part of that wind—

Well, she was, and despite everything he'd learned until this moment, he found himself thinking and feeling things that would have been completely unlike the boy he'd been a fortnight ago. *Soft,* was what he would have called what he was becoming now, but what he was now knew that there was nothing *soft* about where he was tending. If anything, it was hard . . . as in *difficult.*

And *difficult* were the things he was learning, and the things he was going to learn, though truth to tell, it was no more work than he was used to setting himself. Physical exertion? The weapons' work he was doing, the riding, none of it was as hard as roof walking. Book learning? Ha! It was mostly reading and remembering, not like having to figure out a new lock. Even the figuring—the *mathematics,* they called it—wasn't that bad. Since he could already do his sums, this new stuff was a matter of logic, a lot like figuring out a lock. The real difference was that he was obeying someone else's schedule and someone else's orders.

Yet he'd run to Bazie's schedule and Bazie's orders, and thought no worse of it, nor of himself.

For every objection his old self came up with, the new one—or Cymry—had a counter. And if there was one thing he was absolutely certain of, it was that he would not, could not do without Cymry. She didn't so much fill an empty place in him as fill up every crack and crevice that life had ever put in his heart, and make it all whole again. To have Cymry meant he would have to become a Herald. So be it. It was worth it a thousand times over.

And once again, just as when he'd been with Bazie, he was *happy.*

He hadn't known what happiness was until Bazie took him in. Moments of pleasure, yes, and times of less misery than others, but never happiness. He'd learned that with Bazie, and since the fire, he hadn't had so much as a moment of real, unshadowed happiness.

Now it was back. Not all the time, and there were still times when he thought about the fire and raged or wept or both. He wasn't going to turn his back on these people, not until he figured out what their angle was. But for the most part it was back, like a gift, something he'd never thought to have back again.

After that, he knew he couldn't leave. Out there, without Cymry, he'd go back to being alone against the world. In here, with her, there was one absolutely true thing he was certain of. Cymry loved and needed him, and he loved and needed her. The rest—well, he'd figure it all out as it came.

But he woke every day with two persistent and immediate problems to solve. When his fingers itched to lift a kerchief or a purse, he wondered what would happen if he gave in to the urge—and when Kris and Jeri accepted him without question as one of themselves, he worried what would happen when they (and the rest of the Trainees) learned he'd been a thief. Cymry might be the center of his world, but he'd had friends before in Bazie and the boys, and he liked having them. He didn't want to lose the ones he was getting now.

He woke one morning exactly six days after he had arrived, a day when he knew the rest of the Trainees would begin coming back in, signaling the beginning of his real classes tomorrow, although it would probably take two or three more days for all of them to make it back. It helped, of course, that they all had Companions, and however long their journeys were, they would travel in a fraction of the time it took an ordinary horse to cross the same distance. He had met most of his teachers, and even begun lessons designed to allow him to fit into the classes with some of them. He had no idea how many of them—besides Alberich and Teren—knew his background either.

And eventually, it *would* come out. Secrets never stayed secret for long. Eventually someone would say something.

He had worried over that like a terrier with a rat; in fact, he'd gone to bed that night thinking about it. And when he woke, it was with an answer at last.

Whether it would be the *right* answer was another question entirely. But he knew who to consult on it.

The Collegium cook, a moon-faced, eternally cheerful man called Mero, had turned up three days ago. The Collegium bells signaling the proper order of the day had resumed when Mero returned. So now, when Skif awoke at the first bell of the day and went down to the kitchen at the bell that signaled breakfast, he would join Kris and the girl Jeri and some of the teachers around a table in the kitchen for a real cooked meal. With so few to cook for, Mero declined help in cooking, but afterward they all pitched in to clean up. Some of Skif's daydreams about food were coming to pass—Mero even made homely oat porridge taste special.

After breakfast came Skif's first appointment of the day. It wasn't exactly a class . . . especially not this morning.

And this morning, he could hardly eat his breakfast for impatience to get out to the salle, where some of the weapons training was done. He cleared the table by himself so that he could leave quickly.

He ran to the salle, a building that stood apart from the rest of the Collegia, and for good reason, since it needed to be a safe distance from anywhere people might walk, accidentally or on purpose. The Trainees from all three Collegia learned archery, and even some of the Blues, the students who weren't Trainees at all. And some of those archery students were, to be frank, not very good.

Skif, although he had never shot a bow in his life, had proved to be a natural at it, somewhat to his own surprise. Seeing that, Alberich had tried him with something a bit more lethal and less obvious than an arrow. He'd tried him in knife throwing.

Skif had been terrifyingly accurate. Where his eye went, so did whatever was put in his hand. He had *no* idea where the skill had come from—but at least his ability to *fight* with a knife, or with the blunted practice swords, was no better than anyone else's.

Alberich had promised something in the way of a surprise for him this morning, and Skif was impatient to see what he meant, as well as impatient to speak with him.

When Skif arrived at the salle, Alberich was throwing a variety of weapons at a target set up on the other side of the room. Alberich was a hair more accurate than Skif, but Alberich's skill came from training, not a natural talent. Nevertheless, Skif watched with admiration as Alberich placed his weapons—knives, sharpened stakes, and small axes—in a neat pattern on the straw-padded target. He didn't interrupt the Weaponsmaster, and Alberich didn't stop until all the implements he'd lined up on a bench behind him were in the target.

The salle, a long, low building with smooth, worn wooden floors, was lit from above by clerestory windows. This was because the walls were taken up with storage cabinets and a few full-length mirrors. For the rest, there wasn't much, just a few benches, some training equipment, and the door to Alberich's office. For all Skif knew, Alberich might even have quarters here, since he hardly ever saw the Weaponsmaster anywhere else.

"So, you come in good time," Alberich said, as the last of his sharpened stakes slammed into the target. He turned toward Skif, picking up something from the bench where his weapons had been. "Come here, then. Let us see how these suit you."

"These" proved to be little daggers in sheaths that Alberich strapped to Skif's arms, with the daggers lying along the inside of his arms. Once on, they were hidden by Skif's sleeves, and he flexed his arms experimentally. They weren't at all uncomfortable, and he suspected that with a little practice wearing them, he wouldn't even notice they were there.

"Of my students, only two are, I think, fit to use these," Alberich said. "Jeri is one. It is you that is the other. Look you—" He showed Skif the catch that kept each dagger firmly in its sheath—and the near-invisible shake of the wrist that dropped it down into the hand, ready to throw, when the catch was undone.

Skif was thrilled with the new acquisition—what boy wouldn't be?—but unlike most, if not all, of the other Trainees, he had seen men knifed and bleeding and dead. Men—and a woman or two. Even before he left his uncle's tavern, he'd seen death at its most violent. And he knew, bone-deep and blood-deep, that *death* was what these knives were for. Not target practice, not showing off for one's friends. Death, hidden in a sleeve, small and silent, waiting to be used.

Death was a cold, still face, and blood pooling and clotting on the pavement. Death was floating bloated in the river. Death was ashes and bones in the burned-out hulk of a building.

Death was someone you knew found still and cold, and never coming back. And these little "toy" daggers were death. *Not* to be treated lightly, or to be played with.

But death was also being able to stop someone from making you dead.

"Can you kill a man?" Alberich asked suddenly, as Skif contemplated the dagger in his hand.

Skif looked up at the Weaponsmaster. As usual, his face was unreadable. "Depends on th' man," Skif replied soberly. "If you're talkin' in cold blood, I'd a took Jass down like a mad dog, just 'cause he killed m'friends, and I'd'a done it soon as I knew who his master was. In the dark. In the back. An' if somethin' happens, an' his master *won't* come up on what's due him—mebbe I'd do him, too. If you're talkin' in hot blood, if I was come at myself—someone wantin' me dead—aye, I'd kill him."

Alberich nodded, as if that was expected. "So. When are you going to display these to your friends?" he prodded. It *sounded* casual, but it was prodding.

Skif shook his head. "These—they're for serious work. Not for showin' off. 'Less you order me, Master Alberich, I ain't even gonna wear these, 'cept t' practice. That's like balancin' a rock over a door t' see who gets hit. I ain't got a hot temper, but I got a temper like anybody else. Losin' temper makes people do stupid things."

Death was a fight over nothing, and a lost temper, and blood where a simple blow would have served the same purpose. Over and over again, in the streets outside Exile's Gate, Death came when tempers worn thin by need or hurt, anger or drink, flared and blades came out. Alberich, in his guise of the sell-sword, was one of the few in those taverns that Skif had ever seen who went out of his way to avoid killing—to avoid even causing permanent harm.

Alberich gave a brief nod of satisfaction, and went on to drill Skif in the use of his new weapons. He said nothing more as the knives went into the target again and again; he was satisfied that Skif was going to be sensible, and dismissed the question as answered. That was another thing that Skif had come to realize about Alberich in the last week. Where other people—even a few Heralds—were inclined to harp on a subject that worried them, Alberich examined the subject, asked his questions, made his statements, came to his decisions, and left it alone.

If he trusted the person in question.

And he trusted Skif.

That was a very, very strange realization. But when he had come to it last night, it had been the catalyst for his own decision this morning.

"Master Alberich," he said, when the knives had been taken off and wrapped up in an oiled cloth to keep the sheaths supple and catches rust free. "I got a thought. Sooner or later some'un's gonna let it slip what I was. An' that's gonna cause some trouble."

Alberich gave him one of those very penetrating glances, but said nothing.

"But I think that you want t'keep at least part of what I can do real quiet."

Now the Weaponsmaster nodded slightly. "Have I not said it? Your skills could be—more than useful."

Skif clasped his hands behind his back. "So I had an ideer. What if we go ahead an' let *part* of it out? Just that I was on th' liftin' lay. 'Cause there's this—ain't too many as does the roof work an' th' liftin' lay, an' if people know I done th' one, they won't look for t'other." He grinned. "I can turn it into a kinda raree-show trick, y'ken? Do th' lift fer laughs. I'd like—" he continued, with a laugh, "—t'see yon Kris' face when I give 'im his liddle silver horse back, what he keeps in his pocket."

Alberich raised one eyebrow. "You have the itching fingers," he said, though without accusation.

"A bit," Skif admitted. "But—what d'you think?"

"I think that you have the right of it," Alberich replied, and Skif's spirits lifted considerably. "It *is* your skill in other things, and not as the picker of pockets, that is of primary value, at least for now. And when you have your Whites, the novelty of your past will have worn off, those within the Circle will not trouble to speak of it, and most outside the Circle will never know of it. So if there is a thing to be taken amidst a crowd of strangers, you will likely not find eyes on you."

That made perfect sense. One of the pickpockets Skif knew had spent an entire year just establishing himself as a lame old beggar who was always stumbling into people. Then when no one even thought twice about him, he began deftly helping himself to their purses, and there wasn't a man jack of the ones that were robbed that even *considered* the lame old beggar was the culprit.

Alberich's eyes looked elsewhere for a flicker of time, then returned to him. "Those who need to know what you are about," he said, "Will know. The rest will see an imp of mischief." He leveled a long gaze at Skif.

Skif shrugged. "Won't keep nothing," he said, quite truthfully. "Never took more'n I needed t'live comfortable, or Bazie did. That was Bazie's way—start t' take more, get greedy, get caught."

"A wise man, your Bazie," Alberich replied, with nothing weighting his tone.

Skif shrugged again. "So, I don' need nothing here. Livin' better than I ever did. An' you brought me my stuff."

With the purse of money, left in the loft at the Priory. . . .

And when that money runs out, what then?

"If there is need for silver to loosen tongues, or even gold, the Queen's coffers will provide," Alberich said gravely, giving Skif a sudden chill, for it seemed as if the Weaponsmaster read Skif's mind before Skif even finished the thought. "And for the rest—for there are Fairs, and there are taverns, and perhaps there will be the giving and receiving of gifts among friends, there is the stipend."

"Stipend?" Skif asked.

"Stipend." Alberich smiled wryly. "Some of ours are highborn, used to pocket money, some used to lavish amounts of it. We could forbid the parents to supply it, but why inflict hardship on those who deserve it not? So—the stipend. All Trainees receive it alike. Pocket money, for small things. Since you *have* money already—"

He paused.

And I am not asking you where it came from, nor demanding that you give it back, said the look that followed the pause.

"—then you will have yours on the next Quarter-Day, with the others."

"Oh. Uh—thank you—" Skif, for once, felt himself at a loss for words. Blindsided, in fact. This wasn't something he had expected, another one of those unanticipated *kindnesses*. There was no earthly reason why the Heralds should supply the Trainees—him in particular—with *pocket money*. They already supplied food, clothing, wonderful housing, entertainment in the form of their own games, and the Bardic Collegium on the same grounds.

Why were they doing these things? They didn't have to. Trainees that didn't have wealthy parents could just do without pocket money.

But Alberich had already turned away. He brought out a longer knife, and was preparing the salle for another lesson in street fighting. *That,* Skif could understand, and he set himself to the lesson at hand.

"It's a fool's bet," Herald-Trainee Nerissa cautioned a fascinated Blue four weeks later. "Don't take it."

But the look in her eyes suggested that although honesty had prompted the caution, Nerissa herself really, truly wanted to see Skif in action again.

Eight Trainees, two from Bardic Collegium and six from Herald's, and three Unaffiliated students, were gathered around Skif and a fourth Blue in the late afternoon sunshine on the Training Field.

The group surrounding Skif and the hapless Blue were just as fascinated as Nerissa, and just as eager. Skif himself shrugged and looked innocent. "Not a big bet," he pointed out. "Just t'fix my window so's the breeze can get *in* and them—*those*—moths can't. He says he can, says he *has*, for himself and his friends, and I don't think it'd put him out too much."

"It seems fair enough to me," said Kris. "Neither one of you is wagering anything he can't afford or can't do." He pointed at the Blue. "And *you* swore in the Compass Rose that Skif could never pull his trick on you, because you in particular and your plumb-line set in general were smarter than the Heraldic Trainees."

The Blue's eyes widened. "How did you know that?" he gasped.

Kris just grinned. "Sources, my lad," he said condescendingly, from the lofty position of a Trainee in his final year. "Sources. And I never reveal my sources. Are you going to take the bet, or not?"

The Blue's chin jutted belligerently. "Damn right I am!" he snapped.

"Witnessed!" called four Herald Trainees and one Bardic at once, just as Alberich came out to break the group up and set them at their archery practice.

At the end of practice, once Alberich had gone back into the salle, virtually everyone lingered—and Skif didn't disappoint them. He presented the astonished Blue with the good-luck piece that had been the object of the bet, an ancient silver coin, so worn away that all that could be seen were the bare outlines of a head. The coin had been in a pocket that the Blue had fixed with a buttoned-down flap, an invention against pickpockets of his own devising, that he was clearly very proud of.

In a panic, the boy checked the pocket. It was buttoned. He undid it and felt inside. His face was a study in puzzlement, as he brought out his hand. There was a coin-shaped lead slug in it.

Skif flipped his luck piece at him, and he caught it amid the laughter of the rest of the group. He was good-natured about his failure—something Skif had taken into consideration before making the bet—and joined in the laughter ruefully. "All right," he said, with a huge sigh. "I'll fix your window."

As the Blue walked off, consoled by two of his fellows, Herald-Trainee Coroc slapped Skif on the back with a laugh. "I swear, it's as good as having a conjurer about!" the Lord

Marshal's son said. "Well done! How'd you think of slipping him that lead slug to take the place of his luck piece?"

Skif flushed a little; he was coming to enjoy these little tests and bets. Picking pockets was something he did fairly well, but he didn't get any applause for it out in the street. The best he could expect was a heavy purse and no one putting the Watch on him. This, however—he had an audience now, and he *liked* having an audience, especially an appreciative one.

"I figured I'd better have something when Kris told me that Henk had been a-boasting over in the Compass Rose, an' told me I had to uphold the Heralds' side," Skif replied, with a nod to Kris. "We've all seen that luck piece of his, so it wasn't no big thing to melt a bit of lead and make a slug to the right size. After that, I just waited for him to say something I could move in on."

"But when did you get the coin?" Coroc wanted to know. "I mean, Alberich broke us up right after he took the bet, and you didn't get anywhere near—"

Coroc stopped talking, and his mouth made a little "oh" when he realized what Skif had done.

"—you took it off him *before* the bet!" he exclaimed.

"When there was all that joshing and shoving, sure," Skif agreed. "I *knew* he'd take the bet; after all that about his special pocket, he'd never have passed it up. He figured it'd be a secret I wouldn't reckon out, and I'd lose. But even if Kris hadn't told me, I'd have figured it anyway," he added. "The button shows, when you look right, and he ain't no seamstress, that buttonhole ain't half as tight as it could be." That last in a note of scorn from one who had long ago learned to make a fine buttonhole. "Anyway, I had to have the slug, 'cause I knew once he took the bet he'd be a-fingering that pocket t' make sure his luck piece was there."

"It's a good thing you haven't shown up a Gift other than moderate Thoughtsensing," Kris laughed, "or he'd have been accusing you of Fetching the thing!"

Skif preened himself, just a little, under all the attention. If having Skif around was entertaining for his fellow Trainees, the admiration each time he pulled off something clever was very heady stuff for Skif. He'd begun beautifully, a couple of days after full classes resumed, when Kris's best friend Dirk had asked innocently where he'd come from and what his parents did. He'd put on a pitiful act, telling a long, sad, and only slightly embellished story of his mother's death, the near-slavery at his uncle's hands, his running away, and his tragic childhood in the slums near Exile's Gate. All the while, he was slowly emptying goodhearted Dirk's pockets.

"But how did you *live?*" the young man exclaimed, full of pity for him. "How did you manage to survive?"

By this time, of course, since everyone in the three Collegia loved a tale, he'd drawn a large and sympathetic audience.

"Oh," Skif had said, taking Dirk's broad hand, turning it palm upwards, and depositing his belongings in it. "I turned into a thief, of course."

Poor Dirk's eyes had nearly bulged out of his head, and this cap to a well-told tale had surprised laughter out of everyone else. Word very quickly spread, but because of the prankish nature of Skif's lifting, there wasn't a soul in Herald's Collegium, and not more than one or two doubters in Bardic and Healers', that thought him anything other than a mischief maker, and an entertaining one at that. Those few were generally thought of as sour-faced pessimists and their comments ignored.

Not, Skif thought to himself somberly as he accepted the accolades of his fellows with a self-effacing demeanor, *but what they mightn't be right about me, 'cept for Cymry.*

Except for Cymry. That pretty much summed it up. *Everyone* among the Heraldic Trainees was willing to accept Skif as a harmless prankster because he'd been Chosen, because Companions didn't Choose *bad* people. And if anyone among the teachers thought differently, they were keeping their doubts to themselves.

"Time to get to the baths," Kris reminded them. "Otherwise the hot water's going to be gone." That sent everyone but Skif on a run for their quarters. Skif lingered, not because he didn't care about getting a hot bath, but because Alberich had given him an interesting look that he thought was a signal.

He made certain that no one was looking back at him, then sidled over to the salle entrance. Alberich was, as he had thought, waiting just inside.

"Working, and working well, is your plan of misdirection," the Weaponsmaster observed calmly.

"So far." Skif waited for the rest. There had to be more; Alberich wasn't going to give him a look like that just to congratulate him on his cleverness.

"Would it be that you would know the voice of Jass' master, heard you it again?" Alberich asked.

Skif felt a little thrill run through him. So Alberich *was* going to use him! He wasn't just going to have to sit around while the Weaponsmaster prowled the slums in his sell-sword guise.

"I think so," Skif said, after giving the question due consideration. "But, he'd have to be talking—well, he'd have to be talking like he thought he was way above the person he was talking to."

"Condescending." Alberich nodded. "That, I believe, I can arrange. There is to be a gathering of Lord Orthallen's particular friends tonight. Get you to that place without challenge, I can do. It is for you to get yourself into a place of concealment where you can hear and observe, but not be noticed."

"Oh, I can do that!" Skif promised recklessly. "You just watch!"

"I intend to, since it will be myself at this gathering, as guard to Selenay with Talamir," Alberich replied. "I wish you at the door into the Herald's Wing at the dishwashing bell."

He turned and retreated into the shadows of the salle, and Skif whirled and ran for the Collegium.

He got his bath—lukewarm, but he hardly noticed—and ate without tasting his supper, in such haste that he came close to choking once. He was in place long before the bell rang, and Alberich, arriving early, smiled to see him there. And to see him in the uniform of a page, the pale-blue and silver that all of Selenay's pages wore.

"Come," was all he said, and he didn't ask where Skif had gotten the uniform. As it happened, he hadn't stolen it, he'd won it, fair and square. Another little bet. He'd had the feeling that he might need it at some point, and he was still small enough to pass for one of the pages without anyone lifting an eyebrow.

Won't be able t'pull that much longer, though, he thought with regret. He'd learned a lot, impersonating a page in Lord Orthallen's service, and he hoped to learn more, slipping into the Palace proper.

"I trust you know how to serve," Alberich murmured, as they walked together down the corridor, servants whose duty it was to light the lamps passing by them without a second glance.

Skif just snorted.

"I should like to note," Alberich went on, as they made a turn into the second half of Herald's Wing, "that I specified you be in a place of concealment."

"Hide in plain sight," Skif retorted. "When does any highborn look at a page?"

"Unless it is his own kin—a point you have made. Well, this may serve better than having you lurking in the rafters." Alberich nodded a greeting to a Herald just emerging from his room; the other saluted him but showed no sign of wanting to stop and talk.

"Can't see nobody's face from the rafters," Skif pointed out.

They made another turning, into a section that looked im-

mensely old, much older than the Collegium or the Wing
attached to it. Skif looked about with avid curiosity; they must
be in the Old Palace now, the square building upon which all
later expansions had been founded. The Old Palace was ru-
mored to date all the way back to the Founding of Valdemar,
and it was said that King Valdemar had used the old magics
that were only in tales to help to construct it. Certainly no one
in these days would have attempted to build walls with blocks
of granite the size of a cottage, and no one really had any idea
how the massive blocks could have been set in place to the
height of six stories. There were even rumors that the blocks
were hollow and contained a warren of secret passages. Unlikely, Skif thought, but it would be impossible to tell, unless
you knew where a door was, because the outer walls were at
least two ells thick, and you could tap on them until you were
a graybeard and never get a hollow echo.

Alberich stopped, just outside a set of massive double
doors. "This, the reception chamber is. The reception will be in
slightly less than a candlemark. Your plan?"

"Set an' ready," Skif said boldly. "You go do whatever
you're gonna do, an' leave me here."

Alberich nodded, and continued on his way. Skif checked
the door of the chamber, and found it, as he had expected,
unlocked.

He slipped inside.

The walls were plastered over the stone, and the plaster
painted with scenes out of legends Skif didn't even begin to
recognize. Candle sconces had been built onto the walls to provide light later, and there was an enormous fireplace truly
large enough to roast an ox. There was no fire in it now, of
course, but someone had placed an ox-sized basket of yellow,
orange, and red roses between the andirons as a kind of clever
fire substitute. The room looked out into the courtyard in the
center of the Old Palace; here the walls were not of the massive
thickness of the outer walls, and the windows ran nearly floor

to ceiling, with a set of glass doors in the middle that could be opened onto the courtyard itself. There were sideboards along the wall, covered with snowy linen cloths, set up to receive foodstuffs, though none were there yet except two baskets of fruit. Candles and lanterns waited on one of the tables, though none had been put in their sconces and holders, nor lit. Skif took a tall wax taper, and went out into the corridor, lighting it at one of the corridor lamps. He then went about the room setting up the lights, quite as if he'd been ordered to do so. There seemed to be too many lanterns for the room, so after consideration, he took the extras out into the courtyard and hung them on the iron shepherd's crooks he found planted among the flowers for that purpose.

Roughly a quarter-candlemark later, a harried individual in Royal livery stuck his head in the door and stared at him. "What—Did I order you to light the lamps?" he asked, sounding more than a bit startled.

Skif made his voice sound high and piping, more childlike than usual. "Yes, milord," he replied, with a bob of his head. "You did, milord."

The man muttered something under his breath about losing one's mind as the hair grayed, then said, "Carry on, then," waving a hand vaguely at him.

Skif hid his grin and did just that. It was one of the things he'd learned impersonating a page at Lord Orthallen's. If a boy was doing a job (rather than standing about idly), people would assume he'd been set the task and leave him alone. Even if the person in charge didn't recall setting the task or seeing the boy, that person would take it for granted that it had just slipped his mind, and leave the boy to carry on.

When the upper servant appeared again, with a bevy of boys clad just as Skif was in tow, Skif was relieved to see that none of them were the boy he'd won his uniform from. That had been his one concern in all of this, and with that worry laid to rest, he paid dutiful attention to the servant's instructions. He actually paid more attention than the real pages, who fidgeted and poked each other—but then, they were yawningly familiar with what their duties were, and he wasn't.

The food arrived then—tidbits, rather than a meal, something to provide a pleasant background to the reception. He managed to get himself, by virtue of his slightly taller stature, assigned to carry trays of wine glasses among the guests. That was a plus; he'd be able to move freely, where Alberich would be constrained to go where the Queen did.

When all was in readiness, the doors into the courtyard (now nicely lantern-lit, thanks to Skif's efforts) and the doors to the corridor were flung open, the page boys took their places, and the guests began to trickle by ones and twos into the room for the reception.

ALBERICH stood at Selenay's right hand as she circulated among Lord Orthallen's guests. He wore his formal Whites, something he did only on the rarest of occasions. He was not at all comfortable in what, for the first two decades of his life, had been the uniform not only of the enemy, but of the demon lovers. Only three people knew that reason, however; to tell anyone but Selenay, Talamir, and Myste would have been to deliver a slap in the face to those who had rescued and cared for him and taken them into their midst.

Sometimes, though, he did wear the uniform, when the need to do so outweighed personal discomfort. In this case, he wore his Whites because he would be far more conspicuous in his favored dark gray leather than in his Heraldic uniform.

Talamir stood at Selenay's left, where he could murmur advice into her ear if she needed it. Alberich stood on her right, where his weapon hand was free.

He watched everyone and everything, his eyes flicking from one person to the next, and he never smiled. This evidently bothered some, though not all, of Lord Orthallen's guests—the ones who had never seen Alberich before and only knew of him by reputation. Those who frequented Court functions were used to the way he looked at everyone as if he saw a potential assassin.

He did, however. *Everyone* was a *potential* assassin. Of course the likelihood that any of them actually were assassins was fairly low. But he was the Herald who had saved Selenay from death at the hands of her own husband, cutting the Prince down with the Prince's own sword. He saw treachery everywhere, or feigned that he did, and when he looked at someone he didn't know with suspicion in his eyes, that person tended to get very nervous.

Sometimes he wished that he didn't have quite so formidable a reputation. Sometimes he wished that he could just *look* at someone and not have them flinch away.

That was about as likely at this point as for him to turn as handsome as young Trainee Kris.

That was what Herald-Chronicler Myste said, anyway, looking at him from behind those peculiar split-lensed spectacles of hers that forced her pull her head back to peer down her nose when she was reading and tilt her chin down to peer through the top half when she was looking at anything past the length of her arms. "What do you expect?" she'd ask him tartly. "The man who'll cut down a prince wouldn't hesitate at putting a blade in the heart of a man of lesser rank. But for the gods' sake don't ever try smiling at them. You aren't any good at faking a smile, and when you try, you look as if you were about to jump on people and tear their throats out with your teeth."

A pity Myste was perhaps the Herald who was the most inept with weapons in the entire Circle. He could do with a dose of her good sense here tonight. Not that she'd enjoy it, of course. She would far rather be where she could avoid all this interminable nonsense, in her quarters, either writing up the current Chronicles or going over old ones, a glass of cold, sweet tea at her elbow.

Where she would probably knock it over at least once tonight. Hopefully when she did, the glass would be empty. If it wasn't, well, at least the papers on her floor were discards, unlike the ones piled all over Elcarth's office.

Alberich pulled his attention back to the reception. The heat wave had finally broken, though the thick stone walls of the Old Palace kept every room in it comfortably cool even during the worst of the heat. With the doors open, there was a pleasant scent coming from the roses in the courtyard. No one had gone out there, though, for Selenay and Orthallen were in *here*. No matter how tired anyone's feet got, he wouldn't leave where the power was.

If Alberich's gaze rested more often than usual on a particular page, circulating among the guests with a tray of wineglasses, probably no one was going to notice. It was a very ordinary-looking boy: small, dark, curly-haired. If he moved more gracefully than the usual lot, that wasn't likely to be noticed either. Alberich was pleased with the way he was looking up at the people he was serving—not staring enough to make him seem insolent, just paying respectful attention. Very good, very smooth. The boy must have done something like this before, many times, though Alberich doubted it had been for any purpose other than to filch food from whatever noble household he had infiltrated.

Lord Orthallen, on whose behalf this reception was being held, also circulated among the guests quite as if he was the one who was the host, and not the Queen. This particular festivity was a reward for those who had helped Orthallen to conclude a set of delicate negotiations that would ultimately benefit the Crown substantially, according to Myste. Alberich was not at all clear on just what those negotiations were, only that they had involved a number of men (and a few women) of vastly disparate backgrounds, many of whom had personal differences with each other.

One thing they all had in common, though. They were all very, very wealthy.

That much showed in their costumes, rich with embroidery and of costly materials, and in their ornaments, heavy gold and silver and precious gems. The details didn't matter to Alberich, though Myste would have been studying them with the eye of one who would be recording every subtle detail later in her writings. That was the problem of living around a Chronicler; he never knew just what detail, what secret that *he* assumed was just between them would end up in one of her Histories, to be goggled at by some other generation of Heralds to come.

Right now, he was in the unusual position of having part of his attention devoted to something other than Selenay and her welfare. He watched that one small boy, not as a hunter watched prey, but as the prey watches a hunter, alive to every nuance in his behavior, waiting for the slightest sign that the boy recognized a voice he'd only heard once.

When he told the boy that he could arrange for him to hear words spoken in tones of condescension, he had not been promising more than he could deliver. Although these people had worked together for Orthallen's cause, they had not forgotten rank and perceived rank and all of the tangle of quarrels that had made it so difficult to get them to work together—they had merely put those things aside for the moment. And although they were now basking in the unanticipated presence of Royalty, those things still remained. Where the Queen gazed, all was harmony, but the moment that she took her attention away, the claws were unsheathed, though subtly, subtly, with a care not only for the Queen's presence, but for the watchful eye of her guardian.

Who might misinterpret what he saw. And in Alberich's case—

Well, no one wanted Alberich to misinterpret anything.

So rather than bared claws and visible teeth, there were mere hints of rivalries and competitions, mostly carried out in tone and carefully chosen words.

Oh, there would be condescension in plenty, among those able to read tone and words so exactly that they could choose to ignore what they heard or exaggerate the offense. Small wonder the crude bully Jass hadn't heard what the boy had read in his master's tone. The wonder was that the boy had read it so accurately.

Well. Every Herald, every Trainee, is a wonder, small or great.

It could be that this boy was—or would be—more of a wonder than most. There were still those—not Heralds, mostly—who doubted the wisdom of having a thief as a Trainee. And the boy was not yet committed to becoming a Herald; Alberich, so apt at reading the unspoken language of gesture and tone, knew that better than any. If it had been a case of trusting to the boy by himself to come around, to learn to trust, to understand what it was they were doing, Alberich would have been the first to say, "No. He is a danger to us, and cannot be trusted past his own self-interest." But there was more than that; there was the Companion. And so, Alberich was always the first, not the last, to say "Peace. He will be ours, soon enough."

The boy was good; *very* good. Alberich had no difficulty in imagining him moving through a crowd of just about any sort of folk save, perhaps, the highest, and remaining completely unnoticed. He was, after all, a pickpocket; that was the way of the game. The unobtrusive prospered; the rest wound up in gaol. Watching the boy was the only entertainment he had, though, and in the end the reception was, as such things generally were, deadly dull. These people were small; in the normal course of things, no matter how wealthy they were, they would never have seen Selenay except from the back of the

Audience Chamber, or at most, stood before her for a few, brief moments while she passed some judgment in their favor or against them. They would never have watched as she bent that cool, thoughtful gaze on each one alone, never have heard her inquiring as to the details of their lives. For that moment of reflected glory, they were content to be restrained and to keep their masks firmly in place, their smiles unwavering.

And although the boy had shown a moment or two of hesitation, there was no sudden recognition. The reception came to its predictable end when Selenay had had a private word with each and every one of Orthallen's guests, and withdrew, along with Talamir and Alberich. And after that, the guests would depart swiftly, there being nothing there to hold them. The boy Skif would have to extricate himself from the toils of the Page Master as best he could.

And when he did—just as swiftly as Alberich had reckoned he would—he found Alberich waiting for him in his own room.

Alberich had taken some thought to the needs of boys and had brought with him something *other* than the things, good though they were, that lay in Mero's free pantry. He had gone down to the Palace kitchen, and commanded some of the dainties that Selenay's Court feasted on. He calculated that having had such things paraded beneath his nose all night, the boy would not be emotionally satisfied with bread and cheese, however good those common viands were, and if he was anything like Alberich had judged him, he had not filled himself at dinner.

So when Skif pushed open his own door, there was Alberich, beneath a lit lantern mounted on the wall, sitting at his ease in the boy's chair, the covered platter beside him on the desk.

The boy started, but covered it well. "Didn' think t'see you afore the morrow," he said matter-of-factly as he sat down on his bed.

"Good service demands immediate reward," Alberich replied, and uncovered the platter.

Then pulled out the two glasses and half-bottle of wine from beneath the chair. The boy gaped at him—then shut his mouth and looked at the wine. There was a brief flash of greed there. But thankfully, no *need*. Good. That was one thing that Alberich had worried about. Trouble with drink started early among those who lived near Exile's Gate. Alberich had seen children as young as ten caught by the addiction of drink, there.

"I didn' think we was allowed—" Skif began, though his nose twitched as Alberich uncorked it, and he was young enough that his yearning showed, a little more. He must be getting very weary of the spring water, fruit juice, ciders, teas and milk that were all the Trainees were ever offered.

"It is only half a bottle, and I intend to share it with you," Alberich replied, pouring the glasses full and handing him one. "That is hardly enough for even an innocent to be drunk upon. I suspect you've had a deal stronger in your time, already."

The boy accepted the glass and to his great credit, took a mouthful and savored it, rather than draining the glass. "So *this's* what all the fuss is about," he said, after he allowed the good vintage to slip down his throat. "*This* is what the good stuff's like."

"It is," Alberich agreed. "And now, I fear, it is spoiled you'll be for the goat piss that passes itself off as wine near Exile's Gate."

"Dunno how you drunk it, and that's for certain-sure; I allus did my drinkin' a little higher up the street," Skif replied, putting his glass down and reaching for the nearest tidbit, a pasty stuffed with morels and duck breast. Of course, he didn't know that until he bit into it, and as it melted on his tongue, the boy's face was a study that very nearly made Alberich chuckle. He didn't, though; children's dignity was a fragile thing, and this lad's rather more so than others.

"They been passin' those under my nose all night, and if I'd known how they tasted—" Skif shook his head. "This is too much like reward, Weaponsmaster. The plain fact is there were three men that sounded *something* like the one we want, and not one I'd be willin' t'finger."

"Reward is not exclusively earned by accomplishing a task," Alberich noted, pushing the platter toward the boy, but taking a pastry himself. He hadn't eaten any more than the boy had, though Selenay had nibbled all evening, and he wanted something in his stomach to cushion the wine. "Sometimes reward is earned just in the making of the attempt."

"Huh." Skif chose a different dainty, and washed it down with wine. "Now what d'we do?"

"I will try and find another opportunity to put you where you can observe some of the ones I suspect," Alberich told him. "If I do not, it is that you will go to hunt on your own. Yes?"

Skif shrugged, but Alberich read in the shrug that he had considered doing so, if he had not already made an attempt or two. "I got cause," was all he said, and left it at that.

"Meanwhile—I hunt in a place you cannot, for no boy, however disguised, would be permitted to the discourses of the Great Lords of State," Alberich continued.

Skif cocked his head to the side. "Shut the pages out, do they?" he asked shrewdly, and sighed. "Not like I ain't busy."

A most unchildlike child, Alberich reflected later, as he left the boy to finish his feast. But then, most, if not all, of the children from *that* quarter were more-or-less unchildlike. They'd had their childhood robbed from them in various ways; Skif's was by no means the most tragic. He'd *had* a loving mother, for however short a time he'd had her. He'd had a kind and caring guardian and mentor in the person of the thief trainer. That was more, much more, than many of his fellows had.

And if Selenay had even an inkling of the horrors in the twisted streets of her own capital, she would send out Heralds and Guard and all to scour the place clean. There would be a grim forest of gallows springing up overnight.

And her own people would speak her name with hate—and it would be all in vain, for half a candlemark after we'd gone, the scum would all be back again. This was the cost of welcoming any and all who sought shelter under Valdemar's banner. Sometimes what came in was not good. Not all, or even many, of the former Tedrel mercenaries who had remained in Valdemar were of Bazie's stamp.

Alberich sought his quarters—he actually had quarters both with the other Heralds and in the salle, but the latter was less convenient tonight. It was too late, or not late enough, for a visitor; his room was empty, and in a way, he was relieved. He was not fit company tonight; there was too much of a mood on him.

It was more of a relief to get himself out of the Whites and into a sleeping robe, and then into bed. There had been a double reason for the wine this evening; it was not only to prove to the boy that Alberich considered him—in some things—to be an adult. It was to make certain that tonight, at least, he would not be slipping out to snoop and pry on his own. That Taltherian wine was strong stuff; Alberich might have made certain that the greater part of the bottle went inside *him,* but there was more than enough there to ensure that Skif slept.

For that matter, there was more than enough there to ensure that Alberich slept, he realized, as he went horizontal and found a moment of giddiness come over him. It came as something of a surprise, but one he was not going to have any choice but to accept.

Then again, neither would Skif.

Which thought was a safeguard, of sorts.

Skif lay back against a bulwark of pillows propped up against the wall and headboard of his bed, and stared out at the night sky beyond his open window. Not that he could see much, even with his lantern blown out; the lower half of the window was filled by a swath of cheesecloth stretched over a wooden frame that fit the open half of the window precisely. You couldn't slip a knife blade between the frame and the window frame.

Trust a Blue to be that fiddly.

It worked, though. Not a sign of moth or midge or fly, and all the breeze he could want. He thought he might want to dye the cloth black though, eventually, just to get that obtrusive white shape out of the way.

The wine Alberich had brought had been a lovely thing, about as similar to the stuff Skif had drunk in the better taverns as chalk was to cheese. He'd recognized the power with the first swallow, though, and he'd been disinclined to take chances with it. He'd stuffed his belly full of the fine foods Alberich had brought, which slowed the action of the wine considerably, which was good, because he wanted to think before he went to sleep.

He put his hands behind his head and leaned into his rather luxurious support.

Luxurious? Damn right it is. When the best my pillows have been till now was straw-filled bags? This place was pretty amazing, when it came right down to it. Maybe for some people the uniforms were a bit of a come-down, but not even the worst of his was as mended and patched as the best of his old clothing. And for the first time in his life to have boots and shoes that actually *fitted* him—

Didn't know your feet wasn't supposed to hurt like that, before.

His room had taken on the air of a place where someone lived, in no small part because of Skif's little wagers. Mindful of the impression he was hoping to create, he always wagered for something he knew wouldn't put the person who was betting against him to any hardship. So in many cases, particularly early in the game, that wager had been a cushion against a small silver coin—which, of course, Skif knew he wasn't going to lose. Skif preferred sitting in his bed to study, unless he actually had to write something out, and any Trainee could make as many cushions for himself as he cared to—fabric and cleaned feathers by the bagful were at his disposal in the sewing room as Skif well knew. Palace and Collegia kitchens went through a lot of fowl, most of which came into the complex still protesting. The Palace seamstresses bespoke the goosedown for featherbeds, the swansdown for trimming, and the tail feathers for hats. Wing feathers went off to the fletchers and to be made into quill pens. That left the body feathers free for the claiming, so there were always bags full of them for anyone who cared to take worn-out clothing and other scrap material to make a patchwork cushion or two.

Skif now had nearly twenty piled up behind him. And for those whose pockets ran to more than the stipend, some of the more top-lofty of the Blues, he'd wagered against such things as a plush coverlet, a map to hang on his wall so that he wouldn't need to be always running up to the Library, and, oddly enough, books.

The plush coverlet was folded up and waiting for winter to go on his bed, the map made a dark rectangle on one whitewashed wall, and the bookcase—the bookcase was no longer empty.

He'd never disliked reading, but he'd also never had a lot of choice about what he read. It had never occurred to him that there might be other things to read than religious texts and dry histories.

Then he discovered tales. Poetry. Books written to be read *for pleasure*. It wasn't the overwhelming addiction for him that it was with some of the Trainees, who would have had their nose in a book every free moment if they could, but for him, reading was as satisfying as a good meal, in his opinion.

And a book made a very, very useful thing to demand on a wager. It made him look a great deal more harmless in the eyes of those highborn Blues.

So now his bookshelves held two kinds of books; his schoolbooks, and the growing collection of books he could open at any time to lose himself in some distant place or time. And the room now had personality that it hadn't shown before.

But that was not what he wanted to think about; it was what had happened at that reception tonight. The whole thing had been good, in that it proved Weaponsmaster Alberich had every intention of using him. But it hadn't gotten them any results. And what could be done within the wall around the Palace wasn't anything near enough, and he knew that Alberich knew that it wasn't enough. One end of the trail might be here, but the other was down near Exile's Gate. Here, there was likely only one person, the man behind it all. There—well, there were a lot of people, there had to be, and plenty of 'em with loose tongues, if you could catch 'em right, or get enough liquor into 'em.

Now, Alberich *could* go down there, fit in, and be talked to. He'd already proved that. *But* the question was not whether he'd be talked to, the question was *who* would talk to him. Jass had spoken to him, sold him information, and now Jass was dead. Had anyone made that connection? Skif didn't know, and it was certain-sure that no one was going to tell Alberich if they had. Take it farther; if Alberich pressed too hard and in the wrong direction, someone might decide he was too dangerous to let alone. Now, old Alberich wasn't very like to get himself in serious trouble, not with Kantor to come rescue him at need, but if a white horse came charging into Exile's Gate and carrying off a fellow who was hard-pressed in a fight, there weren't too many folks down there that *couldn't* put two and two together and come up with the right number.

There was that, but there was more. The kinds of people that Alberich would talk to were the bullyboys, other sell-swords. If he was lucky, possibly the tavernkeepers would talk to him. They wouldn't necessarily have the information he needed. There was, however, another set of people who *might*. The whores, the pawnbrokers, the people who bought and sold stolen goods—they all knew Skif, and *they* knew things that the folks who practiced their trades in a more open fashion might not.

Come to that, Skif knew a few of the other thieves who might trade a word or two with him. You never knew what you were going to find yourself in possession of when you were a thief. It might could be that one of them would have run across something to put Skif on the trail.

Particularly intriguing was that thread of information that Alberich had let fall—how the trade in children stolen off the streets and the trade in slaves taken by bandits might be linked. It made a certain amount of sense, that, if you assumed that the slavers were all working together.

Skif hummed to himself tunelessly as he considered that. Who would know, if anyone did? There were always rumors, but who would be able to give the scrap of foundation to the rumor?

One by one, he ran down the list of his acquaintances, those who had always seemed to know where to start, when you were looking for someone or some*thing*—most particularly, those who had pointed him on the trail of Jass. And he dragged out all of the tag bits of information he'd been given that hadn't led him to Jass, but into other paths that had seemed at the time like dead ends.

At the moment, he couldn't imagine anything more bizarre than that he, reclining at his ease in his own room of a wing attached to the Palace itself, should be running down the lists of those who owed him favors (and those whose cooperation could be bought) in the most miserable quarter of Haven. Nevertheless—

Alberich does it all the time. So I ain't the only one.

None of the things he'd been told seemed to lead him to child stealing, nor could he think of anyone *he* knew likely to really know anything other than just rumors. Reluctantly, he found himself thinking that if there was one black blot in the alleyways of Exile's Gate that might hide part of the answer, it was his own uncle Londer. Londer Galko always skirted the fringe of the quasilegal. Londer was not brave enough to dare the darkest deeds himself, but Skif could tell, even as a child, that he yearned to. The older Londer got, the less he dared, but the more he yearned.

Bazie had hinted, more than once, that Londer would have sold Skif in a heartbeat if Skif hadn't already been registered on the city rolls. And even then, if he could have manufactured a believable story about Skif running away—

Skif was not at all surprised now that half-witted Maisie had been illegally under-age—perhaps not for the employment at the Hollybush, but certainly for the uses that his cousin Kalchan had made of her. She hadn't *looked* under-aged, what there was of her was woman-sized, but Londer had to have known. Skif wouldn't be surprised now to learn that Londer himself had sampled Maisie's meager charms before passing her on to his son. Londer had never given his sons anything he hadn't already used (Beel being the exception, but then the idea of Londer attempting the life of a priest was enough to make a cat laugh) and Londer didn't exactly have women lining up to keep him company. In the years since running off, Skif had learned a lot about his uncle, and he'd learned that when it came to women, Londer had to pay for what he got. Since he'd already paid for Maisie, it followed that he'd probably seen no reason why he shouldn't have her first. Not that he'd shown any interest in anything too young to have breasts, but half-wits often matured early, and Londer probably wouldn't even think twice about her *real* age if he'd taken her.

Londer had more-than-dubious friends, too, even by the standards of Exile's Gate. And after the raid on the Hollybush—well, he'd lost what few friends he had around there. Not only because of Maisie, but because he had laid all the blame on his own son, and left him to rot and eventually die in gaol. Kalchan had never recovered enough even to do the idiot's work of stone picking, and Londer had done *nothing* to help him recover. Business was business, but blood was blood, and people didn't much care for a man who disclaimed responsibility for things that people knew he was responsible for because his unconscious son couldn't refute them. A good thing for Londer that his son never did wake to full sense and died within three moons. The case against Londer died with him, and Skif could only wonder who Londer was friendly with *now*, given how many people that callousness had offended. Or had that just freed his uncle to edge a little nearer to those dark deeds he secretly admired?

Given all of that, Londer *probably* didn't engage in child snatching for his own puerile entertainment. But that didn't mean he didn't help it along, just because he got a thrill out of doing so. He probably had been frightened enough by his brush with the law not to do anything so dangerous for his own profit either. But it was increasingly likely, in Skif's estimation, that he knew something about it. The Hollybush hadn't, by any means, been Londer's only property. He owned warehouses in places where there wasn't anyone around to notice odd things going on at night.

So, a very good place to start would be with his uncle. Skif knew the ins and outs of Londer's house, for more than once, he'd contemplated getting some of what he considered that he was owed out of his uncle. He'd eventually given up on the idea, for the fact was that anything Londer had of value was generally too big to be carried off easily. But because of that, Skif knew the house, and he knew the twisty ways of Londer's mind almost as well as he knew the house.

The best way to get information out of him would be to frighten it out. Londer was good at keeping his mouth shut, but not when he was startled, and not when he was genuinely frightened.

So Skif set himself to figuring out exactly how he could best terrify his uncle into telling Skif *everything* he might know or guess about the child stealing and the slavery ring.

In his bed, in the dead of night, Skif decided. Skif was short, even for a boy his age—but a shadowy figure dressed in black, waking you up with a knife to your throat, was likely to seem a whole lot bigger than he actually was. And a hoarse whisper didn't betray that he was too young for his voice to have broken yet.

Alberich had brought the all-black night-walking suit when he'd collected Skif's clothing. *Skif* knew a way into Londer's house that not even Londer knew about. Good old Londer! Every window had a lock, every door had two, but he forgot completely about the trapdoor onto the roof. All Skif had to do was get into the yard and shinny up the drainpipe from the gutters. Once on the roof, he was as good as inside.

Right enough, if Londer knew anything, Skif would have it out of him. But he needed a suitably convincing story for his black-clad terrorist to ask the questions he needed the answers to. *I'll say I'm lookin' for m'sister,* he decided. *That's a good story, an' Londer'll probably believe it.*

Now, getting from here to there.

He'd be able to get out of his room easily enough; no one checked beds to see that people were in them around here. The trouble was, how was he to get out of—and more importantly, back inside—the Palace walls?

:Me, of course,: Cymry replied in his head. He jumped; then

smiled sheepishly. *:Nobody is going to stop a Companion and her Chosen.:*

:You don't mind?: he asked, hesitantly. After all, this wasn't precisely going to be a sanctioned excursion.

:Mind?: he felt her scorn. *:You just try and do it without me! You wouldn't have a chance.:*

Well, she was probably right.

:But what do I do with you while I'm sneakin' around?: he asked.

She chuckled. *:I'll take care of that. Trust me, I can always insinuate myself into someone's nearby stable. But I'm not having you so far away that I can't come to your rescue if I have to.:*

He was both touched and a trifle irritated. Did she think he couldn't take care of himself? He'd been *taking* care of himself for the past year and more! She hadn't been around then!

Now she sounded contrite. *:Of course you can take care of yourself, I never doubted that. But your uncle might have guards—:*

He laughed, silently. *:Londer? Old cheap Londer? Not a chance. What he has got is dogs—but he's too cheap to get trained ones, so he just gets nasty ones and keeps 'em hungry to keep 'em mean. Which means—?:*

Cymry knew; bless her, she got it at once. *:They'll eat anything you throw in front of them.:*

He grinned. *:And I know where to get plenty of poppy syrup. Put 'em right to sleep inside a candlemark, then I slip inside and give old uncle a surprise.:*

:Then what will you do?: she asked soberly. *:When you leave? You aren't—:*

:I'm gonna make him drink poppy hisself,: Skif reassured her. *:No way I'm taking a chance on hitting him hard enough to make sure he stays knocked out. Besides, with that thick head of his—I'd probably break what I hit him with before I knocked him out.:*

He felt her sigh gustily. :*Good. Then this will all work. And what then?*:

:*Then*—: he closed his eyes, but couldn't yet see a direction for himself. :*It's early days to make any plans. I'll figure on what to do after I hear what old Londer has to say.*:

And that would have to do, for now.

SKIF looked down on the silent, darkened oblong that was his uncle's yard from the roof of his uncle's house. The roof-tree was not the most comfortable place he'd ever had to perch, but better to rest here than inside the house. Down there somewhere in the shadows were five lumps of sleeping canine that had been completely unable to resist juicy patties of chopped meat mixed with bread crumbs soaked in poppy syrup. Poor miserable animals, Uncle Londer would probably be even harsher with them after their failure to stop him.

This was the halfway point, and Skif paused for a breather while he could take one. He'd gotten out of the Collegium through his window, out of the Complex openly on Cymry's back, as if he was going out into the city for any perfectly ordinary reason.

Well, perhaps not *ordinary*, since Trainees as young as he was generally didn't go out to the city after dark. But he'd made sure to look serious, as if someone had sent for him, rather than overly cheerful, as if he expected to find himself in, say, the "Virgin and Stars" tavern that night. No one questioned him, and Heraldic Trainees (unlike the common-born Blues or the Bardic Trainees) were not required to give a reason for leaving the Complex at whatever hour, probably because it was generally assumed that their Companions would not agree to anything that wasn't proper.

Once in Haven, Cymry found an unguarded stable near Uncle Londer's house—unguarded because it was completely empty and beginning to fall to pieces, symptom of a sudden change in someone's fortune. There he had changed into his black clothing, feeling distinctly odd as he did so. It seemed that the last time he'd worn this was a lifetime ago, not just a couple of moons. But where he was going, that uniform was a distinct handicap.

He hadn't swathed his face and head, or blackened exposed flesh with charcoal just then. He'd still had to get the chopped meat, the bread and the poppy syrup, and not all in the same market square, just so no one would put him and the ingredients together if they were questioned later. That was why he'd left the Collegium early. Markets stayed open late in the poorer parts of town, for the benefit of those whose own working hours were long. Skif had no trouble in acquiring what he needed, and he made his final preparations in that stable by the light of the moon overhead.

Then, and only then, did he finish dressing, and with the treated meat stuffed into cleaned sausage bladders which he tied off, and then put into a bag, he had slipped out alone into the darkness.

The key to making sure that all five dogs got their doses was to send the bladders over the wall at long intervals. The first and strongest dog wolfed down his portion, then staggered about for a bit and fell asleep. When Skif heard the staggering, he sent over the second bladder; by that time the strongest dog was in no condition to contest the food, and the second strongest got it. It took a while, but Skif was patient,

and when he couldn't hear anything other than dog snores, he
went over the wall and up the gutter to the roof.

Now he sat on the rooftree with his back against one of the
chimneys, using its bulk to conceal his silhouette, and took
deep, slow breaths to calm himself. His gut was a tight
knot—a good reason for not eating much tonight. And he was
thirsty, but thirsty was better than being in the middle of a job
and having to—well. This would be the first time he had ever
entered a house with the intention of confronting someone.
Normally that was the *last* thing he wanted to do, and it had
him strung tighter than an ill-tuned harp.

So he ran over what he needed to do in his mind until he
thought he'd rehearsed it enough, and Mindcalled Cymry.

:I'm going in,: he told her.

:You know what to do if you get in trouble,: she replied,
for they had already worked that out. Skif would get outside,
anywhere outside, and she would come for him. She swore she
could even get into the yard if it was needful. How she was to
get over that fence, he had no notion, but that was *her* problem. Bazie had taught him that once you put your confidence
in a partner, you just *trusted* that he knew what he was doing
and went on with your part of the plan. Because once the plan
was in motion, there was nothing you could do about what *he*
was responsible for, anyway, so there was no point in taking
up some of the attention you should be paying to your part of
the job by worrying about him.

He slipped over the rooftree to the next chimney; the hatch
into the crawl space was just on the other side of it. It wasn't
locked—it hadn't been locked for the past five years that Skif
knew of. Even if it had been, it was one of those that had its
hinges on the outside, and all he would have had to do would
have been to knock the hinge pins out and he could have lifted
it up from the hinge side. He left it open, just in case he had to
make a quick exit and couldn't use the route out he'd planned.

The space he slipped down into was more of a crawl space

than an attic, too small to be practical to store anything. He crawled on his hands and knees, feeling his way along until he came to the hatch that led down into the hallway separating all of the dozen garret rooms where Londer's servants slept, six on one side of the corridor, and six on the other.

Well, where the servants Londer had would have slept, if he'd had more than the three he kept. Like everything else Londer had, his servants were cheap because no one else would have them, and he worked them—screaming and cursing at them all the while—until they dropped. His man-of-all-work was a drunkard, so was his cook, and the overworked housemaid was another half-wit like Maisie. None of them was going to wake up short of Skif falling on them, which obviously he didn't intend to do.

Not that he was going to take any chances about it.

He found the hatch, which had a cover meant to be pushed up and aside from the hallway below. He lifted it up and put it out of the way, then stuck his head down into the hall and took a quick look around.

As he'd expected, it was deserted, not so dark as the crawl space thanks to a tiny window on either end of the hall, and silent but for three sets of snoring.

He actually had to stop and listen in fascination for a moment, for he'd never heard anything like it.

There was a deep, basso rumbling which was probably the handyman, whose pattern was a long, drawn out sound interrupted by three short *snorks.* Layered atop this was a second set, vaguely alto in pitch, of short, loud snorts in a rising tone that sounded like an entire sty full of pigs. And atop that was a soprano solo with snoring on the intake of breath and whistling on the exhalation. One was the housemaid and the other the cook, but which was which? The housemaid was younger, but fatter than the cook, so either could have had the soprano.

All three were so loud that he could not imagine how they managed not to wake *themselves* up. It took everything he had to keep from laughing out loud, and he wished devoutly that he dared describe this to one of the Bardic Trainees. They'd have hysterics.

At least now he knew for certain that the last thing he needed to worry about was making a noise up here.

He grabbed the edge of the hatch and somersaulted over, slowly and deliberately, lowering himself down by the strength of his arms alone until his arms were extended full-length. His feet still dangled above the floor, so he waited for the moment when the chorus of snores overlapped, and let go, hoping the noise would cover the sound of his fall.

He landed with flexed knees, caught his balance bent over with his knuckles just touching the floor, and froze, waiting to see if there would be a reaction.

Not a sound to indicate that anyone had heard him.

Heh. Not gonna be hard figuring which rooms are empty! That had been a serious concern; he *needed* to find an empty room with a window, get into it, get the window unlocked and opened for his escape, because now that he was inside, he knew that there was no way he was going to get out the way he came in. If there had been a ladder to let down from the crawl space, that would have been ideal, but there wasn't.

By great good fortune, the room nearest the drainpipe he wanted to use was one of the empty ones—no thief could survive long who wasn't able to tell where he was inside a house in relation to the outside without ever being inside. Out of the breast of his tunic came one of his trusty bladders of oil, and he oiled the hinges to the dripping point by feel before he even tried to open the door.

There was a faint creak, but it was entirely smothered in snores; the door opened onto a completely barren room, not a stick of furniture in it. Moonlight shone in through the dirty window, finally giving him something to see by. After the absolute dark of the crawl space and the relative dark of the hallway, it seemed as bright as day.

Moving carefully with a care for creaking floorboards, he eased his way over to the window, and out came the oil again. When catches, locks, and hinges were all thoroughly saturated, he got the window open wide, checked to make sure he could reach the drainpipe from its sill, and left it that way. He did, however, close the door to the room most of the way, just in case one of the three snorers woke up and felt impelled to take a stroll. They were too dimwitted to think of an intruder, but they might take it into their heads to close the window, which would slow his retreat.

The servants' stair lay at the end of the hallway, and it was just the narrow sort of arrangement that Skif would have expected from the age of the house. In this part of the city, land was at a premium, so as little space as possible within a home was "wasted" on servants' amenities. But fortunately, whoever had built this stair had done so with an eye to *silence* in his servants, and had built it so sturdily that it probably wouldn't creak if a horse went down it.

Not even Londer's neglect could undo work that solid, not in the few years that Londer had owned the house anyway.

Down the stairs went Skif, and now he had to go on the memories of a very small child augmented by as much study of the house from outside as he had been able to manage. Londer's bedroom, as he recalled, and as study of the house seemed to indicate, was on the next floor down, overlooking the street. A curious choice, given that street noise was going to be something of a disturbance and would *certainly* be obtrusive early in the morning. But Londer wanted to see who was at his door before they were announced, and the other choice of master bedroom was over the kitchen and *under* the servants' rooms. Altogether a poor choice for someone who probably knew all about the snorers' chorus and didn't want it resonating down into his bedroom. Nor would he want the aromas of the cook's latest accident permeating his bedroom and lingering in the hangings.

He stifled another laugh as he felt his way down the stair, tread by tread.

He could only wonder what Londer had thought when he discovered the amazing snoring powers of all three of his servants.

This stair should come out beside the room just over the kitchen that Londer used for his guests. Important guests, of course, not people like his sister and her young son. They'd lived in one of the garret rooms, though Skif couldn't remember which one, since they hadn't lived there for long.

When he reached the landing, once again he stopped and listened. Aside from the now faint chorus from Snore Hall above, there was nothing.

He took a precautionary sniff of the air, for a room that was occupied had a much different scent than one that had been shut up for a while. If Uncle had a guest that Skif didn't know about, the guest became an unforeseen complication, a possible source of interference.

But the scent that came to his nose was of a room that had lain unused for a very long time; a touch of mildew, a great deal of dust. And when he emerged from the stair he found himself, as he had reckoned, in the dressing room to that unused guest suite.

The dressing room led directly to the corridor, and probably the reason that the stair came out into it at all was the very sensible one of convenience for the original master and builder of the house, who probably *would* have chosen this suite for himself. Water for baths would come straight up the stair from the kitchen in cans, to be poured into the bath in the dressing room. If the master was hungry and rang for service, his snack would be brought up in moments, freshly prepared.

This corridor was short; it ran between the old master suite to two other sets of rooms. It extended the width of the house and had a window on either end, with the staircase leading downward for the family's use on Skif's right. Three doors let out on it, besides the one that Skif stood in. The one on Skif's side led to a second bedroom separate from the master suite, probably intended for a superior personal maid or manservant. The two opposite were probably for guests or children in the original plan. One was now Londer's, and heaven only knew what he did with the other.

Skif put his ear to the door nearest him on that side.

It was definitely occupied, although the slumberer was no match for the trio upstairs. Just to be sure, Skif eased down the corridor and checked the other.

Silent and, as turning the door handle proved, locked as well.

He returned to Londer's room, took a steadying breath, and took out—

—another bladder of oil. Because he did not want Londer to wake up until Skif's knife was at his throat.

Only when the hinges were saturated did Skif ease the door open, wincing at the odor that rolled out.

Well, the old man hasn't changed his bathing habits any.

After the cleanliness of Bazie's room, the Priory, and the Collegium, Skif's nose wrinkled at the effluvia of unwashed clothing, unwashed sheets, unwashed body, rancid sweat, and bad breath. It wasn't bad enough to gag a goat, but it was close.

If this wasn't so important, I'd leave now. It made his skin crawl to think of getting so close to *that* foul stench, but he didn't have much choice.

Londer had his windows open to the night air, so at least he could see. And at least he wasn't going to smother in the stink.

He took a deep breath, this time of cleaner air, and slipped inside.

Londer didn't wake until the edge of the knife—the *dull* edge, did he but know it—was against his throat. Skif had tried to time his entry for when the moon was casting the most light on the streetward side of the house. In fact, moonlight streamed in through the windows, and Skif could tell from the sheer terror on Londer's face that he was having no trouble seeing what there *was* to see of Skif.

"Don't move," Skif hissed. "And don't shout."

"I won't," Londer whimpered. "What d'you want from me?"

Londer shivered with fear; Skif had never seen anyone actually *doing* that, and to see Londer's fat jowls shaking like a jelly induced a profound disgust in him.

"You can start," hissed Skif, "by telling me what you did with my sister."

Londer looked as if he was going to have a fit right there and then, and Skif thought he might have hit gold—but it turned out that Londer had just gotten rough with one of his paid women, and he thought that Skif was *her* brother. Not but that Skif was averse to seeing him terrified over it, but that wasn't the street he wanted to hound his uncle down.

So he quickly established that the apocryphal sister was one of the children snatched off the streets, and the interview continued on that basis.

Skif must have looked and sounded twice as intimidating as he thought, because Londer was reduced in very short order to a blubbering mound of terror and tears. Skif would have been very glad to have the Heraldic Truth Spell at his disposal, but he figured that fear was getting almost as much truth out of Londer as the Spell would have.

Unfortunately, there was very little to get. Londer knew some of what was going on, as Skif had thought; he knew some of the men who were doing the actual snatches, what their method was for picking a victim, how they managed it without raising too much fuss, and where they went with the victims afterward. Which, as Skif had guessed, was one of Londer's own warehouses. But who the real powers *behind* the snatches were, he had no idea; his knowledge was all at street level. Even the warehouse had been hired by a go-between.

Which was disgusting enough. Londer whimpered and carried on, literally sweating buckets, trying to make out that the poor younglings grabbed by the gang were better off than they'd be on the street. Sheltered and fed, maybe, but better off? *If* they were incredibly lucky and not at all attractive, they'd find themselves working from dawn to dusk at some skinflint's farm, or knotting rugs, sewing shirts, making rope, or any one of a hundred tasks that needed hands but not much strength.

If they were pretty—well, that was something Skif didn't want to think about too hard. There had been a child-brothel four streets over from the Hollybush that had been shut down when he was still with Bazie—there were things that even the denizens of Exile's Gate wouldn't put up with—but where there was one, there were probably more. The only reason why this one had been uncovered was because someone had been careless, or someone had snitched.

But by far and away the single most important piece of information that Skif got was that the man who was in charge of the entire ring always came to inspect the children when they were brought to the warehouse. It seemed he didn't trust the judgment of his underlings. If there was ever to be a time to catch him, that would be it.

When Skif had gotten everything he thought he could out of Londer, he took the knife away from the man's throat. Londer started to babble; an abrupt gesture with the knife shut him up again, and Skif thrust a bottle made from a small gourd at him.

"Drink it," he ordered.

Londer's eyes bulged. "Y'wouldn't poison me—"

"Oh, get shut," Skif snapped, exasperated. "I'd be 'shamed to count ye as a kill. 'Tis poppy, fool. I've got no time t' tie ye up an' gag ye, even if I could stummack touchin' ye. Now drink!"

Londer pulled the cork with his teeth and sucked down the contents of the bottle; Skif made him open his mouth wide to be sure he actually had swallowed it, and wasn't holding it. Then he sat back and waited, knowing that it was going to take longer for the drug to take effect on the man because of Londer's fear counteracting it. Meanwhile, his uncle just stared at him, occasionally venturing a timid question that Skif did not deign to answer. If he really *was* someone out to discover the whereabouts of a young sister, he'd spend no more time on Londer than he had to, and tempting as it was to pay back everything he owed Londer in the way of misery, such torment would not have been in keeping with his assumed role.

And it might give Londer a clue to his real identity.

So he stayed quiet, focusing what he hoped was a menacing gaze on the man, until at long, long last, Londer's eyelids drooped and dropped, his trembling stopped, all his muscles went slack, and the drug took him over.

Only then did Skif leave the room, taking the bottle with him.

His exit via the garret room and the drainpipe was uneventful, as was his exchange of clothing in the stable and his escape from that part of town. It almost seemed as if there was a good spirit watching over him and smoothing his way.

He said as much to Cymry, once they were up in among the mansions of the great and powerful.

:I wish you'd gotten more information, then,: she replied ruefully. *:I hate to think that much good luck was wasted on essentially trivial knowledge.:*

"Not as trivial as y'might think," he replied thoughtfully, for a new plan was beginning to take shape in his mind. It was a plan that was fraught with risk, but it might be worth it.

And he was *not* going to carry out this one alone. . . .

"Out late, aren't you, Trainee?" said a voice at his stirrup, startling him. He looked down to discover that Cymry had brought him to the little gate in the Palace walls used by all the Trainees on legitimate business, and the Gate Guard was looking up at him with a hint of suspicion.

:Tell him the truth, loon,: Cymry prompted, as he tried to think of something to say. He hadn't expected that Cymry would try to take them in the same way they'd gone out.

"I had t'see my uncle in Haven," he said truthfully. "He didn't think he was gonna live. There was summat I needed t'hear from him."

:Very good. He really didn't *think you'd leave him alive, did he?:*

The Guard's demeanor went from suspicious to sympathetic. "I hope his fears weren't justified—"

Skif stopped himself from snorting. "I think he was more scared than anything else," he replied. "When I left, he was sleepin' off a dose of poppy, and I bet he'll be fine in the morning."

:Lovely. Absolute truth, all of it.:

Evidently the Guard either had relatives who were overly convinced of their own mortality, or knew people who were, because he laughed. "Oh, aye, I understand. Well, I'm sorry you're going to have your sleep cut short; breakfast bell is going to ring mighty early for you."

Skif groaned. "Don't remind me," he said, as the Guard waved him through without even taking his name. "Good night to you!"

He unsaddled Cymry and turned her loose, and slipped into his room again via the window, thus avoiding any potentially awkward questions in the hall. He'd had the wit to clean himself up thoroughly at that stable, so at least he needed to do nothing more than strip himself down and drop into bed— which he did, knowing all too well just how right that Guard had been.

Tomorrow, though . . . he had to arrange an interview with the Weaponsmaster. The sooner, the better.

All during his classes the next day he had only half his mind on what was going on. The other half was engaged in putting together his plan, and as importantly, his argument. Herald Alberich wasn't going to like this plan. It was going to be very dangerous for Skif, and Skif knew for certain that Alberich would object to that.

During Weapons Class, Skif managed to give Alberich an unspoken signal that he *hoped* would clue Alberich to the fact that he needed to talk privately. Either he was very quick on the uptake, or else Cymry had some inkling of what was going on inside Skif's head and put the word in to Alberich's Kantor; in either case, just as class ended, Alberich looked straight at Skif and said, "You will be at my quarters here at the salle, after the dinner hour."

The others in the class completely misconstrued the order, as they were probably intended to. So as they all left for their next class, they commiserated with him, assuming that something he had done or not done well enough was going to earn him a lecture.

"I know what it is. It's that you dragged yourself through practice. Whatever you were doing last night to keep you up, you shouldn't have been," Kris said forthrightly. "You've got rings like a ferret under your eyes. If you thought *he* wasn't going to notice that, you're crazed."

"He'll probably give you a lecture about it, is all," opined Coroc.

"I suppose," Skif said, and sighed heavily. In actuality, he really wasn't *that* tired, although he expected to be after dinner. That was probably when it would all catch up with him.

"Whatever it was, it can't have been worth one of Alberich's lectures," Kris said flatly.

Skif just yawned and hung his head, to feign sheepishness that he in no way felt.

His next class was no class at all, it was a session in the sewing room, where he couldn't stop yawning over his work. The other boys in his classes had twitted him about his self-chosen assignment on the chore roster, until he pointed out that he was the only boy in a room full of girls. They'd gotten very quiet, then, and thoughtful—and stopped teasing him.

Today he was very glad that this was his chore, because the girls were far more sympathetic about his yawns and dark-circled eyes than the boys had been. Not that they let him off any—but they did keep him plied with cold tea to keep him awake, and they did make sure he got the best stool for the purpose—one that was comfortable, but not so comfortable that he was going to fall asleep.

A quick wash in cold water while the rest of them were having hot baths woke him up very nicely, and he hurried through his dinner, now as much anxious as eager. Alberich wouldn't like the plan, but would he go along with it anyway? It was probably his duty to forbid Skif even to think about carrying it out, even though it was the best and fastest way to get the man they were both after.

Well, Alberich could forbid him, but that wouldn't stop him. He just wouldn't use *that* plan; he'd come up with something else.

So as he walked quickly across the lawn, with the light of early evening pouring golden across the grass, he steeled himself to the notion that Alberich would not only not like the plan, but would put all the resources of the Collegium behind making sure Skif didn't try it alone.

Well, I won't. I dunno what I'll do, but I can't do that one alone, so there 'tis. He didn't need Cymry warning him against it; the entire plan depended on having someone else—by necessity a Herald or Trainee—standing by. There was not one single Trainee that Skif would dare even bring down to Exile's Gate quarter in the daytime, much less at night. So it would have to be a Herald, and the only one likely to agree to this would be Alberich. Which brought him right around to crux of the matter again.

He entered the salle, and went to the back of it, where one of the mirrors concealed the door to Alberich's other set of quarters. It was no secret that they were there, but it wasn't widely bruited about either. Maybe the concealed door was older than Alberich, who knew? Skif could think of a lot of reasons why hidden rooms might come in handy.

He tapped on the wall beside the mirror, and it swung open as Alberich pushed on the door from within.

He stepped inside. Alberich closed the door behind him and brought him through a small room that served him as an office and contained only a desk and a chair. On the other side of a doorway to the left were the private quarters, a suite that began with a rather austere room that contained only two chairs, a ceramic-tiled wood stove, and a large bookcase. Alberich gestured to the nearest chair. The sole aspect of the room that wasn't austere was the huge window along one wall, made up of many small panes of colored glass leaded together, forming a pattern of blues and golds that looked something like a man's face, and something like a sun-in-glory. It looked as though it faced east, so it wasn't at its best, just glowing softly. Most of the room's illumination came from lanterns Alberich had already lit. Skif made a note to himself to nip around to the back of the salle some time after dark; with lanterns behind it, the window must be nearly as impressive as it would be from within the room in early morning.

But Alberich didn't give Skif a chance to contemplate the window, though, since his chair had him facing away from it. A pity; he'd have liked to just sit there and study it for a time. Someone had told him that the Palace chapel had several windows like this, as did the major temples in Haven, but this was the first time he'd seen one close up.

The Weaponsmaster barely waited for him to settle himself.

"So, your little excursion into the city last night bore some fruit?" was Alberich's question.

Good, he's already gotten everything from Cymry and Kantor and maybe the Guard but the "who" and maybe the "why." That was a bit less explanation he'd have to give. "I visited m'uncle Londer Galko," Skif said, then smiled. "Though he didn't know 'twas me. Went masked, and in over roof. *You* know. I scared him pretty thorough, good enough I figger he told me the truth."

As well Alberich should know, since he'd been the one who brought Skif's things from his old room, and had probably examined every bit. Skif experienced in that moment a very, very odd sensation of *comfort.* It was a relief to be able to sit here and be able to be himself completely. It was like being with Cymry, only a more worldly sort of Cymry.

"That was wise." Alberich leaned forward, resting his elbows on his knees, and looked thoughtful. "I would not have thought of Londer Galko as a source of information for our needs."

"I didn' either, till I stopped lookin' for a man what needed a building burned, and started thinkin' about what I picked up while I was lookin' for him," Skif replied. "An' put that with what you tol' me about the slavers. There's summat snatchin' younglings off the streets—not many, just the ones that have-ta sleep there. More of 'em than you thought, I bet. You don't hear 'bout it, 'cause they ain't the kind that'd be missed."

"We hear more than you might think," Alberich put in, but also nodded. "Although if this is true, we are not hearing of most of them. Go on."

"Londer ain't the kind t'get his fingers where they might get burned, not after that mess with th' Hollybush, but if there's somethin' dirty goin' on, he probably knows summat about it. He likes bein' on the edge of it, not so close he gets hurt, close enough he can kind of gloat over it. So—I paid 'im a visit." Skif launched into a full explanation, frankly describing everything he had done last night, leaving nothing out. He hadn't, after all, done anything that he'd been forbidden. Nobody had put a curfew on the Trainees, no one had told him not to leave the Collegium grounds, he hadn't stolen anything. All he'd done was to terrorize one filthy old man who'd been the cause of plenty of misery himself over the past several years.

Still—

Alberich didn't look disgusted, and he didn't look annoyed, but Skif got a distinct impression that he was poised between being amused and being angry. "You—" he said at length, leaning back in his chair and pointing a finger at Skif, "—are the sort who would find a way around *any* order, so I shall not give you one. This information interesting is—useful, possibly—"

"But if I was to go out all ragged an' kip down on th'street where I know they's been snatching?" Skif asked. "While you kept a watch? It'd be more'n useful, I'm thinkin'. We got what we need for the makings of a nice little trap. An' it's one you can't set without a youngling for bait." He stabbed his thumb at his chest. "Me. You *daren't* use anyone else."

Alberich's face went very, very still. "If you did not Mindspeak with Cymry—" he said, very slowly.

"But I do. An' you got Kantor. So 'tween them we can Mindspeak each other. An' I got some ideas that'll keep me from gettin' coshed, 'cause I know how they been workin'," Skif replied, and sat back himself. "You'll know when I get took, an' you can follow. You'll know when th' man hisself shows up. We can do more'n figger out who he is. *We can catch 'im.*"

"It is very dangerous. You could be hurt," Alberich pointed out immediately. "You can attempt to protect yourself, but that does not mean you will succeed."

"Then I get hurt," Skif dismissed, feeling his jaw tense and his own resolve harden. "It'll be worth it."

Alberich half-closed his eyes and laced his fingers together, occasionally looking up at Skif as though testing his mettle. If this long wait was supposed to test his patience as well, it wasn't going to work that way, for the longer Alberich thought, the better Skif reckoned his odds to be.

And when at last Alberich spoke, he knew he'd been right.

"Very well," the Weaponsmaster said. "Let me hear the whole of this plan of yours. I believe that you and I must do this thing."

19

SKIF widened his eyes pleadingly and held out his bowl to anyone who even glanced at him. He certainly looked the part of a beggar boy. He hadn't worn rags like these since he'd been living at the Hollybush. It was a good thing that it was still very warm at night, or he'd be freezing in the things. They were more hole than cloth, and he couldn't imagine where Alberich had found them, couldn't imagine why *anyone* in the Collegium would have kept them.

At least they were clean. His need for authenticity didn't run to dirt and lice, and fortunately, neither did Alberich's; a little soot smeared across his forehead, chin, and cheekbones provided the illusion of dirt, and that was all that was required.

This time the place where Skif's transformation had taken place had been supplied by Alberich, not that Skif was surprised at the Weaponsmaster's resources. Alberich couldn't have walked out of the Complex in his sell-sword gear, after all.

Alberich brought him to an inn where a Herald and a Trainee could ride into the stable yard unremarked. No surprises there; the innkeeper greeted him by name, and they took Cymry and Kantor to the stable, to special loose-boxes without doors. Then came the surprise, in the form of a locked room at the back of the stable to which Alberich had the key, and which contained both a trunk of disguise material and a rear entrance onto an alley. A beggar boy slipped out that entrance into the shadows of dusk somewhat later, and after him, a disreputable sell-sword whose face would be moderately familiar in the Exile's Gate quarter. Another purpose for all that soot on Skif's features was to disguise them. It wouldn't do for him to be recognized.

Skif made his way quietly to Exile's Gate itself; then as if he had come in the Gate, he wandered the street in his old neighborhood, training his voice into a tremulous piping as he begged from the passersby. Mostly he got kicks and curses, though once someone gave him an end of a loaf, and two others offered a rind of bacon and a rind of cheese. Beggars here got food more often than coin, though there was little enough of the former. Skif went a little cold when he thought about a child trying to live on such meager fare.

He got a drink at a public pump and wandered about some more as the streets grew darker and torches and a few lanterns were put up outside those businesses that were staying open past full dark. There were streetlights, but they were very few and often the oil was stolen, or even the entire lamp. He was ostensibly looking for a place to sleep on the street, out of the way of traffic. Actually he knew exactly where he was going to go to sleep, but he had to make a show out of it, because the child snatchers were almost certainly watching him. He also kept hunched over, both to look more miserable and to look smaller. The younger the children were, the more timid they were, the better the snatchers liked them.

And behind him, going from drink stall to tavern, was Alberich. There was great comfort in knowing that.

:Kantor says Alberich is very surprised at how good you are at this.:

:A thief that gets noticed doesn't stay out of gaol long,: he replied, though he was secretly flattered. Now, if he'd *really* been trying to make his way as a beggar, *he* would never be doing it this way. He'd have bound up his leg to look as if he'd lost it, or done the same with an arm. No sores, though; people around here would stone him into some other quarter for fear of a pox. Then he'd stand as straight as he could and catcall the people passing by, a noisy banter that was impossible to ignore. He'd be cheeky, but funny, and not insulting. People liked that; they liked seeing a display of bravado, especially in a cripple. He'd be making a better go of it than this thin, wistful waif he was impersonating. And the child snatchers would avoid him. A child like that would never tame down, and would cause nothing but trouble.

In his persona of woeful beggar child, he had a single possession that was going to make this entire ruse work—a wooden begging bowl. Perfectly in character with what he was, no one would even remark on it. And it was going to keep him from being knocked unconscious, because it was much deeper than the usual bowl and fit his head exactly like a helmet. Once he curled himself up in his chosen spot for the night and pulled his ragged hood over his head, he'd slip that bowl over it under the rags. When the snatchers came along and gave him that tap on the head to keep him from waking up when they grabbed him, he'd be protected.

He also had weapons on his person; his throwing daggers were concealed up his sleeves. Alberich hadn't needed to tell him to bring them. Having them made him feel a good deal safer, although his first choice of weapon wouldn't have been one that you threw at the enemy. Or it wouldn't have been if he wasn't so certain of his own accuracy. It was very unlikely that he'd be searched. These beggar children never had any-thing of value on them. If they once had, it was long snatched by those older and stronger than they were.

As he trudged away from the streets where people were still carrying on the minutiae of their lives and toward the ware-houses and closed-up workshops, he felt eyes on him. The back of his neck prickled. The warehouse section of Exile's Gate was where most of the children had vanished from, and he knew now, with heavy certainty, that the snatchers were somewhere out there watching him, waiting for him to settle.

Alberich was out there, too, and had taken to the same co-vert skulking as Skif's stalkers. He was hunting the hunters, watching the watchers, to make sure that if anything went wrong, Skif wouldn't be facing it alone.

:He's seen two of them, anyway,: reported Cymry.

He would never, ever have attempted this by himself, or even with someone who didn't also have a Companion. The key to this entire plan was that Kantor and Cymry could Mind-speak to each other, keeping Skif and Alberich aware of every-thing that was going on.

The buildings here were large, with long expanses of blank wall planted directly on the street—you didn't want or need windows in a warehouse. There weren't a lot of places where a tired child could curl up to sleep. But where there *was* a doorway that was just big enough to fit a small body, or a recessed gate, it was dark and it was quiet, and no one was likely to come along to chivvy one off until dawn. Mind, any number of adult beggars knew this too, so the first few places Skif poked his nose into were occupied, and the occupants sent him off with poorly-aimed blows and liberal curses. He lost his bacon rind to one of them, not that he fought for it.

But when he did find a place, it was perfect for the child snatchers, and thus perfect for his purposes. It was a recessed doorway, a black arch in a darkened street, with no one in sight in either direction.

He sat down on the doorstep and pretended to eat his crust and cheese rind, then with a calculatedly pathetic sigh that should be audible to his stalkers, he curled up with his back to the street and his rags pulled up over his head. If that wasn't an invitation, he'd turn priest.

As he stirred and fidgeted, "trying to get comfortable," he slipped his wooden bowl over his head, exactly as he had planned. Once he had, he felt a good deal safer, and the back of his neck stopped prickling so much. There had been the possibility that the snatchers, lured by how harmless he seemed to be and the loneliness of the street, would try for the grab before he curled up for the night. He was glad their caution had overcome their greed.

Gradually he stopped moving around, as a child would who was settling into sleep. He wouldn't find a tolerable position on this stone doorstep anyway, not after he'd gotten accustomed, not only to a bed, but to a *comfortable* bed.

Spoilt, that's what I am.

Once "asleep," he held himself still as a matter of pride, although the stone under his hip was painfully hard and his arm was getting pins and needles. Eventually, he *had* to shift off of that, but when he moved, it was only the formless stirring that a child would make when deeply asleep. He *should* be asleep; the beggar child he was counterfeiting was in the midst of one of the better moments of its short life. It had a full belly, a quiet place to lie down, it was neither too cold nor too hot. No one was going to chase it away from this shelter until morning, and if rain came, it wouldn't even get too wet. Never having known a soft bed, the stone of the doorway would be perfectly acceptable since countless feet had worn the step down in a hollow in the middle into which Skif's body fit perfectly.

Well, he hadn't had to sleep on the street, ever. That was partly because he was smart, but there was no telling how much he'd accomplished was because he'd been lucky. Mostly, he liked to think, it was because he'd been smart—though if Bazie hadn't taken him in, his life probably would have been a lot different. Harder, maybe. It depended on what he would have done after Beel warned him away from the Hollybush. If he'd gone back to Beel, he'd have had to make a statement against his uncle—

That could have gone badly for him. He'd known that even when he'd been that young—it was the reason he'd run off in the first place. Maybe he'd have been safe in Beel's Temple, maybe not. Finding out which could have been bad.

If he'd run, though . . . *I think maybe I'd have hidden in the storage room of Orthallen's wash house*. Then what? He didn't know. How long could he have gone on, sleeping in hidden places, stealing food from kitchens in the guise of a page?

Cymry interrupted his speculations. *:Kantor says they've all gotten together. There are three of them,:* Cymry reported, interrupting his thoughts. She sounded indignant. *:Three of them! For one little child!:*

Skif wasn't surprised. A pretty child, or one that was strong, was a valuable commodity. Having two to make the snatch and one to stand guard meant they could grab it with a minimum of damage to the merchandise. *:That's so one can be a lookout in case their target's gone inside a yard or something,:* Skif told her. *:But I have to agree. Even two seems kind of much for someone my size.:*

:It's disgusting.: He had to smile at the affronted quality in her words. *:Not that the whole thing isn't disgusting, but—:*

:I understand,: he told her. And he did. It was disgusting. He could think abstractly about a child as "merchandise," but the minute he allowed himself to get outside of those abstractions, he was disgusted.

:Skif, be ready; they're moving in.:

He heard them in the last few paces; if he'd really been asleep, particularly if he was an exhausted child with a full belly, it wouldn't have disturbed him, but he heard their soft footfalls on the hard-packed dirt of the street. They were cautious, he gave them that, but waiting for them to finally make their move was enough to drive him mad. He had to grit his teeth and clench his muscles to *stay put* when every instinct and most of his training screamed at him to get up and defend himself.

Then they were on him, all three of them in a rush.

He was enveloped in a smelly blanket. Instinct won over control and he felt the mere beginnings of a reaction—but before he could even move, much less come up fighting, someone hit him a precise blow to the head.

The bowl took most of it, as he'd anticipated, but his head and ears still rang with it. In fact, for just a moment, he saw stars. He went limp, partly with intent, partly with the shock of the blow, and when he could move again, he regained control over himself and stayed properly limp.

They didn't dally about. They bundled him up cocoonlike in the blanket, one of the snatchers threw the bundle over his shoulder with a grunt of effort, and they were off at a lope. Whoever had Skif must have been a big man, because he carried Skif as if he was nothing.

Cymry did not ask "Are you all right," because she knew he was. And what she knew, Alberich knew. So there was no point in wasting time with silly questions, when Alberich needed to concentrate on following Skif's captors, and Skif had immediate concerns of his own to deal with. Skif concentrated on breathing carefully in that foully smothering blanket, staying limp, and keeping up the ruse that he was as completely unconscious as that blow to the head should have rendered him. This was the hardest part of the plan—to literally do nothing while his captor carried him off, and hope that Alberich could keep up with them. They only had to get to their goal, which might or might not be Londer's warehouse. Alberich had to stay with them while remaining unseen.

Not the easiest task in the world; Skif had shadowed enough people in his life to know how hard it really was.

He'd have to get the bowl off his head, too, at some point in the near future, or they'd figure out he wasn't what he seemed and he wasn't unconscious. Definitely before he got unwrapped, or he'd be in a far more uncomfortable position than he was now. So as the man jogged along, Skif worked his hands, a little at a time, up toward his head.

The blanket smelled of so many things, all of them horrid, that he hated to think of what had happened in it and to it. It wasn't so much a blanket as a heavy tarpaulin of something less scratchy than wool. Was it sailcloth? It could be. He wasn't so tightly wrapped up in it that he couldn't move. He'd been "sleeping" with his arms up against his chest, so he shouldn't have too far to work them to get his hands on that bowl. . . .

He was glad he hadn't eaten much, since his head and torso were dangling upside down along his captor's back, the stench of the blanket was appalling, and the man's shoulder essentially hit him in the gut with every step. If there was a better recipe for nausea, he didn't know it. He'd have been sick if he hadn't been cautious about not eating much beforehand.

Bit by bit, he worked his arms higher, moving them only with the motion of the man who carried him, slowly working his hands up through the canvas towards the bowl. Then, at long last, with the tips of his fingers, he touched it.

With a sigh of relief, he pushed with his fingertips and ducked his head at the same time as the man stumbled. The bowl came off his head and fell off into the folds of the blanket. He was rid of it, and now he could—

—not relax, certainly. But wait, be still, try to ignore the reek of the blanket, and remember the next part of the plan.

:It looks as if your uncle's warehouse really is the goal,: Cymry said.

He wished he could see. *Hellfires, I wish I could breathe!*

But if Londer's warehouse was the goal, it couldn't be very much longer. Alberich was supposed to have scouted the place during the day, so he'd be familiar with the outside, at least. Skif just wished that the Weaponsmaster was as good at roof walking as he was—if only they could have switched parts—

Don't worry about your partner. If he says he can do something, and you've got no cause to think otherwise, then let him do his job and concentrate on yours.

Well, that was easy to say, and hard to do, when it all came down to cases.

It seemed forever before the men stopped, and when they did, Skif was gritting his teeth so hard he thought they might splinter with the tension. They knocked on the door, quite softly, in a pattern of three, two, and five.

:*Got it,*: Cymry said. :*Alberich doesn't know if he's going to try going in that way, but if he does, that will make it easier.*:

The door creaked open. "Got 'nother one?" said a voice in a harsh whisper, with accents of surprise. "Tha's third'un tonight!"

"Pickin's is good," said the man to Skif's right, as the one carrying him grunted. "Got'r eyes on two more prime 'uns, so le's get this'un settled."

"Boss'll be right happy," said the doorkeeper, as the men moved forward and closed the door behind them.

"Tha's th'ideer," grunted the man with Skif.

They moved more slowly now, and to Skif's dismay there was a fair amount of opening and closing of doors, and direction changes down passages. This place must be a veritable warren! How was Alberich supposed to find him in all of this if he got inside?

:*Let us worry about that,*: said Cymry—right before there was the sound of another door opening, then the unmistakable feeling that his captor was descending a staircase.

Descending a staircase? There's a cellar to this place? There isn't supposed to be a cellar here!

Skif was in something of a panic, because part of the emergency plan figured in the Companions coming in as well as Alberich, and the Companions were not going to be able to get down a narrow, steep set of stairs into a cellar.

He had to remind himself that he was *not* alone, he was armed, and he was probably smarter than any of these people. No matter what happened here, sooner or later they would *have* to take him outside this building, and when they did, he could escape.

Even if he and Alberich couldn't actually catch the head of this gang of slavers right now, so long as Skif could get a good look at him, they'd have him later.

What's the worst that can happen? he asked himself, and set himself to imagining it. Alberich wouldn't get in. He'd be held for a while, maybe with other children, maybe not. The master of this gang would inspect them; Skif could make sure he saw enough he *would* be able to pick him out again. Then—well, the question was how attractive they found him.

He had to stop himself from shuddering. Just by virtue of being healthy and in good shape, he was as pretty as most of the street urchins they'd been picking up. Which meant there was one place where they'd send him.

Now the panic became real; his throat closed with fear and he had trouble breathing. *Oh, no—oh, no—*

In all his years on the street, he had never really had to face the possibility that he might end up a child-whore. Now he did, for if he couldn't get away from these people, or they found out what he was doing—

His imagination painted far worse things than he had ever seen, cobbled up out of all the horrible stories he had ever heard, and his breath came in short and painful gasps. He went from stifling to icy cold. What if their—the *brothel* was here, in this building? They wouldn't have to take him outside. They wouldn't have to move him at all. He wouldn't get a chance to escape—they could keep him here as long as they wanted to, they could—they *would!* strip him down first and find his knives. What would they do to him then? Drug him, maybe? Kill him? Oh no, probably not that, not while they could get some use out of him—

Don't panic. Don't panic.

How could he *not* panic?

:Chosen—we won't let that happen. We'll get to you, no matter what—:

But how *would* they? How *could* they? It would take a small army to storm this place, and by then—

The man carrying him got to the bottom of the stair and made a turning. "This brat's awful quiet," he grunted to his fellow. "Ye sure ye didn' 'it 'im too 'ard?"

"No more'n the rest uv 'em," the other snapped. " 'E's breathin', ain't 'e?"

"Aye—just don' wanta hev'ta turn over damaged goods. Milord don't care fer damaged goods." The man hefted Skif a little higher on his shoulder, surprising him into an involuntary groan, caused as much by desperation as by pain.

"There, ye see?" the second man said in triumph. "Nothin' wrong wi' 'im. 'E's wakin' up right on time."

"Les' get 'im locked up, then," said the one from the door.

There was the sound of a key turning in a lock, a heavy door swinging open. Then, quite suddenly, Skif found himself being dumped unceremoniously onto something soft.

Well, softish. Landing knocked the breath out of him, though he managed to keep from banging his head when he landed. He heard the door slam and the key turn in the lock again before he got his wits back.

He struggled free of the stinking confines of the blanket, only to find himself in the pitch dark, and he was just as blind as he'd been in the blanket. He felt around, heard rustling, and felt straw under his questing hands. The "something soft" he'd been dumped on was a pile of old straw, smelling of mildew and dust, but infinitely preferable to the stench of the blanket.

He got untangled from the folds of that foul blanket, wadded it up, and with a convulsive movement, flung it as far away from himself as possible. The wooden bowl that had saved his skull from being cracked clattered down out of the folds of it as it flew across the room.

Which wasn't far, after all; he heard it hit a wall immediately. His prison *was* a prison then, and a small one. He got onto his hands and knees, and began feeling his way to the nearest wall. Rough brick met his hands, so cheap it was crumbling under his questing fingers, a symptom of the damp getting into it.

He got to his feet, and followed it until it intersected the next wall, and the next, and the next—and then came to the door.

A few moments more of exploring by touch proved that this wasn't a room, it was a cell; it couldn't have been more than three arm's lengths wide and twice that in length.

Not a very well-constructed cell, though. Rough brick made up the walls, and the floor was nothing more than pounded dirt with the straw atop it. And when Skif got to the door, he finally felt some of his fear ebbing. The lock on this door had never been designed with the idea of confining a thief. He could probably have picked it in the pitch-dark with a pry bar; the throwing daggers he wore were fine enough to work through the hole in the back plate and trip the mechanism.

I can get out. That was all it took to calm him. These people never intended to have to hold more than a few frightened children down here. As long as they thought that was what he was, he'd be fine. If *this* was their child brothel, he could get out of it.

:Or you can jam the lock and keep them out *until we get in,:* Cymry pointed out, and he nearly laughed aloud at what a simple and elegant solution she had found for him. Yes, he

could, he could! Then help could take as long as it needed to
reach him. Even if they set fire to the warehouse to cover their
tracks, he should be safe down here. He remembered once,
when one of the taverns had caught fire, how half a dozen of
the patrons had hidden in the cellars and come out covered in
soot but safe—and drunk out of their minds, for they'd been
trapped by falling timbers and had decided they might as well
help themselves to the stock.

    :Will you be all right now?: Cymry asked anxiously.

    :Right and tight,: he told her. And he would be, he would.
He had to be. Everything depended on him now.

    He would be.

He heard the men enter and leave again twice more, and each
time a door creaked open somewhere and he heard the thump
of some small load landing in straw. He winced each time for
the sake of the poor semiconscious child that it represented.

    Between the first and the second, Cymry told him that Al-
berich had gotten into the building, but could tell him nothing
more than that. It was not long after that the men arrived with
the second child—and soon after that when the cellars awoke.

    There was noise first; voices, harsh and quarrelsome. Then
came heavy footsteps, and then light. So much light that it
shone under Skif's door and through all the cracks between
the heavy planks that the door was made up of.

    Then the door was wrenched open, and a huge man stood
silhouetted against the glare. Skif didn't have to pretend to
fear; he shrank back with a start, throwing up his arm to
shield his eyes.

    The man took a pace toward him, and Skif remembered his
knives, remembered that he didn't dare let anyone grab him
by the arm lest they be discovered. He scrambled backward
until he reached the wall, then, with his back pressed into the
brick, got to his feet, huddling his arms around his chest.

The man grabbed him by the collar, his arms and hands not being easy to grab in that position, and hauled him out into the corridor and down it, toward an opening.

The corridor wasn't very long, and there were evidently only six of the little brick cells in it, three on each side. It dead-ended to Skif's rear in a wall of the same rough brick. The man dragged Skif toward the open end, then threw him unceremoniously into the larger room beyond, a large and echoing chamber that was empty of furnishings and lit by lanterns hung from hooks depending from the ceiling. Skif landed beside three more children, all girls, all shivering and speechless with fear, tear-streaked faces masks of terror. Facing them were five men, four heavily armed, standing in pairs on either side of the fifth.

Was this the hoped-for mastermind behind all of this?

"'Ere's th' last on 'em, milord," said the man who'd brought Skif out. "The fust two ye said weren't good fer yer gennelmen. This a good 'nuff offerin'?"

Skif looked up from his fellow captives. For a moment, he couldn't see the man's face, but he knew the voice right enough.

"Very nice," purred the man, with just an edge of contempt beneath the approval. "Prime stock. Yes, they'll do. They'll do very nicely."

It was the same voice that had spoken with Jass in the tomb in the cemetery. And when "milord" came into the light, Skif stared at him, not in recognition, but to make sure he knew the face later. If this man was one of those that had attended Lord Orthallen's reception, Skif didn't recall him . . . but then, he had a very ordinary face. What Bazie would have called a "face-shaped face" with that laugh of his—neither this nor that, neither round nor oblong nor square, nondescript in every way, brown hair, brown eyes. He could have been anyone.

The man was wearing very expensive clothing, in quite excellent taste. That was something of a surprise; Skif would have expected excellent clothing in appalling taste, given the circumstances.

Milord—well, the clothing was up to the standards of the highborn, but something about him didn't fit. Since being at the Collegium, Skif had met a fair number of highborn, and there was an air about them, as if everyone they met would, as a matter of course, assume they were superior. So it was second nature to them, and they didn't have to think about it. This man wore his air of superiority, and his pride, openly, like a cloak.

So what, exactly, was he? He had money, he had power, but he just didn't fit the "merchant" mold either. Yet he *must* have influence, and *someone* must be feeding him information, or he never would have been able to continue to operate as successfully and invisibly as he had until now.

The man gestured, and one of the four men with him grabbed the shoulder of the girl he pointed at, hauling her to her feet. She couldn't have been more than eight or nine at most, thin and wan, and frightened into paralysis. The man walked around her, surveying her from every angle. He took her chin in his hand, roughly tilting her face up, even prying open her mouth to look at her teeth as tears ran soundlessly down her smudged cheeks, leaving tracks in the dirt. He didn't order her to be stripped, but then, given that she wasn't wearing much more than a tattered feed sack with a string around it, he didn't really need to.

"Yes," the man said, after contemplating her for long moments, during which she shivered like an aspen in the wind. She was a very pretty little thing under all her dirt, and Skif's heart ached for her. Hadn't her life been bad enough without this descent into nightmare? How could a tiny little child possibly deserve this?

And this was the man who had ordered the deaths of Bazie and the two boys with no more concern than if he had crushed a beetle beneath his foot. This man, with his face-shaped face—this was the face of true evil that concealed itself in blandness. No monster here, just a man who could have hidden himself in any crowd. He would probably pat his friends' children genially on the head, even give them little treats, this man who assessed the market value of a little girl and consigned her to a fearful fate. He was valued by his neighbors, no doubt, this beast in a man's skin.

Skif hated him. Hated the look of him, the sound of his voice, hated everything about him. Hated most of all that he could smile, and smile, and look so like any other man.

"Yes," the man said again, with a bland smile, the same smile a housewife might use when finding a particularly fat goose. "Pretty and pliant. This one will be very profitable for us."

"Oh—it is that I think not, good Guildmaster," said a highly accented voice from the doorway. Skif's heart leaped, and when Alberich himself walked through the door, sword and dagger at the ready, it was all he could do to keep from cheering aloud.

THERE was a moment of absolute silence, as even the Guildmaster's professional bodyguards were taken by surprise. But
that moment ended almost as soon as it began.

The man who'd brought Skif out bolted for the door behind
the Guildmaster, disappearing into the darkness. All four of
the bodyguards charged Alberich, as the Guildmaster himself
stood back with a smirk that would have maddened Skif, if he
hadn't been scrambling to get out of the way. He pushed the
three little girls ahead of him into the partial shelter of the
wall, and stood between them and the fighting. Not that he
was going to be able to do anything other than try and push
them somewhere else if the fighting rolled over them.

Not that *he* was going to be able to do anything to help
Alberich. He knew when he was outweighed, outweaponed,
and outclassed. This fight was no place for an undersized and
half-trained (at best) adolescent. Besides, Alberich didn't look
as if he needed any help, at least not at the moment.

The Weaponsmaster had been impressive enough in the

salle and on the training ground; here, literally surrounded by four skilled fighters, Skif could hardly believe what he was seeing. Alberich moved like a demon incarnate and so quickly that half the time Skif couldn't see what had happened, only that he'd somehow eluded what should have killed him—

Still—four to one—maybe he'd better do something to try and drop the odds.

Skif slipped the catches on his knives and then hesitated. The combatants were all moving too fast and in unpredictable ways. He'd never practiced against anything but a stationary target; if he threw a knife, he could all too easily hit Alberich, and if he threw a knife, he'd also throw away half of his own defenses.

:Skif, get the children out now!:

Cymry's mental "shout" woke him out of his indecision; with a quick glance to make sure the Guildmaster (what Guild was he?) was too far away to interfere, Skif grabbed the wrists of two of the three—the third was clinging to the arm of the second—and pulled them onto their feet. Then he got behind them and slowly—trying *not* to attract the eye of their chiefest captor—he herded them in front of him, along the wall, and toward the door that Alberich had entered by.

One of the three, at least, woke out of her fear to see what he was trying to do. She seized the wrists of both of the others and dragged them with her as they edged along the wall. Her eyes were fixed on that doorway; Skif's were on the fight.

It was oddly silent, compared with the tavern- and street-fights he was used to. There was no shouting, no cursing, only the clash of metal on metal and the occasional grunt of pain.

And it was getting bloody. All of the bodyguards were marked—not big wounds, but they were bleeding. It *looked* as if the four bodyguards should bring Alberich down at any moment, and yet he kept sliding out from beneath their blades as Skif and his charges got closer and closer to their goal. Skif wanted to run, and knew he didn't dare. He didn't dare distract

Alberich, and he didn't dare grab the attention of the Guild-master.

Ten paces . . . five. . . .

There!

The girl who was leading the other two paused, hesitating, on the very threshold, her face a mask of fear and indecision. She didn't know what lay beyond that door—it could be worse than what was here.

"Run!" Skif hissed at her, trusting that Alberich had already cleared the way.

The girl didn't hesitate a moment longer; she bolted into the half-lit hallway, hauling the other two with her. Skif started to follow—hesitated, and looked back.

There was a body on the floor, and it wasn't Alberich's. While Skif's back was turned, the Weaponsmaster had temporarily reduced the odds against himself by one.

But Alberich was bleeding from the shoulder now. Skif couldn't tell how bad the wound was, and Alberich showed no sign of weakness, but the leather tunic was slashed there, and bloody flesh showed beneath the dark leather whenever he moved that arm. Skif's throat closed with fear. Somewhere deep inside he'd been certain that Alberich was invulnerable. But he wasn't. He could be hurt. And if he could be hurt—he could die.

At that moment, the Guildmaster finally noticed that his prizes had escaped.

"Stop them!" he shouted at his men. *"Don't let them get away!"*

Skif froze in the doorway; but he needn't have worried. No one was taking orders now. The fighters were too busy with Alberich to pay any attention to Skif, although they redoubled their efforts to take the Weaponsmaster down.

:Skif, run! Get out of there now!: Cymry cried.

"No!" he said aloud. He couldn't go—not now—he *might* be able to do something—

The lantern flames flickered, and shadows danced on the walls, a demonic echo of the death dance in the center of the room. It was confusing; too confusing. Once again Skif felt for his knives and hesitated.

Alberich was tiring; oh, it didn't show in how he moved, but there was sweat rolling down his face. He had taken another cut, this time across his scalp, and blood mingled with the drops of sweat that spattered down onto the dirt floor with every movement.

Skif *still* didn't dare throw the knives, even with one of the opponents down. He edged away from the door, and looked frantically for something *else* he could throw.

Alberich's eyes glittered, and his mouth was set in a wild and terrible smile. He looked more than half mad, and Skif couldn't imagine why his opponents weren't backing away just from his expression alone, much less the single-minded ferocity with which he was fighting. He did not look human, that much was certain. If this was how he always looked when he fought in earnest, no wonder people were afraid of him.

No wonder he had never needed to draw a blade in those tavern brawls.

Skif's eye fell on a pile of dirty bowls stacked against the wall on the other side of the doorway—the remains, perhaps, of a meal the child snatchers had finished. It didn't matter; they were heavy enough to be weapons, and they were within reach.

He snatched one up and waited for his opportunity. It came sooner than he'd hoped, as Alberich suddenly rushed one of the three men, making him stumble backward in a hasty retreat. That broke the swirling dance of steel for a moment, broke the pattern long enough for Skif to fling the bowl at the man's head.

It connected with the back of his skull with a sickening *crack* that made Skif wince—not hard enough to knock him out, but enough to make him stagger, dazed.

And that moment was just enough for Alberich to slash savagely at his neck, cutting halfway through it. The man twisted in agony, dropping to the floor, blood *everywhere* as he writhed for a long and horrible moment, then stilled.

Skif froze, watching in fascination, aghast. Alberich did not. Nor did the two men still fighting. They reacted by coming at Alberich from both directions at once, and in the rain of blows that followed, Alberich was wounded again, a glancing slash across the arm that peeled back leather and a little flesh—but he delivered a worse blow than he had gotten to the head of the third man, who dropped like a stone. At which point the first man who'd been felled stood up, shaking his head to clear it, and plunged back into the fray.

Skif shook himself out of his trance and flung two more bowls. Neither connected as well as the first; the first man remaining was hit in the shoulder, and the second in the back. But the distraction was their undoing, for they lost the initiative and Alberich managed to get out of their trap, nor could they pin him between them again.

The fight moved closer to the Guildmaster—Alberich got the second man in the leg, leaving his dagger in the man's thigh, and the bodyguard staggered back.

Skif threw his last bowl, which hit the man nearest the Guildmaster in the side of the face. Alberich saw his opening, and took it, with an all-or-nothing lunge that carried him halfway across the room.

Skif let out a strangled cry of horror—

If any fighter Skif had *ever* seen before had tried that move, it would have ended differently. But this was Alberich, and he came in *under* the man's sword and inside his dagger, and the next thing Skif knew, the point of Alberich's sword was sticking out of the man's back, and the man was gazing down at Alberich with an utterly stupefied expression on his face.

Then he toppled over slowly—

But he took Alberich's sword with him.

And *now* the Guildmaster struck.

Because he had done nothing all this time, Skif had virtually forgotten he was there, and had assumed that he was harmless. Perhaps Alberich had done the same. It was a mistaken assumption on both their parts.

The Guildmaster moved like a ferret, so fast that he seemed to blur, and too fast for Alberich, exhausted as he was, to react. The Guildmaster didn't have a weapon.

He didn't need one.

Skif didn't, *couldn't* see how it happened. One moment, Alberich was still extended in his lunge; the next, the Guildmaster had him pinned somehow, trapped. The Guildmaster's back was to the wall, his arm was across Alberich's throat with Alberich's body protecting his. Both of Alberich's hands were free, and he clawed ineffectually at the arm across his throat. The Weaponsmaster's face was already turning an unhealthy shade of pale blue.

"Kash," the Guildmaster said, in a tight voice. "Get the brat."

But the last man was in no condition to grab anyone. "Can't," he coughed. "Leg's out."

Given the fact that his leg had been opened from thigh to knee, with Alberich's dagger still in the wound, he had a point. The Guildmaster's gaze snapped back onto Skif.

"Well," he said, in that condescending voice he'd used with Jass, "I wouldn't have expected the Heralds to use bait. It's not like them to put a child in danger."

Skif bristled. "Ain't a child," he said flatly.

"Oh? You're a little young to be a Herald," the man countered in a sarcastic tone. Then he punched Alberich's shoulder wound with his free hand, making him gasp, and putting a stop to Alberich's attempts to claw himself free. "Stop that. You're only making things more difficult for yourself."

"What has age to do with being a Herald?" Alberich rasped.

Skif said nothing, and the man's eyes narrowed as his arm

tightened a little more on Alberich's throat. "Be still, or I will snap your foolish neck for you. A Trainee, then. But still—that's *quite* out of character—unless—"

He stared at Skif then, with a calculating expression, and Skif sensed that he was thinking very hard, very hard indeed.

It was, after all, no secret that the latest Trainee was a thief. But what that would mean to this wealthy villain—and whether he'd heard that—

Then the Guildmaster's eyes widened. "Well," he said, and his mouth quirked up at one corner. "Who would have thought it. The Heralds making common cause with a common thief. Oh, excuse me—you're quite an uncommon thief. Old Bazie's boy, aren't you? Skif, is it?"

Skif went cold with shock and stared at the Guildmaster with his mouth dropping open. *How'd he know—how—*

The Guildmaster smirked. "I make it my business to know what goes on in my properties, as any good landlord would," he said pointedly. "Besides, how do you think that cleverly hidden room got there? Who do you think arranged for the pump and the privy down there?"

"But you *killed* him!" Skif cried, as Alberich tried to move and turned a little bluer for his trouble.

"I had no intention of doing so," the Guildmaster pointed out, in reasonable tones. "That was Jass' fault. If he'd *obeyed orders,* everyone would have gotten out all right, even Bazie."

Since Skif had heard the truth of that with his own ears, there was no debating the question of whether Jass had gone far beyond what his orders had been. But—

How would Bazie have gotten out in time, even so? How? The boys couldn't have carried him—

The Guildmaster interrupted his thoughts. His expression had gone very bland again. He was planning something. . . .

"You've been very clever, young man," he said, in a voice unctuous with flattery. "I don't see nearly enough cleverness in the people I hire—well, Jass was a case in point. Now at the moment, we seem to be at a stalemate."

Alberich writhed in a futile attempt to get free. His captor laughed, and punched the shoulder wound again, and Alberich went white. "If I kill this Herald," he pointed out, "I lose my shield against whatever you might pick up and fling at me. *You* can't go anywhere, because Kash is between you and the door. Stalemate."

Skif nodded warily.

"On the other hand," he continued. "If you decided to switch allegiances, I could strangle this fool and we could all escape from here before the help he has almost certainly arranged for arrives."

Skif clenched his jaw. In another time and place— "An' just what'm I supposed to get out of this?" he asked, playing for time to think.

Cymry was oddly silent in his mind. In fact—in fact, he couldn't sense her at all. For the first time in weeks he was alone in his head.

"What do you get? Oh, Skif, Skif, haven't you learned *anything* about the way Life works?" the Guildmaster laughed. "Allow me to enlighten you. No matter what these fools have told you, the *only* law that counts is the Law of the Street. What you'll get is to be trained by me, in something far more profitable than the liftin' lay."

"Oh, aye—" Skif began heatedly.

"No. You listen to me. *This* is what is real. These are the rules that the real world runs by." He stared into Skif's eyes, and Skif couldn't look away, couldn't stop listening to that voice, so sure of itself, so very, very rational. "Grab what you can, because if you don't, someone else will snatch it out from under you. Get all the dirt you can on anyone who might have power over you—and believe me, *everyone* has a past, and things they'd rather not have bruited about. Be the cheater, not the cheated, because you'll be one or the other. There's no such thing as truth—oh, believe me about this—there are shades of meaning, and depths of self-interest, but there is no *truth.*"

Skif made an inarticulate sound of protest, but it was weak, because *this* was all he'd seen at Exile's Gate, *this* was the way the world as he had always known it worked. Not the way it was taught in the Collegium. Not the way those sheltered, idealistic Heralds explained things—

"And there is no *faith* either," the Guildmaster continued, in his hard, bright voice. "Faith is for those who wish to be deceived for the sake of a comforting, but hollow promise. Think about it, boy—think about it. It's shadow and air, all of it. Cakes in the Havens, and crumbs in the street. *That* is all that faith is about."

The priests—oh, the priests—how many of them actually *helped* anyone in Exile's Gate in the here and now? Behind their cloister walls and their gates, they never went hungry or cold—they never suffered the least privations. Even the Brothers at the Priory never went hungry or cold. . . .

Skif's heart contracted into an icy little knot. Alberich's eyes were closed; he seemed to be concentrating on getting what little air the Guildmaster allowed him.

"Throw your lot in with me. *I* won't deceive you with pretty fictions. You'll obey me because I am strong and smart and powerful. You'll learn from me to be the same. And maybe some day you'll be good enough to take what I've got away from me. Until then, we'll have a deal, and it will be because we *know* where we stand with each other, not because of some artificial conceit that we *like* each other." He laughed. "The smart man guards his own back, boy," the insidious voice went on. "The wise man knows there is no one that you can trust, you take and hold whatever you can and share it with *no one,* because no one will ever share what he has with you. *Hate* is for the strong; love is for the weak. No one has friends; *friend* is just a pretty name for a leech. Or a user. What do you think Bazie was? A *user.* He used you boys and lived off of *your* work, kept you as personal servants, and pretended to love you so you would be as faithful to him as a pack of whipped puppies."

And that was where the Guildmaster went too far.

Bazie, thought Skif, jarred free of the spell that insidiously logical voice had placed on him. *Bazie* had shared whatever he had, and had trusted to his boys to do the same. Bazie had taken him in, with no reason to, and every reason to turn him into the street, knowing that Londer would be looking for him to silence him.

And Beel—Beel had protected him, Beel *could* have reported a hundred times over that Skif had fulfilled his education, but he didn't. And when Beel could have told his own father where Skif was, he'd kept his mouth shut.

And the Heralds—

Oh, the Heralds. Weak, were they? Foolish?

Skif felt warmth coming back into him, felt his heart uncurling, as he thought back along the past weeks and all of the little kindnesses, all unasked for, that he'd gotten. Kris and Coroc keeping the highborn Blues from tormenting him until Skif had established that he was more amusing if he wasn't taunted. Jeri helping him out with swordwork. The teachers taking extra time to explain things he simply had never seen before. Housekeeper Gaytha being so patient with his rough speech that sometimes he couldn't believe she'd spend all this time over one Trainee. The girls teasing and laughing with him in the sewing room. The simple way that he had been *accepted* by every Trainee, and with no other recommendation but that he'd been Chosen—

Cymry.

Cymry, who had filled his heart—who still *was* there, he sensed her again, now that he wasn't listening to the poison that bastard was pouring into his ears. Cymry, who cared enough for him to wait while he listened—*to make his own decisions,* without any pressure from her.

No love, was there? Self-delusion, was it?

Then I'll be deluded.

Did the Guildmaster see his thoughts flicker across his face? Perhaps—

"Kash, now!" he shouted. The wounded bodyguard lunged, arms outstretched to grab him—

But Skif was already moving before the bodyguard, clumsy with his wounds and pain, had gotten a single step. He jumped aside, his hands flicking to each side as he evaded those out-stretched arms.

And between one breath and the next—

The bodyguard continued his lunge, and sprawled face-down on the floor, gurgling in agony, one of Skif's knives in his throat.

The Guildmaster made a strangled noise—and so did Alberich.

The arm around Alberich's throat tightened as the Guild-master slid down the wall.

Skif's *other* knife was lodged to the hilt in his eye.

But Skif's dodge had been deliberately aimed to take him to Alberich's side. The Guildmaster had been a stationary target. And at that range, he couldn't miss.

In the next heartbeat he had pried the dead arm away from the Weaponsmaster's throat, and Alberich was gasping in great, huge gulps of air, his color returning to normal.

Skif helped him to his feet. "You all right?" he asked awkwardly.

Alberich nodded. "Talk—may be hard," he rasped.

Skif laughed giddily, feeling as if he had drunk two whole bottles of that fabulous wine all by himself. "Like that's gonna make the Trainees unhappy," he taunted. "You, not bein' able to lecture 'em!"

The wry expression on Alberich's face only made him laugh

harder. "Come on," he said, draping his teacher's arm over his shoulders. "We better get you outside an' get back to where th' good Healers are afore your Kantor decides he's gonna put horseshoe marks on my bum."

They got as far as the door when Skif thought of something else. "I don' suppose you *did* arrange for help, did you?"

"Well," Alberich admitted, in a croak. "It comes *now.*"

:Cymry?:

:Half the Collegium, my love.:

Skif just shook his head. "Figgers. Us Heralds, we just keep thinkin' we gotta do everything by ourselves, don't we? We can't do the smart thing an' get help fixed up beforehand. Even you. An' you should know better."

"Yes," Alberich agreed. "I should. *We* do."

We. It was a lovely word.

One that Skif was coming to enjoy a very great deal

A Herald he didn't recognize brought Skif his knives, meticulously cleaned, as the Healer fussed over Alberich right there in the street, which was so full of torches and lanterns it might have been a festival. Well, a very grim sort of festival.

It actually looked more like something out of a fever dream; the street full of Heralds and Guards, more Guardsmen swarming in and out of the warehouse, a half-dozen Heralds and their Companions surrounding Alberich—who flatly refused to lie down on a stretcher as the Healer wanted—while the Weaponsmaster sat on an upturned barrel and the Healer stitched up his wounds. Four bodies were laid out on the street under sheets; one semiconscious bullyboy had been taken off for questioning as soon as he recovered. Not that anyone expected to get much out of him. It wasn't very likely that a mere bodyguard would know the details of his master's operations.

No one had sent Skif back to the Collegium, and he waited

beside Alberich, between Kantor and Cymry, listening with all his might to the grim-voiced conversations around him. Most of the Heralds here he didn't know; that was all right, he didn't have to know who they were to understand that they were important. He did recognize Talamir, though, who seemed considerably less otherworldly at the moment and quite entirely focused on the here and now.

"This is going to have an interesting effect on the Council," he observed, his voice heavy with irony.

Alberich snorted. "Interesting? Boil up like a nest of ants, when stirred with sticks, it will! Sunlord! Guildmaster *Vatean!* Suspect *him,* even I did not!"

"Gartheser is going to have a fit of apoplexy," someone else observed. "Vatean was here was here at his behest in the first place."

Hadn't they noticed he was here? This was high political stuff he was listening to!

:They know,: Cymry told him. *:But you're a Herald, even if you aren't in Whites yet. You proved yourself tonight. No one is ever going to withhold anything from you that you really want or need to know.:*

Well! Interesting. . . .

"Gartheser will be a pool of stillness compared to Lady Cathal," Talamir observed, with a sigh. "He was a Guildmaster after all, and she speaks for the Guilds."

"Oh, *Guildmaster*, indeed," someone else said dismissively. "Becoming a Master in the Traders' Guild. . . ." He left the sentence dangling, but everyone—including Skif—knew that the requirements for Mastery in the Traders' Guild mostly depended on entirely on how much profit you could make. Provided, of course, that you didn't cheat to make it. Or at least that you didn't get *caught* cheating.

"He was," Talamir pointed out delicately, and with a deliberate pause between the words, "quite . . . prosperous."

"And now, know we where the profits came from," Alberich

said harshly. "It is thinking I am that Lady Cathal should be looking into profits, and whence from they come."

"*And* Lord Gartheser," said Talamir. "Since Gartheser wished so sincerely to recommend him to the Council."

"There is that," observed someone else, in a hard, cold voice. "And *now* we know where the leak of Guard movements along Evendim came from."

"It would appear so," Talamir replied thoughtfully, "Although . . . it is in my mind that Lord Orthallen was equally, though less blatantly, impressed with the late Guildmaster's talents. . . ."

But a flurry of protests broke out over that remark; it seemed that the idea of Lord Orthallen having anything to do with all of this was completely out of the question.

Except that Skif saw Talamir and Alberich exchange a private look—and perhaps more than that. Looks weren't all that could be exchanged when one was a Herald, and far more privately.

I wonder what all that's about.

And Lord Orthallen had "particularly" recommended Jass to Vatean. . . .

Well, if he wanted to know—

No, he didn't. Not at all. He knew quite enough already. All of this was going right over his head, and anyway, there wasn't anything one undersized thief could do about it even if he did know.

Or—if there *was* something one undersized thief could do about it, he had no doubt that Alberich would have a few words with him on the subject. *And maybe a job.*

So, perhaps his roof-walking days weren't over after all.

Better get myself another sneaky suit.

:I believe that Alberich already has that in mind,: said Cymry.

The little group continued to paw over the few facts they

had until they were shopworn, and even Talamir, whose patience seemed endless, grew weary of it.

"Enough!" he said, silencing them all. "There is nothing more we can do until we *know* more. The boy and Alberich have told us all they know. Herald Ryvial and our picked Guardsmen-Investigators are on their way to Vatean's home even now, and if there is anything to be found there, rest assured, they will find it. Every known associate of Vatean will be under observation before sunrise, *long* before word of his death leaks out—"

"Uncle Londer," Skif interrupted wearily. Now that the excitement was wearing off, he was beginning to feel every bruise, and was just a little sick.

"And the man Londer Galko will also be observed," Talamir continued smoothly. "Because he clearly knew a great deal about the child stealing although he is not connected with Vatean in any way."

Now he looked at Skif, and put a hand on Skif's shoulder that felt not at all patronizing. Comradely, yes, patronizing, no. "Trainee Skif is weary to dropping, Herald Alberich is in pain, and *we* are fresh and have constructive work ahead of us. I suggest we send them back to their beds while we get about it, brothers."

There was a murmured chorus of assent as the Healer put the last of the stitches into Alberich's scalp wound, and the Heralds magically melted away, leaving Skif and Alberich alone in a calm center in the midst of the bustle.

"You won't travel in a stretcher as you *should,*" the Healer said wearily, as if he had made and lost this same argument far too many times to bother again. "So the best I can do is order you to back to the Collegium and to rest."

"Teach from a stool I will, tomorrow at least," Alberich told him.

The Healer sighed, and packed up his satchel. "I suppose

that's the most I can get out of you," he said, and looked at Kantor. "Do what *you* can with him, won't you?"

The Companion tossed his head in an emphatic nod, and Skif added, "Jeri an' Herald Ylsa can run th' sword work for a week—an' Coroc an' Kris can do archery." Kantor nodded even more emphatically.

Alberich glared at him sourly, made as if to shrug, thought better of it, and sighed. "A conspiracy, it is," he grumbled.

"Damn right," Skif said boldly. And when Alberich got to his feet and made as if to mount, Kantor stamped his foot, and laid himself down so that Alberich could get into the saddle without *mounting.* When his Herald was in place, Kantor rose, and shook his head vigorously.

"You make me an old woman," Alberich complained, as Skif got stiffly into Cymry's saddle and the two of them headed up the street away from the scene of the activity, riding side by side.

"Naw," Skif denied, very much enjoying having the fearsome Weaponsmaster at a temporary disadvantage. "Just makin' you be sensible. Ye see—" he continued, waxing eloquent, "there's th' difference between a Herald an' a thief. Ye don' have t' *make* a thief be sensible. All thieves are *sensible.* A thief that won't be sensible—"

"—a thief in gaol is, yes, please spare me," Alberich growled.

But it didn't sound like his heart was in it, and a moment later he glanced over at Skif. "That was one of your mentor—Bazie—that was one of the things he told you, yes?"

Skif nodded.

"And now, revenge you have had."

True. Jass was dead, Vatean was dead; the two men responsible for Bazie's horrible death were themselves dead. Skif's initial bargain with himself—and with the Heralds—to work with Alberich because they had a common cause was over.

"Regrets?" Alberich prompted.

Skif shook his head, then changed his mind. "Sort of. There weren't no *justice.*"

"But it was your own hand that struck Vatean down," Alberich said, as if he were surprised.

It was Skif's turn to bestow a sour look. "Now, don' you go tryin' that sly word twistin' on *me,*" he said. "I know what you're tryin' t'do, an' don' pretend you ain't. No. There weren't no *justice.* Th' bastid is dead, dead quick an' easy, he didn' have t'answer fer nothin', an' we ain't never gonna find out a half of what he was into. I got revenge, an' I don' like it. Revenge don' get you nothin'. There. You happy now?"

But Alberich surprised him. "No, little brother," he said gently. "I am not happy, because my brother is unhappy."

And there it was; the sour taste in Skif's mouth faded, and although the vengeance he thought he had wanted turned out to be nothing *like* what he really would have wanted if he'd had the choice, well—

I am not happy, because my brother is unhappy.

That—*that* was worth everything he'd gone through to get here.

"Ah, I'll get over it," he sighed. "Hey, I get t' boss you around fer a week, eh, Kantor? That's worth somethin'."

Once again, Kantor nodded his head with vigor, and Alberich groaned feelingly.

"This—" he complained, but with a suspicious twinkle in his eye, "—is putting the henhouse in the fox's charge."

"Rrrrr!" Skif growled, showing his teeth. "Promise. Won't have *too* much chicken."

"And I suppose you will insist on going into Whites, now that a hero you are," Alberich continued, looking pained.

"Hah! You *are* outa your head; th' Healer was right," Skif countered. "What, me run afore I can walk? Not likely! 'Sides," he continued, contemplating all the potential fun he could have over the next four years in the Collegium, "I ain't

fleeced a quarter of them highborn Blues yet, nor got all I can
outa them Artificer Blues!"

Alberich regarded him with a jaundiced eye. "I foresee—
and ForeSight *is* my Gift—a great deal of trouble, with *you* at
its center. And that no Trainee in the history of Valdemar will
have more demerits against his name, before you go into
Whites."

"Suits me," Skif replied saucily. "So long as I have fun
doing it."

"Fun for you—yes," Alberich sighed. "Fun for the rest of
us, however, extracting you from the tangles you make—"

"It'll be worth it!" Skif insisted, once again feeling that
giddy elation bubbling up inside him, as he felt the warmth of
acceptance encircle him and hold him at its heart.

And in spite of present pain and future concerns, Herald
Alberich gave him a real, unalloyed smile. "Oh, there is no
doubt it will be worth it," he said, and Skif had the sense that
he meant more than just the subject of Skif's future mischief.
He meant Skif's very existence as one of the Trainees now and
Heralds to come, no matter who objected, or how strenuously,
to the presence of a thief among them. He confirmed that with
his next breath.

"Welcome, very welcome, to the Collegium, Skif. It seems
we were always right to take a thief."